Mistakes Were Made

Also by Meryl Wilsner

Something to Talk About

Mistakes Were Made

A Novel

MERYL WILSNER

ST. MARTIN'S GRIFFIN
NEW YORK

First published in the United States by St. Martin's Griffin, an imprint of St. Martin's Publishing Group

MISTAKES WERE MADE. Copyright © 2022 by Meryl Wilsner. All rights reserved. Printed in the United States of America. For information, address St. Martin's Publishing Group, 120 Broadway, New York, NY 10271.

www.stmartins.com

Designed by Gabriel Guma

Library of Congress Cataloging-in-Publication Data

Names: Wilsner, Meryl, author.
Title: Mistakes were made : a novel / Meryl Wilsner.
Description: First edition. | New York : St. Martin's Griffin, 2022.
Identifiers: LCCN 2022013551 | ISBN 9781250841001 (trade paperback) |
    ISBN 9781250841018 (ebook)
Classification: LCC PS3623.I577777 S66 2022 | DDC 813/.6—dc23
LC record available at https://lccn.loc.gov/2022013551

Our books may be purchased in bulk for promotional, educational, or business use. Please contact your local bookseller or the Macmillan Corporate and Premium Sales Department at 1-800-221-7945, extension 5442, or by email at MacmillanSpecialMarkets@macmillan.com.

First Edition: 2022

10 9 8 7 6 5 4 3 2 1

For Tash McAdam & Zabe Doyle,
who loved this book from its beginnings

One

CASSIE

A stranger caught Cassie's arm as she moved past him toward the bar.

"Hey, beautiful, lemme buy you a drink." The guy's grin was cocksure, like he knew he was going to get what he wanted.

Cassie flipped her long blond ponytail over her shoulder and gave the man a syrup-sweet smile, blinking at him through her lashes. "Let me go before I break your arm."

"Jesus," the guy said, but he let go.

He muttered something about her being a bitch as she walked away, but Cassie didn't care. She wasn't there to make friends. In fact, she'd picked this bar specifically so she wouldn't see anyone she'd have to talk to. It was across town from campus, which meant the Lyft ride cost more than she'd have liked, but it was worth it to get as far away as possible from her college's Family Weekend. Cassie didn't even understand why Keckley held Family Weekend in early October. They'd barely been at school a month. Did people really need to see their families that often? She hadn't seen her mom since Christmas last year, and she was doing just fine.

Cassie made it to the bar without any more strangers putting their hands on her. There were three open stools, and she pushed herself up onto the middle one. The bartender didn't ask for ID, just made her a dark and stormy then left her alone. Cassie was perfectly happy getting slowly drunk by herself in a bar where she knew no one.

That was, until she spotted this woman.

Definitely woman, not girl or chick. She was probably twice Cassie's age, and honestly, Cassie wasn't typically a cougar hunter—she could appreciate an older woman, sure, she just usually wasn't the type to pursue one—but this woman was way too hot to worry about any age difference. Plus, she was alone, and Cassie swore she looked lonely.

Cassie's eyes raked the woman's body: sensible peep-toe heels, strong calves, a dress that fell a bit lower on her thighs than Cassie was hoping. It hugged the woman's curves just right, though—hips Cassie wanted to hold on to and tits she wouldn't mind getting her hands on either. Then there was shoulder-length brown hair with a hint of blond highlights, like it was summer at the beach and not autumn in the New River Valley, a strong jawline, and bright eyes—staring right at Cassie. The older woman leaned against a wall, a barely there smirk on her face.

Cassie blushed but didn't look away. The woman quirked an eyebrow and honest to God, it sent a shiver down Cassie's spine. She quirked an eyebrow right back, letting a slow grin work its way across her face. It was the other woman who broke eye contact as she ran a hand through her hair with a chuckle. She glanced over again, raising her drink. They toasted each other from across the bar, then the woman looked away, like there was anything more interesting in this place than Cassie Klein.

It wasn't a rejection; it just felt like maybe the woman thought all Cassie wanted to do was check her out. That was not all Cassie wanted to do.

She flagged down the bartender.

"The woman over there?" She gestured subtly, and the bartender nodded. "Whatever she's drinking, send her another from me."

She watched him make it and was thrilled to see it was whiskey, neat. A no-nonsense kind of drink.

The woman's eyebrows popped up when the bartender placed the drink in front of her. She bit her bottom lip as she smiled, looking over at Cassie, who tipped her glass and let her eyes wander to the open stool beside her. The woman chuckled. But she gathered her purse and started heading over.

"Thanks," she said, sliding onto the stool next to Cassie and sipping her drink.

Cassie grinned. "My pleasure."

She didn't say more, too busy ogling the woman. She hadn't gotten her fill from across the bar, apparently. It was even better up close, the woman's pale skin somehow glowing even in the low light. Her eyes were strikingly blue—thin eyeliner making them stand out even more.

Cassie licked her lips. "I'm Cassie."

"Erin," the woman said. She offered her hand and Cassie shook it. She didn't bother trying to make the handshake a seduction, but Erin's hands were soft and she liked it.

"Nice choice of drink," Cassie said.

Erin smirked. "What's yours?"

"Dark and stormy right now," Cassie said, "but I'm easy."

Erin ducked her head as the apples of her cheeks went rosy. Cassie liked the juxtaposition of Erin's smirk and her blush, like the woman was confident but not used to being hit on.

Cassie hadn't planned on hooking up with anyone tonight, but plans could change, and Erin was hot, and it was sure to make her less annoyed about Family Weekend.

"I like your dress," she said.

Erin looked down like she needed to remind herself what she had on. She said thanks without looking back up.

"You're fucking amazing in it," Cassie said.

That got Erin's attention, her eyes snapping to Cassie's.

"Are you always this bold?"

Cassie shrugged. Why play games? There were no stakes here. Erin was a hot stranger; she didn't have the power to hurt Cassie. There was no reason to pretend she wanted to go slow. Plus: "It's working, isn't it?"

Erin's cheeks were still flushed, but she grinned and returned the compliment. "You don't look half bad either."

Cassie was only in jeans and a racer-back black tank, her bomber jacket on her stool beneath her, but still, "I know."

She smirked and Erin rolled her eyes—she was smiling, though, so yeah, being bold was definitely working. Cassie wondered how far she could push it. Could she get away with suggesting they go someplace less crowded?

Before she got the chance, Erin excused herself to go to the bathroom. Cassie watched her leave, jealous of the way that purple dress clung to her ass. Right before Erin reached the hallway where the bathrooms were, she looked back at Cassie, making eye contact before she turned the corner.

Well. That was an invitation if Cassie had ever seen one.

She paid—for her and Erin both—as quickly as she could, slipped her jacket on, and headed for the bathroom. The other patrons were now a bunch of assholes standing around cockblocking her—or, more accurately, clamjamming her. She weaved her way around tables and through the crowd, ducking under two people's beers as they toasted something.

Inside the women's restroom, Erin stood at the sink washing her hands. Cassie only did a cursory check of the stalls before pushing her against the counter and kissing her. Erin didn't seem surprised, fisting Cassie's jacket with still wet hands to pull her even closer.

Cassie had thought she'd have to hold back, ease into it, but Erin kissed hard enough that their teeth clinked together. She slid her tongue into Cassie's mouth like an apology and twisted to reverse their positions. Cassie stumbled, slamming her hip into the counter. She broke the kiss to curse. Erin didn't bother asking if she was okay. Instead, she wrapped her hands under Cassie's thighs and lifted. Water on the counter seeped through Cassie's jeans when Erin set her down.

"Good?" Erin asked, stepping between Cassie's legs.

Cassie barely felt the damp spot on the back of her thigh. "Great."

Erin's mouth was on hers almost before she'd finished the word. The new position meant Erin had to tilt her head up to reach, but that didn't diminish her enthusiasm, kisses rough and biting. Cassie reveled in the not quite swallowed moan when her teeth closed around Erin's bottom lip.

"Oh shit, sorry," someone said.

Erin pulled back, far enough to separate their lips but close enough that Cassie could press a kiss under her jaw. Cassie didn't notice the noise of the bar had gotten louder until the door closed and it was muffled again. She sucked Erin's skin too gently to leave a mark.

"Let's get out of here," she said against the throb of Erin's pulse.

"I just have to pay—"

Cassie bit below Erin's ear and laughed. "Already got it covered, sweetheart."

Erin chuckled, and it vibrated against Cassie's lips. Erin's neck shone, damp from Cassie's mouth, when she pulled away. Cassie eased herself to the ground.

"Let's go."

Erin kissed her once more before leading the way. She held her hand as they weaved through the crowd toward the door; Cassie's lips turned up before she forced them down, annoyed at herself for finding it endearing.

Cassie shivered in the parking lot—from the chill in the air, not the brush of Erin's thumb against the back of her hand. Was Erin taking her home? To a hotel? She wished she could take Erin somewhere, but she only had a dorm. Yeah, it was an apartment with no roommate, but it was still a *dorm*.

When they reached a car, Erin opened the *back* door. Apparently they were doing this here.

Cassie glanced around. Across the lot, four or five people were huddled next to a car. This wasn't private enough to be called private, not public enough to be called public.

Erin gnawed on her bottom lip. "Good?"

"Great." Public or private didn't really matter when Cassie wanted to be the one biting that lip.

She ducked into the car, and Erin followed, slamming the door behind her and climbing directly into Cassie's lap. Cassie reveled in Erin's weight on top of her, the way her dress slid up, the skin it revealed. She wanted the dress off, wanted to see everything, but admittedly the back seat of a car might not be the best place for that. Cassie turned her head to see if anyone was nearby, but she got distracted when Erin pushed her jacket off her shoulders. Erin's dress gaped open in the front, and Cassie slid her hands inside.

"Fuck, you've got nice tits," she said, and Erin's nipples tightened as Cassie pinched them.

She had to let go for a moment when Erin tugged Cassie's tank top over her head.

"If I return the compliment, are you just going to say, 'I know,' again?" Erin asked, both hands squeezing Cassie's breasts through her bra.

Cassie smirked. "No guarantees."

"That's what I thought." Erin rolled her eyes affectionately before finding her lips again.

Cassie's fingers stalled out when Erin kissed her. She was going to be a literal rocket scientist; you'd think she would have enough brainpower to get kissed and feel someone up at the same time, but apparently not. Her hands fell out of Erin's dress and it was all she could do to clutch the older woman's shoulders.

Erin moved her mouth to Cassie's neck and Cassie groaned, "*Fuck.*"

She could feel Erin smile against her skin. *Get it together, Klein.* Cassie let herself lean into Erin's mouth a few seconds longer before getting to business.

Her hands moved to Erin's thighs, then slid up under her dress. Cassie considered teasing, maybe going slow, but she really didn't want to, like, at all, so when her fingers reached Erin's underwear, she pushed past them.

God. Her favorite part of sleeping with someone with a pussy had to be that first touch, when you could feel just how turned on they were, your fingers slipping through their wetness. Erin jerked and bit down when Cassie's fingers glanced off her clit. Cassie yelped.

"Sorry," Erin said, dragging her tongue along Cassie's collarbone.

Cassie swallowed against the feeling. *Focus,* she reminded herself, even though it was impossible not to think about what Erin's mouth would feel like in other places.

Erin nipped at Cassie's neck, but only occasionally, like she was too busy rolling her hips to worry about anything else. Cassie wasn't even really touching her yet, but Erin was busy, shifting around in Cassie's lap, trying to get her fingers where she wanted them. Cassie didn't make her wait.

Yeah, what she had thought earlier about the first touch being the best? That was a lie; this was the best part—pushing inside and feeling Erin squeeze around her fingers, tight and hot and wet. This was everything.

"God," Erin whispered, and Cassie couldn't resist.

"You can just call me Cassie."

Erin glared at her, breaking the look with a moan when Cassie scissored her fingers.

Cassie worked up a rhythm, sliding out and pushing hard back in, and Erin helped, her hips grinding and jumping. Sometimes she leaned down for a kiss, but mostly she held herself upright, riding Cassie's hand urgently.

"More," she groaned, and Cassie added another finger.

Cassie was pretty sure this was the best day of her life. She was three fingers deep in this gorgeous woman who was clenching like crazy, obviously close—she was about to make this *fucking gorgeous* woman come on her fingers in the back of a car, and she couldn't think of anything better.

She kissed Erin, grabbing her ass to pull her harder onto her fingers.

"*Cassie,* fuck," Erin muttered, and then she was coming, shaking and shuddering, eyes closed, mouth open, and Jesus Christ, Cassie had made plenty of people come in her twenty-one years, thank you very much, but Erin was hands down the hottest she'd ever seen.

Erin collapsed on top of her, after, and Cassie wrapped her arms around her. When Erin lifted her head for a kiss, it was soft. Gentle. She made a contented sound in the back of her throat and butted her head at Cassie like a cat preening. It was all kinds of adorable, but Cassie hadn't gotten off yet; she couldn't control the way her hips twitched under Erin's. Erin laughed at her.

"Impatient," she admonished.

"If I was impatient, I wouldn't have let you go first," Cassie said, but it was offset by the way she pushed Erin's hand toward the button of her jeans as they kissed.

Erin readjusted herself, one knee between Cassie's legs, a hand on the seat by Cassie's side to hold herself up. She undid Cassie's pants and pushed her right leg over as far as she could, bumping it against the back of the driver's seat to get more room before she slipped a hand into Cassie's underwear. It wasn't a great angle, even spread out there wasn't a lot of space to move, but Cassie was so ready that it didn't much matter. Erin's fingers slid in, just to the first knuckle, and Cassie's eyes slammed closed.

She opened them again to find Erin staring down at her like maybe her face had the answers to all of life's questions. Cassie surged forward to kiss her, and it pushed Erin's fingers deeper.

"Christ," Cassie said, falling back.

"You can just call me Erin."

Cassie lost her laugh in a gasp.

Erin worked her and watched her, and Cassie wanted more. She unclasped her own bra, and it was worth it for the gleam in Erin's eyes. It was worth it for the way Erin ducked her head, caught a nipple between her teeth, and moaned like she was the one getting touched.

Erin liked to watch, apparently. She kept her eyes on Cassie's face even as she lavished attention on her chest. Cassie wanted to kiss her, wanted her mouth lower, wanted her to keep doing what she was doing, mouth cruel and fingers hard and fast. Cassie said *please* and *Erin* and Erin's eyes flared.

"Touch yourself," she said.

Cassie gasped again. It felt like she was on fire. Her jeans were cramped when she did as she was told and shoved a hand into them alongside Erin's. It was bone-meltingly good. She rubbed circles over her clit, not bothering to start slow when Erin already had her this worked up.

Whenever Erin hit just right, Cassie's gasps turned to whimpers. Erin wasn't just watching, she was *observant,* so it wasn't long until Cassie whimpered at every thrust. She kept losing rhythm on her clit, too distracted by the gravitational pull in her core, the buildup before a supernova. It was only a matter of time before she exploded. On the brink, Cassie stopped rubbing and pressed hard, her whole body clenching until she broke, shuddering around Erin's fingers.

Erin kissed Cassie's temple as she recovered, and Cassie bit the inside of her cheek to tamp down the goofy smile threatening to take over her face. She was always silly and pliable after sex. Erin climbed off her, but it took Cassie a few breaths to remember to move. When they were seated upright, she leaned over for a kiss. Then put her bra back on and stole another.

Erin smiled. "That was nice."

"Definitely," Cassie said, pulling her shirt over her head. "Next time I gotta get at your tits, though."

Shit.

Next time. She should never be allowed to talk this soon after orgasm.

Erin wasn't fazed, thankfully. "No next time, I'm afraid," she said. "I'm only in Virginia for the weekend visiting my daughter at school."

Cassie froze. "You've got to be kidding me."

Erin gave her this confused brow furrow and head tilt and wow, Cassie really didn't need to be wanting to kiss her again.

"Where's your kid go?" There were other schools nearby; maybe Cassie was nervous for nothing.

"Keckley College," Erin said.

Cassie stared at her for a moment. "Yeah," she said eventually. "Me too."

Erin slammed her eyes closed and huffed out a breath. Cassie stayed silent, let her work through this one on her own. Erin pinched the bridge of her nose. "Tell me you're a grad student at least."

"You want me to lie, or . . . ?"

Erin opened her eyes to level her with a look.

"Senior."

Erin groaned. "Christ. You're barely older than my daughter."

Keckley wasn't a big school, and Cassie absolutely wanted to know who Erin's kid was. But curiosity killed the cat, so she wouldn't ask. She'd already said one dumb postorgasmic thing, anyway.

"So, uh," she tried to head off any potential awkward silence, "good news, then. You know where my school is and could give me a ride home?"

Erin just looked at her. Awkward silence not avoided.

"I mean, you're not going to make me take a Lyft looking freshly fucked, are you?"

Erin scoffed. "You do not look 'freshly fucked.'"

"Um, I'm pretty sure I'm *glowing* right now," Cassie said. "Sure as shit feels like it anyway."

The compliment worked like a charm—Erin blushed and ran a hand through her hair, just like she'd done in the bar.

"Fine," she said. "I'll drive you."

They moved to the front seats with as much dignity as they could maintain. Erin put the car in drive and Cassie turned up the radio. If she had to pick between silence, awkward small talk, and music, she was definitely picking music.

Besides, Erin's phone was playing Beyoncé over the Bluetooth, and you never say no to Queen Bey.

"You ain't married to no average bitch, boy," Cassie sang along without thinking.

She cut herself off and cleared her throat. Singing in front of people she'd just met wasn't exactly her thing. But out of the corner of her eye, she could see a grin spread across Erin's face. Cassie swallowed, took a breath, and kept singing.

Neither said anything, even as they arrived on campus. Erin didn't ask where Cassie lived and Cassie didn't tell her. Maybe it was a coincidence, but the parking lot Erin pulled into was the farthest from the freshman dorms. Cassie wondered if her daughter was a freshman, before reminding herself that curiosity killed the cat, and enough pussy had been wrecked already that night.

The brightest light Cassie had seen Erin in was in the fucking bathroom, but even here, under the weak lights of the parking lot filtered through the windshield, the older woman shone. If Cassie were a romantic, she'd say Erin's eyes were like the night sky—she'd never get bored tracing their constellations. But she was absolutely not a romantic, so mostly she was just proud of herself for picking up a woman this hot. And she was never gonna see her again, so Cassie figured she might as well take advantage of the goodbye. She kissed Erin as dirty as she knew how, waited for her to lean closer, over the center console, then pulled away, Erin chasing her lips.

"It's been fun," she said, and climbed out of the car without looking back.

• • • •

Cassie wasn't awake when her phone buzzed the next morning. She ignored it without opening her eyes. No one she wanted to talk to would call her this early. But it rang again, and again after that, and fuck whoever this was, she was gonna kill them.

"The fuck do you want?" she growled as she answered.

"I know it's early, but I need you to come to breakfast with me." Parker.

Cassie rubbed at her eyes. "The *audacity* of you calling before eight on a Saturday. This might be the worst thing you've ever done to me, and yes, I'm including you sleeping with my boyfriend."

Parker was quiet. She never seemed to know how to act when Cassie joked about how they'd met. Eventually, she said, "I'm serious, Cassie."

"Acacia has *got* to be up by now."

Acacia connected them a lot more than Seth, the now ex-boyfriend. She was Parker's roommate and Cassie's best friend since they were kids. She was also a morning person for some inexplicable reason.

"She and her brother are on a hike together," Parker said and Cassie did a full-body shudder. "It'll be a free breakfast—my mom will pay. I just need, like, a buffer. She's too much sometimes, and I thought I could handle it on my own but now I'm spiraling. Please?"

Cassie resolved to never make friends with a freshman again. They were so needy.

Then again, Parker had broken Seth's nose and ended things

when she found out the douchebag had a girlfriend, so maybe she'd earned herself a favor or two.

"When are you picking me up?"

Breakfast was at one of Cassie's favorite restaurants, so by the time they arrived, she didn't even mind being out of bed so early on a weekend. A crowd of people waited to be seated.

"My mom's got a table already," Parker said, scanning the restaurant. "There."

They headed toward a woman sitting alone, facing the window, a cup of coffee steaming in front of her.

"Call her Dr. Bennett if you want to make a good impression," Parker muttered to Cassie.

"I'm great with parents, thanks."

Parker reached the table first, and as her mom stood to hug her, Cassie almost fell over.

"Hey Mom, this is Cassie. Cassie, this is my mom."

Cassie had to give Erin credit; her only tell was the slight widening of her eyes as she extended her hand. Cassie shook it, trying to keep the shit-eating grin off her face.

"Nice to meet you, Dr. Bennett," she said.

Erin squeezed her hand a little too hard. "Please, call me Erin."

Two

ERIN

Erin thanked the waitress for her coffee and the three waters for the table. She wrapped both hands around her mug and left her menu closed. No need to look before Parker and her friend arrived. Erin had found the place on Yelp earlier in the week, so she already knew it had plenty of good offerings. She'd wanted to go to Parker's favorite breakfast spot, but her daughter hadn't had any suggestions—she hadn't made it off campus for breakfast yet.

The restaurant was cute—the yellow walls bright with light from the large windows. Open umbrellas of varying colors and patterns hung upside down from the high ceiling. Erin had had to make her way through half a dozen people waiting for a table to give the hostess her name for her reservation.

Erin missed Parker. Joint custody in high school had been bad enough. Parker had done student government and the science fair and art lessons—both taking and teaching—plus, she'd spent half her time at her father's new apartment. But it was different, with her away at college. Worse.

It'd been barely more than a month, but Erin missed her. She wished she didn't have to share her with Adam this weekend. Though, if Adam wasn't also visiting, Erin wouldn't have been at that bar last night. Even if it was ridiculous she'd slept with a college student, she couldn't bring herself to regret it.

A blush crept onto her cheeks just thinking of the previous night. She had *hooked up* with a college student *in the back seat of her rental car*. Rachel would have a field day with this, but Erin hadn't decided whether she'd tell her. Her best friend had been trying to get her to, well, sleep around a bit for three years now, basically as soon as the divorce was final. Every date Erin had had in the last three years, Rachel made her recount in a full blow-by-blow—sometimes literally, depending on how the date had gone. She would *love* the recap of last night. Erin couldn't even imagine how she would explain Cassie to Rachel. The way Cassie had looked at her, the way she'd touched her, no hesitation.

Erin shook her head and smiled into her coffee mug. She should be thinking about her daughter, not about the cocky woman with the filthy grin who'd bought her a drink.

As though summoned by Erin's thoughts, Parker appeared beside the table.

"Baby!" Erin gushed, leaping up to hug her daughter.

She squeezed her tight, eyes closed, and breathed her in. Her *kid*. Parker smelled like the cheap perfume she'd worn since freshman year of high school. Erin pressed a kiss against the side of her head then let go before she could be reprimanded for holding on too long.

Parker's smile was wide and toothy, and Erin wanted to cry. God, she'd missed her.

"Mom, this is Cassie," Parker said. "Cassie, this is my mom."

It took Erin a moment to shift from looking at Parker to looking at Parker's friend. Her brain lagged, catching on the name but not figuring out why until her eyes landed on Cassie.

Cassie.

Thank God for Erin's mother drilling manners into her since she was a child—her mind might've been a never-ending scream, but Erin didn't miss a beat before extending her hand to shake Cassie's.

"Nice to meet you, Dr. Bennett." Cassie's face was nothing but a self-satisfied grin. She ran her other hand through her blond hair, just as gorgeous and cocky as she'd been last night.

Erin tried not to squeeze too hard. "Please," she said. "Call me Erin."

This could not be happening.

Parker flopped down into the booth, and Cassie slid in beside her. Erin had to put a steadying hand on the bench as she sat down.

This could *not* be happening.

Erin took too big a swallow of coffee. It burned her throat.

Parker was still smiling, and Parker's smile did what it always did: made Erin's heart sing. She loved her kid so fucking much. She could not let this—this—this *clusterfuck* of a situation mess anything up.

"How was dinner with your dad last night?" Erin asked dutifully.

Parker's smile dropped a couple of watts. "Fine."

"Where'd you go?"

Erin didn't care, except she hoped breakfast was better. She and Adam got along for Parker's sake, but it didn't mean Erin wasn't petty.

"An Italian place," Parker grumbled. She changed the subject. "What'd you do last night?"

Erin hadn't looked at Cassie since they'd sat down, but she couldn't miss the way the other woman hid a smirk by taking a sip of water. Something tightened inside her at the sense memory of that smirk.

"Nothing special," Erin said instead of blushing.

Cassie choked on her water. Parker turned and patted her back, and while her daughter was distracted, Erin cocked an eyebrow at Cassie. She was *not* going to let Cassie fuck this visit up.

She meant the look to be a threat, but it wasn't effective; Cassie seemed to take it as a challenge instead. As soon as she had her breath again, she smiled at Erin.

"How long are you in town?" Cassie asked, her bare foot brushing gently against the side of one of Erin's flats.

Erin pressed her lips together. "I fly out tomorrow evening."

"Plenty of time to entertain yourself, then," Cassie said, and her toes curled around Erin's ankle.

Erin's skin must have been bright red. It felt like that anyway—flushed and burning. Was the restaurant always this humid? She preferred the climate of New Hampshire, where she was born and raised, over that of Virginia for a lot of reasons. Added to the list: if they'd been in New Hampshire in October, Cassie wouldn't have been wearing sandals. Erin wouldn't have had to feel the heat of Cassie's skin against hers under the table.

Parker told Erin about her classes, while Cassie perused the menu and played footsie. It was insane, doing this in front of Parker. Not that Erin was doing anything except holding very still. Though perhaps not pulling back counted as doing something. She *wanted* to pull away—not because it didn't feel good, but because it *did*. Cassie's smug smile never left her face, just as bold as last night, and Erin hated that it was still working for her. She should've been mortified. She should've felt awkward and uncomfortable and embarrassed. She'd done a bad thing.

Because that was what this was: bad. How could sleeping with your daughter's friend be anything else?

Parker talked about her studio art class, clearly oblivious to anything going on under the table. Cassie slid her foot up and down Erin's calf as the waitress took their drink orders, and Erin finally forced herself to shift her legs in the other direction, away from Cassie's.

"What about you, Cassie?" Erin asked once the server left. "What are you studying?"

It was easier to look at her now that they weren't touching. Even if the smirk still hadn't left Cassie's face.

"I'm a physics major," she said. "Going into engineering."

"She's going to be an astronaut!" Parker said.

Erin raised her eyebrows. "Oh?"

"I am not," Cassie sighed. "I'm going to Caltech next year to study aerospace engineering, yeah, but I don't even know if I want to do aeronautics or astronautics yet." She must've noticed Erin's complete lack of comprehension because she continued. "Stuff inside the Earth's atmosphere, like planes and sh—stuff, or outside, like, yes, spaceships."

It was laughable that Cassie stopped herself from swearing. As though Erin hadn't already made her curse.

"See?" Parker said. "Astronaut."

Cassie rolled her eyes and gave Erin a grin. Erin couldn't help but smile back.

Parker excused herself to use the restroom after the server took their orders. Once Erin was sure her daughter was out of earshot, she turned to glare at Cassie, who still looked like a cat who'd eaten the canary.

"Cassie," Erin said, voice low and warning, and Cassie's grin went a little feral instead of disappearing like Erin had hoped. "I need you to stop."

"I did!" Cassie protested. "You moved away, and I stopped."

"You need to stop *looking at me like that*."

Cassie furrowed her brow, like maybe she hadn't meant to be looking at her any sort of way. Erin couldn't deny that it was nice— she was less than two years out from forty; it wasn't like it was a hardship to have a twentysomething as obviously attracted to her as Cassie was. If only it were that simple.

"That is my *daughter*." Erin's shoulders slumped. "She already spends half her time hating me for divorcing her father. Please don't make this harder than it has to be."

She scrubbed a hand through her hair. Cassie bumped a leg against hers under the table, and Erin looked at her, defeated.

"No, I just meant—" Cassie cut herself off. She folded her hands in her lap. Erin would've bet her ankles were crossed under the table. "Sorry. I'll be good."

Erin took a sip of her coffee instead of indulging in a smile. It didn't matter if Cassie was cute.

Parker returned then. Cassie slid farther into the booth instead of bothering to get up and let Parker in.

"Whacha talking about?" Parker asked.

Cassie didn't miss a beat. "Just trying to get your mom to tell me embarrassing stories about you as a kid."

"There are none," Parker said, her nose in the air. "I was a perfect child."

Erin snorted. "She was a manipulative little shit."

Cassie burst out laughing, and Erin had to take another sip of coffee.

"She still is," Cassie said. "She brags all the time about how her ability to convince professors to have class outside on nice days is unparalleled."

"I am not manipulative." Parker tossed her hair. "I'm persuasive."

Cassie and Erin laughed at her, and Parker gave a goofy grin.

"Whatever," she said. "Cassie, you're coming to a cappella tonight, right?"

"To see you sing and make eyes at that girl from The BarBelles? Wouldn't miss it for the world."

"What's that now?" Erin smiled as Parker groaned. "Does my daughter have a crush?"

Parker stared daggers at Cassie. "Why did I invite you to breakfast again?"

"My wonderful personality, I think it was."

Cassie smiled like butter wouldn't melt in her mouth.

By the time they finished, the crowd waiting for tables extended onto the sidewalk in front of the restaurant. Parker and Cassie headed outside while Erin went to the counter to pay. She watched them through the window. Parker giggled at something Cassie said. Erin let out a happy sigh.

Breakfast had gone well—so much better than she'd expected

once she laid eyes on Cassie. Parker was happy and talkative, Cassie was charming and funny. It'd been easy. So much of Erin's relationship with her daughter wasn't, since the divorce. Parker had always been a daddy's girl. She and Erin were too much alike not to butt heads. But with Cassie between them, they'd talked and laughed and that knot of anxiety in Erin's chest had loosened.

Who would've thought it would end up being a good thing that Erin's one-night stand came to breakfast?

That part was still too ridiculous for Erin to process. She'd freak out about it at her hotel later, when she had time to think. For the time being, she just smiled as she rejoined Cassie and Parker out front.

The way Cassie grinned at her made Erin feel like the only person in the world, despite the crowd of waiting patrons around them. Cassie must have really not been paying attention to their surroundings, though, because while she was busy smiling at Erin, she stumbled off the curb.

Erin didn't stop to think. She was just there, an arm around Cassie's waist, holding her up until Cassie could get her feet underneath her.

"Good?" Erin asked. She couldn't help but think of the last time she'd lifted Cassie off the ground, when she'd set her on the counter and pushed her knees wide.

"Great," Cassie said, looking at Erin's mouth.

It took Erin a moment to let go.

With Cassie's long hair down, Erin noticed, for the first time, an unnatural tint to it.

"Is that pink?"

"Streaks, yeah," Cassie said, a hand coming up to tug on a lock. "Too much work to keep up a whole head of color."

"It looks good."

When Erin finally took a step away from Cassie, the rest of the world came hurtling back, Parker looking between them, her brow furrowed. Erin pretended not to notice.

Cassie took a different, more direct route. "What?" she snapped.

"There's the Cassie I know," Parker said. "You don't let anyone but Acacia touch you."

Cassie ducked her head and Erin pressed her lips together. She was *definitely* going to freak out about this at her hotel later, but for now, she let herself enjoy the way Cassie's cheeks reddened.

"I just met your mom. Didn't want to be rude."

Parker laughed. "When has that ever stopped you from doing anything?"

Erin took the opportunity to change the subject. She didn't want to give Parker too much time to think about the way Cassie behaved around her.

"It was lovely to meet you, Cassie."

Cassie's smile was free of hunger for once. "You, too."

"I'll see you tonight at the concert?" Erin asked. "Promise you'll show me which one is Parker's crush?"

"Mom!"

"I will," Cassie said, eyes sparkling. "But Erin? Parker makes it obvious all on her own."

Parker grumbled as Erin laughed.

Parker met Erin in front of her dorm after dropping Cassie off at her apartment. Erin had seen the room when she and Adam had brought Parker to school, but it hadn't been decorated then. And though she'd caught glimpses while video chatting with Parker, it was better in person. Twinkle lights lined every wall. Parker's half of the room was orderly and clean, posters perfectly straight and evenly distanced. Acacia's side wasn't messy so much as less controlled—a giant corkboard with photos and sticky notes and ticket stubs tacked all over it. Erin didn't mean to pry, but her eyes snagged on a picture of a much younger Acacia, braids in her hair instead of the shaved head she had now. Beside Acacia in the picture, unmistakable even though the photo was from maybe ten years ago—

"Is that Cassie?" Erin asked.

"Yeah," Parker said. "She and Acacia grew up together."

Cassie was just a kid in the photo, her straw-blond hair piled on top of her head in an absolute rat's nest. She was too skinny, like she hadn't been well fed or had just had a growth spurt. Erin felt like she was intruding, somehow, looking at the picture. She turned to Parker, who nodded toward the photo.

"That's like their first picture together, I think," she said. "They've been best friends since they were like nine and ten."

Erin went rigid. Cassie had said she was a senior. "Cassie's only a year older than you?"

"What?" Parker said, distracted as she put her breakfast leftovers inside the mini fridge under her bed. "No. She's a year older than Acacia, who's two years older than me."

"Acacia's not a freshman?"

"Oh," Parker said like she only just understood Erin's original question. "No. Didn't I tell you she transferred in as a junior? We're just both first-year students. That's why they put us together."

Erin let out her breath, relieved. Fucking a college student was bad enough, but fucking a *sophomore* was unthinkable.

"So you met Cassie through Acacia?"

Parker stood and straightened her comforter, her back still to Erin. "Sort of."

Erin chewed her bottom lip and waited, hoping for more without having to pry. Parker sighed and turned around.

"That guy I met who I thought . . . whatever. That guy from the beginning of the semester—"

"The guy you punched?" Erin cut in. She secretly loved that Parker had given the asshole what he deserved. "The one with a girlfriend?"

Parker nodded. She crossed her arms in front of her.

"Cassie was the girlfriend."

Erin didn't say anything.

"I told you I didn't know," Parker said, defensive. "I ended it as soon as I found out he had a girlfriend. And even after they broke up, I'm not—"

"I know, baby, I know," Erin said. "I'm sorry. I didn't mean to—I wasn't judging you. Just taking in the information."

"Okay."

What Erin had been doing, actually, was wondering if that made it better; was it less of a betrayal, somehow, that she and Cassie had slept together, given that her daughter had had a thing with Cassie's boyfriend? She hated herself for the thought.

"So whatever, this is my room," Parker said. "It's just a dorm. C'mon, I wanna show you the studio."

Magnolia trees lined the path from the residential to the academic side of campus. Parker called hello to some kids lounging in low branches of the tree closest to her dorm. They told her to break a leg tonight.

Erin loved the way Parker fit in easily here, even with how different it was from where she grew up—plenty of southern accents and a smaller student body than Parker's high school. The campus stretched from the freshman dorms on the farthest edge of one side to the library on the other, that magnolia-lined path all the way through. Buildings branched off from it, many with white columns in the front that made them look more like mansions than academic buildings. Walking the entire path took less than fifteen minutes.

Parker talked the whole time, and Erin wasn't going to remember half of the facts and stories told in rapid-fire succession, but she wasn't about to interrupt. It was harder being an empty nester than she liked to admit. Erin had gotten the house in the divorce. The big, silent house. Not that Parker didn't call—every Sunday, like the dutiful, perfect daughter she was. Erin just missed her, missed her voice in person, not over a tinny cell phone speaker.

That voice went quiet, reverent, as Parker led Erin into the art building. Their footsteps echoed in the empty hallway. Erin felt a little reverent herself, getting to see the place where Parker spent so much of her time.

Large windows filled two walls of the studio and provided plenty of natural light. Empty easels took up most of the room, individual drop cloths under each. A counter with a huge sink in the middle of it ran along one wall. Splotches of paint marked the countertop. There was an old-school boombox that Erin imagined got plenty of use. At home, Parker had always listened to music at ridiculously high volumes when she painted.

Parker led Erin to a group of tall skinny cubbies in the corner of the room.

She pulled a canvas out of one, the tips of her ears going red.

"It's gorgeous," Erin whispered.

She'd told her the same thing about every piece of artwork since before Parker was coloring inside the lines. It was true, every time.

"Maureen—the professor—she's been trying to get me to major in art."

"You've barely been here a month," Erin said. "You've got time to decide."

Parker slid the canvas back into the cubbyhole labeled with her name. "Yeah. Right."

She sounded disappointed. Erin tried to fix it.

"I mean, I can see why she'd want you to," she said. "You've always been absurdly talented. I just don't want you to feel like you have to pick right away. College is a time to figure out who you are and what you want. It's your first time away from home. You can do—"

"Oh my God, Mom, I know, I've heard your inspiring college speech like nine hundred times."

"You have to let me mom you at least a little, now that I don't have as many chances to do it," Erin said. "You know I'm going to be hideously embarrassing cheering at your concert tonight, right?"

Parker groaned theatrically, but she was laughing, her previous discontent gone.

Three

ERIN

Erin should've felt worse about this situation than she did.

She *fucked* one of her daughter's friends! Rationally, she knew how absurd that was.

This was just . . . not a thing that happened. People didn't sleep with their children's friends—at least not the type of people Erin knew. Jesus, her mother would've *killed* her. Getting divorced had been bad enough, now a sex scandal?

It wasn't going to be a *scandal*, obviously. No one in Nashua knew anything about it. Only Erin and Cassie knew. And that was how it was going to stay. No one could ever know. She had considered telling Rachel when it was a standard one-night stand, but now? No. This was a secret Erin needed to take to her grave.

Here was the thing, though . . .

It was great sex. No, "great" was not the proper adjective. It was outstanding, unbelievable, history-making, world-shaking sex. It couldn't just have been that Erin hadn't slept with a woman since college. Erin had had good sex—even since the divorce, she'd had good sex. She'd never had sex like that. Which didn't even make sense because it had been in the back seat of a car. Who has the best sex of their life in a parking lot in the back of a rental?

Cassie wasn't even old enough to rent a car.

Erin should've been embarrassed.

Erin should not have been sitting on the edge of her hotel room bed, wondering if there was a way for it to happen again. She should not have been considering changing her clothes. There was no reason she couldn't wear what she wore to breakfast to the a cappella concert.

Then again, she left tomorrow. If she didn't change, then she'd overpacked. It would've been a waste, really, if she didn't change.

In a fit of pique yesterday morning, Erin had thrown her favorite jeans into her suitcase. The ones Rachel always said made her ass look amazing. She hadn't needed to pack them, and she definitely didn't need to wear them. She'd packed the jeans for Adam, to remind him how hot his ex-wife was. Adam was not the reason Erin edged them up her legs.

She wasn't doing anything wrong. It wasn't a crime to want to look nice. It hurt no one to distract Cassie with a little cleavage. Sure, maybe Erin was thinking more about how Cassie didn't get to see her boobs last night, how it was a lot easier to pull a shirt over her head than take a dress off—but it wasn't like anything was going to happen. They were going to be in an auditorium filled with people.

There was a chance she wouldn't even see Cassie, Erin realized as she found a seat. She left the aisle seat open next to her, even though Cassie had probably already arrived. She'd be sitting with Acacia or any number of age-appropriate friends. Erin looked for her anyway.

Erin would've had a hard time finding Parker in a crowd this big; she had no chance of finding someone she'd only met twice. In the bar—and in the bar's parking lot—the light had been too low for her to even notice the pink streaks in Cassie's hair. The crowd here was boisterous, a steady hum of noise punctuated by occasional shouting or shrieks of laughter. It skewed young. Young enough that Erin wanted to look away. She'd *slept* with a *college student*.

Just as she decided it was too late—past the time the concert was supposed to start—Cassie walked right by her.

Erin didn't pause before saying her name.

Cassie turned around, grinning when she laid eyes on Erin. God, she was pretty. Erin swallowed. Smiled. Gestured to the seat next to her.

Cassie's hair was in a braided ponytail. A few strands had come loose, dangling around her face. She was in the same clothes from breakfast, but they were a mess now. Something black was smeared across the front of her plain white T-shirt. She must have wiped the same thing off her hands onto her jeans, streaking along her thighs. She looked like a mechanic after a long day, and Erin's entire body was suddenly too hot.

Cassie spared a glance toward the front of the auditorium before sliding into the seat beside Erin.

"Hey," she said, stretching one leg out into the aisle.

Whoops went through the audience as the lights went down. The stage door opened, and the crowd noise rose to a crescendo as the first group walked out.

"You made it just in time," Erin said.

She was grateful for the timing, actually, as it saved her from small talk. Her tongue felt thick in her mouth. She tried to focus on the group onstage, not the way Cassie's hands fidgeted in her lap, not the sense memory of those hands on her body. The singers were all boys—men—*guys*. Their opening song was "Billie Jean."

This didn't need to be weird. Cassie had promised Erin she'd point out Parker's crush—how would she do that if they didn't sit together? That was all this was. There was no reason for Erin to be hyperaware of Cassie's movements as she did something on her phone, then pulled her canvas jacket closed over her stomach. There was no reason for Erin to want to tell Cassie that she didn't have to hide the stain on her shirt, that Erin liked the idea of Cassie getting dirty.

Three songs went by before Cassie said anything else. And when she did, it was: "Sorry if I stink."

Erin tried not to laugh. What a way to start a conversation.

"I was in the shop all day," Cassie continued. "Didn't have time to get all dolled up."

Her eyes flicked to Erin's chest. Erin wore a V-neck that showed a hint of cleavage, but it was still just a T-shirt—she was hardly dolled up. The attention made her bold. She dragged her eyes up Cassie's body.

"You are a little dirty, aren't you?"

Honest to God, Cassie's jaw dropped.

Erin turned back to the stage instead of giggling. She felt like a schoolgirl. Like she was flirting with someone for the first time, giddy and fluttery.

Cassie didn't reply, but she relaxed in her seat, her foot shifting a little closer to Erin's. Close enough for Erin to have noticed, but not close enough to be an explicit move. They both had plausible deniability.

They stayed not quite touching for the rest of the first performance. The second group to the stage was Parker's—the Sky High Notes. Cassie sat up straight, put two fingers in her mouth, and wolf whistled. It was loud enough that Erin laughed, delighted. Cassie slid her a grin, and Erin made a decision.

As Sky High Notes started their first song—a Disney medley Parker had gushed about on their past three Sunday phone calls— Erin adjusted in her seat, her thigh pressing against Cassie's.

There went plausible deniability.

They should have done this during the previous group's performance. It probably made it worse to touch Cassie while Parker was onstage. But it gave Erin an extra little thrill. Her whole life, she'd followed the rules. Maybe she would've been more of a rebel if she'd realized breaking them would feel this good.

In the break between songs, Cassie interlaced her fingers and stretched her arms in front of herself, palms out. She cracked her neck.

"Ouch," Erin said. "Is that normal?"

"Long day in the shop. Just a little sore. Do you mind?" Cassie settled her arm around Erin's chair.

"Not at all."

By the end of the next song, Erin's back was pressed into the curve of Cassie's arm.

"Parker says she's got a mini solo in this next one," Erin said.

Cassie nodded. "That's a big deal for a freshman in her first concert."

Parker was good at everything she'd ever done. Erin was so proud of her, even while she also wished Parker would slow down. Not grow up so quickly, not push herself so hard. Erin knew her daughter could do anything, but she wanted her to just *be* for a while.

She couldn't say any of that to Cassie, obviously, so she said nothing.

When Sky High Notes finished, Cassie and Erin cheered so loudly that Parker noticed, laughing and blowing a kiss their way. Erin pretended to catch it in the air, determined to be the embarrassing mom. She couldn't tell from where she was sitting if Parker rolled her eyes, but she hoped so.

Before the next group came on, Cassie brushed her hand over Erin's leg. Erin started in surprise.

"I'm gonna run to the bathroom," Cassie said, voice low.

Erin swallowed. Nodded. She didn't watch Cassie go. Ten seconds ago, she was being Parker's embarrassing mom, and now she was pressing her lips together and trying to keep her breath steady.

Last night, it had been easy to join Cassie at the bar, easy to be suggestive as she went to the bathroom. Cassie had wanted it, obviously, and Erin had, too. She'd needed the distraction, hadn't wanted to think about her ex-husband and wonder who her daughter loved more. Cassie looked hot, and she didn't hide her interest. Erin hadn't thought very hard before leading her to the rental car.

But today was different.

Today, Erin knew Cassie was in college. She knew she was her *daughter's friend.* She knew exactly what a bad idea it would be to follow her.

She followed her anyway.

Erin didn't even know where the bathrooms were. Keckley was not a big school; this wasn't a big building. The noises fell away behind her as she ducked out of the auditorium, finding the doors she'd come in earlier to her left. The right led to a hallway, but it'd been blocked off for performers only. Erin's eyes darted around. She was taking too long. Cassie was going to think she wasn't coming.

Finally, she caught sight of a sign that said RESTROOMS with an arrow pointing down a set of stairs she hadn't noticed earlier. Erin's feet carried her quickly down.

Cassie loitered at the end of the hallway on the lower level. She disappeared through a door before Erin finished descending the stairs.

There was no one else to be seen, so no one could prove if Erin's pace ended up somewhere between a power walk and a run.

The door Cassie had gone through was to an accessible, single occupancy, all gender restroom. Erin took a moment to be glad her kid was going to such an inclusive school before remembering she *really* didn't want to be thinking about Parker right now.

She slipped inside the bathroom and locked the door behind her.

Cassie was already against the counter, like she expected Erin to lift her onto it for a second night in a row. Erin just looked at her. She was *gorgeous,* that golden hair against her tanned skin, long lashes framing her dark blue eyes. There was not a single wrinkle on her face.

"We shouldn't," Erin said, because it was true.

Cassie nodded, but she didn't blink. "I know. It's wrong, and we shouldn't, and—"

Erin kissed her.

Erin kissed her because it was wrong and they shouldn't but she *wanted* to. Lately she'd been trying to do the things she wanted, to make up for lost time.

Her reasons didn't really matter, though. Not when Cassie's tongue was wet and warm enough to melt everything in its way. She kissed like she'd never been worried she wasn't good at it. Erin tried to keep up, tried to do everything she'd done last night that made Cassie gasp. Kissing her way down Cassie's jaw worked just as well today.

"We shouldn't fuck in here," Cassie said like that would convince Erin of the opposite.

Erin laughed against Cassie's neck. "We're not going to."

She'd decided that already. She could only make so many bad decisions during a single a cappella concert. Thinking of the concert reminded her that they needed to be back sooner rather than later. She dug her teeth into the thin skin over Cassie's collarbone. Cassie let out a whimper—it should've been illegal how hot that was.

Cassie's hands tightened their grip on Erin's hips and she pivoted them, switching positions, pushing Erin back against the counter for once. Erin lifted herself up onto it and Cassie stepped between her legs. She kissed her. And kissed her and kissed her and kissed her. It felt like everything they'd done last night turned upside down. Erin was the one on the counter, and they weren't moving too fast; they weren't moving fast at all. Cassie's fingernails were scratching softly against Erin's scalp while she explored just how Erin liked to be kissed. That must've been what she was doing, anyway—fast then slow, wet turned to chaste, deep to teasing.

Erin liked it all.

And no, they weren't going to fuck in this bathroom, but that didn't mean they couldn't take this a little bit further.

"Ca—ah—" Erin broke off when Cassie bit at her jaw. "Cassie?"

"Mm-hmm?" She bit again.

Erin shuddered, and she felt Cassie's responding grin against the side of her face.

"Wasn't there something you wanted to do?" When it didn't seem to click, Erin added: "*Next time?*"

Cassie tugged Erin's shirt over her head before Erin could blink.

She stared at Erin's chest, jaw slack and eyes hungry, and suddenly the needlessly sexy and somewhat uncomfortable bra was totally worth it. Cassie's fingers made quick work of the back clasp, and then Erin was fully topless. She almost shrunk back, aware of the harsh fluorescent lights and the decade and a half she had on the woman in front of her. But Cassie just stared some more, the saliva clicking in her throat when she swallowed.

"*Fuck,* you've got nice tits," she breathed.

She'd said it last night, too, but it felt more real now. Erin believed it now. Cassie's hands cupped her, squeezing more gently than Erin would've liked, but before she could instruct her any differently, Cassie's lips were on her. She rolled one nipple between her thumb and forefinger and sucked the other into her mouth.

Erin tried not to gasp. *"Fuck."*

"Glad you wore a shirt this time," Cassie said, but the words were muffled from the way she didn't take her mouth off Erin's skin to say them. "Easier access."

"I thought you'd appreciate it," Erin said before she thought better of it.

Cassie bit down, and Erin's head dropped back, thumping into the mirror. Cassie swirled her tongue gently, her hand coming up to cradle the back of Erin's head.

Erin hadn't meant to say anything. She hadn't meant to tip her hand quite so obviously. Now Cassie knew this wasn't so much something that just happened as it was something Erin had thought about.

Maybe this had been inevitable from the moment Erin had decided to wear a shirt instead of a dress. Maybe it had been inevitable from the moment Cassie had started flirting this morning.

Cassie marked her. Erin hadn't had a hickey since well before the divorce, but Cassie was leaving them now. Sucking and biting and soothing the sting with her tongue. She had enough sense to keep her mouth low, only on skin that would be covered when Erin put her shirt back on.

Erin got a hand in Cassie's hair. The braid came out of its elastic, and Erin threaded her fingers through the loose ponytail. When Cassie sucked a hickey too high on Erin's chest, Erin tugged. Cassie moaned, and Erin swore she felt it on her clit.

One of Cassie's hands had worked its way between Erin's ass and the counter. She slid it around to the button on Erin's jeans. Erin caught Cassie's wrist and kissed along her jaw.

"We're not doing that." She sucked right beneath Cassie's ear, considered leaving marks of her own.

"Erin—" Cassie broke off as Erin bit at the tendon standing out on her neck.

Erin had to stop. She had to get her mouth off Cassie's skin while she still could. She took a deep breath and pressed their foreheads together.

"I'm serious," she said with her eyes closed. "We should get back."

Cassie bumped her nose against Erin's. "I thought we weren't worrying about what we should and shouldn't do."

Erin laughed, gently enough that it was mostly breath. She pulled back. Cassie's pupils were blown wide. Her lips were swollen, her hair sex-mussed. Erin wanted to mess it up further. She thought about her kid instead.

"You've got to point out the girl Parker has a crush on, remember?"

Mentioning Parker did its job. Cassie stepped back.

"I'll leave first?" she said.

Erin chuckled as she slid herself off the counter. "Just tell me if anyone's out there."

Erin put her bra back on as Cassie fixed her ponytail. Purpling welts covered Erin's chest, a map of everywhere Cassie's mouth had been. Seeing them in the mirror made Erin clench.

When they were presentable again, Cassie kissed her instead of checking the hallway.

"Where are you staying?"

Erin could've told her. It could've been that easy.

But there was letting yourself have what you wanted, and then there was hedonism.

She kissed Cassie one last time. "Let's go."

That was it. This could never happen again.

They slipped into their seats right before The BarBelles came on, having missed the entire third group. Cassie gestured to a girl with more stage presence than the rest of the group combined.

"That's her."

"She's cute," Erin said. "Parker's got good taste."

"Like mother, like daughter."

Erin rolled her eyes like she didn't find Cassie totally charming.

Four

CASSIE

By the time the concert ended, Cassie had sufficiently calmed down. She and Erin had kept their hands, thighs, arms to themselves for the rest of the performance, so she could breathe again. They stayed in their seats while the auditorium emptied around them. It was rude; they were on an aisle. But getting up meant accepting this whole thing was over.

Cassie finally stood when Acacia came strutting up the aisle with a grin on her face. She'd shaved off her relaxed hair when she came to school, and Cassie was still getting used to it, but Acacia somehow looked so much more *herself* than she had before.

"There you are!" She tugged Cassie into a hug. "I thought you weren't gonna show up and I was going to have to help Parker hide your body."

"Really, Kaysh?" Cassie said, using the nickname she'd had for her since they were little. "You wouldn't protect me from her?"

"Hey, you and me go back, but you know she gets scary!"

Erin laughed beside Cassie, and Acacia turned to her.

"You must be Dr. Bennett," she said. "I'm Acacia."

Erin shook her hand. "Call me Erin. I've heard a lot about you."

"A lot of terrible things, probably," Cassie said. Acacia punched her in the shoulder, harder than necessary. "Hey, where's your big brother?"

"He had some work to do. He'll meet us later," she said with a look that meant the work he had to do was likely buying them booze. Emerson had been buying them alcohol since long before Cassie was legal.

"Hiiiiiii!" Parker appeared, practically tackling Acacia in a hug. "Thanks for coming!"

There was the requisite doting on the star of the concert while Parker told them to stop—the giant grin on her face telling them otherwise.

As they headed toward an exit, Cassie realized what an idiot she was. If she'd wanted a proper goodbye, she should have done it in the bathroom. They were sure as shit not going to get one now. For one terrifying moment, she wished she was a hugger, because at least then she'd get to touch Erin again.

Okay, you're done. She shut it down. She'd just wished she was a *hugger.* This had clearly gone too far. Erin was a good kisser, but that was ridiculous. *Get ahold of yourself.* She'd say goodbye to Erin and move on. Emerson better be buying a lot of booze.

Except God hated her, or something, because instead of getting to flee and put all of this behind her, she heard Parker shout, "Daddy!" and watched her catapult herself into the arms of the man waiting by the door.

Of course Parker's dad was here. Cassie had known that. Parker being with her dad was what allowed her mom to be in the fucking bar last night.

Cassie wiped her hands on her jeans—which she'd forgotten were streaked with grease from the shop—and chanced a glance at Erin, who was looking elsewhere, jaw clenched tight.

"Hey baby," her dad said. Then, with much lower enthusiasm, "Erin."

"Adam." Erin's spine was stiff. Cassie wasn't sure she would've noticed if she hadn't seen how Erin was earlier, loose and grinning and at ease. Now she was ramrod straight and unblinking.

Parker was still grinning like a thousand-watt bulb, hanging off her dad's arm. "Daddy, you remember Acacia from when you dropped me off. This is my other best friend, Cassie."

Best friend? They'd barely known each other a month. Then again, the only person Cassie hung out with more than Parker was Acacia. She'd gotten out of bed before 8 A.M. on a Saturday for Parker.

Everything with Erin seemed worse if Cassie and Parker were *best* friends.

"Nice to see you again, Acacia, and nice meet you, Cassie," Adam said, running a hand through his shaggy hair. He was so not hot enough for Erin. "Are your families here?"

"My brother is running an errand," Acacia said. "We're going to meet up with him later."

"And yours, Cassie?"

She didn't want to talk about her family, or lack thereof, especially not to Adam, who looked like a mediocre white man who had never not gotten his way. "Nope."

Adam's smile faltered, just a little, at her lack of enthusiasm. "They didn't make the trip to see their daughter for the weekend?"

"Nope," she repeated.

She was an only child who'd never met her father and hadn't seen her mom in almost a year. Adam didn't deserve to know any of that. *Parker* didn't even know all of that. Acacia stepped closer to Cassie, best friend instinct or something. Cassie didn't know why, but she looked at Erin, whose face was creased with concern.

"Shoot," Adam said. "I would've liked to take everyone out for a drink or something. Bond over the beautiful girls in our lives."

"Well, my mom's an alcoholic, so I'm sure she would've loved that, too."

Cassie shouldn't have said it. But well meaning or not, Adam was obnoxious, and Erin looked in pain, and Cassie really didn't want to be here anymore.

Adam laughed like he thought it was a joke, and Parker finally let go of his arm.

"Anyway," Acacia said, "it was nice to meet you, but we've got to go meet my brother. Great job tonight, Parker."

"Thanks," Parker said. She looked at Cassie. "I'll catch up with you guys later, okay?"

"Sure," Cassie said.

She considered asking about The BarBelles girl—Sam, she thought her name was—but some childish part of her wanted that to be a joke with Erin only. She said nothing instead, felt small and petulant. Acacia brushed their arms together and turned to Erin.

"It was really nice to meet you," Acacia said.

"Thanks again for breakfast, Erin," Cassie said.

Erin put a hand on her shoulder, and it took a lot of effort not to lean into it.

"Anytime, Cassie. It was great to get to know you," Erin said.

Cassie had no idea what that meant. She didn't know why Erin was touching her, either. Parker had been right at breakfast that Cassie didn't usually like to be touched, but she liked the warmth of Erin's hand through her shirt. Adam looked like he wanted redemption, somehow, like he wasn't sure how the conversation had gotten away from him, and Cassie really needed to get out of here. Acacia tugged her away by an arm.

"C'mon, babe, the booze isn't going to drink itself," Acacia said once they were out of earshot.

"Kaysh, he was—"

"I know," she said. Then: "Am I wrong, though, or is Parker's mom kind of a MILF?"

Cassie sputtered. "Oh my God."

"I'm just saying!"

"Can we talk about literally anything else?"

"Okay, okay. Let's go get you drunk."

"You're my best friend," Cassie said as Acacia pulled her toward the dorms.

Acacia *was* her best friend. She had been since they'd met on a playground before either had hit double digits. Cassie had been too young to be unsupervised, but that had never stopped her mom.

Their first meeting, Cassie and Acacia had battled to see who could swing higher. A year younger, Acacia's little brown legs had already been longer than Cassie's dirty white ones, but the extra height couldn't overcome Cassie's sheer will. She had pumped her legs like she was going to launch herself into the sky.

When Acacia's mom had said, "You here all by yourself?" Cassie had crossed her arms and said, "*So?*"

But when Mama Webb—of course this was before Cassie knew her as Mama Webb—had offered Cassie a sandwich out of their picnic basket, she hadn't said no. The Webb family had been a fixture in Cassie's life ever since. Acacia, obviously, but Mama Webb and Mr. Ben and Emerson, too.

That was what Emerson was: a fixture. Like furniture that came with her dorm apartment. Always there. Cassie had never thought of him in any sort of romantic way, and she didn't the night of the a cappella concert, either. It was just that she got good and plastered. That was why they ended up making out half the night. That and maybe the fact that she'd wanted to forget about Erin.

She expected Acacia to be pissed, maybe, but instead Kaysh spent Cassie's entire hangover teasing her about it, which Cassie supposed was a slightly better outcome than her being angry. And making out with Emerson had been a *much* better way to spend the night than thinking about Erin.

Without distractions like Emerson, though, she ended up thinking about Erin kind of a lot. Not all the time, but enough that it bothered her.

It started with—well, Cassie had had a rough start to her week and she was looking for a little stress relief. It only made sense that she thought of her most recent super-hot experience to help her get off. That was what she meant to do, anyway, think of the experience, not of Erin specifically, but it all got a little muddled in her brain.

Then in her bio class, she wondered what kind of doctor Erin was. She thought through any conversations with Parker about her parents, but she didn't talk about them much. Cassie only knew Erin was a doctor and Adam was an engineer, and they both had spent a lot of Parker's childhood working. She wondered if that meant Erin was a surgeon, long hours and holidays on call.

When the professor released the class, Cassie realized she'd been zoning out thinking about Erin for almost ten minutes. Shit.

The next weekend came, and she found a party giving away free jungle juice. She went alone, without Acacia or Parker or anyone, and she didn't plan on getting wild. But free jungle juice was free jungle juice.

She ended up dancing with *Gwen,* of all people. Gwen might not have hated Cassie, but they weren't anything like friends. Back when Cassie was a sophomore, her ambition may have gotten the best of her in a game of capture the flag, and there *may* have been an explosion as Gwen and her friend neared Cassie's team's flag. It had been more smoke and loud noises than anything that would've hurt anyone, but it certainly hadn't endeared Cassie to her then-RA. Yet here they were, at the same party even though Gwen had started at the grad school this fall—getting her master's in social work, Cassie was pretty sure. Here they were, dancing together, Cassie's hands wandering a little too much.

When Gwen took Cassie's hand off her ass and led her outside, Cassie thought she was getting lucky. She did not expect Gwen to dodge her attempt at a kiss.

"Gimme your phone," Gwen said.

Cassie unlocked it and handed it over, not sure why she wanted it but still hoping they were going to make out.

"Which of your friends has a car and is most likely to be sober on a Friday night?"

"Parker," Cassie answered without a thought. She was working on a painting due Monday.

Gwen scrolled through Cassie's contacts. Before Cassie could get her shit together enough to figure out what was happening, Gwen was giving Parker the address to the party and telling her she'd wait outside with Cassie until she arrived.

"What the fuck?" Cassie snapped when Gwen handed back her phone.

Gwen's gaze was flat, unimpressed. "You obviously need someone to take care of you, and it's not going to be me."

Cassie sputtered. She didn't need anyone to take care of her, hadn't for a long time. She just wanted to hook up with someone. It didn't even have to be Gwen; she was just pretty and older and seemed to have her shit together. Cassie refused to think too hard about why she was attracted to that sort of thing right now.

"Fuck you," she said, turning to go back inside and find someone else to make her night interesting.

Gwen put herself between Cassie and the house.

"Your friend is coming to pick you up."

Cassie practically growled. "Get out of my way."

"No."

Cassie didn't bother trying to maneuver around her. She considered walking away—heading toward campus on her own—but she was drunk and the idea of Parker chasing her down, catching her on the side of the road, was a lot more humiliating than waiting for her.

Parker thought it was funny and teased her the whole way to campus. At least that saved Cassie from having an obnoxiously sincere heart-to-heart about why she was getting drunk and hitting on older girls. She really didn't want to talk about it.

Except she must have, because the first weekend in November she talked Acacia into a nostalgic movie night where they watched *How to Train Your Dragon,* just the two of them. Right before the battle against the Red Death, Cassie paused the movie.

"I have to tell you something."

Acacia picked the last of the popcorn from the bowl in her lap. "Shoot."

Cassie sighed. "Kaysh. It's like. A thing."

They'd gone through too much vodka for her to better communicate how important this was. Acacia seemed to get it anyway; she set the bowl on the coffee table and turned to sit cross-legged on the couch, devoting her full attention to Cassie.

"What is it?"

Cassie ran her fingers through her hair. "No, you know what, it's not a big deal, don't even worry about it."

"Klein," Acacia said, and it was a command.

"Okay, but like—" Cassie took another swallow of her vodka tonic. "You can't tell anyone. Or judge me. Or hate me."

"Cassie, you know I'm never gonna hate you."

Cassie did—for the most part. Her mom wasn't around, and her dad had never been around, and most of her friends had left her for Seth even though he'd cheated, but Kaysh—she was the only one who had always been there. So Cassie knew Acacia wouldn't hate her, but she also knew that Acacia and Parker were best friends—not Acacia and Cassie–level best friends, but best friends nonetheless. But Cassie needed to tell someone, and it wasn't like she could tell Parker.

"Okay, but no one," she repeated. "Not Emerson, not Donovan, not Parker."

They were the only three she might've told—brother, boyfriend, best friend—but she *couldn't.* Acacia nodded solemnly.

"Before I knew who she was," Cassie started, because that was *absolutely critical* information for Acacia to have. She let the rest come out all in one rushed breath. "I kinda accidentally slept with Parker's mom."

Acacia was silent.

Then she laughed. She laughed and laughed and reached over to throw unpopped popcorn kernels at Cassie.

"You're so dumb," she said. "I thought you had something real going on."

Cassie stared at her, helpless. She finished her drink.

"Babe . . ." Acacia's smile slowly dropped off her face. "Wait, are you not kidding?"

Cassie could only muster a tight-lipped shake of her head.

"Holy shit, Cassie."

If Cassie had been anyone else, that was when she would've started to cry. But she wasn't *crying* over some woman she'd slept with once. That wasn't why she'd told Acacia. She just needed to not keep the secret anymore.

"You slept with Parker's mom?"

Cassie swallowed. "I didn't know she was her mom at the time."

Acacia took a deep breath. She looked toward the ceiling, like she was trying to figure out the details without having to ask.

"When?" she finally said.

"Family Weekend," Cassie answered. "Friday."

Acacia's eyes went wide. "Friday? Friday like the day before you went out to breakfast with her and Parker? The day before you sat next to her at the a cappella concert?"

Cassie nodded.

"Fuck, Cass," Acacia said. "How did you even sit next to her? God—you didn't do anything then, did you?"

"No," she said immediately. "I mean—we just, like a little, in the bathroom—"

"What the *fuck,* Cassie?"

Cassie wasn't going to cry over some woman she'd slept with once, but she might over how angry her best friend was with her.

Well, she *wouldn't,* obviously, but she was drunk and Acacia had her hands balled into fists, her mouth turned sharply down. Cassie had thought she'd be shocked, yeah, but not *mad.*

"Why would you tell me this? What am I supposed to do with this information?"

"I don't know, Kaysh. Nothing. You're not supposed to do anything with it. I just needed to tell someone."

"Oh, you needed to tell someone you fucked Parker's mom before you knew her, then did it again at *her daughter's a cappella concert?*"

"No! God, we didn't do it at the concert," Cassie said. "We just made out and I felt her up, Jesus."

"Because that's so much better?"

"Yeah, actually, it is," Cassie snapped.

Acacia stared at her. Cassie saw the exact moment her glare started to soften, and it wasn't long until she was cracking up like she had when she thought Cassie was joking.

"Oh my God," she wheezed, could barely breathe from laughing so hard. "Oh my God, you fucked Parker's mom and now you're hung up on her. This is *hilarious.*"

Cassie got up. She needed another drink if she was going to deal with this.

"I am not *hung up* on Erin," she said, setting her glass down a little too hard on the kitchen counter.

Acacia laughed some more. "You so are, though!"

Cassie left the tonic out and threw back some vodka from the bottle.

"You're so hung up on her, you had to tell me about it weeks later. Have you been thinking of her this whole time?"

"No," Cassie bit out the lie immediately.

She drank some more, grateful for the warm way it made her head spin.

Acacia finally stopped laughing. She rose from the couch and came into the kitchen. Her big brown eyes were full of way too much understanding.

"Cassie," she said quietly.

Cassie tried to glare at her, but the look probably came across more desperate than anything.

"C'mon, babe," Acacia said, taking the vodka bottle out of Cassie's hand and putting it on the counter. "Come tell me about it. Feel free to skip over the details, though."

Cassie followed her to the couch. They sat down again, Acacia still holding Cassie's hand. Cassie told her everything. Acacia was silent until Cassie mentioned stumbling off the curb and Erin catching her.

"Shit, Klein, you are so fucked."

"What?" That was like, the least bad part of this story. She'd fucked her friend's mom and played footsie with her while at the same table as her daughter, but letting Erin catch her before she faceplanted was what fucked Cassie over?

"So distracted staring into this woman's eyes you fall over? And don't mind when she catches you? With most people, you'd rather eat pavement than let them put their hands on you. I was mostly kidding about you being hung up on her, but damn."

"Whatever," Cassie said, because wanting to fuck her again and being hung up on her were two very different things.

Acacia went back to quiet listening until Cassie finished her story. She smirked before she opened her mouth, and Cassie knew she was going to hate whatever Kaysh said next.

"So you made out with my brother because you were sexually frustrated about Parker's mom?" she said. "That is too good."

"I hate you," Cassie said.

Acacia beamed. "Actually, you don't."

"Actually, I do."

Five

CASSIE

Actually, she didn't.

She loved Acacia, because Acacia was the best friend she'd ever had. Acacia was stubborn and self-righteous and a little wild, but she was the most loyal person Cassie knew. And she was on her side.

She didn't tell Parker. Didn't tell anyone. She didn't bring Erin up again, unless Cassie did first. Even then, she was the perfect friend—let Cassie whine a little bit, offered some comfort, then told her, "You really need to get laid. Like, by someone who isn't Parker's mom."

Cassie knew this, but she didn't do it. Spending too much time in the shop was a better way to get her mind off Erin than sleeping with someone else would've been. She'd probably *compare* them, which would be worse. Plus, the shop was more productive. She had reasons to spend too much time there that didn't include thinking too much about Erin. Namely: Caltech. At the beginning of ninth grade, her school had students take one of those absurd "what career are you suited for" questionnaires. It had told Cassie to be a race car driver or a plumber. It told her that she had problems with authority and wasn't built for academia. After, she'd googled "careers making planes" then "best aerospace engineering schools." She found Caltech, and never looked back.

But it was about more than proving the test wrong. She'd always wanted to fly. As a kid, she'd spent entire summers outside, sunup to sundown. She climbed every tree she could. She rode her bike, a little farther each time, until she knew every street in a ten-mile radius of their town. It was about freedom, and going fast, and getting away. All things she still wanted to do. She'd never been out of the eastern time zone. California seemed dazzling. Sunshine and palm trees and a whole other ocean. More than two thousand miles from the trailer she grew up in. It was a different world.

Working in the shop was better than hanging out with people anyway. She didn't like that many people. Leaving Acacia behind in Greensboro freshman year had been one of the hardest things she'd ever done. Keckley was a small school, but it was still full of strangers. Going from a best friend who'd known her basically since before she'd known herself to a place she knew no one had Cassie retreating into herself. She'd found Seth, and fell into a friend group, but she'd still always felt on the outside of it.

In the shop, though, Cassie fit. Her head didn't go quiet, exactly, it just focused. Numbers and calculations and how to make whatever she was working on go faster. She never felt sad or scared or lonely. She didn't worry about money. Things just made sense in the shop. She *belonged*. In a way she never had anywhere else. Certainly not in Greensboro, which wasn't even that small, but felt it. Everyone always knowing her business, or thinking they did.

She was that poor girl with clothes from Goodwill. She was the skinny white kid who tagged along with the homeschooling Black family. In high school, Cassie was the promiscuous bisexual who probably wouldn't be into chicks if she'd had a father figure. After her third speeding ticket, cops acted like she was reckless with her life, instead of understanding she just liked going fast.

And it always came back to her family life, or lack thereof. No one ever understood that Cassie was over it, past it, better without them. Her mom had never once chosen her, not over drugs or alcohol or some scraggly dude who often looked like *he* would've chosen Cassie, if he'd had the chance. People never knew what to do with that—most hadn't in Greensboro, so she decided not to give people at Keckley a chance to not get it. She didn't share. She'd tell stories of Acacia and Mama Webb and her favorite classes in high school. She'd skip over the absent mom and never-known father and the way she'd wanted to get out of that town so badly.

Seth had known. Cassie had told him enough that he understood, mostly. She'd opened up. Look where that had gotten her.

Weird homeschooling family or not, the Webbs were her saving grace. Who knew what kind of trouble Cassie would've gotten into without them? Mama Webb's warning *Cassandra Maureen Klein,* and Mr. Ben's quietly raised eyebrows when she and Acacia were pushing things too far, as if saying *You sure you want to do this?* or his heavy sigh, the physical manifestation of *I'm not mad, just disappointed.*

Who knew what kind of rut Cassie would get stuck in now, if Acacia didn't drag her out of the workshop Friday night, force her into a shower, and demand she come to a party?

That was how Cassie ended up in someone's house with way too many people, everyone drunk and loud and rowdy. She was watching beer pong when Parker came tumbling into her.

"Cassie, Cassie, Cassie," Parker giggled. "Cassie. You need to take my phone."

"We pregamed the same amount, princess," Cassie said. "How are you already this drunk? Why do I need to take your phone?"

Parker ignored the first question. "You need to take my phone so I don't do something stupid like text Sam inappropriate things I want to do to her, okay? Okay, great."

She slipped her phone into Cassie's pocket and headed back to the living room-slash-dance floor.

Cassie would not be joining. She'd never been one for rhythm, saw more grace in fuel injectors than in the way people in the living room were writhing against each other. Everyone was pressed together. Cassie did *not* need that many people touching her, thank you. Parker, meanwhile, had already disappeared in the crowd, back to Acacia's side, likely; Kaysh had loved dances since her mom stopped homeschooling her and she'd finally been allowed to go. Cassie slid her hand into her pocket next to Parker's phone and went looking for a bit of quiet.

The thumping bass was muffled in the backyard, at least, though there were still plenty of people around. Cassie slipped to the corner of the porch, as secluded as she could get. She kept her hand on Parker's phone the whole time. Parker was trying to break her habit of drunk texting, so instead she'd picked up a habit of handing her phone off to Cassie or Acacia. For all the self-control that girl had while sober, get her drunk and she lost every ounce of it. Last week, playing king's cup in Parker and Acacia's room, Cassie hadn't paid enough attention. Parker had pickpocketed the phone back, shot off a text to *Seth* before Cassie could stop her. She knew to be vigilant now.

Then Cassie had a really stupid idea.

It was a hideously stupid idea; she knew it was. There was absolutely no good reason to get Erin's number out of Parker's phone. She would never be able to explain to Parker why she had it if she ever found out. There was no way she would ever even use it.

That rationalized it for her, though. She wasn't actually going to text Erin or anything. But wouldn't it be funny if she had her number? There was nothing wrong with having it if she didn't use it.

She saved it under MILF first, because she was drunk and that was hilarious, but it also kind of seemed like she was asking to get caught. So she switched it to Aaron, spelled wrong so if Parker saw it she wouldn't get suspicious. Yeah, drunk Cassie could scheme with the best of them.

So now she had Erin's phone number. Not that it mattered, because she wasn't going to do anything with it. She totally wasn't. That'd be ridiculous.

She headed back inside before she could come up with any other really stupid ideas.

On the way to the living room, some people she'd never met before offered her shots in the kitchen. It's not like she was going to say no.

Her new friends poured her a tequila shot and someone procured lime slices and salt. Acacia swore tequila made Cassie do dumb things, but Cassie was pretty sure it was more the *amount* of tequila. A shot or two couldn't hurt. They toasted to the basketball team that had apparently won, then threw the shots back and bit quickly into the slices of lime. It was cheap tequila—cheaper than Cassie'd had in a while, but she still liked it, liked the burn of the alcohol and the lime both. Everyone poured another, and they started arguing over what they should toast to next. Cassie lasted through maybe thirty seconds of that before taking her shot alone, to a chorus of groans.

"C'mon, dude, that's no fun," one of them said.

She waved them off and continued toward the living room. She'd take their booze but she wasn't going to hang around with people who would rather fight about what to cheers to than take their fucking shots.

She was pretty drunk now, a little wobbly. She wondered where Parker and Acacia—

Well, okay.

Cassie had totally done her job, Parker's phone still clenched in her fist. There was no way Parker had texted Sam any inappropriate things she wanted to do to her. And yet there the two were, doing some pretty inappropriate things against the wall in the living room. Cassie shook her head. They were disgusting. But, like—also kind of hot, Parker's hips pushing hard into Sam's and Sam's hand on Parker's neck. They were going to be so embarrassed tomorrow. Cassie was embarrassed for them already, even though no one seemed to be paying any attention. Cassie went back outside to avoid looking at how much tongue was involved in their kisses.

She stumbled out the front door, narrowly avoiding tripping over some kids making out on the stoop. Apparently everyone but her was getting some tonight.

She shot off a text to Acacia.

Cassie [Today 12:43 AM]
If Parker starts having sex in the living room, you're in charge of putting a stop to it

There. Responsibility passed on.

She leaned against a car parked at the edge of the driveway. You'd never know the size of the party from here—she couldn't see the kids on the stoop, and the music wasn't loud enough to even tell what song was playing.

Cassie looked up at the stars, her eyes finding the W of Cassiopeia in the northern sky, like always. A matching pattern was tattooed on her right shoulder. She followed the line of one of the Ws to a small star above it. For Acacia's sixteenth birthday, Cassie had bought it and named it after her, so they could be by each other's sides forever. Acacia had called her a sap, but she had also *teared up,* so who was really the sap?

Cassie could stare at the night sky for hours. Parker joked about her becoming an astronaut, but she thought about it sometimes— what it'd be like to be up there, closer to the stars and yet still so far away. Space might as well be endless. It made her feel inconsequential, in a good way. Like all the ways she fucked up down here didn't matter. The stars wouldn't mind. She could get hammered and get Parker's mom's number and the universe wouldn't ever stop expanding.

She didn't share Parker's habit of drunk texting. Never had. Tonight, though, she was looking at the stars and thinking about Erin and feeling reckless. And so what if she was feeling a little turned on, too? You try drunkenly watching hot girls make out.

Erin didn't even have her number, so it wasn't like she'd know it was Cassie texting. It wouldn't be a big fuckup. Just something fun to do instead of wondering if Acacia had separated Parker and Sam yet.

(336) 555-0157 [Today 12:55 AM]
I can't stop thinking about your tits

As soon as she sent it, she was overcome with the giggles. She'd drunk texted Parker's *mom*. She was just leaning against this car, cracking up to herself. Her night could not have gotten more ridiculous.

Aaron [12:56 AM]
Excuse me?

Shit. She *texted back*?
Cassie stared at her phone, felt like the text stared right back at her. She could imagine Erin glaring at her. She could imagine the look in her eye, angry, but not uninterested. Cassie's fingers moved before her brain could catch up.

(336) 555-0157 [12:57 AM]
They're so fucking nice. You're so fucking hot

Before Cassie could even think about what a bad idea this was, her phone rang. It actually *rang*. Erin was *calling her*.
She couldn't let it go to voicemail—she'd set it up when she started applying to internships and graduate schools, all professional *Hello, you've reached Cassie Klein*. She couldn't let Erin know it was her. Her phone was vibrating in her hand and she had to make a decision, if she waited any longer it would be made for her, and shit, this was why you should never ever drunk text anyone, she swore she

was never going to do it again—this felt anything but inconsequential now. She took a breath and accepted the call.

She didn't say anything. She couldn't. She pressed mute and listened.

"Who the hell is this?" Erin's voice sounded tired and gravelly and *pissed*. Cassie's head swam. "Why would you think it was appropriate to text me at one in the morning? Why would you think I give a fuck if you can't stop thinking about my tits? Go ahead and jerk off to them, because you're sure as hell not going to see them. I'm not interested in some coward who can only send me creepy messages in the middle of the night."

Cassie wasn't a fucking *coward*. Okay, it might have been creepy to send a message like that to someone who didn't have her number—shit, now that she considered it, she'd probably come across as a complete jackass. But she was no coward. Erin was still breathing angrily on the other end of the line, and Cassie was about to unmute and show how brave she was. She wasn't sure if it was fortunate or unfortunate that before she got the chance, Parker and Acacia came traipsing down the driveway. Cassie frantically hit end call and fumbled to put her phone away.

"Cassie!" Parker shouted, and Cassie was drunk—obviously she was drunk, she'd texted Parker's mom, Jesus, what had she been *thinking*—but Parker was drunker.

Cassie finally got her phone in her pocket, but it was too late.

"Cassie, who were you talking to?" Parker was still shouting.

"No one. I was looking through pictures." Cassie avoided Acacia's stare.

"Seems shifty," Parker slurred. She barreled into Cassie, almost making her slide off the car. She reached for Cassie's phone, but she was too drunk to be coordinated, and Acacia pulled her away gently.

"Definitely shifty!" Parker announced. Then gasped, comically loud. "Are you secretly boning someone?!"

Cassie was grateful for the low light and how alcohol made

her skin flush; hopefully the other two couldn't see how hard she blushed. She still wouldn't look at Acacia.

"Yeah, Parker, I'm secretly boning someone," she said, deadpan.

"Who?" Parker tried for her phone again.

"Parker, babe," Acacia said, tugging her away. "Let's get you home."

Parker narrowed her eyes at Acacia. "You're being shifty, too."

"No, I'm trying to take care of your drunk ass," Acacia said. "You better be able to walk back to campus."

"I don't wanna!" Parker whined.

Cassie ran with the subject change and started for campus. "It's like two blocks, princess."

Cassie tried to slow her pulse. Erin hadn't called back, at least. Cassie wasn't sure what would happen if she did. She'd be fucked, basically.

She couldn't keep calm if she thought about it for another second, so she turned toward Acacia, who was walking with Parker behind her. "Did you manage to separate her and Sam before any clothes were shed?"

Acacia let out a noise halfway between a scoff and a laugh. "Barely."

"Find a room next time, Bennett," Cassie said.

Parker glared at her. "Maybe I'll just go outside, call her on the phone, yeah? Like you with your secret fuck buddy."

"Parker, I don't think Cassie has a secret fuck buddy," Acacia said. Cassie looked at her gratefully, but she was staring back like she knew exactly who Cassie had been on the phone with. "She spends too much time with us or in the shop to be fucking anyone."

"You don't know she's in the shop when she says she is!" Parker said. "Why are you sticking up for her? You should be on my side, since you picked hers with the whole getting between me and Sam thing."

Acacia ignored her and continued glaring at Cassie. Back in high school, they'd shared third hour—Acacia came out of homeschool into advanced English. They used to have entire conversations from across the room with just looks. Silent girl talk, or whatever. It had been fun at the time, but now Cassie wished Acacia couldn't read her so well. She looked at her feet instead of her friend.

"Oh my God," Parker gasped. "It's *you*."

Okay, now she'd gotten Cassie's attention. Parker's eyes flitted between Acacia and Cassie, and Cassie was still avoiding Acacia's glances, so it almost made sense that what Parker came up with was, "You two are secretly boning!"

Acacia burst out laughing so quickly Cassie was offended. "Oh yeah, Parker, Cassie and I are totally boning."

"Hey," Cassie said. "Is the idea of sleeping with me that ridiculous?"

Acacia kept laughing. "Um, yeah? I'm with Donovan and you've been my best friend for nine hundred years and—you know." She gave Cassie another look.

"You're terrible liars and you're definitely having a secret affair. I'm going to tell Donovan."

"You do that, sweetie," Acacia said.

There were worse things than Parker thinking Cassie was sleeping with Acacia. Like, you know, Parker knowing who had actually been on the phone.

"We're definitely fucking," she said, with a little too much bravado. "You totally caught us."

Parker smirked. "I knew it. I don't even want to know anything else, because ew, but I totally knew it."

They got Parker into the dorm without incident. She tried to collapse onto Acacia's bed first, would climb into her own only if Acacia and Cassie got in with her. Fitting three girls in a twin bed was not easy. Acacia ended up mostly on top of Cassie. Parker cackled at first, but then she started looking at them with these really sincere eyes. She took Cassie's face in her hands.

"Cassie," she said seriously. "Cassie, Cassie, Cassie."

"Yes, Parker?"

"You're my best friend."

"I thought I was your best friend," Acacia said.

Parker let go of Cassie's face with one hand to pat Acacia's. "You're my best friend, too."

Cassie realized maybe that was true. Somewhere along the line, the three of them had morphed into some kind of unit. Parker and Kaysh had been tight since they moved in together, but somehow, even though their introduction was Parker sleeping with Cassie's boyfriend, Cassie and Parker had become just as close. Cassie didn't even mind that she was squished up against Parker's side.

"It's okay that you guys are secretly boning," Parker said.

Acacia snickered, and Cassie had a hard time keeping a straight face.

"You can bone anyone you want," Parker continued. "As long as it makes you happy. I don't care who you're boning as long as you're happy."

That took a decidedly unfunny turn, hitting a little too close to home. Cassie rolled out from under Acacia and stood next to Parker's bed.

"Whatever, drunky," she said. "I'm sleeping in Kaysh's bed."

"Of course you are," Parker giggled.

Cassie took it further. "I guess we'll just do it in the bed next to you."

"Ew," Parker said. "But like, whatever floats your boat. Just make sure I'm asleep first, please."

That request wasn't hard; Parker was snoring before Cassie and Acacia even got situated. When they did, Cassie against the wall and Acacia snuggled beside her, Kaysh clicked the light off. And immediately rounded on Cassie.

"Please tell me what I thought was happening earlier wasn't happening," she whispered.

Cassie groaned. "I don't know what you're talking about, Kaysh."

"Shut up," Acacia said. "You didn't actually drunk dial her, did you?"

"No." It wasn't a lie.

"You know I can check your phone, right?"

Acacia reached for it on the bedside table, but Cassie scrambled over her and got it first. She deleted the texts and recent calls.

"I fucking knew it," Kaysh said. "What the hell were you thinking, Cass?"

"I didn't call her," Cassie said quietly. "And you can't prove anything."

She closed her eyes and held tight to her phone and refused to answer any more of Acacia's questions.

• • • •

Things went surprisingly well after that. Erin never called back and Parker was too embarrassed about her public display of horniness to think much about anything else, and even Acacia let it drop. Cassie didn't delete Erin's number, but she didn't look at it again, either. School got too busy to worry much about drunken mistakes.

Thanksgiving arrived right when Cassie needed it. She couldn't wait for Mama Webb's cooking. Acacia's mom made the best mac and cheese in the world, that was all there was to it. And Cassie would kill for her cornbread dressing. After a start to the year that had not at all been what she'd expected it to be, Cassie was ready to immerse herself in her Thanksgiving traditions—primarily getting stoned off good weed provided by Emerson and eating way too much food. She and Acacia would clean the kitchen after the meal but before pie, and everything would be as it should.

Cassie and Acacia were driving Parker to the airport, then taking her car the rest of the way to Greensboro. They were running late, because Acacia had said goodbye to Donovan like he was going off to war instead of to Louisiana for four days.

At the curb for departures, Cassie hugged Parker while Acacia pulled her suitcase from the trunk.

"Hey, you don't have any plans for Christmas, right?" Parker asked. "Nothing happening over winter break?"

Cassie bristled. Just because she wasn't visiting Emerson in Chicago with Acacia didn't mean she didn't have plans. She had a lot happening over winter break. It was called booze and bad movies.

"No," she said anyway. "Why?"

"You know how my mom and I don't always get along." It was the first time Parker had mentioned Erin since Family Weekend, so no, Cassie didn't really know anything about their relationship. "I'm spending Thanksgiving with my dad so most of winter break I'll be at my mom's. And I love her, I do, but we're too similar, or something, because we do *not* get along living in the same house. Like sometimes it's fine but sometimes it is *not*. And the thought of three weeks alone with her is insane. So I asked for an early Christmas present."

She paused to hug Acacia.

"Love you," Acacia said.

"Love you, too."

Cassie cleared her throat. "Parker. You were saying?"

"Oh right," Parker said like she lost her train of thought, but her nonchalance was too obvious for Cassie to believe her. "Anyway, my parents are going to fly you to New Hampshire for break."

"What?" Cassie stared at her. Parker looked over her shoulder to the short line of people at security. "What are you talking about? That's gotta be like, hundreds of dollars."

"I was good this year," Parker said. "Santa helped out."

"Parker, I'm serious. That's way too much."

"I gotta go so I don't miss my flight. Love you both! You're my best friends! See you after Thanksgiving!" Parker grabbed her suitcase and started heading inside. "And the ticket is already bought; you're coming for two weeks. Bye!"

She was inside before Cassie could process her words enough to respond. She had to settle for angry text messages.

Cassie [Today 3:35 PM]
This is ridiculous. It's too much. Your parents can't pay for me to visit

Parker [3:35 PM]
Too late, it's nonrefundable and they'll never let you pay them back

Cassie [3:36 PM]
What if I had plans?

Parker [3:36 PM]
We're best friends, babe. I already knew you didn't

Cassie [3:37 PM]
I don't want your pity.

Parker [3:37 PM]
That's nice. You don't have it.

Parker [3:41 PM]
Just say thank you and spend winter break with me. It's gonna be awesome

Parker [3:42 PM]
My mom makes such good food

Cassie sighed. That was the thing, right there. She could get over the presumptuousness of Parker buying the tickets before asking her. She didn't even care that it was a lot of money; she had no problem with rich people spending their money on her. But the idea of sharing a house with Erin for two weeks?

Cassie threw her phone into the center console and crossed her arms and stared out the window.

"You wanna talk about it?" Acacia asked. She'd been silent since they left the airport, letting Cassie process or something.

"It's whatever," Cassie grumbled.

She turned up the radio. Then turned it down.

"Did you know about this?" she asked.

Acacia nodded. "You're gonna have fun."

Cassie wasn't so sure.

"You can't fuck Parker's mom while you're staying with her for winter break."

"I'm aware of that, Acacia."

"But you're going to want to, like, the whole time you're there."

Cassie was aware of that, too.

Kaysh tapped her thumbs against the steering wheel. "Remind me again why you can't just keep it in your pants?"

"I can—I should—I will," Cassie insisted. "I will."

Acacia glanced over at her. Neither of them said anything.

"Erin's just, like, super attractive, okay?" Cassie said eventually; Acacia's patient quiet had always made her say too much. "And she's pretty funny—I mean, we just made fun of Parker mostly, but whatever—you know how I feel about funny people."

"Yeah, your panties drop."

She wasn't wrong.

"Just don't fuck Parker's mom." She paused, then added, "Again."

Cassie groaned. "I *know,* Kaysh. I'm not going to."

They drove in silence for a while. It was just over two hours to Greensboro—they'd be there in time for dinner. Cassie would've liked to focus on the home cooking she was going to get all weekend, but the idea of two weeks in Erin's *house* was not something her brain could set aside.

"She can't even be that mad at me, though," Cassie broke the silence. "Parker, I mean."

"What?"

"She can't be that mad at me for sleeping with Erin. She said I can bone whoever I want as long as I'm happy. Plus, she slept with Seth."

Acacia stared at her for so long Cassie had to remind her to watch the road.

"She fucked your boyfriend so you get to fuck her mom?"

"Yeah," Cassie said, because that only seemed fair, right? "Quid pro quo."

"That's not how that works."

"Actually, that's exactly how that works."

"Her mother, Cassie."

Cassie shrugged. "You know she's a daddy's girl anyway."

Acacia punched her in the shoulder, but at least she kept her eyes on the road. "That is so not the point."

"Quid pro quo," Cassie said again, rubbing her arm where Acacia's fist connected. She smirked. "Tit for tat."

Acacia hit her again. "Stop thinking about Parker's mom's boobs!"

Cassie did, mostly.

Two hours later, Mama Webb, Mr. Ben—Cassie still couldn't call Acacia's dad just by his first name—and FloJo the dog met them in the driveway when they arrived. Dinner was chicken-fried steak with rice and gravy. For dessert, they cut the chocolate cream pie a day early. It wasn't like Mama Webb didn't have three other kinds of pie for tomorrow, anyway.

At the end of the night, though, Cassie was back to thinking about Erin. She was in Emerson's room—his flight from Chicago was in the morning—instead of bunking with Acacia like she usually did. The privacy gave Cassie space for her mind to spiral.

She wanted to ask Erin what the hell she'd been thinking, wanted to know how they were supposed to spend two weeks together without Parker noticing anything. They'd barely made it through breakfast—and that had been before Erin dressed for the a cappella concert with the express plan to let Cassie touch her boobs. This was insane. Why would Erin have agreed to it?

She could ask.

Cassie had her number. She pressed Aaron in her contacts and held her breath as it rang.

Six

ERIN

Erin told no one. She'd gotten back from Virginia and Rachel had asked if she'd seen any hotties—that was a direct quote—and Erin had rolled her eyes rather than admitting anything.

The entire reason Erin had let what happened at the a cappella concert happen was she thought she'd never see Cassie again.

What happens at Family Weekend stays at Family Weekend, right?

Except when it comes to stay in your house for winter break. More than that, really—what happened didn't stay at Family Weekend because it came back to New Hampshire with Erin: she couldn't stop thinking about Cassie.

She went on a date with someone Rachel suggested, and the woman was nice and interesting, and they had no chemistry whatsoever.

That was the problem with Erin and Cassie. Their chemistry was explosive. It felt dangerous. They made out in the bathroom at her daughter's a cappella concert. Cassie made her do ridiculous things.

No, that wasn't right. That sounded like she blamed Cassie, and not herself. She was the adult in the situation—she should've been reasonable. She obviously didn't think it the fuck through. Cassie was an adult, too, of course, but Erin never thought of that when she berated herself. She'd done a lot of stupid shit in her early twenties—marrying Adam came to mind—so she couldn't blame Cassie. It wasn't Cassie fucking things up; it was that chemistry.

Wednesday night, as Erin got off work, she checked the status of Parker's flight, even though Adam was the one picking her up from the airport. She wouldn't get to see her daughter until Friday. Before Erin could see whether the flight was landing on time or not, her phone rang.

Texting Asshole was calling.

Two weeks ago, when Erin had received those late night texts about her boobs, she'd saved the number in case they tried anything again.

"Hello?" she answered warily.

"Why the hell are you flying me up there for winter break? How did you possibly agree to this?"

Erin stayed silent. *Cassie.*

"Well? Do you have some kind of explanation or not?"

Cassie was demanding and indignant and just hearing her voice made Erin go warm all over. Not that she'd ever admit it. She had no idea how to handle this.

She stalled for time. "Cassie?"

"What?" Cassie was all snarl.

"So this is *your* number."

Cassie huffed. "Obviously."

"Yes, well, I didn't know that when I got an inappropriate text at one in the morning a few weeks ago."

The line was silent, and Erin gave herself a point on a scoreboard in her mind.

"Whatever," Cassie said eventually. "I was drunk. Were you? When your daughter suggested I come live with you for two weeks? That's the only situation I can imagine where you would've thought saying yes was a good idea."

Erin had considered saying no. She'd *wanted* to say no. If there were any reason to say no besides *I've been thinking of her fingers inside me for a month and a half,* Erin would've done it. As it was, she'd told Parker that of course Cassie could come stay, grateful her daughter asked over the phone instead of video chat. Erin definitely wouldn't have been able to sell a realistic smile.

She wondered if she could sell the performance she was about to put on.

After a steadying breath, she forced herself to chuckle. "Seriously, Cassie?"

"Oh, excuse me for not wanting Parker to know I fucked her mom."

"And you think she'll know that if we sleep under the same roof? Are you so irresistible that I won't be able to control myself around you, and I'll give it away?" Erin put a cruel edge into her voice that she *hated*. "Honestly, Cassie, our past didn't weigh heavily on my decision to give my daughter what she wants for Christmas. I haven't exactly spent the last two months thinking about you."

Erin bit the knuckle of the hand not holding the phone and waited to see if she pulled it off.

Cassie said nothing.

"The correct response to someone letting you stay in their house for the holidays is *thank you*," Erin said. "It will be fun. There will be good food and presents and we will all act like adults. Think you can handle that?"

Cassie sounded exactly as small as Erin meant to make her feel when she said, "Fuck you, Erin."

She hung up on her.

Erin let out her breath. *Fuck.* She shook her arms out like that would get rid of the feeling of disgust that had settled over her. She had to do it. She had to. Cassie was going to be staying with her for two weeks regardless of how either of them felt about it; Erin needed to nip it in the bud. Ruin it before they even saw each other, or who knew what they'd do.

Because Cassie was right. It was *absurd* that she was visiting. Erin honestly didn't know how they were going to manage it. How was Parker not going to realize there was . . . whatever there was between them. History and attraction—*magnetism*. The kind that pulled Erin toward Cassie even when she didn't want it to.

Erin was working on her relationship with her daughter. It'd been almost four years since the divorce—the divorce Parker blamed mostly on Erin's work. But they were okay. Better than okay, lately, with Parker at school. She called every Sunday and she always seemed excited about it, like she was doing it because she wanted to and not because her stupid, needy mom wanted her to. They hadn't had a real conversation about the divorce. Erin had tried, when it was happening, but Parker had been too hurt, too emotional. Erin hadn't tried again. She hadn't explained that yes, she chose work over Parker's father, but not for nothing. She chose a job that made her feel good over a man who didn't. She chose her job the same way she chose Parker, back when she was twenty years old looking at a positive pregnancy test. She knew she wasn't supposed to. She knew people would judge her for it. But she'd figured out what she wanted and she held tight to it.

She needed to have the conversation with Parker. Because she needed her daughter to know that was how she should live, how she should make decisions. And Erin needed her to know it before she was thirty-five and almost fifteen years into a marriage that never should have happened to begin with.

Erin was still working on herself. Actual therapy and the type of therapy Rachel gave her—encouraging Erin to put herself first and also fuck whoever the hell she wanted. It was helping. But she still cared too much about what people thought. She was trying to teach her daughter not to, trying to teach her to do whatever the hell she wanted from the beginning, and not have to learn how when she was pushing forty. Erin was trying to teach her daughter the opposite of what her mother had taught her.

The point—Erin took a long time to get to it, but it did exist—
the point was she could *not* sleep with her daughter's friend. Rachel's
advice aside—Erin could not sleep with Cassie again, and Parker
could not find out it had ever happened in the first place. Erin was
learning to hold on to things she cared about and Parker was what
she cared about most. She couldn't fuck that up.

Friday evening, Erin picked Parker up at Adam's. Normally she
would've texted from the driveway and waited for Parker to come
out, but it'd been too long since she'd seen her. Erin met her daughter at the door and hugged her until she complained about it.

"Aren't you going to be cold in that?" Erin asked.

Parker wore the coat Erin had bought her for school—a denim
jacket lined with sheepskin. It was made for Virginia, not New
Hampshire.

Parker rolled her eyes. "Oh my God, stop, I'm fine."

Erin tugged once on Parker's ponytail. Parker swatted at her
hand, but smiled as she lugged her suitcase to the trunk of Erin's
Subaru Forester.

In the car, Parker asked, "How was working Thanksgiving?"

"Slow," Erin said. She knew by now Parker didn't want more
information than that.

She couldn't have told Parker more even if she had pressed. Normally Erin spent down time during slow shifts working on the free
clinic she was campaigning the hospital to open next fall, but on
Thanksgiving the shift had been slow enough Erin spent most of it
zoning out while she was supposed to be charting, staring into space
and feeling guilty about being rude to Cassie. Cassie didn't deserve
her derision.

It had been vindicating, actually, to hear Cassie was anxious about
visiting. Erin had worried that this . . . *thing* was one-sided. That
would've been worse: to have an unrequited crush on a college student. Though Erin wasn't sure it counted as a crush, exactly. "Crush"
felt like too innocent a word. Her thoughts were anything but.

She wasn't allowed to think about this anyway, especially not right now, on the way to dinner with Parker. She wasn't allowed to think about it at all over Thanksgiving weekend, which had certain family traditions, even if they weren't all a family anymore. Saturday night meant games at the Turners'. Erin had known Melissa and Jimmy since they were high school sweethearts, long before they had kids: Caleb and Noah, carbon copies of Jimmy with their tight coils of dark hair, and Mae, whose auburn waves favored her mother. Erin, Melissa, and Rachel had been friends for almost half their lives now. The first two took Lamaze class together when they were pregnant with Parker and Caleb, their kids destined to be best friends long before they were born.

Along the way, Adam and Jimmy had also become best friends. Adam was already at the Turners' when Parker and Erin arrived. Rachel was, too, though, which meant Erin was handed a drink before she had to do anything more than wave at Adam.

"Aunt Rachel's on top of it tonight," Parker teased.

"I know," Rachel said, wrapping her arms around Parker before she'd even taken her jacket off. "What would your mother do without me?"

"Be more sober, probably," Erin said, but she reveled in the bite of the whiskey. Rachel had always had a heavy pour.

"Be less fun, exactly," Rachel said. She hugged Erin next, while Parker flitted off to Caleb's side.

Any time Rachel razzed her for being a stick-in-the-mud, Erin considered telling her about Cassie. Not tonight, though. She didn't want to know what Rachel would think of how Erin had shut things down. She *definitely* didn't want to know how Rachel would've suggested dealing with Cassie being under Erin's roof for two weeks.

The alcohol helped take her mind off that. It helped her get prepared for the games, too, which everyone here took way too seriously. Taboo wasn't so bad—Erin had minored in English; she knew plenty of synonyms. By the time they got to charades, though, she was glad she had a second drink.

Kids versus Grown-ups. With Parker and the three Turner kids, the adults had an extra player, but Parker started the trash talk early, saying the grown-ups would need the help. Adam's first turn demonstrated she was absolutely correct, but it didn't mean she had to say it.

Noah's turn was next. The youngest Turner was a born performer. After demonstrating the answer was six words of song lyrics, he leapt into motion, galloping around the room like he was at a rodeo, one hand holding an imaginary saddle between his legs, the other twirling an imaginary lasso.

"'Mustang Sally'!" Mae called out.

Parker snorted. "Yeah, 'cause we're all nine hundred years old."

"I'm on your team," Mae said.

Caleb ignored his younger sister. "Also that's the title and not the lyric."

"Ride, Sally, ride!" Mae shouted instead.

Rachel joined in on the heckling. "It's six words. Do you not understand the rules of the game?"

But Noah had stopped galloping and pointed to Mae before holding up his first finger.

"First word?"

He nodded and pointed again.

"My first word or your first word?"

He nodded faster.

"Ride!"

As the other team kept shouting to figure out the rest of the words, Erin felt guilty. Well, dumb and guilty. The "Mustang Sally" lyrics made her think of Sally Ride, then of astronauts, then of Cassie. Like her brain was looking for any excuse.

On Wednesday, for their entire conversation, Cassie had said things that vindicated Erin—she was thinking of her, too, this whole time. Erin said things designed to hurt Cassie. That it was the right decision, that she'd had no choice, didn't make it any easier.

"Mom, it's your turn," Parker said.

Erin looked up. Her daughter waved the bowl at her impatiently.

"I'm going to need another drink first. Let Mr. Turner go. I'll be right back."

Rachel and Melissa offered their glasses for refills as well. Erin collected them and headed to the kitchen as Jimmy began acting out the title of a book. Gin and tonic for Melissa, whiskey sodas for Rachel and herself. Alone in the kitchen, Erin thought about the hurt in Cassie's voice as she had sworn and hung up the phone. She let her pour run almost as heavy as Rachel's had been.

Erin was a people pleaser. Always had been. Her mother had certain expectations of her. Getting pregnant at twenty had not been one of them. When Erin made the final decision about the divorce, it didn't matter that her mom had died two years prior—she knew exactly how the disappointment would have looked on her face. Conflict made Erin cringe. She was working in therapy on figuring out what she wanted to do, instead of just going along with those around her.

But it wasn't conflict that kept Cassie in her head. It was more than Erin's typical discomfort with saying no to someone. Cassie was under her skin.

That very first night, Erin had almost stopped Cassie—not while anything was happening, but after, while Cassie walked away from the car. They were on her daughter's college campus, and Erin almost yelled for Cassie to come back, to the car, to her hotel room, to her. She'd fallen asleep that night regretting she hadn't gotten the woman's number. For the rest of the weekend or the next time she visited or both.

Cassie was a bad decision Erin wanted to make again and again.

Charades, at least, was a good distraction.

Erin was buzzed enough that she didn't blush too hard acting out her clues for *making a splash*. It helped that she and Rachel seemed to share brain cells, and the other woman got *splash* from Erin flapping her arms like a goddamn bird.

The highlight of the night, though, was Jimmy's last turn. He pulled a scrap of paper from the bowl, closed his eyes, and let out the most long-suffering sigh.

"You can always pass," Adam suggested.

But Jimmy opened his eyes and held up two fingers.

"Two words," his team said in unison.

He put two fingers up again.

"Second word," the team said.

It didn't take long to get the second word: *dress*.

Jimmy sighed heavily again, then grabbed his crotch.

A lot happened at once. Erin guessed *Michael Jackson*, Melissa went with *groin*, and Caleb muttered *oh God* as Parker squealed with laughter.

Jimmy grabbed his crotch again, more aggressively.

"Masturbation," Rachel offered.

"Because that goes so well with dress," Erin said.

"Says the person who guessed Michael Jackson."

Jimmy made a fist except for his pointer finger, which pointed at the ground.

"Fingering!" Melissa shouted.

Parker laughed harder, Mae joining in. Noah buried his head in his hands. Jimmy did the same two moves again, grabbing his crotch then pointing toward the ground. Erin was both too buzzed and too focused on getting the clue to worry much about her team looking ridiculous.

"Penis," she said.

Jimmy nodded quickly.

"Man," Adam guessed.

"That's cisnormative," Parker and Caleb said in unison.

"Hand job!" Melissa said.

"Please kill me now," Noah said.

Jimmy pointed to Erin and waved his hand, gesturing for her to keep going.

"Penis?" she said again.

He continued gesturing for more.

Rachel rattled off options. "Dick. Prick. Johnson."

Jimmy reenacted his clue for the second word.

"Yeah, dress, we know," Adam said.

"Dick dress," Erin snickered to Rachel, who was beside her on the couch.

Rachel snapped her fingers like she'd gotten the answer and yelled, "Foreskin!"

At that, Parker fell off the couch.

Somewhere between the girls howling with laughter and the boys begging for the round to be over, Erin's team figured out the answer was *cocktail dress*.

"Foreskin?!" Jimmy was incredulous. "Foreskin?!"

"Erin said dick dress! It made sense!" Rachel insisted.

"Can we please stop talking about foreskin?" Caleb groaned.

Melissa wiped tears from her eyes. "I've had too many children to laugh this hard without a bathroom break."

Rachel poked Caleb in the side. "Is talking about your mom's pelvic floor muscles better or worse than talking about foreskin?"

"Leave the boy alone and let's go raid the fridge," Erin said, suddenly desperately hungry.

Melissa joined them in the kitchen when she was done in the bathroom. They didn't even bother with plates, just stacked full containers of leftovers in the microwave together.

When Erin was married, they'd visit Adam's parents in upstate New York for Thanksgiving every other year. The last three years straight, Erin had spent the Saturday after the holiday in this home with these people. It was her favorite tradition, even if she had a kid in college now and was probably too old to be drunk in her friends' kitchen at midnight eating leftover mashed potatoes.

She was too old for a lot of things, like being hung up on by someone she wasn't allowed to have feelings for. Like being unable to get this woman out of her head. She was too old to not be an adult about the situation.

Erin looked up from her Tupperware full of potatoes to find Rachel and Melissa looking at her.

"Hmm?"

"What is *with* you tonight?" Rachel asked.

Erin furrowed her brow. "What do you mean?"

"Your head is in the clouds. You couldn't even get *Dances with Wolves*!"

Rachel had always been way too perceptive for her own good.

"Maybe that was because of your poor excuse for charades-ing a wolf."

"Charades-ing?"

"Leave her alone," Melissa said.

"Yeah!" Erin said, delighted.

But then Melissa continued, "She's too drunk to make real words."

"Wait a minute, you were supposed to be on my side."

Maybe she was too drunk to make real words. She certainly was too drunk to drive home. Adam's lip curled with disdain when Erin handed Parker the keys, but what was the point of having a kid who could drive if you weren't going to use them as a DD sometimes? Parker didn't mind.

Erin didn't feel like a bad parent for making Parker drive home; she *did* feel like a bad parent for thinking of Cassie on the drive.

Erin had just been so *mean*. Cassie hadn't deserved that. Erin had belittled her. She hadn't needed to. There was a middle ground between being honest and being cruel that she had skipped right over. If she weren't in a car with her daughter, she'd text Cassie.

Explain herself. Or—not explain herself, because she couldn't talk about honesty with Cassie, that was the point, but she'd make it better, somehow.

It was probably a good thing Parker was driving her home.

When she woke up the next morning still thinking of Cassie, Erin sent the text she'd been considering the night before.

Erin [Today 7:03 AM]

I shouldn't have been so rude. Parker is really looking forward to you visiting, and I am happy to have you.

• • • •

Three weeks later, when Parker and Cassie rounded the corner in the airport, Erin had five uninterrupted seconds before Parker caught sight of her. She used them on Cassie. Cassie, who was in gray joggers and a hooded Keckley sweatshirt. Cassie, whose hair was piled in a bun on top of her head, or not quite the top of her head—messy and loose, it teetered sideways with every step. Cassie, who made Erin's heart thump hard against her sternum.

And then Parker saw her and beamed, and Erin couldn't do anything but beam right back.

"Baby!" she called.

Her arms were wide and her daughter rushed into them. It hadn't even been a month since they'd last seen each other, but the hug loosened something in Erin anyway.

Cassie adjusted her backpack over her shoulder. She didn't have a poker face to save her life, and Erin had no idea how they were supposed to do this.

They had an awkward moment of should-we, shouldn't-we before Erin made the decision and hugged Cassie. Maybe she shouldn't have. Maybe it was weird to hug your kid's friend who you'd only met once. Erin had known Parker's other friends since they were little; Nashua was small enough that most of them had gone to the same middle school—small enough Erin had gone to middle school with some of their parents. Cassie hugged her back, though. Erin wished it were uncomfortable; it'd be better for it to be awkward than for Cassie's body to meld itself against hers so easily.

"I'm so glad you're here," Erin said, because Cassie never responded to her apology text, and she really was sorry.

Cassie just nodded at her.

"C'mon let's get our bags," Parker said, already heading away. "You're making pot roast, tonight, right?"

"I swear you only like me for my cooking."

"Nah, the college tuition helps, too."

Erin rolled her eyes at Cassie, giving her a little smile. They could do this. They could be fine. She matched Cassie's pace as they walked toward baggage claim. Cassie played on her phone and said nothing, shuffling along in socks and Adidas sandals.

Before their bags arrived, Parker disappeared to the restroom. Cassie was still focused on her phone. Erin tried not to look at her. The airport was small, only two luggage carousels. Other passengers from the same flight milled around. Erin eavesdropped on a couple with matching gray curls as they bickered about how expensive airline tickets were. Out of the corner of her eye, Erin saw Cassie slide her phone into the pocket of her sweatshirt, before both hands came up to take her hair out of the messy bun. Erin was staring by this point—she couldn't help it. Cassie's movement was like a rock skipping across a flat pond, breaking through the stillness.

"No more pink?" Erin asked.

Cassie looked at her, brows furrowing.

"In your hair," Erin clarified.

"Oh," Cassie said. "Nah. I'm too lazy to keep it up, and I've got grad school interviews in the spring."

"She's gonna abandon us for California," Parker said with a whine as she returned from the bathroom.

"Is she?" Erin asked like it was possible she'd forgotten a single moment of their conversation at breakfast over Family Weekend.

Cassie shrugged. "Assuming Caltech recognizes a good thing when they see it."

"Oh right. That's where you're going to learn to be an astronaut."

Cassie groaned and Parker giggled. It wasn't weird, then, how Erin remembered Parker teasing Cassie about that. It wasn't too friendly for Erin to join in the teasing—Parker certainly looked delighted. Cassie had settled, too, no longer fidgeting and grimacing like she was when they first said hello. Maybe the next two weeks wouldn't be impossible after all.

They all settled in further as they ate dinner. Cassie asked for seconds of the roast and potatoes, though apparently one serving of green beans was enough for her. Parker had always been talkative when she first arrived home—whether from a trip or simply a day at school. Once she'd finished updates of her classes and stopped to take a breath, Erin snuck in a question.

"And what about Sam?"

"Pass the potatoes, please," Parker said as though Erin hadn't spoken.

"Oh, do you not know?" Cassie said, a gleeful smirk on her face. "Your daughter is quite the exhibitionist."

Erin raised her brows and Parker hissed, "*Cassie.*"

"It's not my fault you made out with her in front of like a hundred people!"

Parker's face froze in fury, and Cassie looked relentlessly pleased with herself. Erin bit her lip to hold in her laughter.

"That's fine. I'm not embarrassed about it," Parker said, though her cheeks were pink. She reached to grab the bowl of potatoes herself, then added a scoop to her plate. "Unlike some people—sneaking around with a secret lover."

Erin blinked. What did that mean?

"You never told us who you were talking to that night," Parker continued. "Maybe you're the one who's embarrassed."

Erin didn't know what Parker was talking about, but it didn't seem good—the way Cassie's eyes cut to Erin's and away, as her throat worked to swallow her bite of pot roast.

"We did tell you. My secret lover is Acacia. We've been hiding our love for years."

Parker leveled a look at Cassie. "I was with Acacia; you couldn't have been talking to her. You were off by yourself drunk dialing someone else."

Erin looked at her plate. Maybe she did know what they were talking about. She'd never deleted the texts from that night.

"Maybe I wasn't dialing anyone," Cassie said. She was studiously not looking at Erin. "Maybe Acacia and I were just sexting."

Erin's fork clattered against her plate.

"Shit. Sorry," Cassie muttered. "The dinner table is probably not the best place to discuss sexting."

Parker snickered, and Erin cleared her throat. Cassie could talk about sexting all she wanted—it was that she was actually talking about sexting *Erin*. Sure, Parker didn't know, but Erin did.

"Yes, well," Erin said. "I'd still like to hear more about Sam."

Parker heaved out a sigh. "I'd like to hear more about dessert, instead. Did you make pie?"

"I'm making two pies for Christmas Eve, Parker. You don't need three pies in one week."

"Says who?"

Erin had never been more glad to move on from a conversation.

On the whole, dinner was, embarrassingly, very much like the breakfast the three of them shared in Virginia. Erin tried to focus only on Parker, but not in any noticeable way. She worried both that she was paying Cassie too much attention and too obviously ignoring her. Parker seemed carefree—oblivious, if Erin wanted to be rude about it, but she didn't. She was grateful for Parker's lack of suspicion.

Like at breakfast, they just had to get past the initial awkwardness—which was worse: playing footsie or getting too close to the truth about sexting?—and then it was smooth sailing. Cassie and Erin got along too well, even after everything.

As Erin went to clear the table, Cassie put a hand on her arm. Erin froze.

"What are you doing?" Cassie said. "You cooked. You don't clean up."

A smile spread slowly across Erin's face. She looked at Parker instead of at the way Cassie's cheeks went pink.

"You heard her, Parker," Erin said. "Cleanup's on you."

She sat back down, lounging across her chair like she was getting the royal treatment.

"Why are you being so polite?" Parker asked Cassie. "You're never like this at school."

"I'm a good guest. You're never this much of a baby at school. Being around your mom make you revert back to toddler behavior?"

Parker stuck her tongue out at Cassie, giggling halfway through it. Cassie laughed at her, and Erin's heart did a little stutter step in her chest. This would all be easier if she didn't like Cassie so much.

Seven

CASSIE

Cassie washed and Parker dried and Erin sat on a stool at the kitchen island, chatting away. Cassie was glad her back was to Erin. She couldn't look at her.

Not because of anything in particular so much as because of . . . everything. Because Erin had made her feel awful. Because Erin was gorgeous. Because Cassie wanted to kiss her or fight her or maybe both.

It wouldn't have been terrible to make Erin feel bad, the way Erin had made Cassie feel. Cassie was definitely that petty. But she was afraid it would prove Erin right—that Cassie was childish and had a crush on her.

Plus, even though Erin had been kind of a bitch on the phone, she'd apologized a few days later. And she seemed to be trying to make up for it, or something. She was being nice. Cassie could absolutely be an adult. A good guest. A good *friend,* who didn't sleep with her friends' moms, no matter how hot they were.

That was why it was better to be facing the sink, looking at the suds and not Erin's face. She was really fucking pretty, and Cassie was trying to not let it be a problem.

"Time for the tour," Parker said when they finished cleaning.

They'd dropped their suitcases in the hall when they arrived, too hungry to bother with them. Now Parker grabbed them both without asking and led Cassie up the staircase.

"You've already seen the first floor," she said. "There's a basement, too, where we will be spending New Year's Eve definitely *not* getting drunk."

"I'm not stupid, Parker," Erin called up the stairs. She wasn't joining them on the tour, thankfully.

Parker grinned at Cassie. "Some of my friends' parents think they are perfect angels, so we still act like we don't drink. But my mom's really cool about letting us as long as everyone gives her their car keys when they arrive."

"Nice," Cassie said. The thought of Erin as the "cool mom" was too much.

Parker's room was at the top of the stairs. Paintings and pencil drawings covered her walls. They got steadily better in quality as you looked around the room, like a testament to practice makes perfect. There was a mirror against one wall, with pictures of her friends stuck in the sides. The room was very lived in, even if Parker hadn't actually lived here in months.

"Hey," Cassie said, fingers finding the edge of a photograph right at eye level. It was of her and Acacia, huge grins on their faces, both flicking off the camera.

"Yeah, I put it up at Thanksgiving," Parker said. "I think it really captures both of your personalities."

Cassie felt—loved. Or something. It was gross. "Who even prints photos anymore? Were you born in the nineties?"

"Oh, shut up."

They continued the tour. The guest room where Cassie was staying was next to Parker's, though much more standardly decorated. On the other side of Parker's room was the bathroom, stark white except for the rug in front of the sink, which looked like a bi pride flag. At Cassie's raised eyebrows, Parker gave a half smile.

"When my dad moved out I was kind of a bitch about it," she

said. "During one fight with my mom I accused her of being a slutty bisexual, basically, which is embarrassing on *so many* levels, including the one where I am also bi and fucking hate that stereotype." Parker dragged her toe through the shag rug. "I'm not sure if she got this as a peace offering or to make me feel bad for being a shitty kid, but I kind of love it. We're a house of bis. More so now that you're here."

At least Parker knew her mom was into women. It'd be awful to find that out by learning she slept with your friend. Not that Parker was gonna learn that. Obviously.

Cassie realized she needed to react to what Parker said and smiled belatedly.

"You tired?" Parker asked.

No, just thinking about fucking your mom.

"Yeah," Cassie lied, rubbing at her neck. "Also like, does anyone actually use this bathroom? It's fucking spotless."

There was a candle on the tank of the toilet, a clear glass bottle of soap by the sink, and that was it. No toothbrush or toothpaste. No hair ties on the counter or slipped over the doorknob. Cassie wondered if there was even shampoo behind the frosted opaque walls of the shower-tub combo.

"My mom is obsessed with looking good for company," Parker said. "She's not like this in real life. Here, see."

She led Cassie out of the bathroom to the opposite end of the hallway from the guest room. Parker opened a door before Cassie could process what would be behind it.

"I knew it'd be messy."

Fuck.

When Cassie had fantasized about seeing Erin's room, this was not how it happened. There was a nice bed, way too big for one person. It was made, but hastily, covers askew. A bra hung out of one of the open drawers of Erin's dresser. Cassie looked away. Why did she ever think visiting was a good idea?

"That's pretty much it," Parker said when they were safely back in the hallway. "I'm going to take a shower and go to bed."

"Yeah, I'm going to pass out," Cassie said. "I'm exhausted."

It was true, but she also absolutely did not want to be alone with Erin while Parker showered. Cassie said good night and slipped into the guest bedroom. As soon as she closed the door, she pulled out her phone to text Acacia.

Cassie [Today 9:32 PM]
I'm actually going to die.

Acacia [9:34 PM]
That bad?

It wasn't. And it was only two weeks. Dinner had been fine, not counting that one conversation. But Cassie couldn't tense up every time Erin smiled at her. Erin wasn't flirting. She wasn't interested. She'd made that clear. Which wouldn't be a big deal if Cassie could just get over herself.

Acacia [9:47 PM]
Get some sleep. It'll be better in the morning. No jet lag and stuff.

Acacia [9:48 PM]
Also wtf just control yourself?

Cassie pretty much agreed with all of that.

The next day, Cassie woke up before she wanted to. During finals, she'd lived off coffee and any energy drink she could get her hands on. She needed caffeine.

She mostly stumbled down the stairs, eyes not fully open yet.

The door to Parker's bedroom was still closed. Erin was sitting on a stool at the kitchen island when Cassie walked in. She gave her a smile.

"Good morning."

"Morning." Cassie tried not to sound too grouchy. She stifled a yawn. "Coffee?"

Erin gestured to the pot. "Cups are in the cupboard above it."

Cassie grabbed the first mug she could reach and didn't realize until she was pouring her cup that it said WORLD'S BEST MOM on it. She didn't care. It was everything she could do not to gulp it down steaming and black. She didn't even like black coffee, but it smelled so good, and her head pounded. Erin pushed a carton of cream toward her on the counter; the sugar was next to it. A splash and a spoonful and as Cassie lifted the cup to her lips, Erin interrupted her.

"I hope you don't mind that it's decaf."

Cassie sputtered. "It's *what*?"

Erin's eyes crinkled when she laughed. It'd be pretty if she weren't literally laughing in Cassie's face.

"Teasing," she said.

"That's rude," Cassie said, and drank half her cup in one go.

Erin was still chuckling when Cassie plopped onto the stool next to her. Their elbows bumped together and Cassie immediately pulled hers away.

"Did you sleep well?" Erin asked, getting up to put the cream in the fridge.

Cassie nodded. "Not long enough, though. Parker better have a nap planned into our day."

Erin turned back to Cassie and leaned against the counter toward her, stretching her shoulders. Cassie was now awake enough to remember Erin was really freakin' attractive. The way Erin smiled at her made her wonder if her thoughts were written all over her face. She looked at the coffee left in her cup.

"Don't worry," Erin said. "Knowing Parker, she'll see every single person she wants to see over the course of two days, and then be exceptionally lazy for the rest of break."

"That's what I like to hear," Cassie said. She glanced at Erin, who was still smiling at her. Cassie told herself the warmth in her chest was from the coffee.

"Would you like me to make you something for breakfast?" Erin offered.

Cassie didn't want to sound rude, but: "I'm an adult. I can make my own breakfast."

"You're a guest, Cassie," Erin said. "And I'm a good hostess. And you probably eat horribly at college."

Cassie smirked and responded without thinking. "I've been told I'm very good at eating, actually."

Jesus, why was she so bad at this? She got up to put her mug in the sink so she didn't have to look at Erin.

"I'll believe it when I see it."

Cassie pressed her lips together. Erin must've missed her double entendre, probably because she wasn't expecting a cunnilingus joke before 9 a.m. But when Cassie looked at Erin again, she swore her eyes were sparkling.

If Erin hadn't made it really clear how *not* into Cassie she was, Cassie would've thought she was flirting. She needed to text Acacia—surely she'd say exactly what Cassie needed to hear to make this stop.

"Anyway," she said, and it felt like the most awkward transition ever, but she had to do something. "I'm gonna shower. Get the airplane feel off of me."

"You saw the towels in your room? And Parker showed you where the shower is?"

"Yeah," Cassie said. "I'm good, thanks."

She texted Acacia before she was all the way up the stairs.

Cassie [Today 8:09 AM]
Please tell me not to do anything stupid.

Acacia [8:12 AM]
Dude 1) it is too early and 2) you owe me so much for being this good of a friend to you because I really feel like I'm being a shit friend to Parker.

Acacia [8:12 AM]
But yeah no, don't do anything stupid

Cassie [8:13 AM]
Even if it seems like she was flirting with me?

Acacia [8:13 AM]
Especially then

The problem was it *did* feel like Erin was flirting. Maybe Erin was just that nice, but no one smiled that much in the morning, did they? Even if they did, it was a specific sort of smile; the kind Cassie had first seen across a crowded bar when she got caught staring. Maybe it was just Erin being an adult. Being mature. Maybe she smiled like that at all of Parker's friends. Maybe Cassie just looked at Erin through heart eyeglasses like the ones Acacia loved to take selfies in. It was probably nothing, but it felt like something. It felt like Erin wanted her.

They didn't have pancakes for breakfast in the end, because Parker didn't get up until eleven, and they were meeting Parker's friend Lila for lunch at noon. Cassie had spent the morning cooped up in the guest room on her laptop. She didn't shake off her anxiety until they were out of the house.

After lunch with Lila, an Indian girl who was so pretty it wasn't fair, Parker's friend Caleb, who Cassie had already heard plenty of stories about, joined them for coffee. Lila and Caleb were both easy to get along with, mostly because they liked embarrassing Parker as much as Cassie did. Cassie retold the story of Sam and Parker at the party, adding in some parts about groping she hadn't actually seen, but from the way Parker's cheeks went red, apparently happened.

They were out for hours, and it was so fun that Cassie forgot to be anxious when they came home to Erin in a tight V-neck sweater. She looked really fucking good, and Cassie enjoyed it instead of worrying. They watched TV and during commercials, Parker updated Erin on her friends. Erin grinned as Parker talked about Lila's plans to study abroad next year. Cassie couldn't help but watch her, only a little embarrassed by how blown away she was by Erin's gorgeousness. Erin caught her staring, and her grin went bigger. It was exactly like the night they met, and maybe it was just her good mood, but Cassie was completely unconvinced that Erin wasn't interested in her.

"You look happy," Erin commented when Parker was in the bathroom.

"Yeah," Cassie said. "It was a good day. I'm glad I came."

Erin smiled. "I am, too."

They held eye contact until Parker came back into the room. Cassie knew she was in trouble when she didn't even consider texting Acacia.

Erin made them dinner—it was delicious, again, Parker totally wasn't lying about her mom making good food—and they got ready to meet up with more of Parker's friends. While Parker rummaged through the pantry for snacks to bring, Erin caught Cassie by the arm. Her pulse shot up.

"Here, take my number," Erin said. Her smile had a hint of mischief. "If you need a sober ride home, let me know. Parker tends to lose her phone when she's out with her friends."

"She doesn't lose it," Cassie said as she programmed the number back into her phone, under Erin this time. "She has to give it away so she won't drunk text people."

"Cassie, honestly, could you stop?" Parker yelled from the pantry. "I know you like embarrassing me, but she's my *mom*. Do you have to tell her everything?"

"You can't invite me and then tell me I'm not allowed to have any fun," Cassie called back.

Erin smirked at her. "Do you have to do the same with your phone, so you don't drunk text anyone?"

Cassie ducked her head, trying not to blush. "Nah," she said. "I'm usually pretty good about it."

Parker reappeared, then, three bags of chips in her arms and a glower on her face when she looked at Cassie. "Are you ready?"

"Yeah, let's go."

"Bye, Mom."

"Bye, honey," Erin said. As the door closed behind them, she added, "Make sure you don't text anyone you shouldn't."

"I literally hate you," Parker told Cassie.

"You invited me to be a buffer with your mom! I'm doing a good job!"

"Maybe too good of one."

Cassie grinned. She really hoped that was true.

• • • •

When Cassie came downstairs the next morning, Erin had a cup of coffee ready for her.

"Good morning," she said, offering the mug. "I poured it when I heard you coming downstairs."

It looked like it had exactly the right cream-to-coffee ratio. Cassie's chest felt warm.

"Thanks," Cassie said, taking the cup from her and taking a sip. "It's perfect."

Erin smiled. She sat at the counter and Cassie slid onto the stool beside her. They drank in comfortable silence.

"There are bagels if you want one," Erin said eventually. "I'd rather you not make too much of a mess in the kitchen—I'll be cooking most of the day."

"Most of the day?"

"We've got a lot of people coming over tomorrow," she said. Her voice was a little tight.

"I'll make a bagel and then help cook?" Cassie offered.

Erin's face softened with a smile. "You don't have to, Cassie."

"Don't be ridiculous. Parker's probably not gonna be up for hours. I can help out."

"I . . ." Erin trailed off. "Thank you. That'd be great."

Cassie ate an everything bagel with cream cheese then Erin pointed her to the cookbook on the kitchen island.

"Can I trust you to make the sausage balls?" she asked. "The recipe shouldn't be too tough."

"I can't believe you're making me cook *balls,* but yeah, I can follow a recipe."

Erin laughed lightly. "You can do piecrust if you'd rather, but Parker is very particular about her pies."

"I don't want that kind of responsibility."

Erin put on Christmas music and got to work on the other side of the kitchen.

"Nice of you to join us," Erin snarked as soon as Parker walked into the kitchen.

The sausage balls had come out of the oven twenty minutes ago. The figs Cassie was sautéing in sugar were going dark and sticky, though she didn't yet fully understand the appetizer they were to be a part of.

"Good morning to you, too," Parker said.

Erin huffed. "Cassie's been helping me for over an hour and you're just getting up."

Cassie didn't look up from the figs. She was not getting in the middle of this.

"We're having fifty people here tomorrow," Erin said. "We have to get the house clean and as much food ready as possible, all right?"

"Okay, God," Parker muttered.

She made a face at Cassie when Erin wasn't looking. Cassie shrugged. Erin was kind of being a bitch, but she was stressed, was all.

Parker ate a bagel and then helped with the now-cooling figs. She spread goat cheese on them and then Cassie wrapped each one in prosciutto. Erin left them in the kitchen to go clean the rest of the house.

"She gets like this sometimes," Parker said, "before having people over. Acts like it'll be the end of the world if everything isn't perfect. She usually at least lets me wake up before being so pissy, though."

"It's fine," Cassie said, because it was. It wasn't a big deal.

"She just like—" Parker spread some cheese on a fig too enthusiastically and got it all over her fingers. She didn't clean it off, just reached for the next fig. "She does this stuff, like going all out as a hostess. And it'd be one thing if it seemed like she liked it, but I feel like she just does it because it's what she thinks is expected of her. Like, my grandma was a big hostess, so my mom thinks she's supposed to be."

Cassie went to the fridge for more prosciutto because she didn't know how she was supposed to respond.

"What?" Parker's voice was accusatory. "Are you best friends with my mom now since you've been cooking together? Are you on her side?"

Cassie laughed. "I'm best friends with *you*."

Parker grinned, and Cassie realized that might be the first time she'd ever called Parker her best friend.

"Of course I'm on your side," Cassie continued. "It's not like I give a fuck about what people think about your house. But I'm on your mom's side, too. She made us two bomb-ass meals and lets you sleep in as long as you want. We can help her a little."

"Whatever," Parker said. "I didn't come home to be put to work, you know?"

Cassie cut a strip of prosciutto and gave Parker a little side-eye, not that she was looking.

"She flew me up here," Cassie said. "I figure the least I can do is help make some appetizers."

That shut Parker up, thankfully.

Seriously, Erin *flew her out here.* She'd spent more on Cassie than Cassie's own mom had spent in years. Erin might not have been perfect, but Cassie sure as hell wasn't complaining about a little cooking and cleaning.

That was absolutely not an accurate portrayal of why Cassie was so okay helping with party prep. Erin needed help. It may have been pathetic, but that was reason enough for Cassie to pitch in.

After the figs came prepping shrimp puffs to be cooked right before people arrived tomorrow. Parker had lunch plans with her dad, so once they finished the puffs, she tugged Cassie upstairs as she went to change.

"Do you want to come with?" she asked, flipping through her closet looking for an outfit. "I don't want to leave you here with my mom when she's in such a mood."

"I'm good."

Cassie sat on Parker's bed and leaned back on her arms. Erin wasn't that bad, and certainly no worse than Adam. Cassie thought of his smarmy smile when they met and wanted to punch him all over again.

"I mean, she'll probably be okay because you're not her daughter," Parker said. "But I don't want her to work you too hard."

She can work me as hard as she wants. Cassie fell back onto the bed and stared at the ceiling. Ran a hand over her face.

"Everything I do means there's less for you to do," she said. "So your mom gets less stressed so she's less mad at you and you're less annoyed by her and everyone's happy."

And Cassie was happy, too, both to be around Erin and to not be around Adam.

As Parker headed out the door, Erin said, "Remind your father he's bringing ham tomorrow."

"I know, Mom, you've told me three times already."

Erin sighed. Parker gave Cassie a wave and the door closed behind her. Erin turned in a full circle, eyes darting from the table in the foyer to the entrance to the kitchen to the hallway toward the bathroom.

"You don't have to help," she said, looking very much like she needed help.

"Let's eat lunch," Cassie said. "Then we can work."

"I can't break for lunch," Erin said. "I have to go pick up loaves of bread from the bakery and make the pecan pie; the apple can wait until the morning. I want to mop the floors but we probably don't have time. The downstairs bathroom needs to be—"

"Whoa, Erin," Cassie interrupted gently. "One step at a time."

Her smile was brittle. "There's too much to do for one step at a time."

Cassie wanted to squeeze her arm or something, give some kind of reassurance. She didn't. "Look, I'm going to make us sandwiches, just peanut butter and jelly, nothing fancy. If you're dead set on not taking a break, you can eat it while you mop or whatever."

Erin sighed again and finally relented, following Cassie to the kitchen. She got peanut butter and bread out of the pantry, and Cassie found strawberry jelly in the fridge.

"Why are you so worried about this?" Cassie asked as she slathered peanut butter on two pieces of bread.

Erin gestured, vaguely but wildly. "There are so many people coming over!"

"Yeah, but aren't they your friends? Like, they're not going to care if the floor's not mopped." Cassie heaped strawberry jelly on top of the peanut butter, swirled it together with the knife. "Don't you do this every year?"

"Yes, and I always want it to be perfect."

Cassie slid a plate with Erin's sandwich on it over to her, then joined her on the same stools where they'd had coffee together earlier. Erin took a bite of her sandwich and chewed it slowly.

"If I work hard, I can get mostly everything done," she said. "There's just so much I should do."

Cassie bumped her knee against Erin's. "Fuck should."

The comment made her laugh, and suddenly Cassie remembered the bathroom at Parker's a cappella concert, saying *we shouldn't* right before they absolutely *did*. Cassie pulled her knee away from Erin's and picked at the crust on her sandwich.

"It's going to be perfect because your friends are going to be here and it's going to be fun," Cassie said. She was trying to be good, but the memory of Erin's teeth on her collarbone wouldn't go away. "Parker has told me these things are always fun. It's all going to work out. Don't stress out about it."

Cassie kept her eyes on her sandwich.

"Think I can get that embroidered on a pillow?"

Cassie's brow furrowed. She tilted her head to look at Erin. "What?"

"'Fuck should.' I think it'd be a great pillow."

Her smile was cute and crooked and Cassie spent too long looking at her mouth.

"You could," Cassie said finally, getting up to put their plates in the sink. "But after we do all the things we need to do. I'll text Parker to pick up the bread on her way home. You do the pecan pie, I'm going to work on the bathroom."

Erin kept smiling at her. "I have no idea how my daughter made friends with someone as willing to do housework as you, but I'm really glad she did."

"I am, too."

It was true. For a lot of reasons. Including Erin's crooked smile.

By the time Parker returned from lunch with the loaves of bread, the pecan pie was finished, the bathroom was clean, and Erin and Cassie were laughing over reviews of Roomba-style robot mops on the internet.

"Hi?" Parker said.

"Hey, honey," Erin smiled at her. "Thanks for picking up the bread."

"Yeah, no problem."

Erin turned back to the computer, and Parker gave Cassie a WTF face. Cassie grinned and shrugged, rather proud of herself for getting Erin to de-stress.

"Come upstairs for a sec, Cass," Parker said. "I need help with Acacia's present."

Cassie followed her to her bedroom. Before closing the door, Parker checked the hallway like her mom might somehow be there even though they'd left her in the living room.

"Who is that and what have you done with my mother?" she whispered.

Cassie laughed. "I just talked to her and helped out a little."

"You're a magician. She's never this happy before a party."

"It literally isn't difficult to make your mom happy," Cassie said. "Maybe you're just bad at it."

"I take it back," Parker said. "You're not a magician. You're a jerk."

"You love me."

She rolled her eyes but didn't contradict Cassie.

Eight

ERIN

A decade ago, Erin had taken over her mother's annual Christmas Eve party. And she'd never done it as well as her mom.

She opened her house for the entire afternoon for guests to drift in and out as they pleased, stopping in after seeing family, or while on the way to a Christmas Eve church service. Erin invited everyone they knew, like her mom always had. Their dining room table got pushed against a wall and completely covered with food, even with both leaves in. Erin fashioned a wet bar in the corner of the living room. She made a nonalcoholic punch and provided multiple types of alcohol for people to add to their own glasses if they liked. She made most of the food, too, though guests who were regular attendees tended to bring a dish. Every year, Erin forgot how much work it took.

Her mom had been the perfect hostess. Her house was always spotless, the food was always delicious, and she never let anyone sit long with an empty glass. Even with Cassie's pep talk yesterday, Erin couldn't stop herself from double-checking that she'd gotten all the dust bunnies out from under the living room furniture.

Cassie *had* helped, though. Too much, maybe. Erin felt better every time the other woman smiled at her. Being rude to Cassie on the phone at Thanksgiving was supposed to put an end to any possibility between them. Erin should've left it at that. She should've been okay with Cassie thinking she was a bitch. It'd be smarter than whatever they were doing now. Because they were doing . . . something. Even if Erin wasn't sure what it was. All she knew was it felt dangerous every time their eyes met. Like a lit match. Their eye contact was combustible.

It was better, with a houseful of people. Erin was busy. People arrived at various times, with boisterous hellos as they unwound scarves and pulled off gloves. Those who brought food or drink handed it off to Erin, who did her best to arrange both the table and the refrigerator so nothing would tumble to the floor. Adam showed up at two thirty with the ham and an apology for being late. Erin let it roll off her like water off a duck's back.

She should have been too busy with hostess duties to pay Cassie much attention, but you know what they say about *should*. She told herself this was a hostess duty, too, the way she checked on Cassie from across the room. She saw her tucked away in a corner, chatting with Lila, then later, hovering around the table, picking at the finger foods instead of getting herself a plate. She saw the back of her head, more than anything, which was probably good. Cassie didn't need to notice how often Erin's eyes found her in a room so crowded Erin had taken off her cardigan barely an hour into the party.

After popping more sausage balls out of the oven onto the serving platter, Erin finally made herself a plate—figs and shrimp puffs and some crackers with a whole slab of Brie. She didn't get any ham. The punch was getting low, but she gave herself a break instead of immediately refilling it.

Looking at Cassie wasn't even intentional this time—it was just that her gloomy face stood out against the animated conversations happening around her. Cassie looked like she wanted to be any-where else. Erin was being a good hostess by letting herself be pulled into Cassie's orbit. She couldn't have one of her guests be so obvi-ously displeased.

She sidled up next to her and offered her plate. "Shrimp puff?"

Cassie took one.

"How you doing?" Erin said because she didn't know how to ask what was wrong.

Cassie shrugged. When Erin furrowed her brows, the other woman said, "Could be worse. At least no one has complained that the floors aren't mopped."

Erin's cheeks heated. "Be quiet."

Cassie grinned, her eyes twinkling more than the lights on the Christmas tree behind her. Erin's blush deepened. She hadn't even added any alcohol to her punch. Her skin buzzed just being near Cassie.

"Anyway," she said. "I should go refill the punch."

She fled to the kitchen. It was cooler there, no one else's body heat multiplying around her. Erin took a breath. Before she could get it together, Cassie was there, arms crossed, hip propped against the counter. She must have gotten warm, too—somewhere along the line, she rolled the sleeves of her flannel up to her elbows. Erin focused on opening the ginger ale to make more punch instead of on Cassie's forearms.

"Is everyone here?" Cassie asked. "Is there anyone missing?"

"People arrive at different times," Erin said. "Most of these people will filter out and others will show up. There aren't many who stay the whole time."

Rachel usually did, but she'd headed to Puerto Vallarta after Hanukkah and had been having an intense fling with a local bartender for the past week. Erin was getting regular text updates with more information than she needed.

"Oh, I just wondered if anyone saw that the sidewalk wasn't perfectly shoveled, got offended, and left."

Cassie couldn't keep a straight face, a teasing smirk breaking through as Erin laughed and shoved at her shoulder.

"You're rude."

"I'm just pointing out that I was right. No one cares what your house looks like. They're here for the company. And maybe the food." She grabbed another shrimp puff off Erin's plate and popped it into her mouth.

Thank God Adam came in before Erin could overthink and be mortified at the way she'd shoved Cassie's shoulder. It felt childish, and obvious. Like pulling someone's pigtails on the playground.

Erin was grateful for the interruption, but she hoped Adam hadn't noticed the way she took a giant step backward upon hearing his voice. She hadn't realized they had been standing so close. She went back to the punch while Adam resumed a conversation he'd apparently begun earlier with Cassie.

"I'm serious about the recommendation," he said. "I'd be happy to write you one. It would help to have someone outside of academia speak up for you, and I'm happy to say I'm somewhat well-known."

Erin rolled her eyes as she added lemon juice to the ginger ale–cranberry juice mix. Adam and his fucking opinion of himself.

"I think it's probably more important to have someone who knows my work and what I'm like," Cassie said.

Erin recognized the forced politeness in her voice. She'd had to use the same tone plenty of times when talking to men in medicine.

"I don't know—I write a mean recommendation letter." Adam chuckled. "And I know being female will help you when it comes to admissions, but you need more than the diversity boost."

The cap of the lemon juice bit into Erin's hand as she tightened it with more force than required. Surely her ex-husband did not just say that.

"You're not going to get into Caltech just because you're a girl. If we could—"

Erin absolutely could not let him say one more word. "Adam?" He looked at her like he hadn't realized she was in the room. At least that meant he didn't notice how close she'd been to Cassie earlier. "Can I talk to you for a moment?"

She didn't wait for him to reply, just turned and walked into the pantry that connected to the kitchen. She squeezed her fingers into fists to keep her hands from shaking.

Adam followed eventually, and Erin whirled on him as soon as he was in the small room.

"What are you doing?"

He took a step back. "What do you mean?"

Erin pressed her lips together and flexed her fingers wide. "Did Cassie ask you for a recommendation letter?"

Adam narrowed his eyes. "I offered."

"Seriously, Adam?" Erin's voice snapped, and it was probably too loud—Cassie could be listening, the door to the pantry not fully closed.

"What? I'm not supposed to offer to help our daughter's friends now?"

This conversation was every reason Erin divorced this man. His calm, arrogant certainty.

"You're not supposed to talk to a woman you barely know and assume you know better than her what she needs."

"It's not that I know better than her—"

"You're right," Erin said. "You don't. Especially if you're going to act like she can only get into graduate school because she's a woman."

Adam scoffed and Erin wanted to strangle him.

"If the two of you would just *listen*—"

"Do you even know what she wants to study?"

Adam did what he'd done every time Erin won an argument their entire marriage: he held his hands up like she was attacking him and his voice went all faux ingratiating.

"Fine, fine," he said. "I won't push it . . . but if she ever *wants* a letter of recommendation from an industry-wide known engineer, give her my number."

Erin absolutely would not.

When they left the pantry, Cassie was nowhere to be seen. Erin had to finish mixing the punch. She ignored Adam, who wandered back to the party.

Alone in the kitchen, Erin hung her head and leaned on the counter, palms flat. She and Adam got along well enough most of the time, but he drove her crazy when they disagreed. He'd always made her feel small when she tried to talk about problems. He was so certain in his own worldview, he made her feel like a fool for seeing things differently.

Whatever. Erin rolled her shoulders back and stood straight. She'd finish the punch and find Cassie and apologize, because Lord knew Adam wouldn't.

But she couldn't find Cassie when she returned to the party. Guests were shoulder to shoulder in the living room, Parker enthralling a group of them by talking about a cappella. It was more than halfway through the party, but there was still an inordinate amount of food on the dining room table. Erin stole a prosciutto-wrapped fig as she slipped past. The firepit in the backyard had only drawn a few guests. Erin didn't have to venture outside to tell that one of them was Adam in his puffy black North Face. Cassie was nowhere to be seen.

Erin wondered if she'd overheard, worried she was upset. Not because of any *feelings*—she would've defended anyone against Adam being a misogynist dick like he'd been to Cassie. She just wanted to make sure the other woman was all right.

But her brother arrived then with their dad in tow, and Erin had to play the dual roles of wonderful hostess and perfect daughter.

"Hi, Daddy," she said, offering her cheek for a kiss.

"Sweetheart!"

His coat was cold from outside on her bare arms as they hugged.

As always, her father's first stop was at the food table. Erin teased her brother about his new haircut while their dad loaded up a plate for himself.

"Why do I even visit when you're always so mean to me?" her brother joked.

"Someone has to bring Dad to see his favorite child."

"No chicken wings?" their dad asked.

"Ooh," her brother said. "Are you sure you're the favorite child when you didn't even make chicken wings?"

Erin ignored him. "I know, I'm sorry. I should have made time to make them."

"Please, sweetheart. No apology needed. I tried to get your mother to stop making them for years."

Erin was distracted by her brother making vague gestures behind her dad, which she was pretty sure were supposed to be about him being the favorite child but it was hard to tell. It took her a moment to process what her dad had said.

"Really?"

"She hated them! So much work for such a tiny amount of meat on each one of those things." He reached for a prosciutto-wrapped fig. "These on the other hand? Totally worth the work."

Erin couldn't move on with the conversation. "She hated the chicken wings?"

"The chicken wings, the cleaning, the never knowing how many people would actually show up. There were so many years I would've canceled the thing if she wouldn't have killed me for it."

"You can't *cancel* the Christmas Eve party."

Erin's dad laughed and shook his head. "You truly are your mother's daughter. What would people *think* if you *canceled* the Christmas party?!"

Before Erin could ask what that meant, Parker slid her arms around her grandfather's waist from behind, squeezing him hard. "Pop!"

His granddaughter took all his attention, and Erin's brother's, too, and Erin was left to herself to try to understand this new information about her mom.

For Erin, it wasn't about what people would think. She loved the

Christmas Eve party. Sure, she agreed with her mom on the chicken wings and the cleaning, but not knowing who would show up was half the fun. Every year someone she didn't expect would arrive, and she'd get to catch up with an old friend—or introduce a new friend to her favorite traditions: figs wrapped in prosciutto, holiday punch, and Melissa's lemon-polenta cake.

Had her mom only cared about the party because—what? People might think something was wrong if she didn't host it? Like she was worried about judgmental people. Erin had always thought of her mom as one of the judgmental people. She'd had certain standards she held everyone to; they'd always felt higher for Erin.

If Erin were truly her mother's daughter, Cassie would've never known she was stressed about the party. There would be chicken wings, and the floors would be mopped.

Every year after the party, Erin needed a nap.

It was almost eight by the time she woke up. There was a note on the kitchen counter from Parker—she and Cassie were apparently doing some last-minute Christmas shopping.

Erin heard the front door as she was picking through the leftovers.

"Come eat!" she called.

The air fryer beeped to let her know the wontons were ready. They were the only dish to get an actual plate instead of being served directly from Tupperware.

Only Parker appeared in the kitchen. Erin raised her eyebrows at her daughter.

"She's putting your present upstairs to wrap later."

"Oh my God, Parker, she didn't have to get me a present!"

Parker shrugged and grabbed a wonton off the plate, tossing it back and forth in her hands to cool it down. "She wanted to."

Erin opened the fridge to find the sweet chili sauce. The *woosh* of cold highlighted her warm cheeks. Hopefully Cassie didn't feel beholden to her. She certainly didn't have to buy Erin a gift.

"Speaking of presents." Erin didn't bother getting a dish for the sweet chili sauce; they could pour it. "You both should open your Christmas Eve presents after we eat."

"Can I pick which one to open?" Parker asked.

"Sure," Erin said. "You can pick any present wrapped in purple tissue paper."

"*Mom.*"

"What?"

"I'm just saying we should get to pick which one we open," Parker said. "Instead of having it always be pajamas."

"Who says it's going to be pajamas?"

Parker groaned. "It's been pajamas for the past eighteen years. I've caught on."

Cassie appeared then, coming to sit beside Parker at the kitchen island. She reached straight for the mashed potatoes.

"I always get to open one present on Christmas Eve," Parker explained. "And it's *always* pajamas."

"Oh no, that sounds terrible," Cassie said, scooping potatoes onto her plate. "A new pair of comfy PJs every year. How awful."

"Thank you," Erin said. "See, Parker, some people know how to be grateful."

Parker rolled her eyes. Cassie rolled her eyes right back. She didn't look at Erin.

Erin couldn't help but look at her, though. She hadn't seen Cassie since the conversation with Adam, which still made Erin's hands want to ball into fists. Cassie was quiet—they all were, like the party had taken their socializing energy for the day. But even Cassie's hair seemed flat, the normally rosy glow of her cheeks dampened.

After eating, they moved to the living room for the present opening. Parker grabbed the two presents wrapped in purple tissue paper from under the tree. She clambered onto the couch beside Cassie and held one out to her.

Cassie just looked at her.

"Take your present," Parker said.

Cassie kept looking at Parker, then turned her head to look at Erin.

"I get one, too?" There was the slightest hint of wonder in Cassie's voice.

"Duh." Parker acted like this wasn't a special moment, but it felt like something to Erin.

Cassie took the present.

It was pajamas, of course. Erin had gotten Cassie dark gray flannel pants with little stars all over them and a midnight blue top; Parker's set was light blue. Parker insisted they put them on immediately, which Cassie made fun of her for—"You know, for someone who was complaining about pajamas, you're pretty excited right now." "They're just so soft!"—and took selfies to send Acacia. Cassie made a different ridiculous face for each picture, no matter how many times Parker told her to quit it.

Erin wondered if the smile on her face looked as soft as she felt.

Some days her life was a thundercloud following her around— all of her mistakes, every moment wasted on something she didn't actually want, the way she still cared too much about her mom's disapproving voice even though it no longer existed anywhere but in the back of her mind. But some days—this day—everything was blue sky. Like there were wings on her shoulders instead of the weight of the world.

As lovely as the evening was, Erin didn't want the day to end without addressing the worst part of it. Cassie's door was open after she'd brushed her teeth, but Erin knocked on the door jamb anyway. Cassie looked up and gave her a grin.

"I just wanted to say good night," Erin said.

"Good night, Erin. Thanks for the pajamas."

"Of course."

She took a step into the room. Broke eye contact. She was being awkward. This didn't need to be a big deal. There was no reason for her heart to be in her throat.

"I'm sorry. About earlier. About Adam. He can be . . ." She trailed off and looked at Cassie. "I'm sorry."

"Yeah, it's fine."

Erin took a step closer. "It's *not*."

She wanted to *fix* this, to make it better, somehow. Like she could fix misogyny. Cassie made things so much better for her, yesterday, and she wanted to return the favor.

"Don't worry about it," Cassie said, like it didn't matter. "Thanks for . . . you know. Calling him out."

She'd heard, then. Erin should have been harder on him. Should have called him a dick.

She should not have taken another step toward Cassie, who was looking at the ground now. When her eyes came back to Erin's, her intake of breath wasn't quite a gasp, but it turned into one when Erin leaned in and kissed her.

Parker was in the bathroom down the hall and the door to the guest room was open, and Erin was an idiot, she knew she was an idiot, but she was kissing Cassie anyway. She bit at her mouth and tugged her closer by the hips and Cassie moaned. Erin wanted to moan back. She wanted to be loud. She wanted to press closer to Cassie, wanted inside her. Cassie's hands slipped under Erin's shirt and Erin nodded and bit down. Cassie's fingernails dug in. Erin pushed her leg hard between Cassie's, and Cassie sighed like that was what she'd been waiting for and ground down and—

The bathroom door opened.

Erin was immediately halfway across the room. Cassie looked like she was going to complain before she seemed to remember. *Parker.*

"Don't stay up too late," Erin said exactly like a weird, uncool *mom*. "Santa doesn't visit unless you're asleep."

"God, Mom," Parker said from the hall, "I haven't heard that one since I was like eleven."

Parker was in the doorway then, right there, and Erin smiled at her daughter. It felt like she was watching the scene from above, like this was so fucked up her mind had tried to escape.

"I guess I better get to bed," Cassie said. Her voice was perfectly steady, while Erin was fucking dissociating. "Wouldn't want Santa to skip the house."

Parker laughed. "Night, babe."

"Night."

Erin followed her daughter out of the room, closing the door behind her without looking at Cassie.

"Good night, Mom," Parker said. "Almost Christmas."

"Almost Christmas," Erin said.

Nine

CASSIE

Cassie had never gotten particularly excited for Christmas as a kid. She might have gotten a toy if she was lucky, but mostly it was her mom hauling her to every soup kitchen she could find, like maybe if she fed Cassie three Christmas dinners she wouldn't have to feed her again for a while. When Cassie got older she'd marched into her favorite kitchen and offered to volunteer. They knew her there—she'd been coming for years—but they'd given her a ladle and let her eat in the back when she took a break, away from everyone else.

She didn't hold a grudge, had nothing against the holiday now. But she wasn't the type to bounce out of bed or anything like that. Especially not after last night.

Instead, she lay flat on her back and stared at the popcorn ceiling.

Erin had kissed her.

Erin had *kissed* her. With Parker down the hall.

She still had to wrap Erin's present. She'd planned to wrap it last night, but there was no chance of that once Erin had kissed her. Cassie wasn't good at wrapping gifts to begin with; trying to do it when she couldn't stop thinking about Erin's lips? It probably would've looked like it'd been wrapped by someone without opposable thumbs.

Not that Cassie *wasn't* thinking of Erin's lips this morning. But at least she had some distance from the fact that Erin had *kissed* her with Parker *down the hall*.

Right. Yeah. It was fine. Cassie could totally focus on wrapping Erin's present.

She'd bought it only last night, after the Christmas Eve party. She hadn't thought about getting Erin a gift before then—half because Erin had been such a bitch to her over the phone, and half because Cassie wasn't too good at guest etiquette. Obviously. Pretty sure good guests didn't secretly kiss the hostess.

Regardless, she had the gift now: fancy hot chocolate mix in three different flavors. Parker had balked at the number of boxes Cassie had bought, but it wasn't too much. In fact, sitting cross-legged on the floor of the guest bedroom on Christmas morning, Cassie thought maybe it wasn't enough. What was an appropriate gift for your friend's mom who you'd slept with before knowing the whole "friend's mom" thing, but now that you did know, you still wanted to bang?

She'd also impulse bought several chocolate hearts at the register, little fifty-cent candies. Cassie had eaten three yesterday. The last heart, covered in red foil, lay on her bedside table. Parker had made a face when Cassie chose the white chocolate hot cocoa flavor, so that was the box Cassie opened now, dropping the chocolate heart inside before closing it again. She taped it shut before she could change her mind.

Cassie wanted to kiss Erin again. She didn't know what the fuck Erin was thinking last night, but she didn't care. She didn't need the why. The reasons didn't matter so much as the feeling of Erin's lips against hers, Erin's tongue brushing soft against her lower lip, Erin's hands on her hips and her leg between Cassie's, giving her something to grind against. It was dumb, to have done it with Parker down the hall, but Cassie could admit that was half the fun—there was something about the potential of getting caught. Or maybe that wasn't what made it thrilling—maybe it was more that Erin wanted to kiss her enough to do it while her daughter was nearby. Like Cassie was irresistible.

It wasn't a competition—it was *unhinged* to think of it as a competition, but—Parker was perfect. Smart and talented and rich enough to go to private school, but from a place where the public schools were good enough she didn't have to. Her parents were divorced, sure, but she had them both, loving her, supporting her, paying for her to go to college. Cassie could barely afford community college, much less Keckley, which she could attend only because she'd gotten a full ride. Parker's great-great-whatever uncle had signed the Declaration of Independence. Cassie's mom had told her so little about her dad that Cassie suspected she didn't know who had fathered her. Parker had a solid hometown friend group, and easily fit into friend groups in college. Cassie had Acacia. Cassie had had a boyfriend of three years who hadn't hesitated to try to get in Parker's pants. She had friends who left along with him. The only person who had always been there for Cassie was Acacia, and even she had fallen under Parker's thrall. Which wasn't even bad—Parker was great, and Cassie loved her, too. It was just a lot.

Erin kissing Cassie felt like a win. Seth might have thought their relationship was worthless enough to throw away on Parker, but Erin wanted to kiss her enough that it didn't matter Parker was down the hall.

All the trying Cassie had been doing had gone out the window. Why try not to be into Erin if Erin was into her? It had been less trying and more pretending, anyway, because she couldn't not be into this woman. You could cut yourself on her jawline. Skin like porcelain, so soft and delicate Cassie forgot she wasn't supposed to know what it felt like. Her crooked smile and that mouth. That mouth that she *kissed her with.*

So why should Cassie pretend? Sure, Parker probably wouldn't be cool with it, but what she didn't know wouldn't hurt her. And anyway, like Cassie had reminded Acacia, Parker had told her she could bone whoever she wanted.

Not that Erin and Cassie were going to *bone* while sharing a roof with Parker. A kiss was one thing. Then again, Parker did sleep late . . .

As Cassie considered the possibility of morning sex with Erin while Parker slept, the door swung open and Parker herself came bounding in.

"Merry Christmas!" she shouted, vaulting onto the bed.

Cassie had finished her wrapping, so she climbed back into bed beside Parker, who was grinning ear to ear. Cassie couldn't help but laugh at her enthusiasm.

"Merry Christmas to you."

"I brought you your stocking," Parker said, handing over a red and white knit stocking. "My mom always hung them on my door handle when I was little so I could play with smaller gifts and not wake her and my dad up super early for bigger presents."

Cassie made a noise of acknowledgment, much more focused on the stocking in her hand and the fact that Erin got her gifts. They were simple and small: lotion, nail polish, chocolates. Her grin got bigger anyway.

"Don't you love Christmas?" Parker said.

"You know what? It's not bad."

They headed downstairs, still in their new pajamas. Parker took the steps two at a time and disappeared around the corner. Cassie heard her and Erin wish each other a Merry Christmas. By the time Cassie made it all the way downstairs, Parker was at the kitchen island choosing between flavors of Danish. Erin was at the kitchen window, looking out at fresh snow that had fallen overnight. She turned around and smiled. Cassie wasn't pathetic enough to say her heart skipped a beat, but—well, it was something.

"Merry Christmas!" Erin said, and that smile wasn't any more or less than friendly, but it still took Cassie a second to say Merry Christmas back.

Erin's dark brown hair was unkempt. It'd been down in gorgeous waves for the party yesterday, and it was still beautiful, just slept on, a little flat on one side. Cassie couldn't deal with how good she looked, even early in the morning, but she couldn't look away, either. Erin wore a white short-sleeve shirt and black yoga pants that clung to her in a way that made Cassie jealous. In her hands was a coffee mug, and there was another on the kitchen island next to a glass of milk and the Danishes. Parker had settled on blueberry and grabbed the glass of milk. Cassie set her stocking down and reached for the coffee, which already had the right amount of cream in it.

"Thanks for the presents," she said.

Erin tilted her head, looking confused. "What presents?"

Cassie gestured to the stocking.

"I'm pretty sure Santa is the one who fills the stockings," Erin said with a little smirk.

Parker laughed, sending crumbs of Danish across the kitchen. She covered her mouth.

Cassie arched an eyebrow at Erin. "Seriously?"

Erin shrugged and turned away to refill her coffee mug. Cassie watched her pour and rather liked the idea that she got her gifts without wanting credit.

They moved to the living room for the rest of breakfast. Cassie took the love seat, and Erin and Parker shared the couch. Parker's first pastry had already disappeared; she had a plate with her second. Cassie was slowly eating an apple Danish, looking at the lights on the tree and trying not to think about how Erin kissed. She wanted her so much it felt like it had to be noticeable. Like cartoon heart eyes or something. How was Cassie supposed to be around her without it being obvious?

As soon as Parker finished eating, she grabbed presents from under the tree and started distributing them. Erin and Parker both had a few boxes; Cassie had a small box and an envelope.

"I'll go first," Parker said.

Cassie laughed at her.

"Don't you think Cassie should go first?" Erin asked. "Since she's our guest?"

"Nope!" Parker grinned and ripped into her first present. "Shoes!" She exclaimed as she revealed the box. Her enthusiasm dropped noticeably when she lifted off the top. "Tennis shoes. Great."

"I know you don't think you need them, but you have to take care of yourself," Erin said. "You're always on your feet drawing or painting. You need good shoes."

Parker didn't argue. "Thanks, Mom. Cassie, you're up."

"Nah," Cassie said. "Hostess first."

Erin smiled at her and reached for a present. The one from Cassie was on top of her pile, wrapping paper puffy at the corners. That was the one she grabbed. Cassie was suddenly very interested in the arm of the love seat next to her. As Erin opened the present, Cassie glanced at her, glanced away. It was only hot chocolate, but she still had to stop herself from telling Erin she had the receipt if she didn't like it.

"Oh my gosh," Erin said, and Cassie looked at her. "This is my *favorite* kind. And so many flavors!"

Cassie smiled tentatively, and Erin beamed at her.

"You did good," she said.

"I'm glad you like it."

"I'm definitely stealing some of it this break," Parker chimed in.

Erin chuckled. "We'll see."

"My turn," Parker said, tearing into the envelope in her hands.

Erin and Cassie weren't really paying attention, though, still smiling at each other. Christmas definitely wasn't so bad.

"A gift card to Art Apart?" Parker said. "Babe, you're too great! I've been wanting pens from there for ages!"

"I am too great," Cassie agreed. "Especially because it was definitely my turn to open a present."

"Oops?" Parker said, looking not at all sorry.

Cassie chuckled and reached for her present. The tag read *Cassie* in what looked like a failed attempt at fancy cursive.

Cassie must've made a face, because Erin said, "I know. I can't help my terrible handwriting."

"She's a doctor, what do you expect?" Parker said.

Normally when Cassie got a gift, she ripped the wrapping paper. She loved presents, wanted to know what they were as quickly as possible. But this time, she went slowly. She broke the seal of the tape and unfolded the paper instead of ripping it. Erin was watching, but Cassie couldn't look at her.

It wasn't like Erin was going to give her anything inappropriate. Especially not in front of Parker. There was no reason for Cassie to be nervous, but she was.

Inside the wrapping paper was a box with a lid. She opened it to find a necklace, delicate silver chain and a trinket hanging down. It was a rocket ship. She bit her lip, tamped what wanted to be a huge grin into a small smile.

"It's great," she said, aware that her voice was strained.

"Let me see," Parker said.

"I saw it and thought of Parker calling you an astronaut, and— well, I just thought you'd like it."

Cassie finally looked at her. Color was rising on Erin's cheeks.

"I do," Cassie said. "I love it."

"Let me see it!" Parker repeated her demand.

Cassie passed her the box. Parker's eyes got wide when she saw what it was, but she smiled.

"Ooh, it's pretty!"

As soon as Parker passed it back to her, Cassie put the necklace on.

Erin stammered. "I mean—you don't have to—"

"Shut up, Erin," Cassie laughed. "I want to."

Parker gave her a look, and Cassie ducked her head, fiddling with the necklace.

"Mom, your turn again," Parker said.

Erin got scrub caps with little bi flags on them and a book. Parker got a book, too, and gave Cassie a gift card to an online mechanic shop. It was everything Cassie could do not to get on her computer immediately to look at their huge selection of tools.

Erin offered to get them second Danishes—a third, for Parker—and they agreed wholeheartedly.

When Erin was out of the room, Parker cleared her throat. She didn't meet Cassie's eyes because she was looking at the necklace instead. Cassie swallowed.

"What?" she said.

"I'm sorry if it's weird," Parker said quickly. "The necklace. I know you haven't worn one since Seth's, like . . ."

That was—not what Cassie was expecting. She blinked.

"I can honestly say Seth didn't even cross my mind, babe."

It was the truth. Cassie had absolutely no thoughts about Seth and the star necklace she used to wear. Parker looked like she didn't believe her. Cassie shrugged.

"It's a cool necklace," she said, tugging at the charm.

• • • •

"What up, losers?" Acacia's voice came over the speakers before her video kicked in.

"That's it, Kaysh," Cassie said. "I'm returning your Christmas present."

Acacia's face appeared on their screen. "Don't lie—you haven't even bought my present yet. You're waiting for the sales."

"How would you know?"

"Because you've been doing it for the past decade," Acacia said. "Anyway. Parker, how are you, babe?"

"Good," Parker said with a grin. "How's your Christmas so far? Emerson get you anything good?"

"Fuck yeah. He gave me money to cover the class to get my motorcycle license."

Cassie wolf whistled. "You'll look hot in leather, Kaysh."

"Just promise me you'll wear a helmet," Parker said.

Acacia rolled her eyes. "Duh, Parker. I don't have a death wish."

"Good, because I won't hesitate to pull the plug if I have to," Cassie said.

"Thanks, boo."

"Anytime," Cassie blew a kiss to the computer screen.

"So what'd you guys get?" Acacia asked.

They rehashed their morning and present hauls. When Cassie mentioned the necklace, Acacia gave her a look that Parker noticed, but thankfully misinterpreted.

"I know," she said. "I thought it was weird because the last necklace she wore was from Seth, but she claims it's not weird."

"It's not weird; it's cute," Cassie said. She held the necklace up to the webcam. "See?"

"It is cute," Acacia said. "Does this mean you accept that you're going to be an astronaut?"

"I accept that I may be working on rocket ships that in reality look nothing like this necklace."

"Boring," Parker said.

"You're exceptionally uncool, you know that?" Acacia said.

"I do, thank you."

They managed to take up well over an hour chatting with Acacia, though it'd been less than a week since they were all together. Emerson and Mama Webb popped their heads in, too. By the end of the call, Cassie's cheeks hurt from smiling. It was the best Christmas she'd ever had.

Ten

ERIN

Erin sat in her home office, but she wasn't working. The mystery she was currently reading was open on her desk. It'd be more comfortable to read in the living room, but that was too accessible. She'd hidden in her office since she woke up, almost an hour earlier.

It was 8:37 A.M. when she finally heard someone come downstairs. Cassie, probably. Parker hadn't gotten up before ten for all of break.

Yesterday, listening to Parker and Cassie video chat with Acacia, Erin had made a decision. Well, she recommitted herself to a decision she'd already made.

Nothing could happen between her and Cassie.

Cassie was Parker's friend. It was never more clear than last night—Cassie and Parker and Acacia talking way too loudly over Zoom, giggling and shrieking and acting like Parker had with her friends since she was a kid—albeit with more cursing and dirtier jokes.

Meeting Cassie separately, meeting her *first*, without knowing she knew Parker—Erin saw her differently than Parker's other friends. Erin knew Caleb when he was still in Melissa's stomach. Lila and Madison were in kindergarten with Parker. Parker's friends hadn't just been her friends first, they'd been *kids* first. Erin had met Cassie as an adult. She had known she was young from across the bar. Her smooth, flawless skin and that middle part in her hair. Erin just hadn't realized *how* young.

Not that her age was even the issue. Her age made Erin feel *good*, actually. She hated the way youth was revered in women. Lusted after. But she couldn't deny it felt nice that a college student thought she was hot.

No, it was the small issue of Cassie knowing her daughter. The Christmas video chat with Acacia reminded Erin of that, and she swore to herself—again—that nothing could happen with Cassie.

When Cassie came downstairs, though, Erin still hadn't decided how to make that clear to her. The thought of actually talking about it made her itch. She didn't want to address the choices she'd made since that first breakfast. How could she explain choosing an outfit for the a cappella concert that would be easy access for Cassie? How could she explain following Cassie to the bathroom or kissing her on Christmas Eve? How could she explain any of it while claiming to not want it to happen again? What she *wanted* wasn't the problem. Or—it was very much the problem, because she wanted to do it all again the exact same way. She wanted to keep doing it. Cassie was hot. She had a smirk that made Erin wet, every time, and she used it way too often. She was great in bed—or in the back of the car, anyway, and in the bathroom, too. Her mouth on Erin's chest had made Erin want to forget about the concert, about her daughter, and drag Cassie to her hotel, get her to use her tongue on more interesting places. Two nights ago, with Parker down the hall, Erin had slid her leg between Cassie's. Erin had wanted so much more than they'd had time for.

If it weren't already exceedingly clear, Erin had no idea what she was doing. She'd tried to be nice to Cassie, to make up for being such a bitch on the phone. They should've been able to be friendly. Erin liked getting along with Parker's friends. But she obviously couldn't be trusted. Being nice to Cassie led to flirting with Cassie, which led to whatever the fuck she'd done. It felt inevitable. Like gravity. Erin didn't *mean* to. But Cassie was smart and sly and her smile lit up a room.

And the way she looked at Erin?

Her gaze felt like something physical. The pressure of it, dragging up and down Erin's body. Erin wanted to lean into it.

So yes, what she wanted *was* the problem.

As she heard Cassie move closer—probably after not finding her in the living room or kitchen—Erin's options opened before her like a rapidly approaching fork in the road. She couldn't be honest. But to deny it would be such an obvious lie as to be laughable. Cassie wouldn't believe her.

Or worse, Cassie *would* believe her, and Erin would have to see the look in her eyes when she felt unwanted.

A third possibility: the nuclear option. It'd worked well enough over the phone. If Erin could keep a lid on her guilt, she might be able to pull it off.

"There you are," Cassie said.

Erin did not turn around at her desk. "Here I am."

"Is it my turn to get you coffee today?"

Cassie's voice was so . . . it was *goofy*. Overly enthusiastic in this adorable way that she was probably cringing about. Like she was trying to be flirty but didn't know how to do it and was just pushing forward with enthusiasm. And here Erin was, about to crush that spring of hope.

She held up her mug. "Already got it."

"Oh. Okay."

Erin read the same sentence three times and the silence stretched until she couldn't take it anymore.

"Did you forget where the coffee cups are?"

She could hear the breath Cassie sucked in.

"They're in the cabinet above the coffee pot."

No response. Eventually, Erin glanced over her shoulder, but the door to her office was empty. Good. Cassie clearly picked up on Erin being curt. Maybe that would be enough.

She should not have let Cassie visit. Hindsight is twenty-twenty, but it wasn't like she hadn't seen this coming. This thing with Cassie should've been a ridiculous memory—something fun that happened once at Family Weekend and never again. She needed to go back to her normal life.

Yesterday had been okay. Cassie had given her a kind gift, and hadn't balked over the necklace, even if Erin was sure it was too much. They could get along, be friendly. As long as they weren't alone together.

Erin went back to reading, or tried to, anyway. Her focus was shit. She hadn't made it more than half a chapter before:

"You kissed me."

Erin started at the voice. She turned halfway around before realizing she could *not* look at Cassie right now. She went back to staring blankly at the book in front of her.

"I did, and I apologize," she said. "It was a mistake."

She shuffled some papers around.

"Why?"

"You're a smart kid," Erin said, and she didn't have to see Cassie's face to know she was rolling her eyes. "You don't need me to tell you why it was a mistake."

"That's not what I meant," Cassie said. "Why did you do it?"

Erin sighed. Why did she kiss Cassie? Because her ex-husband was an asshole and Cassie was so much more than what he saw when he looked at her. Because Cassie had calmed her down when she was stressed, made her feel good instead. Because Cassie always made her feel good. Because she wanted to.

She said none of that. She kept her voice flat, devoid of any emotion. "It doesn't matter. It won't happen again."

Please let this be enough.

If being curt hadn't been enough, this wouldn't be either, but Erin wished anyway. She didn't *want* to hurt Cassie, even if it was the right decision. Certainly a better decision than the ones she'd been making lately.

"How many times have you told yourself that?" Cassie asked.

Erin turned around in her chair. What a mistake.

Cassie's blond hair was a lion's mane. Erin wanted to bury her hands in it. She wanted to trail her fingers high up Cassie's bare legs to where her pajama shorts brushed loose against her thighs. Through the thin white tank top, Erin could see Cassie's nipples. Wild hair and pajamas and all, Cassie managed to look both imposing and alluring.

Erin tried to hold on to her affront. "Excuse me?"

"I'm wondering how many times you've lied to yourself about it never happening again," Cassie said. "Surely you told yourself it wouldn't happen again when you found out I went to school with your kid. And then again at breakfast. Probably again after you followed me to the bathroom during the a cappella concert, right? And when Parker invited me to visit—obviously then, with how bitchy you were on the phone. Did you tell yourself it wouldn't happen when you bought this necklace?" Cassie held up the rocket ship pendant hanging around her neck. "When you hugged me in the airport? And now, after *you* were the one who kissed *me*."

She was gorgeous in her indignation. Resplendent. And she was right. She brought up everything Erin hadn't wanted to. She was smart and beautiful and *brave*, making herself vulnerable like this, even if she couched it in resentment.

Nuclear was the only option.

Without giving herself a chance to change her mind, Erin pushed her hair out of her face and shrugged. "Look, Cassie, I'll admit you've been good for my ego. It's nice to know I've still got it."

Cassie's anger wavered. The look on her face leaned more toward despair. Like she couldn't believe this was the route Erin was taking.

"It feels good to catch the eye of a younger woman." Erin's stomach heaved like it was going to rebel. "But this isn't, like, a thing. I don't need some kid with mommy issues obsessing about my feelings, okay?"

Cassie's eyes flashed. Back to anger. Good. That was easier to deal with.

"Are you fucking kidding me?"

"You obviously don't have a good relationship with your mother. It makes sense you'd be drawn to some sort of mother figure. I don't—"

"I don't want you to be my *mom*. I want to fuck you."

Jesus. The way Cassie didn't just know what she wanted, but owned it. Erin had to go through six months of therapy before she even mentioned the word *divorce*.

"Well—I want to fuck you when you're not being such a cunt," Cassie amended. "My relationship with my mom has nothing to do with you. And, not that it's any of your business, but I have an *amazing* mother figure. I'm sure it's different for bitchy, rich Daughters of the American Revolution or what the fuck ever, but blood doesn't mean shit."

With that, she turned on her heel and left.

Erin counted to five before releasing her breath and letting her shoulders slump. She didn't even *know* anything about Cassie's relationship with her mother. It was just the easiest target she could come up with. Easier to make Cassie feel awful, to make Cassie hate her than to admit there was anything between them.

It didn't matter that it made her feel awful, too.

Erin went grocery shopping to get out of the house. When she returned, as she set the bags on the kitchen counter, Parker came into the kitchen.

"I'm about to head to Dad's. Have you seen Cassie today?"

Erin focused on the bags in front of her. "She came down for coffee before I went shopping."

"Did she seem off?"

"I don't think so." She put the milk in the fridge. Nonchalant. Normal. "Why?"

"I don't know. She's usually down here with you in the mornings."

"Only because you're usually asleep," Erin snapped.

That was too defensive. She could feel Parker's eyes on her as she continued to unload groceries.

"Did you do something to scare her off?" Parker asked.

"Oh my God, Parker, what would I have done?"

"I don't know! I'm just asking."

"I went to the grocery store. Did that scare her off? Is she afraid of groceries?"

"Yeah, she's afraid of groceries." Parker rolled her eyes and Erin tried to remember to be reasonable. "Whatever. She just—she's been in her room all morning and she won't come to Dad's with me. It's weird."

"She won't go to Dad's with you?"

"I even told her he probably got her a present she could open, and she still said no."

Erin had counted on Cassie going with Parker today. She was supposed to leave, not to stay here alone with her. Having Cassie in the house was a constant reminder of how terrible she had been to her.

But it made sense that she wouldn't want to spend more time around Adam than necessary after what a dick he'd been to her.

"Just like, be nice to her if she comes downstairs, okay?"

"Of course," Erin said, tucking her hair behind her ears. "Have fun at your dad's."

And then Parker was gone, and Erin was alone in the house with Cassie.

She finished putting the groceries away and tried to work. She *needed* to work. In the New Year she'd be presenting her plans to create a free clinic to the hospital board. There were numbers to crunch and reports to look over. There was information to learn and absorb until it became a part of her. That was how she had always studied in school, and it was what she fell back on as she prepared for her presentation.

It wasn't going well. White papers stood out against the dark walnut of her desk, but she wasn't processing any of the words on them. Parker had left fifteen minutes ago. The house was cavernous, empty, and open, its silence reverberating.

Erin couldn't focus on anything other than Cassie's presence. She might as well not be here for how much noise she *wasn't* making, but Erin suffocated on the knowledge that they were under the same roof.

She needed to say she was sorry. Because she was! And she could be the adult here—Cassie couldn't mope in her room for the rest of break. That would be more suspicious than anything she and Erin had done so far. Erin would apologize and Cassie would get over it and they could move on.

Sure, maybe her guilt factored into it, too. She hated the idea of Cassie hating her. It was like the phone call—Erin chose to be a bitch, and then felt too bad about it not to apologize. But this time would be different. She would apologize but keep her distance afterward. It'd be fine.

Erin pushed away from her desk to go upstairs.

It'd be fine, she told herself again. She'd find Cassie in her room, apologize, move on. By the time Parker came back, Cassie wouldn't be in such a mood, and Parker would be none the wiser.

Too busy thinking over what she wanted to say, Erin didn't notice the door to Cassie's room was open until she stood right in front of it, the room itself empty. Erin looked down the hallway. The bathroom door was closed.

As Erin approached it, the shower turned on.

Fuck.

She had to do this now, or she'd lose her nerve. Maybe Cassie wasn't in the shower yet—the water needed time to warm up, right?

"Cassie?" Erin said through the door, knocking gently. "I want to apologize."

"I can't hear you. I'm in the shower."

Erin opened the door and stepped inside.

She acted without thinking. She must have, right? Erin never would've gone into the bathroom while Cassie was showering if she'd thought it through. But that seemed too easy an excuse. Like if she could pretend she didn't know what she was doing, it made it okay.

"Hello?" Cassie's voice rose over the steam coming from the shower.

"Hi," Erin said.

What was she doing? What the *fuck* was she doing? Who goes into the bathroom while someone else is in the shower?

"Is this okay?" she asked. "Or—I can wait, if you want. We can talk later."

"Uh, no," Cassie said. "It's okay."

Through the frosted shower door, Cassie was nothing more than a vague outline. She looked pink, like the shower was too hot. Erin looked away. She was not going to think about water running down Cassie's naked body. She wasn't going to think about tracing the rivulets with her tongue. About exploring just how wet Cassie really was. She needed to stop being horny and remember why she came in here. *I'd love to come in here.* Great, now she was making horrible puns to herself.

"Erin?"

Erin jumped when Cassie said her name—jumped, like she was surprised, like she had been so busy daydreaming about fucking Cassie that she had forgotten she was in the room—she jumped and smacked her elbow into the doorknob. "Fuck!"

"Are you okay?"

No. She was very clearly not okay.

"Fine," she said, rubbing at her elbow. It was good to have something to do with her hands other than imagine them on Cassie.

The bathroom was a mess—Erin had made sure it was spotless before Cassie arrived, but Parker's toothbrush hung over the edge of the sink, her toothpaste uncapped beside it. There was a hairbrush and no fewer than five hair ties strewn across the counter. Cassie's rocket ship necklace was there, too.

Erin recapped Parker's toothpaste, dropped her brush into the toothbrush holder inside one of the vanity drawers. Why Erin kept the toothbrush holder in a drawer when they had guests was anyone's guess. Could no one know she had good oral hygiene?

"Did you come in here to *clean*?"

The hair ties escaped Erin's hands and scattered across the tile floor. She bent to pick them up.

"No. No. I'm—no."

She had no idea why she'd come in here. She couldn't believe she had.

"I thought you wanted to apologize," Cassie said.

Erin smirked as she looped the hair ties over the doorknob. "I thought you couldn't hear me."

Score one for Erin.

No, Jesus, not score one for Erin. She wasn't supposed to be bantering with her kid's friend. They'd already seen where that led.

Erin stood in front of the sink. The mirror was fogged up. Right. She'd come in because she wanted to get the apology over with. Now that she was actually in the bathroom while Cassie was *naked* in the shower, though, her mind was blank. She forgot everything she'd planned to say. The rocket ship necklace sat on the counter.

"I didn't mean to make you feel—" She swallowed. Cleared her throat. "I did, actually. This morning, and before, too, when you called about Thanksgiving. The point was to make you feel bad. To push you away. But I didn't *want* to."

"That's still not an apology."

Erin took a breath and walked to the shower door. She looked at Cassie, who was still just a blob behind the frosted glass. She couldn't tell if Cassie was looking back, but she must've been, right?

"I *am* sorry," Erin said. "I brought up your mom, and you're right. I know nothing about her or your relationship with her, and that crossed a line. It was cruelty for the sake of cruelty. You didn't deserve that."

It was quiet for a moment, no sound but the water hitting the wall, the floor, Cassie's body.

"I'm sorry I called you a cunt," Cassie said.

Erin normally wasn't a huge fan of that word, but God, she liked hearing Cassie say it.

"I'm sorry I was being a cunt."

"Is there a reason you couldn't wait until after I showered to tell me this?" Cassie suddenly sounded like she had that first night at the bar. Erin didn't know what had changed, but the smirk was back in Cassie's voice. "You talked a big game on the phone about how I wasn't that irresistible and you'd be able to control yourself, but you don't seem to be."

"Cassie," Erin said, a warning or a concession or maybe both.

Cassie opened the shower door.

Erin looked only at her face, at first. Cassie didn't break eye contact. When Erin finally dropped her gaze to Cassie's body, she said her name like a curse word.

In the car, Erin had gotten a good look at her chest—as good as she could get in a dark parking lot, anyway—but Cassie's pants had stayed on. Here, she was fully, gloriously naked. Here, the lighting was just fine. Here, Erin watched water run down Cassie's body and her own mouth went dry. It was the body of a twenty-one-year-old. Erin thought of her crow's-feet, of the soft pouch of her stomach she'd never gotten rid of after giving birth. Cassie had no such flaws.

"Cassie," Erin said again. She had forgotten every other word.

Cassie said, *"Please,"* want dripping from the word, and Erin pulled her shirt over her head.

She didn't have a bra on, nor underwear, as she stepped out of her yoga pants, and Cassie stared like her body was perfect. Erin didn't let her look. The shower was not made for two people, but they fit like puzzle pieces, their edges lining up just right. With the shower door closed behind her, steam billowed around them. Cassie's nipples were hard like it was cold.

Erin's hands found Cassie's hips and pushed until her back was against a wall. Cassie put her hands on Erin's shoulders.

"This is a terrible idea," Erin said. She kissed Cassie anyway.

This. This was why Erin couldn't get Cassie out of her head. The way she bit at Erin's mouth with no regret. The way she clung to her. Cassie didn't cede an inch. She kissed Erin just as hard as Erin was kissing her.

Erin couldn't stop, even though there were other things she wanted to do with her mouth. When she finally moved to nip at Cassie's neck, the other woman let out a moan that made Erin pin her entire body to the wall with just her hips.

"*Christ,* Erin."

Erin sucked hard at the junction where Cassie's neck met her shoulder. Then she moved lower.

Cassie's breasts were perfect. Soft but firm. *Pert.* Not dragged down by decades spent fighting gravity. Erin closed her lips around a nipple. Everything was wet and warm from the shower. Erin bit down harder than she meant to, but Cassie arched into her like she didn't mind at all.

Erin was going to regret this. For so many reasons, but the one she thought of as she moved lower was that she was much too old to be kneeling in a bathtub. She'd have to pop a couple ibuprofen later, because now that she was down there, she planned to stay awhile.

She tapped Cassie's left thigh, then got impatient, lifting the leg herself and draping it over her shoulder. Warm water cascaded down Erin's back, but the heat from Cassie was warmer. Erin leaned into it.

Fuck.

Erin hadn't given cunnilingus to anyone since college. Early college, even, before she and Adam started dating. Almost two decades. She'd forgotten how good it was. She must've. Because it had to be the act itself, rather than Cassie, that made her feel like this. She no longer noticed the bite of the floor into her knees.

Cassie gasped, and Erin opened her eyes. She wouldn't be closing them again, not when she could watch Cassie, one hand in her own hair and the other arm stretched out, flat against the shower wall. Erin's tongue slipped through Cassie's hot wet flesh. She chased the taste deeper. Cassie slapped her other palm against the wall. Her fingers scrambled for purpose and one hand caught the cubbyhole where the body wash and hair products sat. Erin watched her grip tighten right before Cassie's hips rolled harder into her mouth.

Cassie's blue eyes were not on Erin's, but aimed lower, where Erin's tongue dragged through her folds. Cassie's hips rolled again and Erin took advantage of it, sliding her hands around to squeeze the firm roundness of Cassie's ass. Cassie bit her bottom lip and groaned, and Erin came right there, on her knees in the shower, face pressed into Cassie.

She shuddered through one long blink, a tiny explosion that only whetted her appetite for more. When her breath evened out, she sucked Cassie's clit into her mouth. Cassie's hands came up off the wall before slapping down again.

"Fuck, Erin, *yes.*"

Cassie shook and moaned and Erin sucked harder. There was a second where she thought they were going to collapse, Cassie no longer able to hold herself up as she came, but Erin tightened her hands on Cassie's ass and held her up by sheer willpower, refusing to break contact between her mouth and Cassie's center. Cassie got her foot back under her, the heel of the other digging deliciously into Erin's back.

Erin lapped her tongue gently against Cassie's clit. It was as much of a break as she could give her. She didn't know how to stop. She should have brought Cassie to her hotel room two months ago. She should have gone down on her in the bathroom at the concert. She should have taken every opportunity she had to do this.

The tang was stronger now that Cassie had come once. Erin wanted more of it. One hand stayed on Cassie's ass, but the other slipped forward and then back, two fingers sliding smoothly into Cassie on the return trip.

The noise Cassie made reverberated around them.

Erin crooked her fingers and let the hint of her teeth graze against Cassie's clit, and *finally,* Cassie stopped trying to grip the wall and held on to the only thing she could, both hands fisted in Erin's wet hair. Erin nodded her approval and scissored her fingers inside Cassie.

Cassie's second orgasm was the *more* that Erin had been chasing. Bigger, stronger, louder than her first. She spasmed around Erin's fingers. One hand stayed tangled in Erin's hair while Cassie bit the back of the other, though it didn't do much to muffle her moans. Erin did everything she could to draw them out, her tongue busy and desperate, her face messy, slick all the way down her chin. How had she let herself go nineteen years without doing this?

She didn't stop until Cassie pulled her away by the hair. Red sat high on Cassie's cheeks. She let go of Erin's hair but kept tugging at anything she could get ahold of—shoulders, elbows, hips, until Erin was standing. The blue of Cassie's eyes had changed, gone dark, pupils blown wide, but Erin didn't have much time to admire them before Cassie pressed their mouths together.

Cassie's hand found its way between Erin's legs, and before Erin could think, she had two fingers inside of her to the second knuckle.

"*Cassie,*" Erin gasped, her body welcoming the intrusion with no resistance.

Cassie kissed Erin's jaw, underneath it, sucked at the soft skin under her ear. "You're so fucking hot."

She added another finger, and Erin took it. She couldn't stop twisting her hips. It felt pathetic, how easy she was for Cassie. She'd come from nothing, from doing the touching rather than being touched, but now that Cassie was touching her, she was going to come again, even faster than the first time. She hadn't slept with anyone since visiting Virginia. Cassie had been the last person to make her feel like this, and she did it again, so easily. Cassie did something inside Erin—curled her fingers or twisted them or thrust harder, Erin had no idea what except that it *worked,* and she was coming, clutching at Cassie's shoulders and pressing her face into her neck.

They spent longer recovering from their orgasms than they'd spent giving them to each other. They caught their breath together and kissed slow and easy, Erin's hands on Cassie's shoulders and Cassie's cradling Erin's elbows. Finally, Cassie pulled back to laugh.

"I still have to shower, you know?"

Erin replied without thinking, "Turn around. I'll wash your hair."

By the time she processed her words enough to cringe, Cassie had turned. Erin couldn't help but trace a fingertip over the tattoo on Cassie's shoulder blade: five stars in a W shape, connected by a delicate dotted line. Maybe it wasn't incredibly weird to offer to wash someone's hair. Or maybe Cassie was just easy in the afterglow. She was pliable, following the gentlest of touches from Erin to dip her head back under the shower spray and then out of it. Erin squirted shampoo into her hand.

This was definitely weird. Too personal. They'd slept together twice. It wasn't like they were dating. It wasn't like they *could* date. Scratching at Cassie's scalp, fingers combing through her hair—it felt more intimate than the sex. Still, Erin let her hand slip down to massage Cassie's neck, which went limp as Erin pressed a thumb along the base of her skull.

"This might be better than the orgasm," Cassie admitted.

Erin couldn't help but laugh. "Maybe I should get better at making you come."

"Yeah, if you want me to black out."

Erin hid her smile even though Cassie was facing away from her. She rubbed harder at Cassie's neck before tilting her backward to wash out the shampoo.

Before Erin could get the conditioner, Cassie turned around.

"I wanna do yours," she said.

Erin decided to stop overthinking it. Instead, she let herself go as pliant as Cassie had been. Cassie hummed—in approval, maybe. Erin hummed back. It made sense, now, why Cassie suggested this was better than the orgasm. Cassie's fingers were just as skilled in Erin's hair as they had been inside of her.

Cassie slipped a hand around Erin's front, reaching for her.

Erin laughed. "Again?"

"Again," Cassie said. She let go of Erin and pushed the products on the end of the tub to the side. It was flat there, not quite wide enough to be called a bench, but wide enough for her to sit down on anyway. "Rinse your hair out and get over here."

Erin complied, rinsing the shampoo out of her hair before moving to stand in front of Cassie. Her knees remembered their time on the floor, and they were not acquiescing to the idea that she straddle the other woman, as much as she wanted to. Cassie pulled her closer by her hips, leaned in and kissed the exact part of her stomach Erin had been self-conscious about.

"We're wasting water," Erin said rather than think too hard.

Cassie smirked. "Then come quickly, and we'll stop."

Erin's chuckle broke off when Cassie slid her fingers inside her once more.

"When are we gonna do this in a bed?"

Before Erin could respond—

"Oh, *fuck*."

Cassie's tongue was against her clit and Erin had no idea how she was supposed to do this standing up. There was no chance her legs were going to hold her.

Cassie's mouth was exactly as wickedly confident as it always was. Erin was embarrassed at how quickly she'd come for Cassie earlier, but this was going to be faster still, that tongue relentless on her clit and those fingers with their own steady pace inside her. Erin couldn't even tell what Cassie was doing the entire time; she just knew she never wanted her to stop.

Cassie took her mouth off Erin eventually, pressing a kiss to her thigh. "C'mon, sweetheart," she murmured. "We're wasting water."

"Fuck you." Erin laughed, mostly breathless. She couldn't remember the last time she'd laughed with someone while having sex.

"Nope." Cassie pumped her fingers harder. "I'm fucking *you*."

She put her mouth back on Erin's center and Erin couldn't do anything but throw her head back and come.

It took a minute to remember how to exist, think, breathe. They did at least manage to get out of the shower before the water went cold.

As they toweled off, Erin tried to keep her mind from spiraling.

She dug her toes into the blue shag of the rug she'd bought Parker. She'd slept with one of her daughter's best friends in the bathroom they shared. Before Adam moved out, the three of them had shared. The only other time Erin had been on her knees in the tub was cleaning it.

She didn't regret this, though. She should've, but she didn't. Her entire body was loose and relaxed. How was she supposed to regret that?

"I get it if you don't want to do that again," Cassie said. "But I think we should."

Okay. Well. Clearly they were going to have to do that again.

Yes, it was irresponsible and wrong and everything Erin had already worried about, but she was not going to say no to sex that good.

"How are we ever going to do it in a bed if we don't do it again?" Cassie grinned.

"But we need to lay out some ground rules," Erin said.

That was the way to handle this.

Cassie smirked. "Like I promise not to fall in love with you?"

Erin didn't acknowledge the comment. "Like no sex while Parker is in the house."

"Reasonable."

She started towel drying her hair. "No hickeys."

"What if they're somewhere no one can see?"

Her cheeks heated, and she hid them, bending to flip her hair forward and scrub it with the towel. "Okay."

When Erin finished with her hair, Cassie was standing behind her, close enough to touch. In the mirror, Erin could see her own blush extend all the way to the towel wrapped around her. Cassie held on to Erin's hips and kissed her neck.

"Are those all the rules?"

Erin tilted her head to give Cassie more access.

"One more," she said before she got too distracted by Cassie's mouth. "This ends when your visit ends."

Cassie nuzzled under Erin's ear. "I already promised not to fall in love with you, sweetheart," she murmured. "Now can we get on to the leaving-hickeys-where-no-one-can-see part?"

Eleven

CASSIE

The next morning Cassie brushed her teeth before going downstairs. Erin met her in the kitchen with a cup of coffee and a soft smile.

Cassie kissed her gently before taking the coffee.

The kitchen seemed like its own world. Snow fell so lightly outside the window it looked like it was in slow motion. The coffee mug was warm in Cassie's hand, but Erin's smile made her warmer, spreading through her body like molasses, slow and thick and sweet. It felt like they were breaking rules just by looking at each other, like they were getting away with something.

Cassie set her coffee on the counter so she could get her hands on Erin's face. Erin opened her mouth for Cassie when she kissed her, clutched at Cassie's shoulders.

"We agreed not when Parker is home," she whispered when they pulled apart.

"We agreed no sex when Parker is home," Cassie said, nosing at Erin's chin and kissing below her jaw. "We said nothing about making out in the kitchen while she's asleep upstairs."

Fifteen minutes went by before Erin protested again. She slipped out of Cassie's arms and ran the back of her hand over her kiss-swollen lips.

"You're trouble," she said.

Cassie gave her best innocent face. Erin leaned toward her, just slightly, before shaking her head and reaching for her coffee. She took a sip and grimaced.

Cassie laughed. "Gone cold?"

Erin pretended she didn't think it was funny, but Cassie could see a smile as she dumped both their cups down the sink and poured them fresh coffee.

Once Parker was up and she and Cassie were fed, they got ready to go sledding. Cassie ended up in an old pair of Erin's snow pants and a hat with a ball of fluff on top.

"You look ridiculous," Erin said, biting at her bottom lip like she was trying to hold back laughter.

"They're your snow pants, Mom," Parker said. "So it's your fault she looks like this."

"Excuse the both of you," Cassie said. She pulled a pose. "I look great."

"Keep telling yourself that, babe," Parker said.

Cassie jutted one hip out and put her hand on it, pouting her lips. "Maybe winter isn't so terrible if I get to look this good."

Erin failed at holding back her laughter, then, and Cassie couldn't keep a straight face.

Sledding included Caleb and Lila, plus some kids Cassie hadn't met—Scout and Haylee and Madison.

"Ever get sick of hanging out with a bunch of girls?" Cassie asked Caleb.

"Not really, no," he said. "And Madison's genderqueer."

"Sorry, Madison," Cassie said.

"I literally couldn't give a fuck," Madison said.

Cassie grinned. She really liked Parker's friends.

It only took two runs for the hill to look insurmountable. Cassie sat on her sled at the bottom for a while, throwing snowballs at the others whenever they were within range. Madison retaliated after

she pelted them in the side of the head, and Cassie took a snowball
to the chest.

"Wanna stop being a dick and help me build a jump?" Madison
asked.

They both climbed halfway up the hill then used their sleds as
shovels in the snow. The jump ended up way too high to be safe, but
that stopped exactly no one.

Everyone did a drumroll on their sleds before Cassie took the first
run. She sped toward the jump and then—

She was flying, hands clutched to the sides of her sled, wind rushing in her ears. It couldn't have been more than a second or two until
she hit the snow again and continued down the hill, but her heart
felt like it was still in the air. When her sled came to a stop she rolled
off it and made a snow angel, beaming up at the sky. She didn't even
mind the cold.

She trudged up the hill three more times to get that flying feeling
again.

They made it back to Parker's as the sun was setting—granted,
only a little past four. In the laundry room they took off their snowy
boots, jackets, gloves, *everything* needing to dry out. Cassie tucked
her hands under her armpits to keep them warm.

"Hot chocolate?" Parker suggested.

"If Erin will let us."

"If I'll let you what?" Erin asked, coming to lean against the
doorframe.

"Have some of your hot chocolate?"

"I'll even make it for you if you ask nicely," Erin said.

She turned to head for the kitchen before Parker responded.
"Please will you make us some of your hot chocolate, Mom?"

"I'd be delighted to," Erin said. "What kind?"

"Chocolate supreme," Parker said.

Cassie smiled, thinking of the chocolate heart as she eased onto
one of the stools in the kitchen. "White chocolate, please."

Erin put milk on the stove and asked about sledding. Parker started in on a dramatic retelling of Caleb taking the jump too quickly, flying off his sled, and getting his head stuck in the snow. She was halfway through the story when Erin opened the white chocolate cocoa box. Parker was too engaged to notice, but Cassie was watching; Cassie saw the smile creep onto Erin's face. Cassie's insides felt warm even though she could still feel the chill on her cheeks.

Erin looked at her but glanced quickly away. Cassie bit the inside of her lip to keep from smiling too hard.

"Did Caleb hurt himself?" Erin asked, back at the stove stirring the milk. Her cheeks were flushed.

There was no better feeling than making a pretty girl blush.

"No, he's fine," Parker said. "Do we have marshmallows?"

"Probably. Why don't you go look?"

"Because I'm lazy and I don't want them enough to look for them."

"Oh my God," Cassie rolled her eyes and got up. "I'll look."

Their pantry was basically a decent-sized walk-in closet. Cassie smiled imagining Adam's face as he got told off by Erin, here among the cereal boxes and canned goods.

"They're probably up high," Parker called from the kitchen.

"I'll help her," Erin said, adding, "you worthless daughter of mine," and making Parker laugh.

Erin didn't help, though. Instead she came in, barely out of Parker's view, and kissed Cassie. Cassie almost fell over. Erin caught her by the elbow and grinned into her mouth and Cassie felt too big for her body.

"Got 'em," Erin said as she pulled away.

She left with the marshmallows as quickly as she'd arrived. Cassie could still feel Erin's tongue in her mouth.

"How many?" Erin asked Parker as Cassie remembered how to walk and made it back to her place at the counter.

"Three, please," Parker beamed.

"Cassie?"

Cassie blinked. "One's fine."

Erin dropped two into Cassie's mug, sliding a grin her way. Cassie swore she was going to give her a heart attack.

Cassie tried to estimate how far the pantry was from the counter. She got off on doing things she shouldn't, sure, but they hadn't been ten feet from Erin's *daughter*.

Erin hid a grin behind her mug of cocoa.

Cassie let herself get a milk mustache and refused to wipe it off when Parker laughed at her.

The next day began with a good morning kiss and ended with game night at Haylee's. Cassie beat everyone handily in Connect Four until they were no longer willing to play her anymore. They moved on to Life, which quickly turned into Life with booze, and devolved into just the booze part when Parker got mad that she ended up with four sons and flipped the board over.

Next came Mario Kart, then drunk driving Mario Kart—where you had to finish your drink before you finish all three laps or you didn't win. Madison chugged their drink before even starting the race, then came back to take the lead for the last lap. Cassie got a blue shell and ended up sneaking into first place right before the finish line, laughing hard enough to almost fall off the couch while Madison cursed at her.

Things got a little hazy after that. Cassie eventually ended up sprawled across a couch, phone in her hand.

Cassie [Today 12:01 AM]
You said to text if we wanted you to come pick us up and you don't need to but I want you to

Cassie [12:01 AM]
I mean I want you to and I don't want you to

Cassie [12:02 AM]
I mean I want to kiss you

Erin [12:03 AM]
I thought you didn't have a habit of drunk texting.

Cassie [12:03 AM]
I don't

Erin [12:04 AM]
What do you call this?

Cassie [12:04 AM]
It's not a habit. You're just more interesting than Parker's friends

That was mean; her friends were perfectly nice. But Cassie would've much rather been interacting with Erin than anyone here, nice as they may be. She could get drunk with college kids any time. She only had a week left with Erin.

Erin [12:06 AM]
Maybe they'd be more interesting if you actually talked to them instead of texting me.

Cassie was going to reply that that was very definitely not true, but Parker shouted from across the room, "Who are you sexting over there, Klein?"

"Your mom," was out of her mouth before she could stop herself.

Parker rolled her eyes and went back to her conversation with Caleb. Cassie put her phone away.

The next morning, Cassie woke up cramped on a couch with Madison. She didn't quite remember going to sleep last night, and couldn't imagine she'd *agreed* to share a couch. Everyone else was passed out around the room. Parker had a couch to herself, Caleb on the floor beside her. Cassie wished she was still asleep, but it seemed her body had gotten used to waking up earlier than usual. She made her way upstairs in search of breakfast.

She found Haylee's dad, sitting at the kitchen table reading the newspaper.

"Good morning," she said.

"Good morning—Cassie, was it?"

She nodded. "Mind if I snag a cup of coffee?"

"Mugs are in that cabinet," he said. "There's nondairy hazelnut creamer in the fridge."

Cassie turned away to hide her grimace. Nondairy hazelnut creamer. Yum.

She ended up needing the creamer, though, because the coffee itself was burnt and bitter. She wanted to pour it down the sink.

"Can you believe Congress these days?" Haylee's dad asked.

He went on about something he was reading in the paper so Cassie couldn't even escape to a bathroom and get rid of the coffee where he wouldn't see. Instead she was stuck talking to him until Haylee came upstairs. Cassie took the first opportunity she got to book it back to the basement, leaving her mug on the kitchen counter.

Everyone else was at least partially awake by then. Caleb and Madison trash-talked each other as they raced in Mario Kart, Parker a yawning spectator. Cassie threw herself beside Parker on the couch.

"Did you wake up on the wrong side of the bed or something?" Parker asked.

"We slept on couches," Cassie snapped, basically proving Parker's point.

"You hungover, honey?" Parker asked. She was faux sweet and it was all Cassie could do not to take a swipe at her.

She wasn't really hungover, just grouchy. Haylee's house was nice, but Cassie wanted to go back to Parker's, where there was good coffee

and better company—Erin would never try to talk to her about Social goddamn Security before 10 A.M.

When they made it back to Parker's—not until past noon—the
house was quiet; Erin was on shift at the hospital. Cassie tumbled
onto the couch in the living room, leaving the love seat for Parker.

"There's probably an *NCIS* marathon on or something," Parker
said.

Cassie shrugged more violently than the situation warranted, and
Parker sighed at her. She turned on the TV and flipped through
the channels. Cassie fell asleep before Parker settled on a station to
watch.

• • • •

"Wake up, Sleeping Beauty."

Cassie vaguely knew that voice was for her, but she didn't want to
wake up. She burrowed deeper into the couch cushions.

There was laughter, then, and though she was mostly asleep, Cassie knew it was Erin's. She cracked an eye open. Erin stood over her
in blue scrubs.

"I brought lunch home. Get up before it gets cold."

She brushed Cassie's hair off her forehead, and Cassie looked to
the other couch. It had a mess of a blanket on it, but no Parker.

"She was easier to rouse than you," Erin said.

Cassie stretched. "First time for everything, I guess."

As she followed Erin to the kitchen, she was much happier than
she had been pre-nap.

Parker was already eating her burger, two grease-stained bags still
full on the counter in front of her.

"I got you a plain burger, so you could dress it however you like,"
Erin said, pushing one of the bags toward Cassie. "And I hope a
chocolate milkshake sounds okay."

"Sounds great." Cassie's mouth watered at the smell of the burgers
and fries.

"Oh, did the nap fix you?" Parker asked. She told Erin, "She was pissy all morning."

"Maybe I'm just bored of you, princess," Cassie said, squeezing too much ketchup onto her burger. "Two weeks is a long time."

"Ha," Parker said around a bite of burger. "Impossible. I'm too charming."

Cassie rolled her eyes exaggeratedly. She cleaned up the extra ketchup with a fry and *mmm*ed at how delicious it was.

"Fuck, that's good," she said, before remembering she wasn't just with crass college students. "I mean—sorry."

She hadn't meant to swear, but the fry was really good. Erin was studiously not looking at her.

"Ray's is the best," Parker said.

When Cassie took her first bite of the burger, she outright moaned, and it was then that she noticed the blush on Erin's cheeks.

That evening after they'd said their good nights and headed to bed, Cassie did her best attempt at tiptoeing down the hallway. Light shone from beneath the door to Erin's room. Cassie didn't knock, too worried about Parker waking up. She opened the door slowly. Erin was sitting up, lamp on the bedside table on, book in her hand.

"What are you doing?" Erin whispered, but she was smiling.

"I haven't gotten to touch you all *day*," Cassie whined. She slipped into the room and closed the door gently behind her.

Erin chuckled and set aside her book. "Well, now's your chance."

Cassie beamed. Erin shifted over in the bed to make room, and Cassie immediately climbed in. She tried to kiss her before she was fully settled on the bed. It was worth it, the softness of Erin's lips and the way her mouth opened immediately, like she'd missed this, too. Then Cassie's knee slipped off the mattress, and her upper body slammed into Erin.

"Shit," Cassie said, scrambling to get off.

But Erin just laughed and held her there.

I missed you. Cassie didn't say it. It hadn't even been thirty-six hours since they last kissed. But she did miss it, the way Erin kissed and laughed and held on like Cassie was strong, but she was going to be gentle anyway. She got her hands on Cassie's face and pulled a little with her fingertips. She sighed into the kiss, and Cassie smiled and bit down on her bottom lip.

Erin slid one hand into Cassie's hair. She brushed her other thumb back and forth against Cassie's cheek. Cassie let Erin control the kiss, was content with lying atop her and following her lead. Erin was slow, methodical. Like they'd never been. It'd always been quick kisses snuck while Parker was out of the room. They'd never gotten to take their time before now. Erin didn't make a move to go further than these steady, deliberate kisses, fingernails scratching at Cassie's scalp.

But Cassie could take only so much. It wasn't that she didn't like kissing Erin; it was that she did, too much. Erin was good at it. Good at it in a way that had Cassie squirming, a way that she could feel in her bones, a way that made her tingle and shift and push her hips down for more.

Finally, Erin stopped holding Cassie on top of her and let her get both legs back on the bed. Cassie settled in, holding herself half up on one side, more on top of Erin than not.

"I'll go back to my room in a minute, I swear," she said.

"And why exactly would you do that?"

"Um." Erin bit where her neck met her shoulder, and it took Cassie a second to fully respond. "You're the one who said we can't have sex with Parker in the house."

"Does oral sex really count as sex anyway?"

Erin tried to kiss her on the mouth again, but Cassie was laughing at her. Quietly, mindful of Parker, but Cassie couldn't not laugh at her.

"Uh, yeah," Cassie said. "It definitely still counts as sex."

Erin shrugged. "Guess I won't sit on your face then."

Cassie stopped laughing.

"What?"

Erin arched one of her perfect eyebrows. "I was going to, but if you say we can't, I guess I won't."

She was playing her. She was being fake nonchalant about it in a way designed to get Cassie to rush to change her mind. Cassie rushed to change her mind anyway.

"No, it's okay," she said. She kissed Erin, slowly. "I don't think oral sex counts. It's probably fine."

"Yeah?" Erin said with a grin.

Cassie nodded. "Absolutely."

"Then lie down."

Cassie did as she was told.

She flipped herself over, her back against the mattress, but she couldn't stay there—not when Erin was wiggling out of her pajama pants beside her. Cassie propped herself up on her elbows to look. She didn't think she'd ever get enough of Erin's skin. She'd call it milky white if that didn't sound like the opposite of a compliment—who wanted to be called milky? It was absolutely not the right adjective for the gorgeous expanse of Erin's legs.

While Cassie tried to come up with the right word—there was a reason she wasn't an English major—Erin threw one of those long legs over Cassie, straddling her and looking down, their hips flush together. She was glorious. Her hair was a little tousled, and Cassie's fingers twitched with the desire to mess it up more.

Cassie surged upward to get her mouth on Erin's and a hand in that hair. She could feel Erin smile into the kiss. Erin slid her hands under Cassie's Henley. Her fingernails scratched gently at her ribcage and Cassie arched into the touch. Erin's hands shifted, cupping Cassie's breasts briefly, before pulling the shirt up, up, up, and Cassie kept her mouth on Erin's as long as she could, breaking only to get the shirt over her head. Erin's hands came to the nape of Cassie's neck, deftly unhooking her necklace.

"Don't want this in the way," Erin said. She dropped the necklace onto the bedside table. "Now lie back."

Her voice was playful, but the shove she gave Cassie wasn't. The arm holding Cassie up gave out under Erin's push, and she fell to lie flat.

Erin lifted her hips off Cassie's, and Cassie missed the pressure so much she almost complained before realizing Erin was moving toward the head of the bed. Cassie swallowed. She tugged at Erin's shirt before she got too far, and Erin stopped to pull it off. Then her chest was at the perfect level, so Cassie made her wait a little longer while she got her mouth on Erin's nipples.

When Erin was settled on top of her, Cassie had to take a moment. There was Erin's cunt in front of her, slick and shining, and when she looked up she had a fantastic view of Erin's tits. Erin gave her a little smile and it was all Cassie could do not to go buck wild. Instead she took a steadying breath, restraining herself before slowly licking into Erin.

She stayed on her clit at first, swirling her tongue around it. Erin breathed a little heavier. It'd be easy to stay there forever, but Cassie dipped lower and fuck, was it worth it. She got her tongue where Erin was wettest and curled it again and again. Erin gasped and ground her hips down, and Cassie couldn't help but grin against her.

"You taste really fucking good," Cassie said and Erin ground down again, like she was trying to get Cassie to put her mouth back on her. Cassie complied.

She licked Erin slowly, thoroughly, too gently to make her come. As she did, she wrapped her hands around Erin's thighs, then slid one up her back, then squeezed her ass. There was too much of Erin that Cassie wanted to touch; her hands were as busy as her mouth. She couldn't decide where to put them.

Erin kept one hand on the headboard, and one hand behind her, fingertips pressing hard against Cassie's ribs. Occasionally she tugged at Cassie's nipples, but mostly she was holding herself up, and so Cassie decided to leave a hand on her back, to help keep Erin upright. She decided to go at her a little harder, too, decided maybe she wanted to make Erin come more than she wanted to never stop going down on her.

She bit at Erin's clit, sudden, then abandoned it to slide her tongue down to trace her opening. She went inside and was rewarded with Erin's thighs tightening around her head. Gasping, Erin dropped her hand from the headboard to Cassie's hair, holding her in place. Cassie buried her tongue deeper and used her teeth on Erin's clit. Erin pulsed her hips down. Cassie was getting messy, the entire bottom half of her face wet. She didn't stop.

Erin's fist clenched and pulled at Cassie's hair, and her hips stopped pulsing and just stayed ground down, hard against Cassie's face. Her thighs trembled and shook and Cassie held tight to them, didn't let Erin pull away until she was breathless and sensitive, worn out by Cassie's mouth. Only then did Cassie grin and let go so Erin could climb off and collapse next to her.

"Fuck," Erin murmured.

Cassie felt pretty damn proud of herself.

"I'm gonna wipe that grin off your face in a minute," Erin said, not even opening her eyes to look at Cassie.

"I'm looking forward to it," Cassie said, grinning wider.

Erin, well—she lived up to her promise. As soon as her breathing slowed, she was back on top of Cassie, lips on hers and a hand snaking down Cassie's pajama bottoms. She slid a finger into her with no resistance, added another before Cassie had time to think. Cassie tried to swallow back a gasp.

"That's what I thought," Erin said, voice low and smirk obvious even with Cassie's eyes closed.

"Kiss me." Cassie would've liked to think she demanded it, but she was pretty sure she begged. Erin kissed her anyway.

Cassie shuddered. She'd known Erin sitting on her face made her wet—like, obviously—but she hadn't expected this. She was *soaked,* Erin pumping her fingers only a few times before adding a third.

"Is this what you wanted?" Erin asked. "Is this why you were sad you hadn't touched me all day?"

"Yes," Cassie gasped. She bit the back of her hand to keep from crying out.

"You were thinking of fucking me all day?"

"Fuck, Erin, *yes*."

Cassie's body felt heavy, like it was sinking except for where it was anchored by Erin's fingers inside of her.

Erin looked *fascinated* watching her. Cassie had never felt like this during sex, like the other person couldn't bear to look away. It made her feel powerful even while she felt helpless, completely at the mercy of Erin's fingers. She smiled, like an experiment, and Erin beamed down at her, almost but not quite losing her rhythm.

Cassie realized then that they were definitely breaking the rules, even Erin's fake oral-sex-doesn't-count rule. She hadn't thought about it before Erin got her hands on her. Cassie was wound up like a goddamn teenage boy—eager and easy—and that Erin wanted to fuck her enough to ignore how her daughter was down the hall shredded the last vestige of Cassie's self-control. She bit her lip, mostly held in her whine, and came, keeping her eyes open to let Erin watch.

Erin kissed Cassie before she'd finished, body still shaking. Cassie shivered and gasped when Erin pulled her fingers out suddenly. She kissed her again. Erin slid to the side as Cassie tried to catch her breath, but left one leg thrown over Cassie's and her arm heavy over Cassie's stomach. This bed could've swallowed them whole and Cassie would've been fine with it.

"I'll go in a minute, I swear," she said. "I'm just not sure I can move my legs right now."

Erin huffed a laugh and rubbed her face against Cassie's shoulder. "Don't be an idiot. Just stay."

That sobered Cassie pretty quickly.

"Um. But Parker . . . ?"

"Sleeps until noon," Erin said, and reached to click off the light.

Cassie was glad for the sudden darkness and the way it disguised her smile. Erin read her silence wrong, though.

"If you want to go, by all means sneak down the hallway." Her voice had no give to it. "Makes more sense to stay if you ask me."

"I guess if you're gonna twist my arm," Cassie said. She was already halfway to sleep, sated and warm.

"As long as you're not a sleep cuddler," Erin said as though she weren't still pressed up against Cassie.

Cassie fell asleep instead of teasing her about it.

Twelve

ERIN

Something was poking into Erin's ribs, hard and solid and unmoving. She brought her hand up to push it away, but froze upon finding bare skin. She opened her eyes.

Right. Cassie.

Cassie, in her bed. The things Erin had whispered to her last night, three fingers deep. The look on Cassie's face as Erin crawled over her toward the headboard.

Cassie was turned away, toward the pale light drifting through the window, but Erin hid her smile in the pillow anyway. She caressed Cassie's elbow instead of moving it so her bones stopped jabbing into Erin's. The touch roused Cassie. She grabbed Erin's hand and tugged it over and around her.

Cassie yawned. "G'morning."

"Morning," Erin said.

She kissed Cassie's shoulder then pressed her smile there. Cassie shifted toward her, like somehow their entire bodies against each other wasn't close enough. Her skin was so warm. Erin's body hummed.

Erin lifted her head to check the clock on the bedside table. Not quite seven thirty.

"Plenty of time," she murmured, and kissed Cassie.

Cassie's mouth fell open more than she kissed back, like she hadn't been expecting it. Erin reveled in surprising her. She had been predictable, *dependable* for most of her life. This felt better.

It was different from yesterday. More desperate. They'd clearly moved past the no-fucking-while-Parker-was-in-the-house rule, and Erin was sure she'd feel awful about that any minute, but for now she couldn't help herself.

That wasn't the only way it was different.

"You don't taste like mint."

Cassie squinted at her. "Are you saying I have morning breath?"

"Did you brush your teeth before coming to kiss me good morning yesterday?"

Cassie's cheeks went pink, but she held on to her affront. "Of course I did. That's not weird—it's polite."

"So I should go brush my teeth first?" Erin was mostly teasing but admittedly a little nervous she'd made a misstep.

"I didn't say that."

Cassie licked into Erin's mouth, hard and intentional.

"You're an idiot," Erin said. She kissed her again, smiling almost too hard to do it properly.

Clearly neither of them minded if the other had morning breath. They kissed long enough to chase any remnant of it away, kissed until they tasted of each other. The only clothing between them was Cassie's pajama pants, which somehow never got removed last night. Erin pushed them down, then pressed her entire body into Cassie's.

"Again?" Cassie said.

Erin quirked an eyebrow at her. "Are you complaining?"

Cassie shook her head so quickly Erin laughed at her. She pushed her pants the rest of the way off.

It was slow, quiet, sleepy sex. Cassie got her fingers on Erin's clit about halfway through, and they rutted against each other. They didn't get any louder than whispers: *right there* and *Christ* and *you feel so fucking good*. They came at the same time, faces buried in each other's necks, panting.

Afterward they kissed, still slow, languid, melding into each other. Erin shouldn't fall asleep, but how could she do anything else while Cassie's fingers combed so gently through her hair?

"Shit."

Erin breathed deeply, let out a murmur of acknowledgment as she exhaled.

Something pushed her shoulder.

"Erin, wake up!" Cassie hissed.

"Mmm?"

Cassie shoved at Erin's shoulder again, hard enough to move her entire upper body. "It's past ten."

Erin sat bolt upright in bed.

"Shit," she agreed.

Cassie was already out of the bed, hopping on one leg trying to get into her pants.

"Okay," Erin said. "Okay. Parker's probably still asleep."

She climbed out of bed and Cassie immediately hurled a shirt at her.

"Put clothes on!"

Erin caught the soft gray Henley against her face and inhaled. It smelled like the travel-sized body wash that had appeared in the shower this week.

"This is yours." A giggle escaped.

"*No.*" Cassie pointed a finger at her. Her attempt at austerity wasn't particularly effective, given that she was fully topless. "This is not funny! Do not laugh at my potential impending death!"

Erin bit down on what would've been a wave of laughter before throwing the shirt at Cassie. She picked her own up off the floor and pulled it over her head. Her pajama pants were on the other side of the bed. By the time she reached them, Cassie, now fully dressed, was at the window on the side of the room, sliding it open.

"What are you doing?" Erin asked as she put her pants on.

"Is the gutter out here attached well?"

"*What?*"

"Like is it sturdy?"

"Cassie."

Cassie looked out the window toward the ground. "It's not that high up. It'll probably be fine."

She actually stuck one of her legs outside the window, straddling the sill. Laughter rattled in Erin's chest, but she didn't let it out.

"*Cassie,*" she repeated. "I can just check and see if her door's closed. You don't have to *climb out the window.*"

None of this should have been funny. It was exactly why they weren't supposed to have sex while Parker was in the house. But Erin felt ridiculous, like Bugs Bunny in a cartoon, tiptoeing to the bedroom door. Cassie quit examining the sturdiness of the gutter to watch.

Erin opened her door a crack, just enough to see down the hall. Parker's door was still closed. The tension in her body released, and her shoulders sagged in relief. She turned around, closing her door, her teeth biting hard into her lower lip to stop her laughter. Cassie almost smiled at her before furrowing her brow.

"Are we safe?" she stage-whispered.

Erin nodded, not trusting herself to open her mouth.

Cassie pulled her leg back over the sill. She cringed once she was fully inside. "Oh Jesus, I think I pulled something."

Erin couldn't stop it then. She leaned against the door, hand over her mouth, shaking with laughter.

"You were really going to go out the window, huh?"

"I *was* halfway out the window."

"How were you going to explain your broken ankle?"

"I don't know! It was fight or flight!"

The patent ridiculousness of that made Erin double over she was laughing so hard. Cassie looked at her like she'd lost her mind, and maybe she had, focusing on the hilarity of the situation instead of all the ways it could go wrong.

"This is maybe the stupidest thing I've ever done," she said, letting out one last chuckle.

Cassie's face fell. She ran a hand through all that blond hair. "We can stop," she said, almost but not quite a sulk. "If you want."

"God, no," Erin said. She crossed the room to kiss Cassie. "I haven't had this much fun in years."

Cassie ducked her head like somehow that would make Erin not notice her smile.

If Erin let herself, she'd be crushed under the weight of all the *should*s. She should feel bad about this. She shouldn't have slept with Cassie, not even once, but certainly not after learning Parker was her friend, and not with Parker under the same roof. She should be embarrassed. Ashamed. She should stop.

If she thought about it too hard, all of that would get to her. But she refused to let it. She was a grown woman, making her own choices. She didn't have to be perfect, and she was allowed to have fun. That was what this was. She could have fun for the next week, then Cassie would leave, and this would all be a fun memory. Maybe Erin would even tell Rachel about it. Rachel would die laughing at the thought of Cassie attempting to sneak out her bedroom window to avoid Parker. She would be so proud of the shower sex, Erin could imagine her pretending to tear up.

That was all this had to be. Erin would have fun stories and think back on them fondly. Next fall, Cassie would be across the country at Caltech. Who knew if she and Parker would even keep in touch?

Downstairs, Erin and Cassie ended up on opposite ends of the couch, each with their own book. Cassie's was three inches thick.

"You are aware it's the week between Christmas and New Year's and thus you're not actually supposed to do anything?" Erin asked.

"Says the person who had a shift at the hospital yesterday. On a Sunday."

Erin ceded the point. "Okay truce. I won't tease you about reading your textbook before classes even start, and you won't tease me about the trashy mystery novel I'm reading. They're my guilty pleasure." She waved her book in Cassie's direction.

"I don't believe in guilty pleasures," Cassie said. "Like what you like. I'm not embarrassed to be a nerd. You don't have to be embarrassed to read mysteries. Why would that even be embarrassing?"

"I . . . don't actually know, now that you mention it."

Erin had felt bad for not reading "real" books for so long, she'd never really questioned it. Cassie shrugged at her and opened the textbook in her lap, like it was that simple.

That first night in the bar, Cassie's confidence had been sexy as hell. It was more than that now. It was impressive, really, that this woman who was barely old enough to drink was so *certain* of herself and the world around her. She could teach Erin a thing or two.

It was more than an hour later before there was any movement upstairs. Cassie had adjusted on the couch, tucked her toes under Erin's thigh. She pulled her feet back when they heard Parker descending the staircase. She was slow, like she was taking one stair at a time. When she finally shuffled into the living room, she was clutching her pillow to her front with one hand and her comforter together under her chin with the other, the rest of the blanket dragging along behind her. Her nose was bright red.

"Oh, honey," Erin said. She leapt off the couch and pressed a hand against her daughter's forehead. "You're burning up."

"I'm *sick*." Parker's voice was nasally, clearly stuffed up. "Can you make me a bed on the couch?"

"Of course."

It didn't matter that Cassie was still on the couch—she could move. By the time Erin returned from the laundry room with two fresh sheets and a pillowcase, Cassie was on the love seat with the TV remote, eyeing Parker like she had the plague.

Erin spread the king-sized sheet over the couch and tucked it in to the edges of all the cushions. The other sheet went on top. She took the pillow Parker had brought down and switched the case out with a clean one. She fluffed it before setting it on the couch.

"C'mon, baby. Lie down. I'll make you some breakfast."

Erin could feel Cassie's eyes on her, but she didn't care. The mama bear in her always came out when Parker was sick. It didn't matter what Cassie thought of it. Jesus. She had slept with Cassie *that morning,* while Parker had been feverish, probably tossing and turning. And Erin had liked sitting next to Cassie on the couch too much to check on Parker upstairs. She could've brought her medicine and breakfast in bed instead of making her sick kid trudge all the way downstairs.

She tucked Parker in on the couch and headed into the kitchen without looking at Cassie.

It was past lunchtime, but Erin made enough oatmeal for all of them. She still didn't look at Cassie when she handed her a bowl.

"Drink some OJ, too," she told Parker. "I brought you DayQuil."

Parker sat up enough to swallow the two orange pills and eat about four bites before setting her bowl on the coffee table. By the time her head hit the pillow, she was already out.

Erin busied herself cleaning up, taking Parker's dishes to the kitchen, finishing her own oatmeal while she was there. Back in the living room, she adjusted the sheet over Parker and brushed her hair off her forehead. Her skin was clammy. Erin shivered like she was the one with the fever.

Cassie slid up against the arm of the love seat. Erin didn't sit next to her. She couldn't. She sat in the chair across the room and kept her eyes on her daughter.

An *Innocents* marathon was on the TV. It took an entire episode for Erin's muscles to unclench. It wasn't Cassie's fault that Parker was sick. Sure, it felt like a sign, like the universe was pointing out they were doing something wrong, but Erin didn't believe in signs. And she never would have interrupted Parker sleeping in—Cassie beside her on the couch or not.

Every Sunday during the semester, when Parker would call, she'd talk about reading she had to do for class, about essays and paintings and how much she hated the math class she had to take for gen ed requirements. She worked so hard. Erin was going to let her rest.

And she was resting, snoring away on the couch.

Cassie turned up the volume of the TV.

"Just put on captions," Erin stage-whispered. "I don't want to wake her up."

"Why are you babying her?" Cassie asked, but she turned the captions on.

Erin looked over at Parker. Her baby. The best thing she ever did. She was strong and smart and *everything,* and Erin would do anything for her. Erin had stayed in a long-dead marriage for her, had eventually left it for her.

"When you raise a kid, it's so easy to fuck up," Erin said. "You don't mean to, but you do. I can't always control whether or not I do right by her. But in this I can. She feels bad, and I can make it a little better. She deserves so much more, but this I can do."

For a moment, there was no sound but a Folgers commercial on the TV.

"You're too much sometimes, you know that?" Cassie said.

Erin looked at her, for the first time since Parker had come downstairs. "Should I be offended or flattered?"

Even as she asked, she knew the answer just by the look on Cassie's face.

"Flattered," Cassie confirmed. "It's pretty great."

She was still all the way to one side of the love seat. Erin didn't need to join her. She'd had the whole morning beside her, Cassie's toes tucked under Erin's thighs on the couch. She'd spent most of the day lazing about so far—there were still numbers to look over for the free clinic, laundry to be done, anything would be better than sitting next to Cassie while Parker was in the room. But Cassie was still looking at Erin like she put the stars in the sky. Erin crossed the room and joined her on the love seat.

"Love seat" was just the technical term for a piece of furniture that sat two people. Erin had shared it with plenty of people without worrying about what it meant or what anyone would think. There was enough room they didn't have to touch.

They *did* touch, a blanket spread over them both, but that wasn't the point. Parker wouldn't think anything, was the point. If she even woke up while they were still there. It wasn't a big deal.

After a while, Cassie slid her hand over onto Erin's thigh. Erin fought her smile. Cassie's hand inched toward more interesting places, but Erin shifted away.

"Cassie," she barely opened her mouth to say it. "My daughter is three feet away."

She tried not to think about a few days ago, when she had kissed Cassie in the pantry, just around the corner from Parker in the kitchen.

"Yeah, but she's passed out," Cassie whispered.

Erin leveled her with a stare, and it was supposed to be stern, but Cassie bit her lip like she was hiding a smile, and it reminded Erin of everything else she could do with that mouth.

"Okay, okay," Cassie said before Erin could make any more terrible decisions. "I'll be good."

She moved her hand back a safe distance, but kept it on Erin's thigh. By the next commercial break, Erin had tangled her fingers with Cassie's under the blanket.

Parker wasn't 100 percent better the next morning, but it was New Year's Eve, so she spent the day announcing she was *not* sick and she *would* still be having people over that night. Erin spent the day trying to dote on her without being obvious about it. Cassie spent the day trying to stay out of the orbit of Parker's germs.

An hour before people arrived, Cassie sidled up to Erin.

"I know I convinced you things don't have to be perfect for a party, but do we not have to clean up *at all*?"

Erin chuckled. "These kids have seen this house in every level of disarray—and caused it in the first place, sometimes. You'll have to clean up whatever mess you end up making anyway. No sense doing it twice."

Cassie didn't argue.

All the guests had been Parker's friends since they were little. Everyone kicked their shoes off as soon as they arrived, lining them up nicely after many years of getting yelled at for making a mess on the foyer floor. Most of them had come to the Christmas Eve party, too, so they just offered general hellos and handed over their car keys before heading downstairs. Laying eyes on Madison for the first time since the summer, though, made Erin gasp.

"Good God, kid, you're not allowed to grow up this fast," she said.

Madison grinned and rubbed at a jaw that was much sharper since Erin had last seen them. "Probably more about starting T than anything."

"Oh, Madison, I'm so happy for you." Erin hugged them. "But I'm still going to have to demand you stop growing up."

"I'll do my best."

Erin didn't mind spending New Year's Eve alone. Rachel was still in Puerto Vallarta, and Jimmy and Melissa were chaperoning Mae's party, and Erin didn't like anyone else enough to want to stay up until midnight with them. Plus, she was over the idea of the New Year meaning anything. When Erin had made New Year's resolutions, they had never been particularly healthy. Lose fifteen pounds, or worse, do what her mother wanted and lose all the weight she hadn't gotten rid of since having Parker. There had been resolutions about having more sex with Adam, as though that were the issue in their relationship. She'd announced she wasn't making New Year's resolutions anymore when she hit thirty, but she'd still made them in her mind until she'd started therapy. Self-improvement did not exist on a time line. There wasn't so much "new year, new you" pressure when Erin was trying to get better every day.

She wasn't truly alone for the night, anyway—they seemed to be having a battle in the basement over who could be loudest with the noisemakers that were supposed to be for midnight. Even once that was over, the occasional peal of laughter filtered up to Erin. There was an indignant shout she was almost certain was her daughter complaining about whatever game they were playing. Parker hated losing.

Alone upstairs, Erin stretched out on the couch and cracked the spine of her mystery novel. The murderer was the victim's sister. The author wanted her to think it was the husband, but it was the sister. There was still a quarter of the book to go, but Erin was pretty sure. She squinted at the small print of the paperback. Maybe she *should* make a resolution: to get reading glasses.

If she woke up with the book splayed open across her chest, no one had to know she'd taken a nap. She rubbed her eyes and looked at her phone. 11:47 P.M. Perfect timing.

When Parker was little, they would always pop a bottle of champagne in the backyard on New Year's, see how far they could shoot the cork. Tonight, Erin used a folded dish towel to twist the cork, popping it gently into her hand. She turned the TV on to watch the ball drop, but she would've known when it fell anyway thanks to the shouted countdown and all those noisemakers downstairs.

Erin poured herself a glass of champagne. As she took her first sip, she heard someone tromping up the stairs. She had an idea who.

Erin prided herself on her poker face. It was something she'd had to perfect throughout her life. Early on, she learned to keep her face blank rather than roll her eyes at her mother. The skill came in handy dealing with patronizing professors, arrogant attendings, any number of people who doubted, ignored, or underestimated her. She used it when telling patients or their families bad news.

But when Cassie poked her head around the corner, Erin's face broke open into a smile. Cassie came into the room on her tiptoes, like she was sneaking, even with her heavy steps on her way up from the basement. She was cute as hell.

"What are you doing up here?" Erin asked. "The party's downstairs."

Cassie sat so close to Erin on the couch their knees banged together. "Yeah, but I heard the prettiest girl in town was up here."

It was a ridiculous, obviously tipsy line, but Erin's chest swelled with warmth anyway. Her laugh was more a giggle than anything.

"How drunk are you?"

"Not as drunk as a lot of those idiots," Cassie said, taking the champagne glass out of Erin's hand and setting it on the table.

Erin *tsk*ed at her. "I love those idiots, Cassie."

"Yeah, I mean, they're great, don't get me wrong," Cassie said. She waved her arms in a gesture Erin had no idea how to interpret. "But Haylee and Scout have been making out for, like, an hour, and everyone is just letting them shove their tongues down each other's throats in the corner?" She smirked. "I mean, I get wanting to do that, no matter who is around, but I hope I'm a little more discreet about it."

Erin quirked an eyebrow. "The middle of the living room is being discreet?"

"Who said I was talking about you?"

Erin might've taken her more seriously if she'd been able to say it with a straight face.

"You're here, aren't you?" Erin said.

"I just—" Cassie finally seemed to lose some of that confidence she was always walking around with. She scuffed one foot against the carpet. "I mean, it's New Year's," she said eventually. She was looking at the ground when she said, "You're supposed to kiss somebody at midnight."

"God, you're cute."

Erin kissed her. She didn't think about how Cassie was her daughter's friend; she didn't think about how anyone could come upstairs at any moment; she just kissed her. It was soft and sweet and absolutely not a bad way to ring in a new year.

When she pulled away, sooner than she'd like—and sooner than Cassie would like, too, if the way she chased Erin's lips was any indication—Erin asked, "How'd you slip away from the party?"

Cassie blinked like she had to reset her brain after the kiss, and Erin tried not to feel smug.

"I'm gonna FaceTime Acacia from the future. It's too loud down there."

She wet her lips with her tongue, and Erin couldn't look away. She tried to get her pulse under control. She could not make out with Cassie with ten teenagers in her basement. She wouldn't do that with anyone, but she certainly couldn't be doing it with someone closer in age to the teenagers than to her.

"You should FaceTime her, then."

They were still leaned into each other. Cassie jutted her chin out, trying to connect their mouths again, but Erin pushed her backward into the couch. She imagined, for a millisecond, following the push with her body, climbing right into Cassie's lap, in the middle of the living room.

"Call Acacia," she said instead, and shifted away.

Cassie's throat worked as she swallowed. It took her a second before she fished her phone out of her pocket. Erin looked away, like that offered some kind of privacy.

"Hello from the future!" Cassie yelled when Acacia answered.

"How is it?" Acacia asked. "Are you living under water?"

"No, in outer space! You always say I'm gonna be an astronaut but everyone is now!"

Acacia's laugh was bright, even over the phone.

"Hey, where are you? Where's Parker? Where's the party?"

"Parker is downstairs with the party," Cassie said. "I came upstairs to say happy New Year to Erin and to call you."

"Cassie."

There was a warning in Acacia's voice that made Erin look at Cassie's face, and it was like she knew what was about to happen before it did: frantic, useless terror.

"Please tell me you didn't do something stupid like go upstairs to try to kiss her," Acacia said.

Cassie went stiff, completely frozen. A rock sunk into the pit of Erin's stomach, but she put on a big smile as she leaned over, into the frame, and waved at Acacia.

"Hi, Acacia! Happy New Year!" She moved back out of the frame.

The way Acacia's face fell might have been funny if Erin weren't feeling something similar.

"Happy New Year," Acacia said blankly.

"Yeah, Kaysh, I should be getting back to the party," Cassie said. Erin could feel her eyes on her. "Talk to you later."

"Bye."

They hung up. Cassie turned to Erin, but Erin refused to look at her.

Cassie took a big breath. "Look, she doesn't even know—"

"It's fine," Erin said.

She was the one who was frozen now, her jaw set so tight her teeth creaked. How could she have been so *stupid*?

"I'm sorry," Cassie said. "She only knows about that night, at the bar. I told her forever ago, because I couldn't stop thinking about you and I had to tell someone. I didn't know—I didn't know I was going to come here. I didn't know anything was going to happen."

If things were normal, Erin would like hearing that Cassie thought about her so much she had to tell someone. *If things were normal.* Nothing had ever been normal here. Nothing had ever been *okay.* Erin had been pretending because she wanted to justify it to herself, but look where that got her: fucking one of her daughter's best friends while the other knew what was going on. What the fuck had she been thinking.

"It's fine," she said again.

"Erin, I'm serious, would you look at me?" Cassie sounded panicked, and that was the only reason Erin finally looked at her. "Acacia's my best friend. She's not going to—"

"It's fine, Cassie," Erin said one more time.

Acacia was Cassie's best friend. Acacia was Parker's best friend. Cassie was Parker's best friend. Erin was the worst mother in the world.

"Go back to the party before you're missed. Happy New Year."

"Erin—"

"Go back to the party, Cassie."

Cassie went.

Erin didn't finish her glass of champagne. She poured it down the kitchen sink instead, and closed the bottle with a reusable airtight cork.

Acacia knew. Parker's *roommate*.

Parker's roommate knew Erin and Cassie were . . . whatever they were doing. Erin hardly knew Cassie. She should've known better than to trust her. This wasn't going to work itself out just because Erin wanted it to.

The world kept reminding her that this was a bad idea. She should listen. She should be a better person. She had no excuse for this.

You don't need an excuse to feel good. Rachel's voice in her head was never a good sign. Now Erin had Cassie's in there, too, because fuck should, right? Cassie was only here for another week. The holidays were a time for excess.

Besides, Erin had *tried* to be better. It hadn't worked. She didn't seem capable of being nice to Cassie without flirting, but she also couldn't distance herself from her without being cruel. This was the situation that worked best for everyone. Cassie was happy, Erin was happy, and Parker was happy. Not telling your kid something wasn't lying. It was like when Parker asked what *Breaking Bad* was about before she'd turned double digits—Erin had said a chemistry teacher and his family, and that hadn't been a lie. What she didn't know wouldn't hurt her.

It was only for another week.

Thirteen

CASSIE

Cassie didn't wake up hungover, because she'd stopped drinking at midnight, but she still felt nauseated. She chugged the glass of water next to her bed. Acacia had texted seven more times. One *Happy New Year from the past!* and six more variations of *fuck I'm so sorry.* Cassie had already told her it was okay.

It wasn't okay, but it wasn't Acacia's fault. Something had to give, fucking her best friend's mom.

She wanted to apologize to Erin again. She brushed her teeth and went downstairs.

It was silent there. No one else was awake—Parker was sharing her bed with Lila and the rest were passed out in the basement. Erin had a cup of coffee ready for her. Cassie mumbled her thanks and took a sip. It was too sugary. Erin stood a few feet away. Neither looked at the other.

Before Cassie decided whether she wanted to stew in silence or actually address this, Erin said, "I don't want to talk about it, Cassie. I understand, but I don't want to talk about it, okay? Now, are you going to kiss me good morning or not?"

Cassie swallowed. Her body leaned toward Erin before she'd consciously decided what to do. This seemed like a break. She'd be stupid not to take it.

She kissed her carefully. She'd never really tried to put so much feeling into a kiss before, to say *I'm sorry* and *It's okay* and *How did you expect me to do this without telling someone about you?* She cradled Erin's face. Erin bumped their noses together.

Too soon, they heard footsteps coming up the stairs from the basement. Cassie and Erin moved away from each other, and Cassie forced herself to look away.

"Morning, Dr. Bennett. Morning, Cassie," Caleb said as he entered the kitchen.

"Honestly, Caleb, when are you going to start calling me Erin?"

Cassie smiled at the tender frustration in Erin's voice.

Everyone got out of the house pretty quickly. Cassie and Parker were still in their pajamas, getting ready to watch the Rose Parade, when Erin came into the living room.

"I've got to go to the hospital," she announced.

Parker's head snapped in her direction. "What?"

"I told you I was on call, didn't I?" Erin asked, sitting down to slide her feet into her tennis shoes. "They need me."

"It's New Year's Day," Parker said. "We always have chili and cabbage and watch the parade and football."

"I'm sorry, baby," Erin said. "But the chili is already simmering on the stove, stir it every once in a while, okay? You can eat it whenever. I'm sure Cassie will watch the parade and football with you."

She dropped a kiss on Parker's head.

"Love you, sweetie," she said. She nodded in Cassie's direction. "Cassie."

As soon as Erin was gone, Parker huffed. "This is such bullshit. She was on call last New Year's Day. She must volunteer for this."

Cassie didn't reply. Parker looked at her for confirmation.

"Don't you think it's shitty?"

Cassie shrugged. "She was here Christmas Eve and Christmas Day. That's probably more important than watching football on New Year's Day."

Parker sighed.

"It's just stupid," she said. "We used to have a really great time, and it's like she avoids it now."

This was getting more into Erin's past with Adam than Cassie particularly wanted to. But she wasn't a bad friend, so she wasn't going to leave Parker hanging.

"You used to have a really great time like you, your mom, and your dad?"

Parker played with the fringe on the edge of her afghan. "Yeah, I guess."

"Look," Cassie said, "I feel like your parents have had like, the best divorce of all time, to be honest. Your dad brings ham to Christmas Eve at your mom's house. They both obviously love you and get along with each other well enough. I'm not saying your mom avoids New Year's Day with you, because fuck if I know. I'm just saying maybe cut her some slack when it comes to family traditions."

Parker finished braiding a part of the afghan fringe and squinted at Cassie.

"That seems reasonable." It sounded like an accusation.

"Plus, you can't say you invited me to be a buffer because you don't get along, while also complaining that she isn't hanging out with you."

"Yeah, okay, fine," Parker said, before adding, "Actually you have been a good buffer, you know? Like how you got her to calm down before the party instead of obsessively cleaning everything? So. Thanks."

"Yeah," Cassie fake scoffed. "I'm awesome. Thanks for finally noticing."

Parker threw a pillow at her.

They watched the parade and football and Cassie really didn't care about any of it, so she spent the day in and out of sleep on the couch. She played on her phone and pointed out all the inappropriate-sounding things the announcers said. *He saw that hole and he plowed right in.*

They were going for their second round of chili when Erin arrived home, still in her scrubs, looking worse for wear. Cassie served her a bowl and got her a glass of water without being asked. Erin smiled blearily at her. Parker made an effort to be nice; she did a pretty in-depth recount of the parade that made Erin laugh.

Cassie pressed her ankle against Erin's under the table. She wasn't trying to be flirty. She just—she still wasn't sure what ground they stood on. Erin pushed her ankle back against Cassie's. Maybe she was forgiven for telling Acacia.

The next morning, Cassie woke up with a sore throat. More than sore, it was scratchy and raw, and her nose was running. Now she completely understood why Parker was so whiny when she was sick. Not that she was going to be as whiny as Parker, obviously, because she was a good and decent person.

She brushed her teeth and trudged downstairs. Erin had a cup of coffee ready for her.

"Thanks," she croaked, and wished she could kiss her good morning like usual.

"Oh, sweetheart," Erin said immediately, setting down her mug. "Are you sick?"

"M'fine."

Erin held her hands to Cassie's face, one on her cheek and the other over her forehead. "You're hot."

"You, too." Cassie tried for a joke, but she winced at the way her throat cracked.

"Can I make up the couch for you?" Erin asked.

Cassie wanted to say no. She could take care of herself. She just needed to sleep it off, maybe take some ibuprofen. But Erin hadn't taken her hand off her forehead, and Cassie leaned into it without meaning to. Maybe Erin taking care of her wouldn't be so bad.

"Okay."

The whole couch bed thing seemed a lot less absurd when she

was the one getting tucked into it. The sheets were cool and soft against her warm skin. Erin brought her orange juice and Kleenex and ibuprofen.

"You want breakfast?"

Cassie shook her head. "Sleep first."

Erin smiled down at her, and then she was out.

She woke up shivering, even under a blanket that hadn't been on her when she fell asleep. She could hear Parker and Erin in the kitchen. If she were a different person, she'd call out to them, cold and hungry and needy. Instead, she drank the room-temperature orange juice that was still next to her. It hurt to swallow.

What felt like hours later, but was probably only fifteen minutes, Erin came to check on her.

"Oh, you're awake. How are you feeling?" Erin put the back of her hand against Cassie's forehead. "You're still hot."

Cassie shook her head. "I'm freezing."

Erin got her another blanket. Parker came in as Erin was tucking it under Cassie's feet.

"Feel better," Parker said. "I'm getting out of here, away from your sickness."

"You're the one who gave it to me." Cassie's voice was more a rasp than anything.

"Well, I'm not reinfecting myself."

"Don't worry, Cassie," Erin said. "I'll be here if you need anything."

"Your mom's a lot nicer than you, you know that?" Cassie asked Parker.

"That's why she's the doctor," Parker said. "Also why she'll end up sick in like three days."

Parker left—Cassie didn't ask where she was going because talking hurt almost as bad as swallowing. Erin made her oatmeal and brought her more orange juice.

"You want me to find you something to watch?" Erin gestured to the TV.

Cassie shook her head.

"You want anything else to eat?"

She shook her head again.

Erin smiled at her. It could've been out of pity, but Erin was pretty when she smiled, and Cassie was too sick to get upset about anything.

"Can I do anything to make you feel better?" Erin asked.

"You should have a pet—a dog or a big cat or something."

Erin's smile went soft. "Why?"

"Because pets can cuddle you when you're sick without getting sick themselves."

She was aware she sounded pathetic, but her throat hurt and she wanted to snuggle and feel taken care of.

"How's this," Erin said, "I'll sit at the foot of the couch? You can put your feet in my lap while I read over some stuff for work?"

Cassie tried not to seem too desperate when she nodded.

She fell asleep with Erin rubbing absently at the arch of her right foot.

Cassie didn't wake up until almost dinnertime. She was sweating balls and flung all the blankets off.

"Good morning," Erin said from behind the couch. Cassie didn't know how she'd gotten out from under her feet without Cassie noticing.

"I'm hungry."

Erin laughed. "That's probably a good sign."

She had dinner ready. It was literally homemade chicken soup, and Cassie felt, for a moment, almost smitten. Give her a break— she hadn't kissed Erin in more than twenty-four hours; that plus the fever had her a little delirious.

Parker was home for dinner, babbling away about her day, but Cassie didn't hear a thing. She inhaled the soup and drank four glasses of water and was ready for bed again.

"Cassie?"

"Mmm?"

Cassie wasn't fully awake when the bed dipped. She opened her eyes to find Erin next to her, smiling gently. Cassie tried to blink away the sleep blur. The sky outside her window was pink, the sun just beginning to rise.

"I wanted to make sure you were feeling okay before I head in for my shift," Erin said.

"Mmm." Cassie nodded. She swallowed. Her throat still hurt but it was far better than yesterday. "M'okay," she said.

"Good," Erin said, leaning down to kiss her.

"No!" Cassie scrambled back toward the headboard, suddenly more awake. "I still could be contagious or something. I don't want you to get sick."

Erin chuckled. "But we can't have you spending the day pissy with Parker because you didn't get your good morning kiss."

Cassie squinted up at her.

"That's what happened last time I went to work without kissing you good morning," Erin said. "Am I wrong?"

She wasn't, but Cassie refused to acknowledge that.

"I'm not to blame if you get sick."

"Deal," Erin said.

She kissed her. She kissed her long and deep and with enough tongue that if Cassie was even a tiny bit contagious, Erin was getting it. She smirked as she left, and Cassie stared after her dumbly, then collapsed against her pillows once more, heart going faster than she'd like to admit. She fiddled with her rocket ship necklace and fell back asleep with a smile on her face.

The next morning, in the dark, Cassie stubbed her toe on her packed suitcase. Why the hell did her flight have to be this early? At least Erin had a bagel and a travel cup of coffee ready for her in the kitchen. Cassie kissed her soundly—after she'd taken a huge gulp of coffee.

Parker stumbled downstairs as Erin hefted Cassie's suitcase into the car in the garage. She rubbed at her eyes and reached for her coat.

"What are you doing?" Cassie asked.

"'mma drive with you to the airport," Parker said.

Cassie laughed. "No thanks, babe. You look like you want to die being awake this early. Go back to sleep."

Parker looked at her with disbelief—some joy, too, but not until she was sure this was for real. "Are you serious?"

"I'm going to see you in less than a week," Cassie said. "I think I'll live if you don't take me to the airport."

Parker hurled her arms around Cassie. "You're my best friend."

"I'm telling Acacia," Cassie laughed.

"I don't even care," Parker said. "She'll understand when I explain this glorious thing you're doing for me."

"Go to bed, idiot."

Cassie smacked Parker on the ass as she turned to go upstairs.

"Wait," Parker said. "You don't mind, Mom—do you?"

"Of course not," Erin said.

Cassie bit back her grin. "Sleep well, princess."

She disappeared up the stairs and Erin turned to Cassie with a smile. "Ready to go?"

It only took about twenty minutes to get to the airport, and Cassie didn't mean to fall asleep, but Erin rested her palm over Cassie's thigh and her eyes got heavy and the next thing she knew Erin was shaking her awake.

"Erin," Cassie said when she realized they were in a parking garage. "You could have dropped me at the curb."

"Too late."

Erin smiled and Cassie rolled her eyes.

"You're too much."

"I've heard that's a compliment," Erin said.

Cassie took a swig from her travel mug instead of replying.

Erin carried her suitcase for her and Cassie rolled her eyes again, but she appreciated it. Her body hadn't adjusted to the New Hampshire weather, and no part of it wanted to be awake, much less moving. Erin stood close to her all through check-in, and Cassie double-checked her ticket on her phone. She handed Erin her empty travel mug.

"Don't want to steal this," she said. "But I might need more caffeine. Can I buy you a coffee?"

"You'd have to drink it before security. Do you have enough time?"

"There's like no line, Erin. It's fine. As long as you're okay maybe paying for parking? It said it was only free for the first half hour."

Erin quirked an eyebrow and echoed Cassie's words back to her. "It's like four dollars, Cassie. It's fine."

There was a Starbucks near the baggage claim. Cassie bought a vanilla latte for Erin and a caramel macchiato for herself. Their fingers touched when Cassie handed over the cup. Erin smiled at her, and Cassie looked away, her cheeks warm. It was too early.

They sat on a bench by the window, Cassie's carry-on tucked beside them. Neither said anything. What were you supposed to say to your friend's mom at the end of your . . . affair or whatever the fuck they were calling this? Cassie slouched in her seat, stretched her legs out. If her ankle came to rest against Erin's, so be it. Erin's eyes crinkled at their corners, and Cassie was pretty sure she was hiding a smile behind her coffee cup. Cassie's face flushed hotter.

Eventually, there was nothing to do but go through security.

Erin walked her upstairs. It was still too early for the line to be anything other than short, so Cassie and Erin stood off to the side. Cassie shoved her hands in her coat pockets. Erin scratched at her neck.

"So this was fun," Cassie said. She shifted on her feet.

"Don't make this awkward, Cassie," Erin said.

"I'm not!" Cassie protested, knowing she was. "It was fun, for real."

"It was."

"Yeah, I'm really glad you stopped denying my hotness." Cassie grinned.

Erin shoved her shoulder. "You're an idiot."

"So I've been told."

There was a moment where they just stood there smiling at each other, then Cassie wasn't really sure who moved first but suddenly they were kissing.

She was mildly aware that they were in public, but she didn't really care that they were kissing too hard to be family friendly. Almost no one was at the airport. So they were giving the TSA guys a little thrill, who cared?

She was wobbly on her feet when they pulled back, and Erin kept her hands on Cassie's hips until she was steady. Erin grinned like she knew the effect she had. Cassie kissed her again, quick, to wipe it off her face.

"Thanks for bringing me to the airport," she said, hefting her carry-on more securely over her shoulder.

"Have a good semester," Erin said.

Cassie didn't look back until she was through security. Erin was in the same place she'd left her. She gave a wave, and Cassie swallowed thickly before giving a brief nod and turning to go.

Cassie was eating dinner that night, settled in and comfortable in her apartment, when she got a text.

Erin [7:23 PM]
You got me sick

Cassie [7:24 PM]
I told you not to kiss me! It's not my fault!

Cassie [7:24 PM]
I hope you feel better tho. At least it's just like a 24 hour bug

Erin [7:25 PM]
It was worth it ;)

Fourteen

ERIN

Even after five whole years of talking to Carolyn, Erin still felt like she should ask her therapist more about her own life, like she shouldn't take up the entire hour talking about herself, which was literally what she was paying for. She always got over the impulse once she got on a roll, but she stumbled through the first few minutes of conversation.

"Did you have a good holiday?" Erin asked.

"I did, thank you," Carolyn said. "How about you?"

Erin nodded. "It was nice."

"Parker was home, right? Is she still there?"

"She is," Erin said. "I've got her for another week."

"How's that going?"

"Great." It was an instinctual response. Don't admit weakness. Don't let anyone know you're not perfect. Erin took a breath and tried again. "Pretty good, for the most part. She brought a friend home for the first two weeks, which I was worried about, but I think it helped."

"Why were you worried about it?"

Erin had never intentionally lied to her therapist before. It seemed like that defeated the point of therapy.

She was absolutely lying about this.

"I think I was afraid Parker would use her friend as an excuse to not interact with me? Which—I know that doesn't make sense. We're doing well. Better than we have been for a long time. We're past her not interacting with me, I hope."

Carolyn reaffirmed Erin, asked more questions, let her talk. It was a typical therapy session except for the way Erin avoided the thing she needed to talk about the most.

No, that wasn't right. She didn't need to talk to her therapist about Cassie. It was fine! It happened. It was fun. It was over.

Toward the end of session, Carolyn asked if she could make a suggestion. Erin braced herself. Carolyn's suggestions tended to, as Rachel would say, drag her for filth.

"Maybe it's time to have that conversation with Parker."

"What?"

"About the divorce. About the whys. About what you want for her."

It was a conversation Erin had been wanting to have. Or—that wasn't exactly true, either. She didn't want to have the conversation, but she wanted Parker to know.

Parker hadn't forgiven her for the divorce. They'd moved on, but that didn't mean Erin was forgiven. She wanted Parker to understand. The divorce? It was for Erin, yes, but for Parker, too. Erin learned to put herself first because she wanted to model that for her daughter.

"Can't I just write her a letter or something?"

"Sometimes we have to do things that make us uncomfortable for people we love."

Erin knew that, obviously. And she had to have the conversation with Parker eventually. She'd tried, once, during the divorce, but she and Parker were both too close to it then. Erin hadn't been able to talk about it without blaming Adam—to be fair, a lot of the blame lay at his feet. But he was a good dad, and Parker loved him, and she hadn't yet seemed to realize he wasn't perfect. She'd figured that out about Erin long ago.

With some distance from the divorce, Erin refused to be the one to show Parker her father wasn't perfect. The conversation had to be about *her*, not about the divorce.

Erin tried when she got home. Parker asked how therapy was and Erin didn't just say *good* and move on. She tried being more honest.

"Okay," she said, tilting her head back and forth as she tried to find words for the session. "Sometimes I feel like I'm doing it wrong."

Erin's mother would've died at the thought of going to therapy, and she would roll over in her grave knowing Erin actually spoke to her daughter about it.

"It's like that sometimes," Parker said. "Did I tell you I'm going at the student center now?"

"You are?"

"Yeah. Sasha had offered to do virtual visits when I went to school, but I like it better in person."

Parker had been in therapy since the divorce, because Erin had wanted her to have someone objective to talk to. Someone not on Erin's or Adam's side, but on Parker's.

"How's it going?"

"Okay," Parker mimicked her earlier answer. "It's weird having to catch my new therapist up on all my childhood trauma."

"Oh, yes, that sounds horrible. How have you had time to fill her in on all the ways your mother is wretched?"

Parker giggled. Erin flicked water on her before drying her hands.

They could be more honest, more vulnerable, without having to fully bare themselves. Baby steps.

They would have the conversation, eventually.

• • • •

Toward the end of January, Rachel took Erin to lunch and a pedicure for her birthday, as she'd done for years. Erin always picked some place fancy, both because Rachel was paying and because now that she was single, Erin never really got the chance to go to nice restaurants.

In her head, she could practically hear Carolyn's voice asking why she didn't think she was worth nice restaurants on her own.

In between the appetizer and the entrée, Rachel asked the question she asked every birthday:

"What did you learn about yourself in the past year?"

Every birthday Erin was unprepared. She usually forgot the question was coming, but this year she'd thought about it in advance. And she still wasn't sure.

"I'm still learning it, I think, but . . ." It felt ridiculous to say, but it was all she'd come up with. "Fuck should. It doesn't matter what I've been trained to think I'm 'supposed' to do. What do I want? What makes me feel good? What will make my relationships stronger? Those are the questions that matter. Not what *should* I do."

"Yes, fuck, I love this."

"You should've seen me the day before the Christmas party. I was freaking out—"

"As you do."

"As I do. But once Cassie talked some sense into me—I swear Parker didn't recognize me when she got home and I wasn't frantically cleaning anymore."

"Cassie?"

Erin popped another piece of calamari into her mouth. "Hmm?"

"That was Parker's friend, right?"

"Yeah." She nodded. Breathed through her nose. "Yep."

"So you needed some college kid to talk sense into you?" Rachel asked.

Reducing Cassie to "some college kid" made Erin bristle. Before she could figure out if it was possible to say something about it without being obvious, Rachel continued.

"No, yeah, that makes sense. You're a disaster before that party."

Erin rolled her eyes. "Thank you, I really appreciate you being kind to me on my birthday."

"I'm paying for your lunch and your pedicure, bitch."

Better not to address the college-kid comment. Besides, it was accurate, even if it did seem dismissive.

"Well, I was better, this year," Erin said instead. "And it got me thinking about how much I've worried about people's expectations. I'm ready to be done with that."

"I've been trying to convince you to be done with that for as long as I've known you."

"I know, I know, you've always been much smarter than me."

"Nice of you to recognize it."

Rachel wasn't joking—not about how long she'd been trying to convince Erin to stop caring about what people thought. Erin couldn't name a single time Rachel had bent to external expectations. She'd been proudly pansexual since before Erin knew what that meant, before most people knew—then again, maybe that was still the case, thinking about society at large. She'd seemed to always live as herself. She wasn't hiding things away, burying things like Erin had spent so much time doing.

If Erin wasn't worrying about what other people thought, why was she still not telling Rachel—or Carolyn, for that matter—about Cassie?

Well, like Carolyn always said: recovery was a journey, not a destination. And the thing with Cassie was over. There was no reason to talk about it.

Birthday lunch was good, but birthday pedicures were better.

Erin picked out a hot pink polish, too bright for January, but it wasn't like anyone would be seeing her toes. It was a summer color. She was absolutely ready for summer. The last week in January in New Hampshire felt like an entire year away from summer, but Erin needed the reminder that the world wouldn't always be gray and white slush.

The polish was called Hotter Than You. It made her think of Cassie—the confidence in the name, the fading streaks in her hair, her devilish tongue wetting her lips, the flesh between her thighs. Not what Erin needed to be thinking about right now, no matter how much Rachel would love to hear about it. Just because Erin knew every detail about Rachel's sex life didn't mean she was going to share her own.

Rachel picked a dark but bright purple and they climbed into adjacent spa chairs. Erin eased her feet into the water. It was the perfect temperature—almost scalding at first, but just right once her body adjusted. It bubbled around her aching feet.

Erin leaned back into her chair and turned on a massage program. Why did pedicure chairs always have massage settings that felt half like a massage and half like you were being punished? It dug in just under Erin's scapula and she gasped.

"Have I told you lately that I love you?" she asked Rachel.

"Never often enough," Rachel said. "But I'm pretty sure you're the one who gets credit for inventing birthday pedicures."

Erin relaxed further against the chair. "Wow, I'm brilliant."

Rachel chuckled but didn't reply. They'd talked themselves out at lunch—well, they could never talk themselves out, really. Hadn't done it yet in twenty years of friendship. It was more that they knew how to be quiet together. Each other's company was enough without talking. Erin didn't open her eyes until the tech who would be painting her nails sat on a rolling stool near her feet and asked her to take one out of the water. Once she'd appropriately greeted him and confirmed she wanted her nails cut, she closed her eyes again. Quiet music played throughout the salon, and Erin didn't think about anything except trying not to make any inappropriate noises as the massage chair dug into her muscles.

The nail tech was exfoliating her calves, which felt even *better* than the chair, when Erin's phone buzzed beside her.

Cassie [Today 1:37 PM]
I heard it was your birthday

A grin broke across Erin's face. She dipped her chin to her chest and her thumbs flew over her phone.

Erin [1:37 PM]
It might be . . .

An ellipsis, like she was trying to be cute or coy or something. As though she could pull off coy after texting back the same minute.

"Who the hell are you texting?"

Erin dropped her phone. She managed to kick it—with her shin, not her foot—before it landed in the tub, and it clattered across the floor instead, chased by a wave of water. The nail tech sighed.

"Sorry!" Erin winced. "Sorry."

He handed her the phone before reaching for a towel.

"I'd like to amend my question," Rachel said. "Who the *fuck* are you texting?"

Erin's face was probably the color of the nail polish she'd picked out. "My hairdresser texted to wish me a happy birthday."

"I'm sorry, do you want to fuck your hairdresser?"

Erin glanced down at the nail tech, whose eyebrows were raised as he finished wiping up the water she'd splashed everywhere.

"You know women talk about worse shit here," Rachel said, waving her hand like it didn't matter who heard her discussing Erin's sex life. "Out with it."

"There's nothing to be out with," Erin said. "I'd just rather not you start rumors about me and Abbey at the nail salon."

"We are excellent secret keepers, thank you," the woman working on Rachel's nails said. "We don't gossip."

Erin wondered what they'd think if she'd told Rachel the truth.

"I'm sure we are far from the only people who would deserve it," she said. "Anyway, I do not want to fuck my hairdresser. She was being rude about covering gray hairs as I get older."

"That still doesn't explain why you looked like a blushing school-girl."

Rachel never left anything alone in her entire life.

"I don't know what to tell you, Rach. I mean, I did respond, 'oh fuck you,' but I didn't mean it literally."

When had Erin become so good at making up an alibi? Her phone buzzed in her hand with another text. She kept looking at Rachel, who appeared to be analyzing her face for signs of deceit.

"Let me see your phone."

"Oh my God. No. I am not humoring you."

"I don't believe you."

"That sounds like a personal problem."

"You should've seen your face!" Rachel crossed her arms and narrowed her eyes. "If we weren't getting pedicures right now, I would get that phone from you."

Erin believed her. Rachel could be tenacious.

"I'm glad we're getting pedicures then," Erin said, refusing to engage. "I'm going to go back to enjoying mine now. It'd be great if, for my birthday, you could stop being annoying."

She shoved her phone between her thigh and the armrest. Closing her eyes, she leaned back into the massage chair. Hopefully she was conveying complete relaxation.

In reality, her pulse jumped when her phone buzzed again. She cracked an eye open. Rachel was back to playing something—almost certainly Pet Rescue—on her own phone. It was probably safe.

Maintaining the straightest face possible, Erin opened her messages.

Cassie [1:38 PM]
Happy birthday. I hope you get everything you want

How did Cassie even know it was her birthday? Parker must have told her, obviously. But Erin wasn't thinking about her daughter.

She'd been thinking of Cassie even before the other woman texted. It'd been three weeks since Erin had driven Cassie to the airport, but she still thought about her. Too often. She couldn't take a shower without blushing. Well, blushing and wishing Cassie were there with her.

Erin didn't know what to text back. She wanted to flirt. Wanted to say she couldn't get everything she wanted, not with Cassie in Virginia. It was her birthday. She was allowed to daydream about fucking her daughter's friend if she wanted to. She was allowed to pretend she didn't do it most days with no excuse.

All she ended up texting was *thank you*.

Then she deleted the messages. She didn't trust Rachel not to try to rip the phone from her hands the second they got out of the salon.

Fifteen

CASSIE

It was the first week of February and Cassie was thinking about doing something stupid.

She and Erin had texted twice since winter break: Erin's initial text about getting sick, then Cassie wishing her a happy birthday.

And now Cassie was online, looking at 1800flowers.com, thinking about doing something stupid.

Everything was insanely expensive and roses would be too much, right? She shouldn't be doing this. Parker said Erin was working Valentine's Day. What if she didn't want flowers at work? It was all too much and too expensive and too stupid.

Cassie debated for thirty minutes before sending lilies. The ones that were white with dark pink toward the inside of them. As soon as the order went through, she wanted to call the company and cancel it. Instead, she closed her laptop.

"Why don't you come to our anti–Valentine's Day movie night?" Parker asked.

She was sprawled across Cassie's couch, clicking through Facebook on Cassie's computer. Cassie was looking in her fridge, deciding if she was hungry enough to make something or if she should just wait till the caf opened for dinner.

She didn't take her head out of the fridge to ask: "You mean your actual–Valentine's Day date?"

"It's not a date," Parker sighed. "Her friend Gwen's gonna be there."

That got Cassie's attention. "Your girl is friends with Gwen? Like, looks-like-she-could-kill-you-but-you-might-enjoy-it Gwen?"

"She's not my girl," Parker said. "And yeah, the same Gwen you hit on at a party that you were so drunk at I had to pick you up."

Cassie refused to engage on that particular subject. "You and Sam made out in public months ago, how is she not your girlfriend yet?"

Parker took a minute to respond. "You know how shitty I felt after Seth."

"After Seth fucked us both and fucked us both over? And you broke your hand punching him when you found out?" Cassie said, reliving the only good part of that story. "Sure, but the best way to get over someone is to get under someone else."

"Look who's talking," Parker said. "Have you even had sex since Seth?"

Cassie blushed and didn't hide her grin. "Of course I have, princess. Just because Gwen can resist my charms doesn't mean everyone can." It was true—there had been a few weekends in a row of one-night stands after Seth. Erin had been supposed to be another. Cassie headed to her bathroom, because being in the same room as Parker while thinking of fucking her mom was too much. "I gotta pee."

The flowers were supposed to be delivered earlier. Erin should have gotten them by now. Cassie wondered if she liked them.

"I'm just saying you should come," Parker said, raising her voice to carry on their conversation.

"I'm saying if I don't, maybe *you* will come."

Parker let out a noise of exasperation. "You're so annoying."

"You love me," Cassie called.

Her phone buzzed in her hand. Speak of the devil.

Erin [Today 4:23 PM]
Babe. You got me flowers?

Erin [4:23 PM]
They're beautiful.

Cassie's stomach did this swooping thing that was really dumb, but she couldn't help her smile.

Cassie [4:24 PM]
You like them?

She flushed the toilet and washed her hands, singing the chorus of "Truth Hurts" under her breath to count the requisite twenty seconds. When she got back to the living room, Parker stood in the middle of it, looking—shocked, or something.

"What's up?" Cassie asked.

"I gotta go," Parker said.

"I thought we were doing dinner?"

"I can't." She looked at the ground.

Cassie guffawed. "Oh my God, are you having dinner with her, too? This is obviously a date, Parker."

"Whatever, Cassie. Shut up," Parker said, and left.

Cassie laughed at the closed door. Parker was so whipped for someone who wasn't even her girlfriend yet.

Cassie's phone buzzed in her hand.

Erin [4:26 PM]
I love them.

Cassie swallowed, grinning.

Cassie [4:27 PM]
It's okay that I sent them to work?

Erin [4:28 PM]
It's great that you sent them to work. Everyone is jealous of my "secret admirer"

Erin [4:29 PM]
You kicked up the gossip mill here. Everyone is offering guesses for who it is. Most are suggesting an intern in cardiology. Apparently he has an obvious thing for me

Cassie [4:30 PM]
Intern? You're a hit with all the young'uns I guess

Erin [4:30 PM]
Don't sass your elder like that ;)

Erin [4:31 PM]
Anyway I have to get back to work. I just wanted to say thanks.

Cassie [4:31 PM]
You're welcome

Cassie's stomach kept doing the swooping thing. She decided she must be too hungry to wait for the cafeteria and went about making her own dinner.

She definitely didn't spend the entire time she was cooking thinking about how Erin had never called her babe before.

Avoiding the cafeteria was probably a good decision. No one wanted to be in their school cafeteria on a Friday night, especially not when it was Valentine's Day. It seemed pathetic. Sitting in her dorm alone seemed pretty pathetic, too, so she decided to tag along on Parker's stupid date after all.

Cassie [6:07 PM]
Okay fine I'll come. Where are you watching movies?

Ten minutes went by without Parker texting back, and the only reason Cassie didn't send another text telling her to stop making moon eyes at Sam and pay attention to her phone was that then Parker would not text back out of spite. Cassie considered venturing from dorm to dorm—but there were too many possible lounges they could be in, plus the sun had already set. Cassie had no interest in wandering around in the dark cold. Eventually she texted Acacia instead.

Cassie [6:42 PM]
I know you're probably out with Donovan, but do you know where Parker's having her movie night? I'm boooored

She played around on her computer for a while, waiting for someone to text her back. She didn't have Sam's number, and she was maybe too intimidated by Gwen, whose number she still had from when she was Cassie's RA, to text her.

Cassie [7:37 PM]
Yo. Parker. Where are you?

She felt a little sorry for herself, to be honest. She'd never liked Valentine's Day—if you're being romantic only for the sake of a holiday, you're not being romantic—but it was her first Valentine's Day alone in years. It was weird, especially knowing Parker was probably snuggled up with Sam watching movies, and Acacia was likely through dinner and on to "celebrating" with Donovan. Cassie was lonely, was all.

She found some sappy stupid romantic movie starting on TV;

it wasn't actually on the Hallmark Channel, but it looked like it should've been. She tried to watch it to distract herself, but it didn't work particularly well.

She was bored and lonely and Erin was off work by now, she was pretty sure. Cassie could text her. The flowers had gone over well, so texting was probably not a terrible idea. She clicked to the messages app on her computer so she didn't have to switch back and forth between her laptop and phone.

Cassie [8:04 PM]
How was the rest of your shift?

Erin [8:05 PM]
Good. Got off early enough to miss the inevitable patients who tried some new sexual position for Valentine's Day and failed

Cassie [8:05 PM]
Lol is that actually a thing that happens?

Erin [8:06 PM]
Absolutely

Cassie was trying to craft her next message when Erin FaceTimed her. She stared at her computer for a second, then muted the TV, sitting up straight so she didn't look hideous, and answered.

"Hey."

Erin smiled at her through the screen. Cassie's heart absolutely did not start beating faster.

"Hey," Erin said. "I wanted to thank you again for the flowers, and I realized I could just show them to you. They're really sprucing up the kitchen, don't you think?"

She reversed the camera to show the bouquet on the kitchen island. They were prettier than the picture online had been.

"They look great," Cassie said. Erin turned the camera back to herself, and Cassie added, "You look great."

Erin laughed, and even through Cassie's tinny computer speakers, it was a wonderful sound.

"I don't mean to keep you from anything tonight," Erin said.

"Please. My plans for the night are watching this terrible movie on TV, and I am more than happy to be distracted from that." Erin chuckled and Cassie bit her lip instead of beaming. "What are you up to?"

"Cooking dinner for one," Erin said.

They chatted. Just chatted, like it was completely normal to be FaceTiming each other. Erin propped her phone up on the counter, and Cassie watched while she flitted in and out of the frame, chopping vegetables and cooking at the stove and pouring herself a glass of wine. Cassie told her how classes were going, and Erin talked about her day at work—a few mentions of patients, but mostly stories of reactions to the flowers.

"Everyone's convinced it's Ian from cardiology," Erin said.

"I'm going to come up there and give this Ian a piece of my mind."

"Oh, you'd terrify him." Erin laughed. She served herself a plate and moved to the living room. "He's very quiet and looks like he's about twelve. Why anyone believes he's brave enough to anonymously send me flowers is beyond me."

"Eh, it didn't take that much guts," Cassie said.

Erin went quiet, and then, "What was your goal? In sending them to me, I mean."

Her voice was serious, but she was sitting on her couch, halfway out of the frame; Cassie couldn't read her face.

"My goal?" Cassie said. She shrugged, decided honesty was the best policy. "I wanted to make you smile."

Erin leaned toward her camera, and she was definitely smiling. "It worked."

Cassie blushed a little and looked away.

"Okay," Erin said, reaching for something Cassie couldn't see.

It turned out to be the TV remote. "What terrible movie are we watching?"

"I don't even know what it's called," Cassie laughed. She was thankful for the change of subject. "It's on Oxygen."

"Oh, I love it already," Erin said. "What's been happening so far?"

"I've had it on mute, Erin," Cassie said. "I don't know. It seems like this blond lady wants to bang that guy but she doesn't know it yet."

"Thrilling!"

Cassie laughed and unmuted the TV.

They watched the movie together, hundreds of miles apart. Erin pretended she was riveted, offered ridiculous theories about what would happen next. Cassie spent more time watching Erin's face on her computer than the movie on the television.

It was comfortable, and it shouldn't have been. Spending the entire evening FaceTiming with her friend's mom should've been weird, right? But it was nice, especially since everyone else, including said friend, seemed to have abandoned her.

She didn't realize she was tired until she heard Erin saying her name.

Cassie blinked awake.

Erin was smiling gently at her. "Maybe you should go to bed."

"Oh, no, I'm good," Cassie said, sitting up. She couldn't believe she fucking fell asleep. "I gotta see how this thing ends, anyway."

"Cassie," Erin said, still smiling. "The movie's over."

"What?"

"You've been asleep for about half an hour."

"What?" Cassie said. "You just let me sleep?"

"You looked peaceful," Erin said with a shrug. "And your snoring was quiet so it didn't interrupt my movie watching."

"I do *not* snore."

Erin laughed. "Whether you do or not," she said, "I think you'll be a lot more comfortable if you sleep in your bed instead of on the couch."

Cassie rubbed the sleep and blush from her face. "You're probably right," she said. "Thanks."

"Thank you," Erin said, "again. For the flowers."

Cassie's blush came right back. She was tired and couldn't control her reactions, apparently.

"I'm glad you liked them," she said. "I gotta get ready for bed."

"Me too."

"Good night."

"Good night, Cassie."

Her computer froze on Erin's soft smile for a moment before the call fully disconnected. Cassie kind of wanted to stab herself. Erin's smile was beautiful and Cassie wanted to kiss the shit out of her.

She tossed her laptop and phone onto her bed and went to brush her teeth. She kept the water as cold as she could stand to wash her face.

In bed, she stared at the ceiling. She felt weird, all over, and didn't know why. She felt like she got caught doing something she shouldn't, which was stupid, because she neither got caught nor was doing anything that hurt anyone. She felt antsy.

Cassie [11:03 PM]
I also kind of sent the flowers to woo you

Erin [11:04 PM]
To woo me? Cassie, we've already slept together

Cassie [11:05 PM]
Yeah but . . . I know we had rules but I want to do it again. So staying on your good side seems like a good idea

Erin [11:05 PM]
You're doing a good job then

Erin [11:06 PM]
What would you have done if we were in the same city?

Cassie went for broke.

Cassie [11:06 PM]
Hand delivered them and fucked you in an on call room

Cassie [11:07 PM]
Or is that something that only happens in greys anatomy?

Cassie's heart beat probably two hundred times before Erin responded.

Erin [11:08 PM]
It is . . . not something that only happens in Grey's Anatomy.

Cassie [11:09 PM]
No? Has cardiology intern Ian been giving you the eye and nodding toward the on call room?

Erin [11:09 PM]
Cardiology intern Ian can keep his hands to himself

Erin [11:10 PM]
You on the other hand . . .

Cassie grinned. She wouldn't have pegged Erin for a sexter, but the thought was thrilling. She noticed the time, closed her eyes, and made a wish that this ended well. Resting one hand on her stomach, over the tank top, she texted back with the other.

Cassie [11:11 PM]
Would we have to be quick? So no one catches on?

Erin [11:12 PM]
And so I don't get called away for a patient

Cassie [11:12 PM]
I'd push you against the door as soon as you had it locked

Erin [11:13 PM]
God, Cassie, are we really doing this?

Cassie [11:14 PM]
Do you not want to?

Erin [11:15 PM]
I do. I've just never done this before

Cassie [11:15 PM]
You mean had sex in the on call room? ;)

Erin [11:16 PM]
That too

Cassie [11:16 PM]
Wait, seriously?

Erin [11:17 PM]
Seriously

Cassie [11:17 PM]
In that case, I would /definitely/ have you against the door as soon as you locked it

MISTAKES WERE MADE | 193

Cassie [11:18 PM]
I wouldn't want to stop kissing you, but if we have to be quick . . .

Erin [11:19 PM]
Like you could keep your hands off my chest, or your mouth if you had the chance

Okay, Cassie's hand definitely slid into her pajama bottoms. She didn't touch herself, yet. Just got ready.

Cassie [11:20 PM]
It's not my fault you've got great tits

Cassie [11:20 PM]
I'd get my mouth on them for sure

Cassie [11:20 PM]
Probably wouldn't even have moved away from the door before I had your shirt and bra off

Erin [11:21 PM]
I've been thinking of this all day, Cassie. Feels so good

Cassie wasn't sure if Erin meant she'd be thinking about this in the scenario or if she literally meant all of today. Maybe ever since she got those flowers. Maybe she'd FaceTimed Cassie thinking about this, imagining this might come of it.

Cassie ran a finger along her slit and it came back wet.

Cassie [11:23 PM]
Erin I gotta get you into a bed

Erin [11:24 PM]
The bed in there's a twin, you're gonna have to be on top of me

Cassie [11:24 PM]
That's not a problem

Cassie [11:25 PM]
I want your pants off, too

Erin [11:25 PM]
That's not fair. You have too many clothes on

Cassie pushed her pants down over her hips, kicked them off.

Cassie [11:26 PM]
There. My pants are gone

Erin [11:26 PM]
Shirt too, Cassie, I want to see you

Cassie [11:26 PM]
Fuck

She pulled her shirt over her head.

Cassie [11:27 PM]
Okay. Shirt's gone too

She hoped Erin knew she meant it. She hoped Erin knew she had Cassie naked and touching herself. She hoped Erin was doing the same thing.

Cassie [11:27 PM]
Are you wet for me?

Erin [11:28 PM]
Touch me and find out

Cassie [11:28 PM]
I mean now Erin. Are you wet for me right now?

Erin [11:29 PM]
Yes Cassie. Fuck

Cassie's head spun. Her fingers swam around her clit, her flesh hot and slick. The thought of Erin doing the same—she didn't want to bother with the on call room; thinking about Erin touching herself was enough.

Cassie [11:31 PM]
I wish I could feel for myself Erin

Cassie [11:31 PM]
I want to touch you

Cassie [11:32 PM]
I want to taste you

Cassie [11:33 PM]
Could I go down on you there? Or would you need my hand over your mouth to keep you quiet?

Erin [11:34 PM]
I want your fingers inside me

Jesus fuck. Cassie slid two fingers into herself, wished they were Erin's. She rolled her hips.

Erin [11:37 PM]
Cassie please

Cassie [11:37 PM]
Yes Erin God. I want to touch you. I want to fuck you

Erin [11:38 PM]
I'm close

Shit. Cassie pulled her fingers out so she could focus. She brushed them against her clit as she texted.

Cassie [11:38 PM]
I want to hear you come

Erin [11:38 PM]
I told you we had to be quiet

Cassie [11:39 PM]
I'm serious Erin. Call me. Right now.

Erin [11:39 PM]
Cassie

Fuck it.

Cassie called her.

Erin picked up with no more than her breathing, hard and fast.

"Erin," Cassie said.

Erin let out a huff of breath, like she couldn't even make words.

"Erin, fuck, you're so hot." Cassie's fingers moved fast over her clit. "I wish I was there. God, I wish I was inside you. Your cunt feels so good."

Erin whined.

"Erin, please," Cassie said, wishing she had FaceTimed her instead, wishing she could watch this. "Please, baby, come for me, let me hear you."

Erin did.

She'd never been particularly loud, when they'd fucked before, and she wasn't now. Her breath stuttered and Cassie must've been on speaker, she could hear Erin's legs thrashing in her sheets.

Erin choked out, "Oh my God," and she was still coming, this long quiet moan.

Cassie couldn't stop herself; she closed her eyes and said Erin's name and she was coming, too, pleasure melting into her bones.

They caught their breath together over the phone. Cassie's whole body felt soft.

"Goddamn," she said. "You're the best Valentine I've ever had."

Erin laughed at her. "You're not so bad yourself."

"I wish I could have been there for real," Cassie said, stretching. "When we do this again, we're doing it with video—I want to see your face. Show you how wet you make me."

"Christ, Cassie," Erin chuckled. "Are you trying to get me worked up again?"

"See, that's another reason," Cassie said. "If we were together, I could easily make you come more than once. We didn't have enough time for that much over break. I'd like to see how many orgasms I could give you in twenty-four hours."

"*Cassie.*"

Cassie grinned into her pillow. "Fine," she dragged out the word. "I'll let you go to sleep."

"Good night, babe," Erin said. "Thanks again for the flowers."

Cassie *mm-hmm*ed and ended the call. She fell asleep with a smile on her face.

Sixteen

ERIN

Erin didn't wake up until sunlight slipped through the slats of her blinds and fell across her face. She yawned, stretching her whole body, toes reaching for the foot of the bed. She couldn't remember the last time she'd slept so late. A pleasant ache settled between her legs. She yanked the top sheet up over her head to hide her blush from the empty room.

She felt . . . good.

So good. That was the best Valentine's Day she'd had in years. Flowers and an orgasm, from someone who gave them to her because they *wanted* to, not because they had to. That part felt better than it should. Cassie had wanted to make her smile.

They hadn't texted since Erin's birthday, and not since the day Cassie had left New Hampshire before then. But Cassie had been thinking about her. It felt so good to be wanted.

The feeling waned throughout the day. Or, more accurately, it got overshadowed by another feeling.

Because Parker didn't call.

It shouldn't be a big deal—it *wasn't* a big deal, really, except for how she'd called every Sunday since they'd dropped her off at school.

It was fine.

There was no reason Parker would know she and Cassie had sexted on Friday. It was fine that her number was in Cassie's phone; Erin gave it to her over winter break. Cassie was smart enough to delete the messages. It was fine.

Parker had probably lost track of time in the studio. Or maybe she was with Sam—Erin hadn't gotten any juicy details about the girl, but Parker talked about her every call. *Sam's doing this amazing arrangement of "Savage" by Megan Thee Stallion for her a cappella group* or *Sam's going to double major in international affairs and political science. She's, like, so smart.*

Erin was halfway through emptying the dishwasher before realizing it was dirty.

It was just—what if Parker *did* know? What if she knew, and now she was never going to speak to Erin again?

Erin couldn't even blame her. She had no excuses. She was being selfish and irresponsible and inconsiderate. And she'd do it again.

Erin [9:14 PM]
Hope you had a good weekend!

She texted Parker, then immediately worried it was going to come off passive-aggressive. Parker probably didn't even realize she hasn't called. She was allowed to have her own life. She was growing up. She didn't need to call her mom every week.

God, that felt worse than the possibility of her never talking to Erin again.

Erin had reloaded the dishwasher by this point. She checked her phone three times in a two-minute span, then finally opened another message.

Erin [9:34 PM]
Did you have a good weekend?

Cassie [9:35 PM]
Pretty good. But it was all downhill from Friday night tbh

Erin pressed the heel of her hand into her mouth, like she had to hide her smile even though there was no one around to see it.

Cassie [9:35 PM]
What about you?

Erin [9:36 PM]
Pretty much the same

Cassie asked about Erin's work week and talked about her classes. It should've been weird, not easy. Just like FaceTiming on Friday should've been weird. *Sexting* should've been weird. But Cassie was easy to talk to—she seemed to always be listening, like she cared what Erin had to say. That probably shouldn't have been a high bar to pass, but somehow it was.

By the time Erin fell asleep, she'd forgotten that Parker didn't call.

But then Parker didn't call all week. It was probably nothing. The semester was in full swing now; Parker was just busy with schoolwork. Erin tried to not freak out, tried to give her space.

She spent the week texting with Cassie. Not constantly, but steadily. Cassie treated it like Snapchat, basically—which Erin had learned how to use only to monitor Parker's usage in middle school—she sent random pictures: of her notes as she studied, highlighted in color-coordinated ink; of herself pretending to sleep after her morning class, head down on the desk; of her biceps when she was at the gym. Half her face was visible in that last one, and her smirk was unmistakable. Erin had never particularly liked taking selfies—she still didn't, really, but she liked sending them to Cassie. Cassie sent back emojis: fire or heart eyes or once the sweating one.

Sometimes Erin wanted to ask Cassie if Parker had been acting strange, but there were unspoken rules. *Don't talk about Parker* was one of them. Not that Cassie and Erin were particularly good at following rules when it came to each other.

By her Thursday therapy session, Erin was so ready to talk she didn't even stumble over early conversation like usual.

"Parker didn't call on Sunday."

"Oh?" Carolyn said.

"It's not a big deal," Erin said. "I'm sure she's busy. And we had spoken on Thursday, so it still hasn't been a full week since we last talked. It just felt . . ." She sighed. She couldn't tell Carolyn how it felt. "Bad," she finished feebly.

"Why did it feel bad?"

"You know why," Erin said. "Because what if she's mad at me? What if she stops speaking to me again? What if this is the start of something worse?"

"Why would she be mad at you?"

If Erin were a better actor, she would respond immediately, instead of letting the question hang while she swallowed the real reason.

"I don't know," she said eventually. "I'm trying to be better at communicating with her."

"Have you had a miscommunication recently?"

"I don't think so. I don't know. Maybe this counts as a miscommunication. Because probably she was just busy and forgot and yet here I am talking to you about it."

Carolyn gave her an indulgent smile. "You're allowed to talk about whatever you want. Talking to me about something doesn't mean it's bad."

"Right. Of course not."

What was bad was the thing she *wasn't* talking to her about.

Like she was reading Erin's mind, Carolyn asked, "Is there something else bothering you?"

"No. What do you mean?"

"You seem . . ." She did that pause where Erin was never sure if she was searching for the right word or letting the silence stretch so Erin would rush to fill it. "Jumpy."

"I . . ." How did she explain this?

She watched the second hand tick a full revolution on the wall clock. She reached for a couch pillow and clutched it to her stomach. Then she started talking, eyes on the carpet in front of her so she didn't have to look at Carolyn.

She'd thought about telling Carolyn before. Part of it, anyway. She thought she could talk about sleeping with someone new without talking about Cassie specifically. But what was there to talk about besides Cassie? It didn't matter that Erin had slept with someone; it mattered that she'd slept with Cassie. That she liked her enough to do it again and again. She hadn't wanted to deal with that, so she'd said nothing.

Now, she told Carolyn only part of the story, at first. Paused after the reveal: the woman she'd had the one-night stand with was her daughter's friend.

"And then what happened?"

"And then I let her feel me up in the bathroom of Parker's a cappella concert."

That got Carolyn's eyebrows to raise, just briefly, as she took in the information.

"How did that feel?"

Erin smirked, and Carolyn's cheeks went pink.

"I mean—not how did *it* feel, but how did *you* feel about it happening?"

"I know what you meant," Erin said. "I . . . good. To both questions."

"You felt good?" Carolyn asked.

There it was: surprise at Erin's enjoyment of what was obviously a bad decision. She shouldn't have—she knew that. She'd been waiting for Carolyn to agree, but it added weight to her shoulders anyway. She scratched at her neck.

"I don't mean to imply that you shouldn't," Carolyn said. "But you don't always *let* yourself feel good."

"I sure picked a hell of a time to let myself, huh?" Erin gave a humorless laugh. "But I figured no one was going to know. It was just a dumb, fun thing I did for the weekend, and that was it. I hadn't planned on Cassie visiting for winter break."

"What happened then?" Carolyn asked.

She couldn't look at Carolyn's face. Couldn't chance seeing judgment there, even while she hadn't seen any in the entire four years she'd been in therapy. The thing was—she'd never said anything like this before. She talked around it, put it more kindly, but the gist was:

I knowingly and repeatedly slept with my daughter's friend.

Erin laid it all out. The rules they made, then broke. The sexting. All of it.

When she'd finally run out of words, Erin's fingers traced the decorative edge of the pillow she was holding. She glanced at Carolyn's face. There was no judgment there.

"Okay."

Erin practically guffawed. "Okay? That's all? Okay?"

Carolyn gave her a look. "Do you honestly think two consenting adults sleeping together is the most shocking thing I've heard as a therapist?"

Okay, well, when she put it that way it didn't sound quite so absurd.

"This is a little more complicated than just two consenting adults sleeping together!" Erin's voice wasn't quite *shrill*, but it was higher than she'd like.

"It always is," Carolyn said. Then, "How did you expect me to react?"

Erin knew her answer wasn't what she was supposed to say, so she didn't say anything. When it became clear she wasn't going to respond, Carolyn went on.

"My guess? You expected judgment. You assumed judgment. There are people in your life who conditioned you to constant judgment."

Carolyn had treated Erin with kid gloves when she first started therapy. Erin had needed it—a chronic people pleaser trying to figure out how to put herself first. Eventually, once Erin got her feet under her, Carolyn figured out when she could push, when Erin *needed* her to push. She wasn't pushing, here, but Erin was pretty sure she should.

"I want your honest opinion. Not your professional, sugar-coated, better-not-make-my-patient-have-a-breakdown opinion."

"I'm not particularly worried about you having a breakdown."

That made one of them. Maybe everything with Cassie *was* her breakdown. Or her midlife crisis or something.

"You know what I mean," Erin said. "Tell me what you really think about this."

"My honest opinion," Carolyn said, steepling her fingers in her lap, "is that I'm glad you finally told me. You've been circumspect in the New Year. I've been wondering if I should confront you about it. This makes it a lot easier."

Erin ducked her head. If she'd been that obvious with Carolyn, what was she like with Parker?

"I don't want to ask you to tell me things you don't want to," Carolyn said. "But I can't help you with the things you don't share in our sessions."

"I didn't think I needed help with it. I thought it was over."

Carolyn leveled her with a stare. "While you thought it was over, how did the fact that anything happened at all make you feel?"

Erin focused on the fringe of the pillow in her lap. "I . . . guilty. But also . . . proud of myself? I don't know. That sounds ridiculous. It's just—I *know* I've spent too long caring what other people think. I know that. It's something I'm working on. It's something I've been working on since I started seeing you. So yeah, I felt guilty because I know this never should have happened. But it felt good, too. To have done something . . . fun? Stupid? Both. Obviously this is something I did for me—anyone else would judge me for it. I judge me for it. But it feels like progress. I wasn't exactly picking up women in bars a year ago." She grimaced. "Is it weird to measure progress by propensity for a one-night stand?"

Carolyn chuckled at her. "No, I know what you mean. It doesn't seem like your behavior has been driven by anything other than what you want, here."

Phrasing it that way pointed out the selfishness, even though Erin knew that wasn't how Carolyn meant it.

"When is the last time you did something for no other reason than because you wanted to?"

"Well, there's the clinic."

"Respectfully, no." Carolyn shook her head. "The clinic is wonderful, and I know how long you've wanted it. I'm glad you're finally working toward it. But it also objectively does good. There's a lot more happening there than just what you want."

Erin conceded the point. Most of her indulgences were food related, but even then, there were times she made dinner instead of ordering takeout because she knew it was what she *should* do. When was the last time she said "fuck should" before meeting Cassie?

Instead of thinking too hard about it, she changed the subject. "Okay, but what if Parker knows?"

"Why would she?"

"Because she didn't call Sunday."

Carolyn tutted at her. "That's not the answer to why she would know. That's the answer to what are you using to support the conclusion you already jumped to."

So she'd stopped with the kid gloves then.

"Cassie could've told her."

"Why would Cassie do that?"

She'd told Acacia. Granted, that was a *little* different from telling *Parker,* but it worried Erin anyway. Erin hadn't told anyone. Though she felt better now that Carolyn knew. Like she could breathe a little easier.

"Maybe Acacia did," Erin said. "Or maybe she saw the picture I sent Cassie on Valentine's Day."

"Or maybe you're coming up with increasingly unlikely worst-case scenarios when you could just call Parker and see what's up."

Okay, fair. Not that Erin would ever actually call Parker to "see what's up." She wasn't risking hearing an answer she didn't want.

"What do you think would happen if Parker found out?"

Erin spent the rest of therapy catastrophizing. She couldn't decide what would be worse: Parker angry and hurt enough to yell and cry or Parker just cutting off contact. She'd never done well when Parker cried. Adam had to take her to get her shots when she was little, because Erin would have a worse time of it than Parker did.

Even spending a half hour going through worst-case scenarios, leaving therapy, Erin felt . . . at ease. Untroubled. Not carefree, exactly, but like things would turn out okay. Tomorrow maybe everything would be bad again, but today, she'd said it. Someone other than her and Cassie knew it had happened. And the world hadn't come to an end.

That was the thought she kept in mind as she made plans with Rachel to get coffee in the morning. Maybe Erin had expected judgment from Carolyn, and she certainly would from anyone else, but not from Rachel. Never from Rachel.

Even knowing that, Erin had to build up her courage the next morning. She'd already finished the muffin she'd split with Rachel and was most of the way through her cappuccino before finally asking:

"What would you say if I said I was sleeping with someone?"

Rachel let out a hoot that got the entire coffee shop's attention on them. Erin gave her a flat stare, unimpressed.

Rachel shrugged. "You asked."

"I'm serious."

"So am I. You deserve orgasms from someone other than yourself."

Thankfully other customers seemed to have stopped paying attention to them.

"Obviously I want to know everything. Who are they? Where did you meet? When did you start sleeping together? Is the sex good? When can I meet them?"

Erin wasn't going to answer the majority of those. She wanted Rachel to know—maybe. She was pretty sure she wanted Rachel to know, but only about the vague shape of what was happening in her life. She couldn't tell her details; it didn't matter that she was her best friend. Erin was grateful Rachel hadn't been there on Christmas Eve—as soon as she saw Erin and Cassie interact, she was going to know. It's what she did.

"The sex," Erin paused for effect, "is outstanding."

Rachel giggled gleefully. She singsonged, "Tell me more, tell me more."

"This woman is just—"

"A woman! See, I knew getting away from men for a while was going to help! What's she like?"

Erin sighed—she didn't even mean to, but she let out this dreamy sigh at even thinking about Cassie. She shook her head like that would make the feeling go away.

"She's ridiculous," she said. "She makes me do ridiculous things."

"Like what?"

"Like *sext*."

Rachel pressed her lips together hard enough they went white. She was holding back her laughter, which Erin appreciated.

"Honey. Sexting is not ridiculous. You were just in a passionless marriage for too long."

Erin didn't disagree, but still—"She called, at the end of it." Erin glanced around, but the tables nearest to them were empty. "To hear me."

"Oh shit, you mean sexting like legitimately masturbating while texting?"

"What else would sexting be?"

"I sext while I'm grocery shopping."

"What?"

Rachel shrugged. "Sometimes someone wants to sext but I'm busy. It's not like I'm going to rush home and take off my clothes."

That sounded absurd, but Rachel knew a lot more about dating than Erin did, so she'd have to trust her.

"Well," Erin said. "I was not grocery shopping."

"I'm proud of you."

Erin rolled her eyes, even though she knew Rachel was being serious.

"So, phone sex—does that mean she lives out of town? Where have you even been lately? How did you meet her?"

"Okay, no. We're not doing the whole interrogation thing. I just—"

"It's not an *interrogation* to want to know about the person your best friend is seeing."

"I'm not *seeing* her. We're just . . ." Erin trailed off.

"Just fucking?"

Erin wasn't sure what, exactly, they were doing. It wasn't like they were actively sleeping together—the over seven hundred miles between New Hampshire and Virginia kind of put a damper on that. But she couldn't explain that to Rachel.

"Friends with benefits," she said instead.

"Those benefits being orgasms."

"I'm ready to be done talking about this," Erin said.

"Good, then I can tell you about *my* latest hookup."

Rachel launched into a play-by-play of her date last weekend, but for once, Erin didn't particularly mind getting too many details. She'd told two people, now. And the world still hadn't ended.

Then again, Parker still hadn't called.

Seventeen

CASSIE

That week, Cassie talked with Erin more than her other friends. They flirted, but never got into full-on sexting again. Cassie was a little disappointed, honestly. She saved the old messages on her computer in a hidden folder named *biophysics*. She would've named it *spank bank* if she didn't want to be 100 percent sure no one found it.

That she talked to Erin more often than her friends said more about her friends' schedules than how much she and Erin were texting. Parker skipped Monday morning breakfast, which she, Acacia, and Cassie had been eating together since the middle of last semester. Cassie didn't even see her until Wednesday, when Parker arrived at the cafeteria for lunch right as Cassie was leaving.

"Babe!" Cassie beamed. She threw her arms around Parker's neck. "It's been forever."

"Yeah," Parker said. She hugged back gently. "I've been busy."

"Me too," Cassie said. "Projects starting to pile up and midterms soon, you know? When are you doing dinner tonight? I miss you."

"I'm not doing dinner, actually," Parker said. "That's why I'm eating lunch so late. I've got stuff tonight."

"Boo," Cassie said. "Well, when are you free? I want to hang out and bother you about your new lady."

Parker rolled her eyes. "As lovely as that sounds, Cassie, I don't know. I'll text you."

She started to head into the cafeteria.

"I miss my best friend!" Cassie called after her.

"Acacia's your best friend," Parker said over her shoulder.

But Acacia was pretty busy, too, only having time for the occasional meal and never a hangout. It took till Friday night, when she and Cassie went to a party together, for them to get actual quality time. Even then, Acacia snuck away with Donovan eventually, and Cassie was not about to track them down.

In the beginning, Seth had always been Cassie's closest friend at school. They'd hit it off during orientation week and grew their friend group together. Cassie had never been more embarrassed than in the dining hall the day after she'd broken up with him. She'd approached her usual table only to have none of their friends acknowledge her, much less move to make room. The ease with which her friends chose a cheating Seth over her had taken her aback. He'd always been the more charming one, but Cassie hadn't realized she was so forgettable.

It was weird making new friends as a senior. Mostly she relied on Acacia and Parker making friends and including her by default. This group would probably abandon her at the drop of a hat, too, but Cassie didn't mind. She was getting out of here soon, and she'd have Acacia beside her no matter what. Who cared about anyone else?

Well, okay, she did, she guessed, because it *was* fun to have dinner with the whole group Sunday night. Sam and Gwen even joined, flanking Parker, who sat on the other side of the table from Cassie. Both of the girls gave Cassie unimpressed looks, then paid more attention to Parker. The only reason Cassie didn't roll her eyes was she didn't want to piss off Parker the only time they'd hung out in a week.

She figured she could always give her trouble at Monday morning breakfast instead. Except the next morning:

"No Parker?"

Acacia shrugged. "She was working late on something. Wanted to sleep in."

It was one thing to see Parker sparingly for a week. But this was the second Monday breakfast she'd missed in a row. None of them had missed two weeks in a row since they'd started.

"How does she have *another* project due already?" Cassie asked while they waited in the food line.

"Might be the same one?" Acacia answered distractedly. She craned her head to see past the four people in front of them. "Nice! They have breakfast quesadillas."

It couldn't have been the same one—Parker had missed last week because she was desperately trying to finish so she could turn it in on time. Supposedly, anyway. It wasn't that Cassie thought Parker was lying, it just didn't feel right. Cassie had barely seen her since she'd started dating Sam. Dinner last night was the only meal they'd shared, and even then, Sam was there, with her blank stare and perpetual frown for Cassie. Her face lit up like a fucking Christmas tree when she looked at Parker, but Cassie was barely worth a glance.

Whatever. So what if Parker was lying about having a project because she wanted to sleep in with her new girlfriend who couldn't give two fucks about Cassie?

The breakfast quesadillas Acacia and Cassie loaded onto their plates were the perfect level of toasted, the tortillas evenly browned. This early on a Monday the dining hall was mostly empty. Everyone seemed to be shuffling around, unable to pick up their feet before coffee. Acacia, who'd already been on her morning run, marched across the cafeteria to a table in the corner by a window. She sat down a good fifteen seconds before Cassie made it to the table. Just because her best friend was a morning freak didn't mean she had to be.

"Hey, know what I was thinking about on my run?" Acacia said. She didn't pause for Cassie to respond. "You know how at New Year's we FaceTimed, and I accidentally talked about how you wanted to kiss Parker's mom, not knowing she was there? I still feel so bad about that, like, it had to be so messy. And I realized I never even asked how you got out of the situation. Like what could you have possibly said after y'all hung up?"

Cassie blinked at her. Acacia wasn't even paying attention to her, already digging into her quesadilla, talking about this like it was no big deal.

"You were thinking about Erin on your run?"

"Yeah, I don't know how I got there—" She looked at the ceiling as she chewed. "It was kind of a chilly morning so I was thinking about Christmas in Chicago, and how I wore this miniskirt to the New Year's party Emerson took me to, and I refused to wear tights because my legs looked great, but it was fucking freezing, and obviously since I thought of Emerson I thought about how y'all made out, and then—"

"Okay no, yeah, I don't need to know your running thoughts. I would rather not acknowledge you run at all because I'm fairly certain willingly getting out of bed when it's dark out so you can exercise means you're the devil."

"Okay, so whatever. Yeah, I was thinking about Parker's mom on my run. What happened with that?"

Cassie focused on dunking her quesadilla into the pile of ketchup on her plate so she didn't have to look at Acacia.

"I truly cannot believe you would call me the devil when you're dipping your breakfast quesadilla in ketchup, by the way."

"People eat ketchup on eggs. This is normal."

"More people like running than like ketchup on eggs. Pretty sure I'm the normal one."

Cassie took a bite. Dipped it in ketchup again.

"I didn't, uh, really get out of the thing at New Year's," she said.

"What do you mean?"

"I mean she was pretty mad about it and didn't really let me apologize. So we never really talked about it."

"Was it just hella awkward the rest of your visit?"

"I mean. No. Like she still wanted a good morning kiss the next day."

Acacia gave a quick shake of her head like that would change Cassie's words. "Wait, what?"

Cassie lifted her eyes to Acacia's, her face still tilted toward her breakfast. "Me wanting to kiss her didn't exactly surprise her 'cause we, uh, were kind of already hooking up by then."

Acacia closed her eyes and took a deep breath. She ran her hands back and forth over her shaved head. Cassie chewed on her bottom lip and waited for Acacia to blow up. She'd been mad about this when Cassie had only slept with Erin once. This was bound to be worse.

But then Acacia opened her eyes, gave Cassie a humorless smile, and gently said, "Tell me what happened."

Cassie had expected something more along the lines of *Are you fucking kidding me?*

"Uh."

What happened? Nothing, really. They'd just gotten along. Things snowballed from there.

Cassie told Acacia a bit more than that, though. Swirling the juice around in her cup, she told her about Parker's dad being all smarmy and patriarchal—"What a bag of dicks," was Acacia's take—about Erin stepping in, about Erin kissing Cassie later that night. She tried not to smirk when she got to the shower sex.

"I don't need details." Acacia grimaced.

"But they're such good details," Cassie said. Okay, fine, she didn't try *that* hard not to smirk.

"So what's happening now?"

"What do you mean?"

"Between you and Erin."

"Nothing, obviously. We live like a thousand miles apart."

"So after your airport make out you just never talked again?"

"Well." Cassie didn't want to *lie* to her. "I mean, I sent her flowers for Valentine's Day."

Acacia's eyebrows went up.

"We've kind of been texting since then."

Cassie took a bite of her breakfast quesadilla for something to do. She didn't taste it.

Acacia chewed slowly. Swallowed. "Are you going to tell Parker?"

"What?" Cassie sputtered. "No. Why would I?"

"If you're gonna date her mom, it seems like it'd probably be polite to tell her about it."

Cassie almost did a spit take of her orange juice. Her body shook with silent laughter as she managed to swallow it.

When she caught her breath, she said, "Sure, Kaysh, I'm in a long-distance relationship with Parker's mom."

Acacia shrugged like she didn't buy that at all, but she wasn't going to fight Cassie on it.

"Look, I'm not gonna be a bad friend to you and not let you talk to me about her, but I do kinda feel like that makes us both bad friends to Parker."

"I don't need to talk about her," Cassie said. "It's literally not a big deal. And speaking of bad friends—when would I even tell Parker? I haven't seen her in like a week. I know there's a honeymoon stage or whatever, but it'd be cool if she didn't drop her so-called best friends quite so easily."

"Can you really call yourself someone's best friend if you're dating her mom?" Before Cassie could protest, Acacia corrected herself. "Or sleeping with her or whatever?"

"Parker told me I could bone whoever I wanted."

"Sure, but she didn't say you could do it in secret," Acacia said. "If you were boning my mom, I'd want to know."

Cassie grimaced. "Your mom is more my mom than my own mom. Sleeping with her would basically be incest."

"And yet you made out with my brother."

"I keep thinking there will come a time when you don't bring that up and it keeps not being that time."

Acacia grinned. "There will never be a time."

"I hate you."

"You don't."

"I don't."

Acacia walked Cassie to class, even though she didn't have anything till noon. She hugged Cassie goodbye, big, the way Acacia always did and said, "You're a dumbass, but I love you."

"Love you, too, Kaysh."

Acacia wasn't finished. "I'm always going to have your back. I'm just not sure this is the best decision you've ever made."

"Maybe not." Cassie shrugged. "But it's sure not the worst."

"No, yeah, the worst was definitely jumping off the roof of your trailer after you'd made yourself wings you thought would work."

"Okay, I was gonna say dating Seth but I like yours better."

"Ugh, don't make me think of that earthworm."

Cassie cackled. As soon as she and Seth broke up, Acacia started referring to him only as the earthworm, maintaining that he had a little pinhead that made him look like one. Cassie loved it every time.

Over the week, the group text quieted down, Acacia and Cassie keeping up most of the conversation. One time, three days after they'd eaten dinner in a group and two days after Parker skipped breakfast for the second week in a row, Cassie asked, "So, Parker, am I just not gonna see you anymore?"

She sent it right before chem lab when she'd be too busy to hover over her phone, worrying if she'd get a response. When she got out of lab, there were fourteen new messages in the group chat.

They were all Acacia and Parker talking about Parker's latest art project.

Cassie's question went unanswered. She didn't ask it again.

Instead, while Acacia was sitting on the couch in Cassie's apartment, one foot propped on the coffee table as she painted her toes bright red, Cassie asked, "Is Parker pissed at me?"

"Why would she be?"

There was really no reason, except: "'Cause I'm fucking her mom?"

Acacia's head whipped around. Her eyes were wide. "Do you think she knows?"

"No." How the hell could she know? Acacia obviously wouldn't tell, and it wasn't like Erin would, either. "But I don't know what else I did."

Acacia went back to painting her nails. "Why do you even think she's mad at you?"

"We never hang out anymore."

Kaysh shrugged. "She's got a lot of projects going on, and so do you. Things will settle down eventually."

Cassie tried to believe her.

But Parker had just . . . disappeared off the face of the earth. Cassie would've been pissed if she weren't determined not to let it bother her. If anything, she was embarrassed. She'd never used the term *best friend* lightly, and to have used it on Parker only to be dropped as soon as Parker got a girlfriend didn't feel great. In fact, the last time she'd used it on Parker, the other girl had joked that Acacia was Cassie's best friend. Maybe she'd been trying to tell her something.

Any sense of regret Cassie had been feeling about the whole fucking her friend's mom thing faded to the background. Parker was basically not even her friend right now. It'd been two weeks since Parker and Sam officially got together, and Cassie could count the number of times she'd hung out with Parker on one hand—hell, on one finger. And even that had been in a group.

Cassie should've known better. She barely knew Parker. Parker was just a freshman who roomed with Cassie's best friend. Yeah, she and Cassie had gotten along for a while there, but apparently that was it.

But whatever. Cassie didn't need Parker. She'd had to fend for herself for pretty much as long as she could remember.

It wasn't like she was short on ways to spend her time. She had homework and classes, Acacia and work in the shop.

She had Erin.

Not that they were *dating*, or anything. That would be ridiculous.

Seth had been Cassie's first relationship. Not her first anything else, but her first actual relationship. Cassie knew from experience that sleeping with someone did not mean you were dating. People could get what they needed from each other without it being anything other than the physical. Admittedly, it *was* more than that with Erin—Cassie actually liked her, which was a lot more than she could say for most of the people she'd fooled around with.

But liking someone as a person didn't mean you were dating them any more than sleeping with them did. Nor did texting every day. They weren't texting each other *good morning* and *good night* or anything, but it wasn't unusual for Erin to be the first and last person Cassie talked to each day. Acacia could only take so much engineering talk, but Erin seemed to have endless interest. They spent an entire day texting about grad school—Cassie admitted to applying at MIT, plus Georgia and Virginia Tech, even though she was dead set on Caltech. She was confident—cocky, maybe—but not dumb enough not to have a backup.

Erin [11:23 AM]
Have you decided what kind of astronaut you want to be yet? 😊

Cassie liked that Erin included the emoji, like it wouldn't have been obvious she was joking otherwise. It was how she always teased:

gently. It was too damn sweet, and made Cassie feel way too rude for her most of the time.

Cassie went through the pros and cons of aeronautical versus astronautical specialties. Every time she thought she'd figured out which was right for her, she'd come up with another pro for the other one.

Cassie [11:34 AM]
I wanna make things that go fast. That's all I know for sure

Erin [11:35 AM]
You'll figure it out and kick ass in whatever you decide

Cassie grinned. She appreciated people who didn't underestimate her.

Cassie [11:35 AM]
What about you?

Erin lit up when she talked about the free clinic that was opening that fall. They'd just gotten the final approvals, but Erin couldn't shake the feeling that this dream was gonna get pulled away from her at the last minute.

Not all their conversation topics were so heavy though. Sometimes Erin would just complain about patients, or Cassie about classes. Cassie liked to send selfies from the gym, pre-workout, so she was in her sports bra and tight pants but wasn't sweaty yet. Selfies from the shop, though, came after she'd finished working but before she cleaned up—Erin liked her a little dirty. They talked about vacations they wanted to take—Cassie had never left the eastern time zone, so she wasn't particularly picky. Erin wanted to go anywhere warm.

Erin [4:51 PM]

I went snorkeling in the Bahamas once. It was amazing, but I'd love to go scuba diving

Cassie [4:51 PM]

Oh hell no

Erin [4:52 PM]

???

Cassie [4:52 PM]

The ocean is terrifying!!!!! Why do you willingly want to go into its depths?

Erin [4:52 PM]

From the woman who wants to go to space 🚀

Cassie [4:52 PM]

Okay, first of all, I'm not going to space, I'm just going to make things that do. And second, the ocean is way scarier than space!

Erin [4:53 PM]

Absolutely not. Black holes? Possible alien life-forms?

Cassie [4:53 PM]

You wanna talk about aliens? Have you seen some of the organisms that live in the deep ocean? Space is mostly nothing. We don't even know what is in the ocean

Erin [4:53 PM]

You're ridiculous.

Cassie [4:53 PM]
You're the one who wants to go *scuba diving* 🤿

Erin never asked about Parker. Cassie couldn't have told her anything even if she had.

The next Monday, after a weekend without hearing from Parker even *once,* Cassie decided to be the one to skip breakfast. She had class, so she still had to get up, but she didn't have to eat in the dining hall. Lonely Reese's Puffs in her apartment was a pathetic breakfast, but it worked.

Acacia [Today 8:15 AM]
Where are you?

Cassie lied.

Cassie [8:20 AM]
Just woke up sry. Gonna eat here so I can make class on time

Acacia [8:20 AM]
We both know you take .5 seconds to get ready for class. You got time for breakfast

Cassie [8:21 AM]
It's cool. I'll catch you at lunch or something

Cassie didn't ask if Parker was there. It didn't matter. She didn't care. Her Reese's Puffs were delicious, however pathetic, and there was no conspicuously empty seat at her apartment counter, the way there'd been in the cafeteria the past two weeks.

Erin [Today 8:25 AM]
Good morning

Cassie's mood lifted. She held her phone up at an angle, snapped a quick selfie of her eating cereal. Except she almost missed her mouth and ended up with milk dripping down her chin. She sent the pic anyway. It wasn't a great picture, but she'd noticed that while Erin usually sent photos of her coffee mug, or some other inanimate object, every time Cassie sent a selfie, Erin sent one back.

Sure enough, two minutes later, she got a shot of Erin in light green V-neck scrubs at work, wisps of hair already coming out of her ponytail and one eyebrow raised. She was so fucking hot.

Erin [8:28 AM]
I thought you were good at eating.

Sharing a bad selfie was definitely worth that picture of Erin. Cassie wanted to climb right through the phone and kiss that crooked smile.

Cassie [8:28 AM]
Don't act like you don't know that's true

Erin sent back a smirking emoji that made Cassie grin. She ended up late to class.

• • • •

When Parker's name appeared on her phone, Cassie almost didn't believe it.

CUNT CREW
Parker [Today 3:42 PM]
It's been too long since we've had a movie night. Cassie you should come over after dinner

It was the first group text in a week. Cassie didn't even have to scroll that far to find her message asking if she'd never see Parker again.

Here she was, pretending nothing was wrong. Like Cassie had been overreacting the past two weeks. Cassie could admit she wasn't necessarily the best at understanding how friendships worked, but she knew Parker had disappeared on her. Maybe this was her olive branch.

Cassie didn't like doubting herself. So, whatever. A movie night sounded fun. It didn't mean they were best friends or anything. Whatever Parker was feeling mattered less to Cassie than what movie they watched.

After dinner, Cassie stood outside Acacia and Parker's room. A white board hung on the door. Block letters reading DAMN THE MAN, SAVE THE EMPIRE, took up most of it, but there were little embellishments. An unsigned "XO" in the upper left corner, a stick figure skeleton in a casket at the bottom left saying, "I'm so glad I went to college." Cassie used to leave a different drawing every week. She always did it when Parker and Acacia were in class and never owned up to it afterward. Maybe it was obvious it was her now that she'd missed two weeks in a row. Then again, Parker probably didn't even notice, too busy with Sam.

Last month, Cassie would've walked right in. Last month, Parker and Acacia would've been at dinner with her, probably. This month, she looked at the whiteboard and knocked twice.

"It's open!" When Cassie went inside, Acacia threw her hands up at her. "What the fuck? You knock now?"

Cassie shrugged. At her desk, Parker didn't look up from her phone. Cassie could let it go, but she decided to be petty instead.

"Hi, Parker," she said pointedly.

"Hey, what's up?" Parker said it like everything was normal, like it hadn't been more than a week since they'd seen each other. She was still on her phone.

"We haven't gotten Disney+ on your newest email address, have we?" Acacia asked.

Cassie and Acacia had been making new emails to utilize every free trial available over and over again since they were in middle school. They used Mama Webb's Netflix and Emerson had just subscribed to HBO Max, but for things like Disney+ and Showtime, Cassie and Acacia needed acassie142@yahoo.com—or were they on 143?

"I don't think so," Cassie said.

Parker finally set her phone down. She looked at Acacia. "What do you want to watch?"

"Wanna do something really old? Like *Aladdin*?"

"Talk about old. That was my mom's favorite movie as a kid."

Cassie was not going to freeze or go awkward because Parker mentioned Erin. It wasn't a big deal.

Instead of freaking out, she joined Acacia on the couch under her loft bed. The TV, an old twenty-four-inch they'd found at Goodwill, was under Parker's bed across the room. Cassie stretched her feet into Acacia's lap as her best friend signed up for a free trial.

"So how's Sam?" Cassie poked at the bruise.

Acacia eyes flitted to her, then back to the TV. Parker looked at her for the first time since she'd arrived.

"Fine."

That was her entire answer.

"You must be having so much sex," Cassie said just to get a reaction.

Parker blinked at her. "Excuse me?"

"I mean, I never see you anymore, and school can't be keeping you that busy, right?" Cassie grinned like it was funny. She was teasing, yeah, but she also wanted to be a bit of a dick. Because while she didn't particularly like to admit to having feelings, Parker had hurt them. She'd made Cassie feel replaceable—worse: unnecessary. Cassie wanted to get under her skin. "How's Sam in bed? I feel like it goes one of two ways—she's stone cold, or she cries."

Acacia pinched the back of Cassie's calf where Parker couldn't see. Parker didn't bother responding.

"Okay, so did we agree on *Aladdin*?" Acacia asked.

Cassie wasn't done, though. She sat up. Poked harder. "C'mon, princess, at least give me a hint."

Parker rolled her eyes. "I'm not talking to you about my sex life, Cassie."

"But you seriously have to be having a ton of it. We never see you anymore." That might not have been true—Cassie had no idea how often Acacia saw Parker. Maybe the only person who'd been cut from the friendship was her. "Do you and Sam even hang out with anyone, or is it just all sex all the time?"

Out of nowhere, Parker snapped. "Actually, for some of us, it's possible to have an emotional connection with people and not just fuck whoever the hell we feel like."

The room was silent.

Cassie stared at Parker, whose nostrils flared. "What's that supposed to mean?"

Parker didn't say anything initially, and Cassie laughed—this had to be a joke, right? Her laughter made Parker's eyes flash.

"Look, y'all, let's just—" Acacia's tone was placating, but Parker ignored her.

"You've had one serious relationship your entire life and he cheated on you," she said. "You don't know how to be vulnerable with someone. You haven't even tried to date anyone since Seth. You wouldn't have any idea what it's like."

That was a fucking nasty thing to throw in her face.

"It's not like you've had any models of good relationships in your life," Parker sneered.

It reminded Cassie of Erin at Christmas, calling her some kid with mommy issues. Like mother, like daughter, apparently. With Erin, Cassie had left, but with Parker, she got mad.

"Like you have any idea what my life is like, lately, the amount of time you spend with Sam." Cassie knew she shouldn't keep going, but she was pissed. "I could be in a goddamn relationship for all you know. Maybe I have a secret lover after all—you'd have no idea."

Acacia winced. She didn't try to calm either of them.

Parker clenched her jaw. "Fuck you, Cassie."

"Fuck *you*. Go enjoy your 'serious emotional connection' with Sam. Lord knows you're not attempting to connect with any of your friends."

She pushed herself up off the sofa. Parker glared at her. Acacia's face was still a grimace.

"What the fuck, man," Cassie said, and left.

Eighteen

ERIN

It was Tuesday when Parker's name finally lit up Erin's phone. Erin had patients to see, but she ducked into a stairwell and answered the call instead.

"Hey, baby!" She winced as soon as she said it, sounding too enthusiastic, clearly compensating for her terror over what this call could be.

"Hi," Parker said. Did she sound awkward because she knew Erin had fucked her friend or did she sound awkward because Erin had answered the phone like a fitness instructor trying to inspire people at a 5 A.M. workout?

"What's up?" The forced casualness was *obvious*. "I mean, how are you?"

"Why are you being weird?"

Erin laughed, too high pitched. "I'm not being weird. I just haven't heard from you in a bit, that's all."

"Oh my God, I'm sorry I didn't call Sunday, jeez," Parker said. "I was working on a piece and by the time I remembered, it was late."

It had been two Sundays, but Erin didn't point it out.

"That's all right, of course, it's all right," she said in a rush. The tension in her loosened. "I didn't mean to be annoying about it."

"You're always annoying about it," Parker teased, and Erin must have imagined the mean undercurrent in her tone.

"I know, I know, I'm your mom, I'm supposed to be annoying. So, tell me about the painting."

When she was little, Parker had been nervous about school. She'd gone to a preschool that was run out of the teacher's farmhouse. It had been less structured and more like going to a friend's house than to school. So kindergarten scared her. She wouldn't get on the bus the first day, cried until Erin called in late to work so she could drive her. Erin left work early, too, to pick Parker up at the end of the day. She had been ready for more tears.

Instead, the whole drive home, Parker hadn't stopped talking about the finger painting they'd done and how much Mrs. Schecter liked hers.

Asking Parker about art still worked just as well as it had back then.

She told Erin about her piece—a mixed-media project, not just a painting—and Erin relaxed with every word. Parker didn't hate her. She was busy at school, doing well in something she loved. She was happy. It was *good* that she hadn't called Sunday. Erin's baby girl was growing up.

"Anyway," Parker said when Erin ran out of questions about the piece. "How was your week?"

"Some good, some bad," Erin said honestly.

Good, in terms of texts from Cassie. Bad, given that Erin had spent most of it worried her daughter was never going to speak to her again. So good won out, Erin supposed, now that she was on the phone with Parker.

"Anything interesting happen since we last talked?" Parker asked.

Erin almost laughed. The question sounded like how she used to question Parker when she was in trouble. *Is there anything you want to tell me?* she'd say, holding the broken vase she found under some strategically discarded paper towels in the kitchen trash. It was probably her guilt, warping a genuine question into suspicion in Erin's mind.

"Just the usual," Erin said. "We're trying to agree on a time line for the opening of the clinic and it's a lot of back and forth."

"Sounds fun," Parker said like she hadn't heard anything Erin said. "But actually, I gotta go, I'm meeting Acacia for lunch."

"Oh, okay. Have fun! Tell her I said hi."

"Talk to you later."

"Bye, love you."

Parker hung up.

Which was fine! It was a good conversation. It didn't matter that she hung up without saying *love you*. Erin didn't need to let that undo how the rest of the call eased her anxiety.

She was grateful to have to get back to work instead of allowing herself to spiral.

After work, though, she went straight to spiraling.

What if Parker knew? What if that was why she hadn't called for so long? What if that was why she didn't say she loved Erin on the phone?

Carolyn would lecture Erin for ascribing judgment where there was no proof of it. Last week, she'd told Erin to just ask Parker what was going on. The thought was still petrifying.

Erin shouldn't be doing what she was doing with Cassie for a lot of reasons, but if she was going to be this neurotic after every phone call with her daughter, she *really* shouldn't be doing it. Surely this anxiety canceled out some of the happiness that seemed to crop up every time she got a text from Cassie.

Removing Cassie from the situation altogether—what would Erin do if Parker hadn't called her in a week and a half if Erin had never done anything with Cassie? She'd ask probably. She would press. If she thought something was wrong with Parker, she'd want to know. She'd want Parker to know she could talk to her about it. They could talk about things that mattered.

They hadn't lately, though, had they?

Parker hadn't even told Erin what she wanted to study. She loved art, obviously, but whenever Erin brought up a future in it, Parker shut her down. And while Parker knew how Erin's life had changed with the divorce from the outside—Adam had moved out and Erin worked more—they'd never talked about how *she* had changed.

Pushing wasn't going to make Parker open up.

Erin had to open up herself. Carolyn had said maybe it was time to have the conversation with Parker about the divorce more than a month ago. Erin couldn't do it then. Maybe she could now.

She wanted to talk to Cassie about it. She'd told Cassie things Parker didn't know: how important the clinic was to her, how she felt like herself for the first time in more than a decade.

But they didn't talk about Parker. They'd never explicitly agreed not to; they just never had. Like if they didn't mention her, they could pretend they weren't doing anything wrong. So Erin didn't say anything about her decision to talk to Parker. She didn't admit to chickening out the next time Parker called, finally on a Sunday.

But by the Sunday after that, when Parker called, Erin had built up her nerve. They did the usual weekly catch up, and Parker was more loquacious than she'd been their last two phone calls. She talked about Sam, a quiet smile in her voice.

"Does she know that if she hurts you, your mom is gonna fly down there and hurt her right back?"

Parker laughed. "I think Acacia would get to her first."

"That won't stop me," Erin said. "Seriously, though, sweetheart, she sounds great. I'm glad you found someone who treats you right."

"What about you?" Parker said. "Anyone treating you right nowadays?"

They'd never talked about Erin's dating life after the divorce. It'd taken Erin more than a year to give in to Rachel's desire to set her up, and she always did it when Parker was with her father.

"Actually," Erin said. She swallowed. She could do this. "There's something I've been wanting to talk to you about."

The line was silent.

Erin swallowed. "It's not bad. But it's important."

Still no response from Parker.

"Are you there?"

"Yeah."

Erin had thought parenting was hard when Parker was little. Raising a baby into toddlerhood while in med school took everything Erin had, and she'd still messed up, pretty much all the time. Parker had survived, but it felt like barely. To this day, Erin's guilt flared when she caught sight of the scar behind Parker's ear from when she'd managed to launch herself out of a swing at three and a half.

Parenting an almost adult was harder.

Erin was somehow supposed to balance being the grown-up while also recognizing Parker as something of an equal. It'd been a long time since Parker believed her mother to be all-knowing, but Erin was still supposed to have *some* wisdom. She was supposed to teach Parker things she was still learning herself. How to live in this world. How to be a good person. How to take care of yourself.

"I want to explain my decision to get the divorce," Erin said, as plainly as she could.

A beat. "What?"

"It wasn't something I took lightly. It wasn't something I did to hurt you or your father. It wasn't me choosing anything over either of you."

"We're talking about the divorce?" Parker said. "Really? Now?"

"Yes, I—" Erin considered. Barely into the conversation and already a parenting fail. "Actually, you're right. I shouldn't have sprung this on you with no warning. This is a conversation it's important for us to have, but it doesn't have to be right now. Is there another time this week that would work better for you?"

Parker scoffed.

Erin chewed at her bottom lip and waited.

"Whatever. Fine. Let's have the conversation. Go right ahead. Tell me all your great reasons."

"You're my reason," Erin said.

More silence.

Erin couldn't stay still for this. She got up off the couch to pace instead, running a hand through her hair.

"I want you to be happy. More than anything, that's what I want. And I mean really happy, long-term happy. It wasn't what your grandma wanted for me, not really, or if it was, our ideas of happiness were nowhere close to each other's. It never seemed like it was about wanting me to be happy as it was about having a path for me, all planned out. Your dad wasn't a part of that path. You weren't a part of that path. Med school wasn't a part of that path. And so, I spent a lot of time trying to do what she wanted, to make up for how I thought I'd let her down. I don't want our relationship to be like that. Nothing you could do will ever let me down. And I want you to be happy, whatever path you take to get there."

Erin took a breath. She was babbling, obviously, but she needed to get it all out. Now that she'd opened the door, it felt more like floodgates, everything rushing out at once.

Parker broke in now that she finally had the chance. "You want me to be happy, so you got a divorce? That's really what you're trying to say here?"

"Yes." She took another breath. It was simple, really. "How could I teach you to be happy when I wasn't?"

No scoff at least.

"All the things I want you to do? Figure out what you want in life. Find your own path. Make mistakes but actually learn from them. Leave behind what doesn't bring you joy, what you've out-grown. I wasn't doing any of it when I was married to your dad." She was still circling the couch. "I thought I was staying in the marriage for you—so you didn't have to go through your parents divorcing. But, in the end, I left it for you. Because how could I raise you to do all those things when I wasn't doing them myself?"

For the first time in the conversation, Erin wished she could see Parker's face. She might not have been able to get the words out if she'd had Parker's eyes on her, but now she wanted to see them, to know how they looked. Bright blue like the summer sky? Or clear like ice over a pond, which meant tears were coming if they weren't already there. Did the little wrinkle on Parker's forehead come out as she furrowed her brow?

After a minute, when Parker still hadn't responded, Erin stopped walking. She hugged the arm not holding the phone around her, tight.

"I'm sorry," she said. "For doing it. For taking so long to do it. For taking so long to have this conversation." She tacked "I love you so much" on the end.

"I love you," Parker said, quiet, and her eyes must've been icy, be-cause there were definitely tears in her voice. "Thank you, for telling me this."

"I know it's random. I just—I wanted you to know."

"I'm glad you told me." Silence. "All those things you want me to do: are you doing them now?"

Erin considered it. "I'm trying to, at least."

Over the line, Parker sniffed. "I'm . . . happy for you, Mom."

"Yeah?" Erin rubbed hard at her eyes.

"Yeah. It's weird, but I'm happy for you."

Of course it was weird to talk to your mom about why she di-vorced your dad. It was weird for Erin to talk to her daughter about it. But they'd done it. It felt like a lot more than a baby step toward being closer with Parker.

"I love you," Erin said again.

"Okay, enough, let's stop being mushy," Parker said wetly. "Tell me more about the clinic."

That felt like a step, too, Parker asking for more than the bare minimum of information about Erin's job. Erin wiped her eyes and told Parker about the clinic.

Nineteen

CASSIE

If Cassie thought Parker had disappeared *before* their fight, she was really gone, now. A campus of barely a thousand people, and still, Cassie never saw Parker, even in passing. She tried not to care.

So what if Parker thought Cassie didn't know how to be in a relationship? Maybe she was right. Cassie had had one serious partner and he'd cheated on her. All of that was true. It didn't excuse the way Parker had talked to her, like she was stupid. It didn't excuse the way Parker had ghosted once she started dating Sam. Cassie might not know how to be in a relationship, but she knew it didn't mean abandoning your friends.

She didn't need to know how to be vulnerable or be in a relationship to fuck Parker's mom. She imagined, briefly, telling Parker that. It'd only be out of spite though, a *Look, I can be a terrible friend, too*. But if Parker knew what Cassie and Erin were doing, they'd have to stop. Plus, Acacia would murder her, probably, and Cassie might not care about losing Parker's friendship, but she wasn't about to lose Acacia's.

Parker and Acacia were spending spring break together visiting Emerson in Chicago. Acacia had invited Cassie, hesitantly, but Cassie had begged off. Not because it would've been awkward, she and Parker trying to be friendly—or Cassie trying, anyway, she wasn't sure where Parker stood on the whole thing.

She'd begged off because she already had spring break plans.

Two nights in Boston, paid for by United Aerospace Laboratories. They were flying her out to interview for what was basically her dream job.

She'd had to lie, just a little, in the phone interview, about grad school. A company in Boston wasn't gonna hire someone who wanted to go to California at the end of the summer. So Cassie had played up her application to MIT. It wasn't lying, really—she *had* applied to MIT. Lately, it didn't even feel like the worst option.

Caltech was just so *far*.

She'd been away from Acacia for the first three years of college. More than two hours away.

At college, Cassie had never expected to be homesick. She didn't even like her hometown. She went back during breaks only to see the Webbs—hadn't spent a single night in her mom's trailer since she'd headed off for Keckley. Somehow, two months into freshman year, she missed Acacia so much she'd called her crying, just to hear her voice. Acacia had shown up on campus that weekend—a spur of the moment surprise to make Cassie feel better.

They couldn't do that if Cassie went to Caltech.

Cassie would be happy. She'd love what she was studying, and she'd make other friends eventually, probably. But she wouldn't be able to get in a car and drive to Acacia in a day. That knowledge made her second-guess what she'd thought was her dream since she was a kid.

It didn't hurt that she knew, if she got this UAL job, they'd help pay for her to go to MIT.

And maybe it helped that Erin was near Boston, too.

Cassie hadn't told anyone except Professor Upton about the second interview. She hadn't even told anyone about the phone interview—it had been right after Parker, like, snapped at her or whatever. They hadn't been talking, and still weren't, and she and Acacia had been both awkwardly talking about Parker and actively avoiding talking about Parker, so the interview hadn't come up.

Not that Cassie would've said anything, anyway. She didn't want to get her hopes up. If people knew she wanted it and she didn't get it, that'd be so much worse than not getting it without everyone knowing she'd failed.

There was an a cappella concert the weekend before spring break. Cassie almost wished she didn't want to go. It'd be easier if she didn't want to support Parker, if she didn't miss her. But she did, and so she went, sitting in the front row with Acacia and determinedly not thinking about the last concert.

When it was over, Parker met them in the audience, beaming and laughing. She hurled herself into Acacia's arms and latched on to Cassie next. Her body went stiff halfway through the hug. Cassie let her go gently. Parker, face flushed, ducked her head, then looked up at Cassie.

"I'm glad you came."

"I wouldn't miss it," Cassie said. "You were great."

"You were!" Acacia said, preventing the awkward silence that would've undoubtedly come next. "You fucking killed it. And now we're gonna go fucking kill the after-party."

A cappella parties, it turned out, were messy. And loud, because everyone sang all the fucking time. But it was fun, too. Cassie spent most of the night on a couch pressed tight between Parker and Acacia, and even though Parker spent more time singing than talking to her, it was great. They took about twenty selfies together and drank too much, until Parker and Acacia disappeared to the bathroom, leaving Cassie to stake their claim on the couch. She stretched herself across it and scrolled through the pictures they had taken.

They all looked good in all of them, thank you very much, but she found her favorite—they were laughing over something Cassie couldn't even remember anymore, none of them looking at the camera, Acacia almost falling off the couch, Parker's nose pressed against Cassie's cheek. She hadn't sent Erin a picture today, so she sent her this.

Erin [11:58 PM]
My favorite girls!

Cassie felt warm as she slipped her phone into her pocket. The couch was so soft. Her eyes slipped closed. Members of the Sky High Notes were belting Olivia Rodrigo songs, but still, Cassie almost fell asleep before the other two got back.

It was a great way to start spring break, and it just got better from there. Three days later, in Cassie's humble opinion, she'd nailed the interview. She'd worn a black jumpsuit with a red fabric belt and red flats—professional and as femme as she was willing to go.

"I'm glad you're in closed-toed shoes," Joel, the head of the lab, told her. "Means I can take you on a proper tour."

That's right: it wasn't just an interview. It was a lab tour and so many introductions Cassie had already forgotten names and they even took her to lunch. That had to mean something, right? And yet, when she'd asked when she might hear from them, Joel had only said "Soon," with an enigmatic smile. It'd been the low point of an otherwise excellent six-hour interview process.

The day had been long enough that when Cassie got back to her hotel in the late afternoon, even buzzing from the interview, she lay down for a quick nap, which turned into a not-so-quick nap. At least she woke up refreshed instead of wondering what year it was.

She was still in the hotel bed, passively scrolling Yelp reviews on her phone when it rang. It was the UAL number. Cassie gave herself time to take a breath, then answered.

"Hello, this is Cassie."

"Cassie, hey, it's Joel from UAL." This seemed like a really good sign.

"Hey, Joel, how're you doing?"

"Pretty great," he said. "I'm calling because—now, we don't usually do this so quickly, but there was unanimous enthusiasm in the lab today, and we want to offer you the position."

Cassie couldn't stop herself from asking, "Really?"

"Really." Joel laughed. Cassie leapt out of the bed and pumped her fist as he continued, "You'd be an excellent addition to UAL. If you accept, I can't wait to see where you'll take us."

"Of course I'm accepting, Joel," Cassie said. "This is an amazing opportunity. I'm so excited."

"Great. You'll get emails from HR with the details tomorrow, and we'll see you in a couple of months. Feel free to call or email me if you've got any questions."

"Thank you so much."

"Thank you. I look forward to working with you, Cassie."

She ended the call and collapsed back onto the bed. She got it. She couldn't believe it—or she could, sure, she'd totally rocked today, but—she got it. Holy shit. She let out a little scream of joy.

She had to tell someone. Fuck, she was so excited. She *had* to tell someone.

"This is Erin Bennett."

"Erin," Cassie laughed into her phone. "What are you doing right now?"

"Cassie?" She sounded tired. "What's going on?"

"What are you doing?" Cassie repeated. She paced in front of her hotel bed.

"I was—resting," Erin said. "Napping. I worked an overnight yesterday."

"Shit, I forgot. I'm sorry. I didn't mean to wake you. I just—I've got some kind of exciting news!"

Erin was quiet, and then, "Well, tell me what it is already!"

"I got a job!" Cassie practically screamed it. "A really great job. I toured the labs today and killed my interview so hard they offered it to me barely two hours after I'd finished."

"Babe, that's great! What's the job? Where is it? Tell me everything."

Cassie grinned. "It's with United Aerospace Laboratories."

"What?" Erin said. "The one in Boston?"

"The one in Boston," Cassie said. "I'm in my hotel at Copley Place right now."

"You're in Boston right now?"

"That's what I just said, Erin," Cassie said, laughing. "And you should come meet me for a celebratory dinner."

"I can't believe you didn't tell me you were in Boston!"

"I'm telling you now! I didn't want anyone to know in case I didn't get it."

"But you got it."

"I got it." Cassie couldn't stop grinning. "Come to Boston. Let's celebrate."

Erin took a moment to respond. "I can be there in an hour and a half."

"Drive faster."

"Cassie."

"Safe, but fast," she amended.

Erin laughed. Cassie laughed, too, thrilled. She was just so damn happy.

"The Westin at Copley Place," she said. "Let me know when you get close, and I'll come down to meet you."

"What should I wear?"

Cassie's grin widened. "Something sexy."

"Cassie." Erin laughed again. "I mean, do you want to go someplace fancy? What's the dress code?"

"I am way too hype for someplace fancy," Cassie said. "Just dress normally, Erin. You always look great."

"Flattery will get you nowhere."

Cassie cracked up. "That's blatantly untrue."

"Whatever," Erin said, and Cassie could hear the smile in her voice. "I'll see you soon."

"Hurry."

She had an hour and a half, but Cassie got dressed right away anyway. Just jeans and a white T-shirt—she'd throw the blazer from her jumpsuit on before she left. She wanted to look good, because she felt good, and because of Erin. It seemed unreal that she hadn't seen her in more than two months. They texted daily, sure, but like, she actually got to see her. In person. And touch her. Yeah, she wanted to look really good.

She turned on her pump-up playlist on her phone and rocked out as she did her makeup. God, she got an amazing job, and she was about to see Erin. She wasn't sure she could be happier.

She was on the sidewalk when Erin pulled up, hadn't bothered to stop smiling. She climbed into the car, leaned over the console, and kissed Erin. Erin giggled into her mouth.

"Well, hello," she said.

Cassie sat back, grinning. "Hey."

"It's good to see you, too."

Cassie shrugged. "It's been way too long since I've gotten to do that."

"Maybe you should do it one more time, then."

Cassie laughed and kissed her again.

They were probably taking too long in the hotel roundabout, so Cassie made herself stop. She considered suggesting they just go to her room, but her stomach growled.

"Let's go."

"Where are we going?" Erin asked, pulling onto the street.

"What, you don't have any cool places to take me to? You're the one from around here."

"You really think I'm the type to know cool places?"

Cassie considered mentioning that Parker had said she was the cool mom, but bringing up Parker was probably not a good way to get laid.

"To be honest, I'm a little surprised you don't know any place to take a pretty girl," she said instead.

Erin slid a grin toward her. "Well, there is this bar you might like."

Cassie beamed.

She definitely liked the bar. It had good music and nice lighting—not so dark you had to squint, but dark enough to provide some privacy. The corner booth Erin took her to was comfortable, and the beer Cassie ordered was delicious. They put in a food order right away, too, since Cassie's stomach kept grumbling.

"To your *job*," Erin said, raising her glass.

Cassie clinked glasses with her.

"Tell me all about it," Erin said.

"I get to be a huge nerd slash genius in UAL's labs," Cassie said. "And if I'm good enough, I won't even be able to tell you what I'm working on, because they'll put me on classified stuff. I mean, I have to be really good to get there, but—I'm me, so I'll probably get there."

Erin grinned at her. Cassie wanted to kiss her again. Why hadn't they just stayed at the hotel and ordered room service?

"They might not be thrilled if I go to Caltech in the fall, but I'm hoping we can work something out."

"If?" Erin repeated. "Where's that Cassie Klein confidence I'm so used to?"

"It's not about confidence. I mean—UAL has offices in LA and Atlanta, too, so they've said they want to keep me on no matter where I go to school," Cassie said. "I just hope they mean it."

It wasn't about confidence about getting into Caltech, anyway. More like—Cassie was no longer confident that was where she wanted to go. The past month, since she was fighting with Parker, it'd felt like Acacia was slipping away. Not completely—she'd never completely lose Kaysh, she knew, but there was all this distance between them. She didn't want to put any more actual distance between them than necessary. Caltech was literally across the country. The entire fucking country. Georgia Tech was less than eight hours from Keckley. MIT was about ten. Both doable in a day. If Cassie were at Caltech and desperate for Acacia, she'd have no way to get to her.

Cassie hated that it mattered so much. She wanted to take care of herself. She wanted to be an adult. Independent. Capable. Sometimes she thought of how much she depended on Acacia and she felt like she was nine years old again, after the failed attempt at flying off her mom's trailer, the bones of her leg doing something they were absolutely not supposed to do, the way Acacia had said, "I'm gonna go get help. Don't move." Like Cassie had had some other option.

But they were celebrating tonight, so Cassie wasn't going to think about any of that.

"You look great, by the way," she said. "As usual."

Erin laughed. "You do, too," she said. "It's such a nice surprise to get to see you."

"I'm glad you weren't working," Cassie said. "I'm sorry that I totally forgot about your shift last night and woke you, though."

"If you hadn't, I wouldn't be here. I think I'll survive."

"I had to tell somebody. I mean, I should probably let Upton know, too. He's the only one who knew I applied."

"Wait," Erin said. "I'm the only one who knows you got it?"

Cassie grinned. "Yeah."

"I feel special." She had this little smile on her face as she glanced toward the bar, where their waiter was on his way with their food.

Cassie wanted to investigate that smile more, but she was hungry.

Once Cassie had some food in her and could focus, she watched Erin. She was in jeans and a purple blouse, eating and talking and not doing anything spectacular, but Cassie wanted to touch her. Cassie wanted to kiss her and fuck her and just get her goddamn hands on her. She settled for footsie under the table, which made Erin smile some more.

They finished their food and ordered another round of drinks and Erin asked for a dessert menu. Cassie's foot was up in Erin's lap by this point. She knew exactly what she wanted for dessert.

Erin ordered crème brûlée.

"You can't have a celebration dinner without dessert," she told Cassie, then excused herself to the restroom.

When she returned, she joined Cassie on her side of the table. Cassie's hand dropped to Erin's thigh pretty much as soon as it was within reach.

"You know," Cassie said quietly, "I was already planning on dessert."

"Did you want something other than crème brûlée?" Erin asked, all innocent except for the way she almost imperceptibly opened her legs.

Cassie squeezed her thigh, didn't move her hand when the waiter brought the dessert. She let Erin take the first bite. Erin moaned—at how good it was, or maybe just to fuck Cassie up—and Cassie's fingers tightened around her thigh. Erin blinked at her, wide doe eyes and Cassie knew she was doing this on purpose, but it worked. Cassie shifted in her seat.

Erin smiled. "You have to try this. It's delicious."

Cassie squirmed through the entire dessert. Erin made little noises of pleasure, licked the spoon more than she possibly needed to. She radiated heat from her core; Cassie could tell even though her fingers were still a few inches and a layer of denim away. She wanted to be done, wanted the real celebration to start. Wanted to get Erin back to her hotel and lay her naked across the bed. But Erin took her sweet time, finishing, flirting with the waiter over the check until Cassie's fingers dug farther into her leg. Cassie wanted Erin so much she had to stop herself from fidgeting; meanwhile Erin's only tell was the slight flush on her cheeks.

Erin laced their fingers together as they left the bar, and Cassie bit down on her smile. She'd like to be biting down on Erin's neck, the delicate skin there exposed as Erin flipped her hair over one shoulder.

They got two blocks from the bar, turned down the side street where the car was parked, and Erin pushed Cassie up against a building.

Apparently she'd been more affected than Cassie thought.

She kissed hard and dirty, and Cassie let her. Cassie, who normally saw what she wanted and went for it, took it—Cassie just let Erin kiss her. Erin was so good at it, was the thing. The brick wall of the building scratched at the elbows on Cassie's blazer, and Erin's tongue was hot in her mouth.

It was so much and so good, but it wasn't enough. Cassie arched. Erin grabbed her hips, held her in place, and grinded against her.

"Erin, your car—" Cassie gasped.

"Is too damn far away," Erin said, getting her hands under Cassie's jacket. "You drive me crazy all night and then you think I can make it to my car?"

Cassie's head dropped back against the brick. They weren't hidden really. It was just an alcove to an apartment building, and if anyone were to come out or go in—

"Anyone could see."

"Cassie," Erin's voice was rough. "I need to make you come. Right. Now."

Cassie moaned, Erin's mouth on her throat. *"Yes."*

Erin unbuttoned Cassie's jeans.

Cassie was wet, probably had been since Erin had sat next to her. She could feel Erin grin against her collarbone as her fingers slipped around Cassie's clit. Cassie moaned again.

"Shhh," Erin murmured.

Cassie tried to keep her eyes open, but then she saw someone walking past them on the other side of the street, so she closed them and just focused on how good Erin felt.

Erin was obviously not going for anything other than fast and messy. Her fingers rubbed furious circles over Cassie's clit. She was leaving a necklace of hickeys and Cassie was silently begging for more, shoulder blades pressed back into the building while the rest of her body arched forward. She tugged Erin's mouth to hers right before she came, smothered her groan of pleasure with a kiss.

Erin removed her hand from Cassie's pants while Cassie caught her breath. Cassie was leaning against the wall still, Erin's other hand strong on her hip. She'd be upset that Erin seemed to think she couldn't trust her legs, except Cassie wasn't sure she *could*.

"Ready?" Erin asked.

Cassie swallowed. She settled her weight back onto her feet.

"Yeah," she said. "Yeah, sure."

Erin laughed at her, but Cassie couldn't bring herself to care. She felt warm and satisfied and she would get to make Erin feel that way, too, as soon as they got to the hotel. She was definitely ready.

She did not get to make Erin feel that way as soon as they got to the hotel, it turned out.

She snuck a hand into Erin's back pocket on the way to her room, but once they were inside, Erin took over. She slipped Cassie's jacket off and kissed her, walked her backward to the bed without ever breaking the kiss. Erin's weight on top of her felt wonderful, but Cassie really wanted to reciprocate. She kept trying to get Erin's clothes off—she plucked at her top and fiddled with her belt—but Erin always caught her hands.

"Erin," she whined, drawing it out.

She could feel Erin smile into the kiss, but when Cassie reached for her shirt again, Erin pinned her wrists over her head. Cassie kept her arms there even after she let go. Erin's hands found their way to Cassie's belt, and she finally stopped kissing her to ask, "May I?"

"Erin, I want—"

"I want you to keep saying my name, Cassie. And I want to go down on you. You'll get your turn, don't worry."

Cassie tried really hard not to, but she might've whimpered. Erin's lips turned up.

"Yeah," Cassie said. "Yeah, you can. Take them off."

Erin stripped Cassie of her pants with startling efficiency and roaming hands. She paused, once the jeans were off, and Cassie was about to tell her to keep going, but Erin was just taking a break to rub Cassie through her panties.

"Christ."

Erin smirked at her. "You can just call me Erin."

Cassie would've rolled her eyes, but she was too busy pushing her panties down since Erin wasn't in enough of a hurry to. Once Cassie's lower half was naked, though, Erin didn't bother with Cassie's shirt before settling between her legs.

Fuck.

Cassie didn't know how she'd gone so long without this. Erin's mouth was criminally good. Cassie dropped her head back against the pillow, letting out a low moan. Her legs fell farther open.

"God, Erin, I missed you."

Erin laughed, kissed her thigh. "Me?" she asked. "Or this?" She licked straight up Cassie's center.

"Both," Cassie gasped.

Erin must've had a great memory. She did all the things that make Cassie the most crazy. She swirled her tongue around Cassie's clit, dropped it down to slide up into her. She never let Cassie get too close, always stopped and changed whatever she was doing when Cassie's legs started to shake.

"Look at me," Erin demanded, and Cassie didn't hesitate.

The sight of Erin looking up at her as she licked her clit made Cassie want to groan and slam her eyes shut again, but she held eye contact. The look in Erin's eyes was pleased. She would be smiling if her mouth wasn't otherwise occupied.

"Erin," Cassie panted, and now she swore she could actually feel Erin's grin pressing between her legs. "Erin, please."

Erin nodded, and Cassie kept her eyes open when she came.

Cassie shook and shook and Erin kept going. Erin's breath was hot and wet when she pulled back, and then when she bit at Cassie's clit again, Cassie's eyes slammed shut as she came a second time, right away.

"Fucking Christ, Erin," she groaned, because Erin was being gentle, but her mouth was still on Cassie. "Are you trying to kill me?"

"I'm not done yet," Erin said.

Cassie's body gave another shudder.

"You gotta give me a break."

"This is your break," Erin said. She was still tonguing at Cassie, but she avoided her clit.

"Erin," Cassie dragged out her name.

Erin sucked a mark onto her inner thigh. "It's been two months," she said. "Just come for me one more time."

Cassie came *three* more times before Erin stopped. She pulled her shirt and bra off between orgasms three and four to play with her tits. By the end, she'd said Erin's name so many times it had lost all meaning. After, Erin climbed out of bed, padded to the sink—still fully clothed—and returned with a glass of water, and Cassie still didn't have her breath back.

"Take your time," Erin said, smirk evident in her voice.

Cassie would've liked to wipe it right off her face, but she couldn't even move enough to take the glass of water.

"I think I'm dead," she said.

Erin laughed at her.

"I really think you killed me."

"I did not," Erin giggled. "Sit up so you can drink."

Cassie managed to sort of shuffle her way to half sitting, still breathing hard. She gulped at the water.

When she set it down on the bedside table, she asked, "Is it finally my turn?"

Erin grinned. "I don't know. Have you recovered enough?"

"Shut up," Cassie laughed, and tugged Erin into bed with her.

Only after Cassie had licked all traces of her own taste out of Erin's mouth did she start undressing her. Erin's blouse was clingy and her hair got caught it in as Cassie pulled it over her head. Cassie tugged harder instead of being careful, but it did the trick, and she got her hands on Erin's bare skin.

Erin was squirming on top of her, obviously desperate for some kind of friction. Cassie considered making her wait, with how long

Erin had made her wait to touch her, but before she made up her mind, Erin was shuddering, eyes closed and mouth slack, and Cassie just watched.

Eventually Erin blinked her eyes open. Cassie still stared.

"Was that—did you just—"

Erin ducked her head like she was embarrassed. "It's been a while, okay?"

"Holy shit, babe," Cassie said, surging forward to kiss Erin and roll her onto her back. "That was hot as fuck."

Erin grinned and Cassie set about making her do that again.

Erin came twice more, and made Cassie come a *seventh* time before they were done. She lay on top of Cassie afterward, head pillowed on her chest and Cassie's arms wrapped around her.

"This is the best spring break ever," Cassie said.

Erin lifted her head to look up at her. "Yeah?"

"I got a great job, I came seven times—"

"So far," Erin interrupted.

"Oh my God, Erin, let me rest," Cassie huffed and Erin laughed.

"I thought college students were supposed to want to have sex all the time," she teased.

"Sure, but two months without it and then seven orgasms in a row takes a lot out of a girl."

Erin's smile went wide and Cassie realized she'd tipped her hand a bit. She should never be allowed to talk after one orgasm, much less seven. Anyway—Erin had said it'd been a while for her, too, so maybe neither of them had slept with anyone since winter break. Cassie swallowed the sudden flutter in her throat and tightened her arms around Erin. The other woman murmured and lay her head down, her ear pressing into Cassie's sternum so she could probably hear every rapid beat of Cassie's heart.

Twenty

ERIN

Erin woke up before seven. Cassie was sleeping like the dead, as if Erin had worn her out. She might have, given that Cassie admitted to not sleeping with anyone else since winter break. Erin hadn't either, but she didn't feel worn out. Instead, there was a pleasant ache between her thighs as she practically skipped to the nearest Starbucks. It was an unseasonably warm day, even this early.

It was freeing, to be in Boston. On a whim. For a girl. It was . . . impulsive, in a way Erin hadn't been in a long time. Early on in college, she and Rachel would occasionally decide on Friday afternoons that they wanted to go away for the weekend. They'd find the cheapest hotel and most expensive booze they could afford and spend the weekend drunk in a hotel room. But Erin had been a dutiful mom, wife, doctor for so long. Predictable. Expected. This was more fun.

Maybe Erin should've been upset Cassie would be spending the summer in Boston. If she were smart, she'd want distance between them. When Cassie just lived in Erin's phone, it was easier to not think about what they were doing. Seeing Cassie in person—Erin thought of the woman she'd left sleeping in the hotel bed. Cassie's hair spread wide across the pillow.

She knew she was being stupid. She knew she was making a mistake, every time she smiled at Cassie.

It would be different, this time, from what it had been at Christmas. Erin was denying herself then, or trying to. Over Christmas, Erin had been flying by the seat of her pants, trying to figure out how to get through it. Now, she hardly had the excuse of acting without thinking. She'd had months to think about it. She tried not to, and certainly never admitted to. She and Cassie had never acknowledged the change in their relationship, but they'd been texting every day for more than a month. Since Valentine's weekend, there had been a day or two when Erin hadn't talked to Rachel; not a single day passed that she didn't talk to Cassie.

Erin had lost the ability to tell herself this was just sex. There was lying to yourself and then there was straight up delusion, and this fell more in the latter.

So she didn't tell herself anything.

In her marriage, she'd spent so long knowing what she wanted and not allowing herself to have it, not allowing herself to even think about it. When she would think about it, she'd talk herself out of it. She did that too often—second-guessed herself into discontent. So, with Cassie, Erin just . . . didn't think about it. She knew what she wanted, and for once in her life, she let herself have it.

Cassie was spread across the bed, legs on one side, arms stretching to the other, when Erin returned with a drink carrier in one hand and a pastry bag in the other, a copy of the *Globe* tucked under one elbow. Cassie looked up at her.

"Oh."

"Morning." Erin pressed her lips together instead of beaming. Even when it was only the two of them, being this happy felt like it wasn't allowed. "I hope you didn't miss me too much."

Cassie pushed herself halfway up and jutted her chin out. Erin took her cue and dropped a kiss on that mouth. Cassie grinned at her when she pulled away.

"What'd you get me?"

"Coffee," Erin said, holding out the carrier so Cassie's drink was within her reach. "And lemon loaf or zucchini bread. Which do you want?"

"Whichever you don't."

Cassie got herself situated in the bed. She was still naked but made no move to get dressed, sitting with her back against the headboard, the sheet tucked around her torso. Erin shrugged out of her jacket.

"Uh," Cassie said. "You're in my shirt."

Erin looked down. She'd put on the first thing she found on the floor of the hotel room—whatever got her to good coffee fastest. She hadn't realized until now that it was Cassie's white T-shirt.

"Is that okay? I can take it off if you want."

"No," Cassie said immediately. "No, uh. It's fine." Her cheeks were bright pink.

Erin should wear her clothes more often.

Cassie took a sip of her drink. The bliss on her face at the taste was worth teasing her over, but she was still blushing from the shirt thing, so Erin gave her a break instead.

Erin had a shift at the hospital that afternoon. It'd be smart to head back to Nashua early. She wasn't even sure she had a clean set of scrubs. She peeled her jeans off and climbed back into bed with Cassie. She wasn't trying anything, didn't mean to be sexy, but she settled close enough that her body pressed into Cassie's. Just as she remembered Parker saying Cassie didn't like being touched, Cassie threw her leg over Erin's, crossing them at the ankle.

They split the baked goods—took half of each. Erin unfolded the newspaper. She kept the first section and offered the rest to Cassie, who immediately flipped through it to find the crossword puzzle. The quiet was nice. They didn't have to do anything. Didn't have to be careful, didn't have to watch the clock or listen for Parker.

They could've had this in October, if Erin had invited Cassie back to her hotel that night. Then again—maybe not. They wouldn't have had a quiet morning in bed together. Erin would've rushed Cassie out the door. She didn't know her, then, and she'd been nervous that morning, meeting Parker for breakfast. Jesus, imagine if Cassie had spent the night, said goodbye in the morning, and then they'd shown up at the same restaurant. As though it hadn't already been messy enough.

"You'll probably know this one," Cassie said, still working on the crossword. "First female graduate of a US medical school, starts with a—"

"Elizabeth Blackwell," Erin said.

"Nerd."

Erin bumped her shoulder against Cassie's. "As if you can't tell me the first female US astronaut."

"Yeah, but everyone knows Sally Ride," Cassie said. "And I'm not going to be an astronaut!"

"Of course not."

Cassie made a show of ignoring her and going back to the crossword. Erin couldn't help but keep looking at her—she was so damn pretty. Her blond hair a lion's mane and her skin with a glow even in March. Eventually Cassie caught her looking. Erin smiled, felt her face warm.

"This is nice," she said.

Cassie grinned. "You gonna come visit when I live here this summer and bring me breakfast in bed?"

"That's your favorite part of this morning?" Erin raised her eyebrows.

"You got something better?"

"Maybe after you finish the crossword."

Cassie immediately filled the unsolved boxes with random letters, then held it up. "Look. Done."

Erin laughed. "When's your flight?

• • • •

Erin sped the entire way to the airport. They didn't have time for her to park and come in with Cassie. They didn't even have time for Erin to get out of the car—Cassie kissed her hard over the console.

"Thanks, babe, I'll text from the plane."

"Have a good flight!" Erin called after her.

Cassie [Today 1:23 PM]
Had to fight the gate agent so they wouldn't close the door on me, but I made it

Erin's good feeling after seeing Cassie only lasted until she made it home to Nashua. By then, her mind had caught up with her.

Last night, Cassie had talked about Caltech. She had said *if*. Almost twenty-four hours later and Erin was still trying not to read too much into it. It wasn't like they could keep doing this, even if Cassie didn't move across the country for grad school. This morning, Erin had made a mental note to wear Cassie's clothes more often. When was that supposed to happen? That night was their only shot. Even with Cassie in Boston for the summer, it wasn't like she and Erin would get time alone together.

Erin couldn't ask Cassie to go to MIT. She couldn't ask anything of her. Cassie was weeks away from turning twenty-two. She had her whole life in front of her, the entire world in front of her. She could do anything. Erin wasn't about to hold her back.

It'd been *nice*, validating, that a hot younger person was so into her. But Erin couldn't act like they were something they weren't. They weren't dating. They weren't in a relationship. They couldn't be. Even if that was something Cassie wanted, it could never work.

Parker could *never* know Erin and Cassie had so much as flirted. There was no way it could go anything but horribly. Erin cared about Cassie—a lot—but she wasn't willing to lose her daughter.

So, she wouldn't ask Cassie to go to MIT. She wouldn't imagine what it could be like, to keep her close. She would allow herself what she could for the summer, and then she would say goodbye.

This was why they didn't talk about it. This was why Erin didn't think about it.

This was why, at coffee the next week, when Rachel asked how Erin had been, Erin just said, "Good," instead of giving details she knew her best friend would've loved.

Though once she thought about it, Erin realized lately Rachel hadn't been as pushy when it came to her love life. The thought gnawed at her while Rachel talked about her trip to Greece at the beginning of the summer.

Erin expressed the appropriate amount of enthusiasm and interest in Rachel's Greek Isles itinerary, and then blurted out: "You haven't tried to get me to go on any double dates or some other ridiculous thing lately."

"I know you're busy getting everything ready for the clinic." Rachel went with the subject change like it was normal conversation instead of a non sequitur. "Plus, you've got your sexting friend, right?"

Erin blinked at her.

"Do you not?"

It was the first week of April. Erin had told Rachel about the sexting exactly once, and it was right after it first happened. On Valentine's Day.

"How'd you know we were still . . ." She trailed off rather than trying to find a word for whatever was happening between her and Cassie.

"No one smiles at their phone as much as you do if they're not sexting someone."

Erin stared at her. "I know you said you do it at the grocery store or whatever, but we've never sexted while I was *with you*."

Rachel waved a hand like it didn't really matter. "You know what I mean," she said, but Erin didn't.

She hadn't realized she smiled at her phone that often.

"You seem happy lately, is all."

Erin felt her cheeks heat. She tried for nonchalance. "Do I?"

"I like the way it looks on you," Rachel said quietly.

They were having a moment—two friends who had known each other since college, sitting in a coffee shop a decade and a half later, talking about happiness.

"Plus," Rachel said, "last week you were practically glowing. Either you changed your skin care routine, or you got railed."

Ah. Moment over.

At least Rachel didn't mine for more info about Erin's sexting friend. She was relentless when she wanted details, but she also seemed to have a sixth sense for when Erin needed to be let off the hook.

Before the divorce was final, after Adam had moved out, Erin had thrown out her back rearranging furniture. It had been awful— she couldn't stand up or sit down or twist her body without pain shooting up and down her spine. When Rachel came over to check on her, Erin was flat on the floor; her bed was too soft. Rachel, God love her, hadn't asked anything about why Erin decided she *had* to rearrange the furniture right then, by herself. She also had hydrocodone.

Erin remembered when the drugs kicked in. It hadn't so much been that she couldn't feel the pain—the pain was still there, obvious, like a brick, but it hadn't actually *hurt*. Everything felt smooth. She and Rachel ordered pizza, and Erin opened the door and paid the delivery guy and carried the box to the kitchen, all without crying out. She could do anything she wanted, even though her body still knew something was off.

That was what being around Cassie was like. The knowledge that she shouldn't, that it was wrong, that it was a *terrible* idea, was all there. But Erin felt good anyway. She could be fucking everything up, but she felt good anyway.

The next Sunday, on their weekly call, Parker said, "Cassie got this job in Boston."

This was bound to happen sometime: Parker mentioning something Erin had already heard from Cassie. Erin tried to act appropriately unaware. "Did she?"

"Yeah. Some engineering thing, obviously. Apparently it's a big deal."

"Well, that's great for her."

"Yeah. And you know, like, Boston is pretty close. We've been talking about her visiting Nashua on weekends and stuff."

"Of course she can come visit," Erin said. She had no idea how she'd handle being under the same roof as both Parker and Cassie again. "But you don't even know where you'll be this summer yet, do you? Or have you found something?"

The line was quiet. Erin silently cursed herself. She didn't know what she'd done wrong but she must've done something. She'd treaded so carefully around Parker since that first Sunday she hadn't called. Their conversations had been stunted for a while, now, but it had been getting better. Parker hadn't gone quiet and surly on her since they'd finally talked about the divorce. Clearly Erin had messed up, somehow, because her brain had time to anxiety spiral before Parker finally responded.

"I was thinking of, maybe, like, just staying at home this summer."

"Yeah?"

"Yeah. Like, I know I'm supposed to do *something*, but I did stuff every summer of high school, right? Stuff to look good on college applications. So I know I should be preparing for whatever I want to do after college—grad school or a job or whatever. But I don't know what I want to do yet. And school's been kicking my butt. And I kind of just want to . . . relax."

"That sounds like a great idea."

"Really?"

"Yeah. You don't have to have everything figured out right now."

"Oh. Okay."

Again, Erin felt like she'd done something wrong. "Is that not what you wanted me to say?"

"I just thought—you're usually the one pushing me to live up to my potential or whatever. I figured you'd want me to find an internship or go to art camp or something."

"Well, yes, I know you can succeed at whatever you put your mind to," Erin said delicately. "But you're the one who gets to decide what that is. And you also have to make time to have fun. You're allowed to be a kid for a while."

Parker didn't say it, but Erin could tell she was surprised. Rather than let her mind spiral again, Erin joked: "If you don't get a job, though, I'm definitely making you mow the lawn every week."

"Ugh, that might be worse than having to get a job," Parker said with a giggle that made Erin's heart grow three sizes.

Twenty-One

CASSIE

Parker [Today 3:38 PM]
What are you doing tonight? There's a party at the baseball
house

Cassie stared at her phone. After the a cappella concert, the
group chat had been resurrected. Cassie sent her favorite of the pictures they'd taken at the after-party, then Acacia had sent pictures
of her and Parker in Chicago over spring break. Cassie had tried
to keep up the conversation, which mostly meant sending memes.
Occasionally Parker would send "lol" in the group text, or even a
meme of her own.

The last time Cassie had gotten a text solely from Parker to her
was more than a month ago.

She had no plans for the night, but even if she did, she wasn't
going to turn Parker down.

Cassie [3:40 PM]
Sounds cool

She considered asking who was going, just for something else to
say, but she didn't want Parker to think she'd only go if other people

would be there. Her thumbs hovered over her screen, her brain never quite figuring out what to type.

Parker [3:42 PM]
I'm going out to dinner so I was gonna meet Kaysh there. You should walk over with her.

Cassie [3:43 PM]
Awesome, I'll see you there

Parker [3:43 PM]
And it's the baseball house, so there'll probably be free jungle juice

Cassie [3:44 PM]
I'd expect nothing less

Parties at the baseball house tended to get out of hand, and when Cassie and Acacia walked up, it was already loud enough they were sure to get a noise complaint. Parker met them inside, Sam and Gwen in tow, and handed them red Solo cups before even saying hi.

Free jungle juice or not, Cassie should've pregamed. Greased the wheels of social interaction. It had helped at the a cappella party. How drunk did they have to get before that easy friendship came back fully?

Before it got too awkward, Parker suggested dancing, and Acacia was never going to say no to that. If it had been anything else, Cassie wouldn't have said no to Parker, but as it was, she and Gwen begged off. The other three disappeared into the crowd, cups still in hand.

Cassie sipped her jungle juice. It didn't taste like there was alcohol in it, which probably meant she'd be hungover as hell tomorrow.

"Don't get too drunk," Gwen said.

Cassie rolled her eyes. It was the first time they interacted properly since Gwen literally called someone to come take care of drunk Cassie—of course she'd be patronizing about Cassie's intoxication level. "I'm fine, thanks."

"I know. I just want you to have good motor control later."

Cassie slid a glance at Gwen. "What?"

"When I take you home later," Gwen said. "I want you to have good motor control."

Cassie gaped at her. Gwen was so complete in her confidence, she wasn't even looking at Cassie, wasn't even smirking. She was calm, straightforward, certain. Cassie took a gulp of her jungle juice.

"Last time I hit on you, you called a friend to pick me up," she said.

Gwen shrugged. "Last time you were desperate. You don't look desperate now. You look hot."

Cassie *was* desperate last time. Desperate to stop thinking about Erin, even if she hadn't recognized it then. Desperate to have sex with someone else, to have a new memory to warm her on cold nights. Now, she was pretty happy with her memories—of Erin in the shower and the kitchen and her bedroom. Erin pushing her up against a building because she needed it fast, and then taking her time in the hotel.

Now, Cassie didn't know if Gwen was worth the trouble.

"What if I've changed my mind since last time?"

Gwen peered at her. "Why would you change your mind?"

Cassie ran a hand through her hair. She looked at the dance floor, at the throng of bodies. She could see Parker, glancing over at them and quickly away. Cassie looked at Gwen, who was as hot as she'd always been, then back at Parker, who'd texted her for the first time in more than a month for this party, who was dancing with Gwen's—best friend, maybe? Cousin? Cassie wasn't sure what their background was.

"Are you dating someone?" Gwen asked.

"No," Cassie said slowly. She thought of Erin. They weren't dating, obviously, but the idea of going home with Gwen not even two weeks after she and Erin had spent an entire night, well, worshipping each other's bodies, basically—it didn't feel right. "Not really."

Gwen raised an eyebrow. "Not really?"

"I'm not dating anyone," Cassie said. "But I don't want to go home with you."

Now Gwen did smirk. "I don't believe you."

Cassie wasn't sure she believed herself. She'd wanted to hook up with Gwen since before she'd met Seth, and now that she finally had the chance, she was turning her down? It didn't make sense, except for how she couldn't stop thinking about Parker texting her for the first time in so long. Cassie couldn't go home with Gwen the first time Parker reached out to her again.

"I'm not going home with you."

"That's not the part I didn't believe," Gwen said, and walked away.

Not the part—? Cassie rolled her eyes. Gwen didn't believe she wasn't dating anyone? Who was she—Acacia? As though dating someone else was the only reason someone wouldn't want to fuck Gwen? Erin had nothing to do with this—Cassie was trying to be Parker's friend, and given that they'd fought over "fucking whoever the hell you feel like," sleeping with Gwen would be a terrible idea.

At the end of the night, Gwen was the only one sober enough to drive, but she'd found someone else to entertain her, so the other four walked back to campus together. Parker draped an arm over Sam and an arm over Cassie. She was practically dead weight, but Cassie didn't complain.

"This was fun," Parker said between them. "You guys aren't all bad."

Acacia and Sam rolled their eyes at her, but it might've been the nicest thing she'd said to Cassie in months.

• • • •

Thursdays always felt aimless—Cassie had class in the morning but her entire day was free after ten. She went to the grocery store to be productive, but then wandered the aisles, unsure what she wanted to buy.

It was Erin's day off—Cassie had gotten a picture that morning of Erin's hair spilling across her pillow as she lounged in bed. Cassie stared at sixteen different kinds of rice and texted her.

Cassie [Today 1:41 PM]
What are you doing?

Erin [1:43 PM]
This is way too early for a booty call Cassie

Cassie [1:43 PM]
😔 I just wanted to make sure I wouldn't wake you up on your day off

Before Erin could ask what that meant, Cassie was calling.

"Don't tell me you came to Boston without telling me again," Erin said as she picked up.

"No, I'm just bored."

"So what? I'm supposed to entertain you?"

"You're supposed to tell me what to make for dinner—I'm grocery shopping but all I want to buy is chocolate ice cream."

"You gotta get at least one vegetable, Cassie."

"Yeah, so it can go bad in my vegetable drawer and I can throw it out later?"

She meandered to the next aisle, full of baking supplies she absolutely did not need. She walked down it.

"What if you bought vegetables but then immediately used them to make stir-fry for dinner?"

Cassie pretended to be considering it, but she was already heading for the produce section. "That doesn't sound terrible."

"Get peppers and sweet peas," Erin said. "And carrots if you don't have any rotting in your vegetable drawer."

"I know how to make stir-fry, babe."

"You're the one who called me," Erin teased.

Cassie did take her advice when it came to the sauce, though. Erin talked through the recipe as Cassie filled her cart.

"God, now I'm going to have to make stir-fry tonight," Erin said. "I've talked it up so much it sounds delicious."

"It better be," Cassie said. She chose a self-checkout lane. "You better not have given me a recipe for a not delicious stir-fry."

"Well, you know, it all depends on the cook. I can't be blamed if yours isn't as good as mine."

"Oh my God, why do I even like you?"

Erin laughed and Cassie grinned wide enough to hurt.

They kept talking all through checkout and the bus ride back to campus. Cassie updated Erin about her classes and projects, bragged that she'd caught Professor Upton looking at her with this ridiculous Proud Dad face like three times since she'd told him about the job.

Erin talked about her patients—vaguely, HIPAA regulations and all—and Cassie decided she was too hungry to bother putting the groceries away. She wedged her phone between her shoulder and her ear and started cutting up peppers.

She almost dropped her phone, then almost sliced her thumb open, before she finally interrupted.

"Erin, hey, I'm sorry," she said. "I want to hear the rest of your story but let's switch to FaceTime so I have both hands to cook with."

She could have just put it on speakerphone, but maybe she wanted to see Erin's face. Sue her.

"I'll call you back."

Erin hung up and immediately FaceTimed.

"Hey," Cassie said, grinning.

"Hey." Getting to see Erin's smile was way better than hearing it in her voice.

"Okay, so you're going for a consult . . . ," Cassie reminded her, and Erin picked up where she left off.

Erin also started making dinner as they talked. Cassie critiqued her knife skills and Erin laughed at her. It'd been barely two weeks since they last saw each other, but Cassie loved this—sharing their time even if they couldn't share their space.

As they sat down to eat—Cassie on her couch and Erin at the kitchen island—Erin asked, "Got any weekend plans?"

"Nah," Cassie said. "It's the a cappella retreat, so Parker's gonna be gone all weekend." She realized what she was saying as it came out of her mouth. They'd never talked directly about Parker. "You probably know that. Anyway."

Worse than mentioning Parker—Cassie had been going to *complain*. Since Parker was gone, it meant Cassie would have Acacia all weekend without having to worry if she'd ditch her for Parker. Not that Kaysh had done that, but she was definitely amorphously *busy* more often since Cassie and Parker had been fighting. Even if they had been getting along better since the concert before spring break. Parker had even seemed excited at the idea of Cassie visiting from Boston over the summer. Mildly excited, but still.

Cassie tried to push through her awkwardness. "Acacia and I will probably be pretty chill, not get into too much trouble."

"Are you saying Parker is the troublemaker of the group?" Erin was focused on her food, not on Cassie on her phone screen.

"Kaysh and I have been getting ourselves into trouble since we were kids," Cassie said. "I'm pretty sure we're the bad influence on Parker, not the other way around."

"I'm sure Parker causes trouble all on her own," Erin said. "I like to think I'm not a completely oblivious parent, though I'll admit I'd probably rather not know a lot of what she gets into."

Cassie took the opportunity to shift the topic. "What kind of trouble did you get into in school?"

Erin looked at her. Cassie grinned, and she could tell Erin was fighting a smile and then, "Well, there was this one time . . ."

The weekend was chill, like Cassie had expected, but Acacia said that Parker came back from the retreat grouchier than usual. It took till Wednesday for Kaysh to find out why.

Acacia [9:48 PM]
Fuck. She and Sam broke up

Cassie [9:49 PM]
Fuck

When Acacia and Cassie had breakfast Friday morning, Kaysh looked tired.

"She's not handling it well," she said. "You know how she puts responsibility for everything on herself."

Cassie could only imagine. She pushed scrambled eggs around on her plate.

"And, babe, Donovan is taking me away for the weekend," Acacia said. "You have to stay with her."

Cassie stared at her. "What?"

"I wouldn't leave her alone, but Donovan planned this like a month and a half ago," Kaysh said. "I need you to stay with her this weekend."

"She doesn't even like me that much lately," Cassie said.

"Well, she likes herself even less right now. You'll make her feel better. Even if she doesn't think that's what you're doing."

Cassie didn't believe that. But she couldn't say no to her best friend. "Okay."

"Promise me," Acacia said.

"I promise."

• • • •

She wasn't alone with Parker for half an hour before Parker was yelling at her to leave.

"Get out, Cassie! I don't want you here!"

Cassie considered it for half a second, but no. "I don't care if you want me here or not, princess," she said. "I told Acacia I'd be here and I'm going to fucking be here. All weekend."

"I don't give a fuck what you told Acacia—"

"Well, you should," Cassie said. "Because she's my best friend. And you're my best friend. And I'm not leaving you alone while you're sad."

Parker actually looked shocked, and it broke Cassie's heart. She seemed surprised that Cassie hadn't just given up on their friendship. Cassie kind of wanted to punch her, kind of wanted to hug her.

"I love you, you idiot," Cassie said. "I'm staying here. We can talk or watch Disney movies or get drunk or snuggle or anything you want, but I'm staying here."

Parker swallowed. Cassie refused to break eye contact.

"I have homework to do," Parker said, like that was as close to accepting Cassie's attempt at comfort as she could get.

"Great," Cassie said. "I brought my books."

They worked in silence for a good hour, Parker at her desk and Cassie sprawled across Acacia's bed. Eventually Parker flipped her book closed and looked over at Cassie. Her face was wary even as she extended the olive branch.

"I'm on season two of *Scandal,* if you want to watch with me?"

"Yeah," Cassie said immediately. "Yeah definitely."

They were two episodes in when Parker talked in the time between one episode ending and the next beginning.

"I'm sorry I said that thing about you not knowing how to be vulnerable."

"What?"

"That night." Parker's voice was quiet. "I'm sorry I said you didn't know how to be in a relationship."

Cassie was glad they were both focused on Parker's computer, no eye contact necessary.

"You weren't necessarily wrong," she said. "I'm sort of an idiot when it comes to that kind of stuff. Sure had no idea about Seth, right?"

"That wasn't your fault," Parker said.

"It wasn't yours, either."

They fell silent. Cassie thought the moment was over, but then:

"Why didn't you sleep with Gwen?"

"What?"

The next episode was starting, but Parker kept talking. "I saw her hitting on you. I know you think she's hot."

Cassie forced herself not to shift uncomfortably. She kept her eyes glued on the screen.

"I don't automatically sleep with someone just because I think they're hot," Cassie said. It felt too heavy, too much like how this whole thing got started, and so she added, "I mean, I haven't slept with you, have I?"

It made Parker chuckle and push her shoulder into Cassie's, which made Cassie a little braver. She talked over Fitz, who was saying something dumb on the computer.

"I didn't want to sleep with Gwen because I didn't want to mess things up with you," she admitted.

Parker burrowed a little farther under the blankets. Finally, after a long silence, she looped her arm through Cassie's, and Cassie breathed.

"Fitz is really stupid," Parker said.

"Yeah. This show would be infinitely better if it were just Mellie and Olivia being awesome together."

"For sure."

• • • •

They fell into friendship again easier than Cassie expected. After so long with minimal contact, they were back to seeing each other every day: breakfast in the caf, waiting for each other after classes, studying together in the library. It was great, even if it hurt Cassie to realize Parker had never really been "too busy." But she'd rather enjoy what she had now than pout about what happened in the past. They never mentioned it, except once, when Cassie was making Parker crack up with an impression of Professor Crane.

Parker clutched her stomach and said, "You're an asshole, but I missed you."

Acacia grinned. Cassie really didn't care what happened before; she was just glad to have her best friends back.

• • • •

Parker and Cassie were supposed to be studying on the couch in Cassie's apartment, but Cassie was on craigslist and she could see Parker was on Facebook, so she didn't feel bad interrupting.

"How much do you know about neighborhoods in Boston?"

Parker shrugged. "A bit."

"Look at this apartment I found."

Parker leaned into Cassie's side as Cassie clicked through the pictures.

"Do you know if this is a good neighborhood?"

Parker leaned away, back to her own computer. "I really don't know," she said. "You should ask my mom. She knows Boston better than I do."

Cassie looked sharply at Parker, who wasn't paying her any attention. "I should ask your mom?"

"Yeah," Parker said. "She's in the city all the time for patient stuff. Just text her."

Cassie swallowed. Wished Acacia were there. "Just text your mom out of the blue about Boston neighborhoods?"

Parker shrugged. "You have her number, right? Just text her or call her. She likes you enough she'd probably even go take a look at the apartment to make sure the photos aren't bullshit or whatever."

"Right." Cassie picked at her fingernails. "That'd be pretty sweet, actually."

It seemed crazy that Erin might go look at apartments for her. Crazier still that Parker had suggested it. Cassie brought it up on the phone with Erin a few days later anyway.

"So, uh, Parker told me to ask you about Boston neighborhoods." Erin *hmm*ed. "Did she?"

"Yeah." Cassie cleared her throat. "Said you liked me enough to go look at apartments for me?"

"I don't know if I like you *that* much."

Cassie tried to backtrack. "Right, of course, I mean, that's a lot and—"

Erin laughed. "Cassie. Of course I like you enough to look at apartments for you. I don't want you living in squalor."

Cassie's pulse tried to get back to normal. "Right," she said again. Erin was just kidding. They were friends. It still seemed like a lot though. "I have it narrowed down to a couple. Just like—if you could, check them out, maybe?"

Erin's voice was soft. "I'd love to, babe."

• • • •

Acacia walked into her dorm without knocking one Thursday afternoon, announcing, "I'm bored and hungry and if I have to eat another meal at the caf, I'm gonna die. Let's go to Sonic tonight."

With the nearest Sonic almost forty minutes away, going there was always an adventure, one Cassie would normally be all for.

"I can't tonight," she said. "Erin and I are making dinner together."

She didn't think she'd said anything unusual, but Acacia was staring at her.

"What?" Cassie said.

"You're making dinner with Erin? Is she somehow visiting without me or Parker knowing about it?"

"Oh, no," Cassie said. "We're gonna FaceTime and cook together."

"And you think that is normal?"

Cassie rolled her eyes. "She looked at one of the apartments today and is gonna tell me what she thinks."

"God, could you be dating any harder?"

Acacia did this to her like once a week, she swore.

"We're not dating, Kaysh."

"I literally don't understand how you think you're not."

"Because we aren't, and neither of us want to," Cassie said.

"Have you even fucked anyone except Erin since Seth?" Acacia asked.

"Of course I have," Cassie scoffed.

There were plenty of weekends right after Seth where she'd gone home with people. When she thought about it, though—there had been other people since Seth, yes, but since Erin? Since that first night in the bar at Family Weekend? She'd made out with Emerson and tried to feel Gwen up at a party. That was it. She couldn't quite believe it, but that was it.

She didn't like thinking about it, and she didn't like the look Acacia gave her, so she pushed back.

"Even if I did want to date her, how would that work? How would I date my friend's mom who lives in New Hampshire?"

"Oh, I don't know," Acacia said, faux confused. "Probably you'd text her every day and cook dinner together on FaceTime and get a job in Boston to spend time—"

"That's low," Cassie interrupted. "I got the job because it's fucking great. It has nothing to do with Erin."

Acacia's shoulders slumped. "I know, you're right. I'm sorry. But I'm just saying that it's possible—"

"It doesn't matter that it's possible; I don't want to date Parker's mom."

Her stomach twisted. This whole conversation made her uncomfortable. She didn't want to date Erin. She didn't want to date anyone.

"Being aromantic is a thing, you know?" Cassie said.

Acacia glared at her. "Don't commandeer a real identity just because you're afraid of getting hurt."

Cassie decided maybe she wouldn't talk to Acacia about Erin anymore.

• • • •

She did actually manage to avoid talking to Kaysh about Erin. Busy buckling down for finals and arrangements for the summer, they didn't have time for lectures on feelings.

Erin helped her land an apartment that Cassie had no idea how she was going to fill with stuff. It wasn't even a studio. But that was the only bad thing about the place. She'd be able to walk to work, plus the apartment came with a parking spot for when she bought a motorbike once she settled in—she needed something to get her up to Nashua on weekends to hang out with Parker. Among other things.

With only a few weeks of her college career left, Cassie lay spread across the floor of Parker and Acacia's dorm. There were so many things she should've been doing. She closed her eyes instead.

"When are you done with school stuff?" Parker asked.

"Graduation is Sunday, even though I technically still have my calc exam Monday and neurobio Tuesday," Cassie said. "I don't even know if I'm gonna walk."

"Why would you not walk?" Cassie's eyes were still closed, but Parker suddenly sounded like she was paying more attention.

"Who wants to sweat in one of those robes while professors drone on about how we're gonna change the world?" She shrugged. "Though Upton will probably be pissed if I skip it."

"*I'll* be pissed if you skip it, Klein," Acacia said. "I already bought the air horn."

Cassie looked at her best friend, who was studying on the futon, her laptop and textbook open in front of her. "Kaysh, I'm like 90 percent sure air horns are not allowed."

Acacia raised her eyebrows, unimpressed.

"Surely your family's coming, though, right?" Parker asked Acacia.

"My parents are going to a wedding that weekend, and Emerson can't afford it."

It was fine, obviously, that they couldn't come. Cassie had never even asked them. When they had asked about graduation week-end so they could plan their schedule, she'd asked why. She hadn't expected them to come, so it didn't matter that they couldn't. It would've been fun, sure, but no big deal.

"You're absolutely walking, though," Acacia was still talking. "Because *we're* still gonna come."

Cassie scowled. "You're really gonna make me put on that stupid gown just to walk across a stage and get handed something that doesn't even have my diploma in it because I won't officially have passed all my classes yet?"

"Yeah. You're gonna put on the gown, and take pictures, and deal with us making a goddamn fuss about you because graduating from college is a big fucking deal."

Cassie could acknowledge that, if she thought about it rationally.

Objectively. It just felt weird, celebrating something that was only step one in her plan. Couldn't go to grad school if you didn't graduate college first.

Grad school. That was how she'd been thinking about it lately, instead of *Caltech*. She'd *always* called it Caltech. Fake it till you make it or speaking it into existence or something. She'd just . . . never thought she'd go anywhere else.

Now, though, she had acceptance letters from every school she'd applied to. Caltech's came in last week. She still hadn't told anyone.

She didn't have to tell Caltech yes until August. It felt . . . safer, maybe? To wait. She didn't know what her job was going to be like over the summer. What if she realized what she wanted her specialty to be, and Caltech wasn't the best for it?

"Can't we just, like, get brunch and go bouldering or something?" Cassie didn't even like bouldering that much, but she had to tempt Acacia with something.

"We can do those things *and* you can walk."

"Okay, whatever, we can fight about this later," Parker cut in. "I was just asking because my mom was wondering when we were arriving."

Cassie squinted at her. "What?"

"Is neurobio your last exam? Are you done Tuesday?"

"Yes," she dragged out the word, not sure what Parker was plotting.

"I don't finish until Wednesday. You wanna leave Friday?"

"What?"

Parker sighed like Cassie was being insufferable. "When do you want to drive to Nashua? We can do it in a day. It'll be long, but we could make it by dinner."

"No offense, princess, but what the hell are you talking about? Driving to Nashua?"

"Do you have another way you want to get there?"

"I didn't know I was going."

Parker rolled her eyes. "What—you thought you'd fly to Boston and set up your apartment by yourself?"

Well. Yeah. That was one of the many things Cassie was supposed to be doing instead of lying on the floor. She had an alert set for ticket prices. She figured she would have to empty her pockets for a plane ticket, plus luggage fees, packing everything she owned.

"That's what I thought." Parker smirked, not unkindly. "So, you wanna leave Friday? Give ourselves Thursday to get through our hangovers?"

A month and a half ago, Parker was barely speaking to her. Cassie still didn't understand exactly what had happened, but she was so glad they were friends again.

"You really think you can survive with me in an enclosed space for, what? Nine hours?"

"Ten," Parker said matter-of-factly. "And yeah, I'll manage."

• • • •

For graduation, Parker had handled the brunch reservations. It was at Marco's, Cassie's favorite restaurant—the same one she and Parker had gone to with Erin over Family Weekend. That didn't make it weird; they'd been there since, more than once, without Erin.

Parker and Acacia were doing a great job of making a big deal out of graduation, but it fell flat. Cassie still didn't know where she was going for grad school. She wanted to talk it out, but didn't know how. Everyone knew Caltech was where Cassie had wanted to go forever. She didn't want people to think she was getting cold feet because she didn't feel smart enough, or something. Erin was the person Cassie had talked stuff out with lately, but she couldn't this time. Her stomach tied itself into knots considering it. Erin might think Cassie's hesitance about Caltech was about *her,* and that'd be embarrassing. But going to Marco's made Cassie think about that breakfast over Family Weekend. It made Cassie nostalgic, or sentimental, or something. It made her wish Erin could've come for graduation.

Marco's was packed when they arrived, as expected.

"Table for," the hostess paused with a smile, "three."

Parker grinned. "That's us."

"Follow me, please."

Cassie had been going to ask for a kid's menu—for the coloring page and tic-tac-toe game, not the food—but the hostess didn't pick up menus or silverware before turning and leading them deeper into the restaurant. Maybe they had started leaving them on the table instead. But as they weaved through the crowded restaurant, Cassie couldn't see a single open table. It was fully packed. She didn't even know where the hostess was leading them, because unless there was a hidden room, every table had people at it.

"Here you are," the hostess said, stopping at yet another table with people sitting around it.

Except—

Cassie blinked. "What the hell?"

Everyone burst out laughing. Everyone being Parker and Acacia, yeah, but also Emerson and Mama Webb and Mr. Ben. Who were all sitting in Marco's.

"What is happening?"

Mama Webb stood and wrapped her arms around Cassie, who inhaled, even as Mama squeezed her hard enough she could barely breathe. She smelled like home. "I cannot believe you actually thought we were going to let you graduate without us."

"Honestly, Cass," Emerson said, next in line for a hug, but Mama Webb wasn't letting go quite yet. His shaved head matched Acacia's, though he was about a foot taller.

"For someone who's gonna be a rocket scientist, you're pretty dumb."

"I hate you," Cassie said.

She would've, maybe, except he didn't even comment on how her eyes were filled with tears. Mr. Ben didn't, either.

"Hey, baby girl," he said instead, and maybe the tears weren't just in Cassie's eyes so much as running down her cheeks as the closest man she'd ever had to a father held her gently.

They came to watch her graduate. Her *family*. Came to celebrate her. Cassie hadn't even realized it mattered to her. It didn't maybe, not graduation itself. But the Webbs did. She still didn't care about walking across that stage, but knowing these people were gonna be cheering for her? Yeah, that mattered.

• • • •

When Cassie walked across the stage set up on Keckley's football field, Acacia made good use of the air horn. Cassie grinned wide, and didn't even mind that she was sweating bullets in that godforsaken robe. After, she allowed a full half hour of pictures—with Mama Webb and Mr. Ben, with Emerson and Acacia, with all the Webbs together, with just Kaysh and Parker, smiling, laughing, Emerson stealing her cap to wear himself—before insisting she needed to shower and change.

She emerged from the shower to texts from Erin.

Erin [Today 1:27 PM]
Happy graduation day, babe. I'm so proud of you

Erin [1:28 PM]
I also might have gone a little overboard with the graduation present

The next message was a picture of what looked like a brand-new Yamaha MT-03, all black and metallic gray with bright red rims, parked in front of the garage of Erin's Nashua home.

Cassie's fingers flew over her screen to pull up Erin's number, call her, then put the phone on speaker so she could keep looking at the bike.

"Babe! Happy graduation!"

Cassie didn't even let herself enjoy the joy in Erin's voice. "Erin, are you fucking serious? You bought me a bike?"

The words came out with about five question marks after them. Cassie just couldn't believe it. Obviously Erin was rich, but—this was a multi-thousand-dollar present.

Erin was significantly quieter when she responded than when she'd picked up the phone. "Is that too much?"

It was, but how the hell could Cassie say no?

"Parker said it was a lot," Erin kept talking, "but I told her graduating was a lot, and I bet she wouldn't be so skeptical when she was the one getting the graduation gift. I just—I wanted to get you something you needed, and it was basically this or a couch for your new place, and it's not a big deal to get a used couch but I didn't want you on some old motorcycle that was gonna fall apart on you. You don't have to—"

"I fucking love it."

Erin exhaled over the phone. "Yeah?"

"Yeah." Cassie had told the others she'd be quick so they could get a late lunch, and here she was dripping all over her bathroom, naked and staring at the picture on her phone. "I know I can't do it right away because I'm coming up with Parker, but Jesus Christ, I'm gonna fuck you on that bike as soon as fucking possible."

Erin giggled, and it was about the sexiest sound Cassie had ever heard.

"I'm serious," she said. "First I'm gonna finger you on it in your garage, then we're gonna take back roads and I'm gonna sit behind you and talk you into another orgasm while you grind on the seat, the engine making it vibrate right against your clit."

"Jesus, Cassie," Erin muttered. "A simple thank-you would suffice."

Cassie had half a mind to talk her through one right then and there, but her phone buzzed with a text from Acacia telling her to hurry up.

"I gotta go," she said. "But a couple orgasms is a good way to say thank you. And I'm giving them to you as soon as I get the chance, deal?"

"Deal," Erin said. "Congrats on graduating."

Right. Graduating. The reason Erin got the bike to begin with seemed far less important than fucking her on it.

Cassie stayed distracted for the rest of the day with the Webbs, for the rest of her last week at Keckley. She was still trying not to daydream about it as Acacia hugged her tightly at 6 A.M. in the parking lot in front of her dorm, Parker's car loaded up with all their stuff.

"Take care of yourself, okay?" Kaysh said.

Cassie hugged her again.

"Stop getting all sappy," Parker said, adjusting the suitcases in the trunk. "You're gonna come visit us in July."

"Shut it, Bennett," Acacia said and hugged her, too.

A ten-hour road trip with your best friend was a damn good time, even if you were sleeping with that friend's mom on the side. They took shifts driving, rocked out to music, and stopped for lunch at this diner with the best pie Cassie had ever had. After, Parker slept off her food coma while Cassie drove, and they made it to Nashua in time for a late dinner.

The bike was in the garage, and Cassie swore she got wet just looking at it.

She had to wait a whole twenty minutes before she got a chance to kiss Erin. It wasn't near as long a kiss as she'd like, but Parker was only taking their suitcases upstairs. Cassie was staying a couple nights until the weekend, when they'd help her move into her apartment.

Parker came back downstairs, and Erin served them dinner and grinned at Cassie over her wineglass.

This was gonna be the best summer ever.

Twenty-Two

ERIN

When Erin heard the front door open, she turned down the corner of the page she was on, her face already breaking into a smile.

"Parker?" she called, though it was much too early for her daughter to be home from Adam's. "Is that you?"

There was no response. Erin could picture the scene in the foyer: Cassie toeing out of her sneakers, hanging her motorcycle jacket over the coat rack and her keys on the hook next to the spare key to her apartment. Cassie didn't always arrive this early on Saturday mornings, but after the Fridays that Parker spent at Adam's? Yeah, she was always here before ten.

"Is she not home yet?" Cassie's voice came into the living room before she did.

She stood at the edge of the room, hands on her hips. Erin had imagined her entry wrong—she still had her jacket on. It made her look bigger. Tough. Erin's smile grew.

"You know she won't be here before noon."

"Hmm," Cassie said, coming closer. "Whatever will we do with ourselves with all this time we have?"

"I don't know what I'll do with myself." Erin got up off the couch and met Cassie halfway. She slid her hands under that jacket. "I've got some ideas about what to do with you, though."

She and Cassie were dressed and in the kitchen by the time Parker arrived.

"Cassie's here!" Parker shouted as soon as she opened the front door.

"Yeah, 'cause you slept so late, princess," Cassie said. "It's almost one!"

Parker barreled into the kitchen and hugged her, paying no mind to her teasing.

Erin didn't look up from the wraps she was making.

Seeing Cassie and Parker together was always—"bittersweet" wasn't quite the right word, but something like that. Erin loved seeing two of her favorite people happy, but being reminded that her daughter's friend was one of those people—for decidedly not friendship-based reasons—bitter was definitely the right word for that. Acacia was coming to visit for the Fourth, and Erin was absolutely not looking forward to it. She didn't know how much Acacia knew—she and Cassie had never discussed it after the New Year's Eve mishap. The idea of someone who knew, someone who might notice the way Cassie looked at her sometimes, the sly smiles and knowing glances they sent each other—it grated on Erin's nerves.

She did have to admit there was a thrill in being near Cassie with people around, though. After lunch, some of Parker's hometown friends arrived, saying hello on their way to Erin's pool. It was how they spent most weekends, and sometimes weekdays, too.

Cassie was on her back on a pool float when Erin came out of the house in the suit Rachel had made her buy when they went to the Bahamas together. It wasn't *inappropriate*, but she could feel Cassie's eyes on her, even though they were hidden behind sunglasses. The bottoms were black, plain, full coverage. The mismatched top was white, triangles and string ties and admittedly some side boob.

"I hope you don't mind if I share some of the sunshine with you guys," Erin said.

"Of course, Dr. Bennett," Caleb said.

"Caleb, I'm kicking you out of my backyard if you call me Dr. Bennett one more time."

"Aren't you used to how chronically over-polite he is yet?" Parker asked. "Anyway, that lounge is open." She gestured to the chair next to the one where Cassie's stuff was.

It wasn't the lounge chair Erin had planned to take. There were three open—Lila's stuff on one while Parker, Caleb, and Madison sat at the table playing a complicated card game Erin had never had the patience to learn. Walking past an open lounge chair to take the one next to Cassie's would've been too obvious had Parker not suggested it. But given the excuse, Erin was glad to stretch out beside Cassie's chair. Unsurprisingly, Cassie was soon out of the pool.

She "accidentally" dripped water on Erin's bare legs before flopping down next to her. Cassie's sunglasses were still on, but she couldn't hide the way her tongue darted out to lick her lips.

"What's up, doc?"

Erin rolled her eyes. Hard. "Never say that again, Cassie."

Cassie laughed and relaxed on her chair.

Erin wished she'd worn sunglasses herself, so she could drink her fill of Cassie. Her high-waisted bottoms and bandeau top matched, both bright red with white polka dots. She looked so . . . *wholesome,* and yet Erin couldn't stop thinking about riding her face.

Caleb, Lila, and Madison filtered out eventually, sun kissed and damp from the pool as they made their way home for dinner. Erin sat up, swung her legs to the side of her lounge chair, and stretched. She did not look at Cassie, who was being too obvious now that her sunglasses were sitting on top of her head.

"What do you want for dinner?" she asked.

"Burgers," Parker said without lifting her head from the next lounge chair.

"I'll have to go to the store and get buns," Erin said. "Do you want anything else?"

At that, Parker sat up. "I can go."

"You don't have to."

"No, I will," Parker said. "You're cooking. I can pick up buns."

Erin eyed her. "Who are you and what have you done with my daughter?"

"I'm growing up," Parker said. "You raised me well. Good job."

"I suppose I won't argue with that. You can grab a twenty from my wallet."

Parker got up and pulled her cover-up over her head. Erin and Cassie stayed put.

"We need anything other than buns?"

"Sweet tea," Cassie said.

"Pretty sure they don't sell the good stuff in New Hampshire, babe," Parker said.

"Ugh. This state is useless."

Erin pushed at Cassie's chair with her bare foot. "I'll see if I can't scrounge up some homemade stuff for the next time you come."

"Parker, your mom is better than you. She offers solutions."

Erin didn't have to look at Parker to know she was rolling her eyes.

"Text if you need anything," Parker said, and left.

It was like Pavlov's dog. The moment she was alone with Cassie, Erin was ready. Cassie, on the other hand, stayed completely still. She didn't even turn her head. Parker's car started on the other side of the house. The tires crunched down the driveway.

Then Cassie was up, pulling Erin out of her chair.

"Thank God," she said, slipping her hands around Erin's bare waist. "Were you trying to torture me all day?"

Erin laughed and let Cassie's hands wander. "What do you mean?"

"You're in a bikini, Erin." Cassie dropped a kiss on her shoulder. "I thought I would never get to touch you."

"You touched me this morning."

"And then you came out here in a bikini and I wanted to touch you again." She was already tugging at the knot in Erin's halter top.

"The store isn't very far away," Erin said.

"Better get you out of this quick, then."

She didn't really get Erin out of the suit, just untied the top and then got her hand inside the bottom. It was indeed quick—Erin was already wet; she'd been thinking about this just as much as Cassie.

Parker took a long time at the store. Cassie and Erin changed out of their suits and had the burgers on the grill by the time she got back.

Cassie never came up weekends when Parker was at Adam's. Erin worried that was too obvious, but then again, Adam didn't have a pool. Even when Parker was supposed to be at her father's, she spent plenty of time in Erin's backyard instead. The benefits of keeping the house with a pool. One day after Parker had left for Adam's, Erin dangled her legs in the pool and texted Cassie.

Erin [Today 3:23 PM]
I'm in Boston for work. You free tonight? I could stick around for dinner maybe?

They'd met for dinner when Erin was in town before, but she didn't go to the city as often as she wanted to see Cassie. It was easier to lie than to say *I miss you. I want to see you.* Easier to give Cassie an out that wouldn't feel as much like a rejection. Cassie was always free, though.

• • • •

It was almost the end of June before Cassie came up for a weekend at the same time Rachel was over. As soon as Rachel laid eyes on Cassie, Erin knew it was a mistake. She had lasted this long without introducing them, and she should've kept it up. Rachel had no tells—nothing specific that Erin could point to, but she *knew*.

Rachel didn't say anything, though. Not right then, and not later, when Parker announced they were going swimming, then wrapped her hand around Cassie's wrist and tugged. Cassie threw a smile over her shoulder at Erin as Parker dragged her outside. Erin bit her lip instead of smiling back, turned back to Rachel once the door closed behind the girls.

Rachel's head was tilted, and Erin steeled herself for whatever smart-ass thing would come out of her mouth, but she launched into stories about her trip to Greece instead. Erin listened, and laughed, and relaxed.

Over the next half hour, Rachel shared every detail about her favorite meals, activities, hotels, and bartenders in Greece and Erin eventually forgot to worry about it, so of course that was when Rachel tilted her head again and said, "So this is why you didn't tell me?"

Erin tried not to go stiff. "What?"

"That kid out there is why you've been smiling at your phone all the time?"

"She's not a kid," Erin said immediately, only realizing when Rachel's eyes flashed that was the wrong part of the sentence to argue with. "I am not having this conversation right now."

"You are absolutely having this conversation right now," Rachel said. "You could've told me!"

Rachel had at least lowered her voice to an almost-whisper, but Erin kept an eye on Cassie and Parker out the window anyway.

"There's nothing to tell," Erin insisted.

"Are you kidding me?"

She turned to face Rachel.

"Nothing you don't already know," she said. It was . . . vaguely true. "You know I've been sleeping with someone. And now you know who. That's all there is to it."

Rachel gave her a Look, which meant Erin was not going to get out of this conversation.

"You know that's not all there is to it," Rachel said. "You are doing a hell of a lot more than sleeping with her."

Erin did know. Erin had known for a long time, and that was

why she'd never told Rachel everything. Rachel always encouraged Erin's bad decisions.

"It doesn't matter," she said. "Nothing's going to happen."

"Nothing's going to happen? It's already happening, Erin!"

"Rachel, be quiet," Erin shushed.

"Just explain, and I'll shut up."

"There is nothing to explain," she said. "I can't just date my daughter's twenty-two-year-old best friend because she's good in bed."

"Are you serious right now?"

Erin shrugged, palms open at Rachel. Describing Cassie like that felt cruel, but that was how it had started, right? The best sex of her life in the back of a rental car. That was how it should have ended, too. If Erin had been a better person, a better mother, there wouldn't have been anything else. Now, she was in over her head, but back then, she could've stopped it. She should've stopped it before it became something bigger.

Rachel sighed. "You aren't serious, right? You know this is more than that?"

"Of course I know, Rachel," Erin snapped, suddenly at her breaking point. "I know she's clever and funny and kind, even if she would never describe herself that way. I know she makes me laugh more than anyone other than you. I know she's . . . great," Erin paused, defeated. "She's also my daughter's best friend. We cannot have more than this summer, but goddammit I am letting myself have this summer."

She couldn't look at Rachel's face, all empathetic and distressed.

"Erin," Rachel said. "You can let yourself—"

"Please tell me you are not about to try to talk me into dating my daughter's best friend who is barely half my age."

"I'm not trying to talk you into anything, but let's look at the facts." Erin glared at her. "You spend time together, you spend all day texting—"

"We do not spend all day texting."

Rachel ignored her. "I'm not trying to talk you into dating your daughter's best friend because it seems like you might already be doing it. And you're happier than I've seen you in a long time."

"It's not something that can work," Erin said. The sharp edge in her words surprised her. "I don't want to talk about it."

Her voice cracked, then, and she was excruciatingly embarrassed.

"Okay," Rachel said. "Okay, we don't have to."

There was a splash, and Erin looked up to see Cassie surface in the pool. Parker said something and Cassie laughed. Erin's chest clenched.

She couldn't talk to Rachel about it. She didn't even let herself think about it. It was overwhelming. If she thought about it, she'd have to reckon with her choices. Her stupidity. The ways she'd failed her daughter.

Cassie made Erin feel good. Being with Cassie made her feel good. Being around Cassie.

Thinking about what she was doing with Cassie made Erin feel . . . horrendous. Awful.

She wanted to be a good mom. The moment she met Parker, sweaty skin-to-skin contact in the hospital bed, Erin had vowed to take care of her. To keep her safe from everything that could hurt her.

Lately, Erin was the one doing the hurting. She'd hurt Parker in the divorce, worked three years to make up for it, and spent the last nine months doing worse.

Erin didn't deserve to have a good relationship with Parker. She acted like she wanted one. She'd worked to fix the ways it was broken. And then she threw it all away, for what? Sex? Cassie was Erin's midlife crisis. She was a giant mistake.

That wasn't fair—Cassie *was* great. Amazing, even. She was young and brilliant and hilarious, and she had her entire life ahead of her. She was going to change the world. Whoever she ended up with would be incredibly lucky. It was Erin who was the mess. The disaster.

Even when Erin was being gentle with herself instead of pointing out her flaws, this thing with Cassie hurt to think about. Not just in a *What the hell are you doing?* and *If anyone ever found out . . .* sort of way. In a *No chance at a happy ending* sort of way. What was the best outcome here? For Cassie to move across the country. It'd be better, probably—easier—if she and Parker didn't keep in touch. Erin didn't know if she'd be able to handle the occasional Cassie mention on Sunday phone calls. She certainly wouldn't be able to handle another winter break visit. No, the best outcome would be Cassie out in California, telling someone new this wild story about how she'd spent a few months sleeping with her friend's mom. The best outcome would be Erin throwing herself into work at the clinic, which was what she'd *wanted,* what she'd been working at for years, so it didn't make sense that when she thought about it now, it seemed like a consolation prize.

Those were the only acceptable outcomes, really. There wasn't another option. It didn't matter that Erin had long since recognized the tug behind her sternum every time Cassie smiled. It didn't matter that when she got good news about the clinic, Cassie was the first person she wanted to tell. Even if Erin could've ever brought herself to ask Cassie to go to MIT, to exert that much influence on the rest of this twenty-two-year-old's life, they'd still be in the same situation—touching each other behind Parker's back. This summer was perfect. She saw Cassie weekly, and she and Parker were closer than they'd ever been. Three months of this had to be enough. It was all they'd ever have.

Before she left, Rachel hugged Erin hard.

"I love you, you know?"

Erin nodded. She did know. It didn't fix what she'd gotten herself into, though.

"It was nice to meet you," Cassie said.

"You, too, Cassie," Rachel said. "Take good care of my favorite girls, okay?"

Erin chanced a glance over her shoulder but had to look away when Cassie gave a half grin, standing a little taller than usual, like she was proud.

"I always do."

Twenty-Three

CASSIE

Cassie hadn't meant to eavesdrop. She had to go to the bathroom, and she was absolutely not the type to pee in a pool, and so she went inside. Overhearing Erin explaining just how much they were *not* dating was not Cassie's intention.

"I can't just date my daughter's twenty-two-year-old best friend because she's good in bed."

Cassie had fled down the hall to the bathroom and closed the door as quietly as she could.

It shouldn't have been a big deal. She'd told herself that then and was still telling herself now, two days later. It *wasn't* a big deal. She'd said the same thing to Acacia countless times, because they *weren't* dating. But Cassie's chest had tightened at the disdain in Erin's voice. Did Cassie sound like that whenever she told Acacia? Erin had sounded so scornful. Cassie hated it.

She resolved to be nicer to Kaysh about the whole thing. She'd get the chance, too—Acacia was visiting for the Fourth of July, flying in Saturday morning for a long weekend.

Cassie just had to make it through the week first. It was only Monday and she already wanted to be done.

· · · ·

Cassie [Today 7:07 PM]
Finally done at work

She included every tired-looking emoji she could find.

Erin [7:08 PM]
There's a surprise at your apartment to make the day better

Cassie [7:08 PM]
What

Cassie [7:08 PM]
What is it?

Erin [7:09 PM]
I know you're not an English major, but surely you know the meaning of the word surprise?

Erin [7:09 PM]
Ride safely, even though you're excited

Cassie rode safely, if a little quickly. Erin didn't give her any hints. There was nothing in her mailbox or in front of her door, like she expected.

She got inside and everything looked completely normal, though honestly cleaner than she remembered it being.

Cassie [7:29 PM]
???

Erin [7:29 PM]
Check the bedroom

Erin was in the middle of the bed, on top of the blankets, completely naked. The sight froze Cassie at the door. Erin grinned.

"Hi."

"Hi."

Cassie just looked at her for a moment. Erin preened a little, as if she liked that Cassie couldn't stop staring. She was so fucking hot, was all, and Cassie didn't know how she got so lucky. She didn't know what she wanted to touch first. She thought of what she'd heard Erin say to Rachel and her stomach clenched. She thought, *I'll show you good in bed.*

"Don't move," she said, and Erin smirked at her.

The mattress dipped as Cassie sat beside her on the bed.

"I might have gotten started without you," Erin said, sounding more proud than ashamed.

She spread her legs a little, and Cassie could see how wet she was already.

"I told you not to move," Cassie said, her voice low. Erin's smirk faltered.

"You were later than I expected," Erin kept talking, but she wasn't moving anymore.

"And you couldn't wait?" Cassie asked. She ran a hand up one of Erin's calves.

Erin's eyes slipped closed. "I didn't think you'd mind."

Cassie didn't, really. The thought of Erin naked in her bed, touching herself, alone in Cassie's apartment—Cassie didn't mind at all. She traced her fingertips over the inside of Erin's knee; she knew Erin was ticklish there. Erin clenched her jaw and didn't react. Cassie rewarded her by swiping three fingers through her wetness.

Erin reacted then, hips coming up off the bed chasing Cassie's touch. Erin reached one hand toward her own hair—it made it halfway there before she suddenly put it back at her side, clutching at the sheets like she'd remembered she wasn't supposed to move.

"Good girl," Cassie said, and Erin's eyes flew open.

Cassie held eye contact as she slid her fingers next to Erin's clit. Erin stuttered over her breath but didn't look away, didn't move.

"I want to touch you," she said.

Cassie rubbed at her clit.

"I could make you feel good," Erin said, the words not quite coming easily. "You've had a long day."

"How long have you been here?" Cassie said.

"A while."

Cassie stopped touching her.

"Two hours," Erin said immediately.

Cassie stroked her again and Erin let out her breath.

"You've been naked in my bed for two hours?"

Erin shook her head. "When I realized you'd be later than I thought—" She gasped as Cassie's fingers rubbed a fast circle around her clit. "I did a load of laundry. Clean sheets."

God, this woman was too much. Cassie worked two fingers inside her and she moaned.

"I want to touch you," Erin said again. "I know you had a long day. I thought I'd do all the work. Let you relax."

"And what if this is how I want to relax?" Cassie said.

Erin didn't hesitate, "Then you can do whatever you want to me."

Cassie swallowed the sound her chest wanted to make.

She pulled her fingers back, and Erin's hips twitched like she was going to follow, but she didn't, just looked at Cassie pleadingly.

"Don't move," Cassie said again.

Cassie didn't take her time undressing, but didn't hurry. She could hear Erin swallow. She shed her pants and underwear. Erin didn't lift her head when Cassie walked away from the bed, but Cassie could tell she wanted to. Cassie retrieved the harness from her underwear drawer and put it on.

"You can look," she told Erin before reaching for the dildo.

Erin looked up and gasped, watching Cassie adjust the strap-on.

"I can do whatever I want to you?" Cassie asked, stroking the dildo for good measure.

Erin nodded quickly.

"Roll over."

Erin face down, ass up on her bed was a sight Cassie would never forget. She walked back across the room, ran her hand over Erin's ass and the back of her thighs. She caught Erin by the hip and tugged. She wasn't strong enough to pull her, but Erin got the idea and slid to the edge of the bed, dropping her feet to the floor.

Cassie positioned the dildo at Erin's entrance and Erin whimpered.

Cassie didn't move.

She stood with the head of the dildo just barely inside Erin and waited. Erin was fisting the comforter and clenching, again and again, and her hips twitched like she wanted to just push herself backward onto Cassie, but she stayed still.

"Good girl," Cassie said again, and pushed inside.

The noise Erin made was obscene.

They hadn't done this before—used a strap-on. As much as Cassie didn't want to, she went slowly. She needed to be sure of how much Erin could take. She thrust a little deeper each time. Erin never resisted, but Cassie wanted to be sure.

She pushed all the way in and leaned over so her front was pressed into Erin's back. "Does that feel good, baby?"

"Yes," Erin gasped. "Yes, Cassie, please."

Cassie pulled out and thrusted again, added a twist of her hips at the end, and Erin cried out. Her legs were trembling, her hands still clutching the blankets.

"You can move, Erin," Cassie said. "Fuck me back."

Erin let out a sob of relief and rolled her hips back into Cassie. Cassie wasn't going slowly now. She kept her hands on Erin's hips and met her every thrust.

"Cassie," Erin said. "Please. Let me touch you."

"I thought I could do whatever I wanted," Cassie said, gripping Erin's body tight enough to stop her movements.

"Please."

"Come like this, and we'll see."

It didn't take Erin long. Cassie kept up her pace, and Erin was so wet she could feel it on her own thighs, damp and sticky. She never touched Erin's clit, just held her hips and thrusted. Erin buried her moans in the mattress when she came.

"There you go," Cassie said gently, brushing her hand up and down Erin's side. "Now, up."

"Cassie," Erin laughed. "I'm not sure my legs work."

"You're the one who wanted to touch me but if your legs don't work I guess I can just take care of myself."

Erin scrambled up on the bed, turning to face Cassie. Cassie grinned. She'd never—most of the time she would do absolutely anything Erin asked of her; flipping the script was thrilling. She felt powerful. Erin glanced between her legs and licked her lips.

"May I?"

"May you what?" Cassie said.

"I want to clean you up."

Cassie's head jerked into a nod.

Fuck. As though Erin face down ass up weren't enough; Erin on all fours, wrapping her mouth around Cassie's cock was the greatest thing she'd ever seen. Cassie had had plenty of problems with her body throughout the years, but not having a dick had never been one until this moment.

It was so hot Cassie might've blacked out, actually, because she really didn't have any idea how she ended up on her back with Erin sliding onto her. Bending Erin over was fun but this was better—the chance to watch Erin's face, to see the way her eyes fluttered closed and her mouth dropped open. They'd been touching each other all summer, sneaking moments over weekends or when Erin came into the city, but they hadn't had this much time alone together since spring break.

Every time Erin dropped herself onto Cassie, the base of the dildo pushed at Cassie's clit. It shouldn't have been enough, really, but it had Cassie straining, one hand fisted in the blanket and one hand gripping the back of Erin's thigh. She bit her lip to keep back her moan and rolled her hips.

Erin looked at her, tilted her head, curious, and sunk down a little farther. Cassie whimpered.

"Shit, Cassie, are you going to—"

Cassie couldn't do anything but nod. Erin, still grinding on her, leaned down to suck at the sensitive spot above her collarbone. Cassie was so close, pushing up into Erin and groaning and it wasn't fair the way Erin knew how to play her, knew which buttons to push and when and how hard. Erin bit, and Cassie came.

Her hips pulsed and her eyes stayed closed until she heard a gasp, then she opened them to watch Erin come undone. Erin kept their hips flush together, ground down in a figure eight, and let out a long shuddering breath. Cassie had recovered enough to half-sit up and kiss her, because she had to when Erin looked that beautiful.

Erin climbed off her eventually and dropped herself onto the bed next to Cassie. They were still on top of the blankets. Cassie was content to snuggle—not that she'd ever admit that—but Erin started unstrapping the harness. Cassie didn't help much, just let Erin do the work and lifted her hips when prompted. The harness was deposited on the floor next to the bed, and Cassie felt warm and soft with Erin curled next to her. Erin reached between her legs. She was soaked, and Erin chuckled softly.

Cassie stretched languidly as Erin's fingers slid over her. The stress of her day, of her week, even though it was only Monday, was forgotten. God, Erin just made her life so much better.

"I—" Cassie started, and thank God Erin hit her clit right then, because the next words out of her mouth were definitely going to be *love you*.

The thought made her body seize—which Erin read wrong, ran her fingers faster, and even though it hadn't been a precursor to an orgasm, Cassie got there anyway.

"What were you saying?" Erin teased while Cassie got her breath back.

Cassie could tell her face heated from more than just the orgasm, but maybe Erin didn't notice.

"I'm glad I gave you a key," she said. It wasn't a lie, even if it wasn't what she had been going to say. Erin beamed and Cassie's chest clenched and, oh, she was in trouble.

"I am, too," Erin said. "And I'm all yours tonight."

"What?"

"I don't have to be back in Nashua until tomorrow." She grinned.

Of course the first time Erin could spend the night was when Cassie realized she had feelings for her. Cassie closed her eyes and tried to remember how to breathe.

"You stay here," Erin said, getting up. Cassie looked at her. She had a smirk on as though she thought the orgasm was what had Cassie like this. Cassie was not planning to dispel her of that notion. "Do you wanna order food?"

"Chinese." Cassie said. "Orange chicken and I don't care what else. There's a menu from my favorite place on the fridge."

"Okay," Erin said. She leaned down for a kiss. "You recover, and I'll handle dinner."

She sounded annoyingly smug. But thinking she made Cassie come so hard she needed to rest was better than realizing Cassie had feelings for her, so Cassie let her tease.

As soon as she was out of the room, Cassie grabbed her phone.

Cassie [Today 8:42 PM]
Kaysh what the fuck am I supposed to do

Cassie [8:42 PM]
I'm into Parker's mom

Acacia must've been in a fight with Donovan, because she had her read receipts on—she turned them on whenever they fought because she was petty, and Cassie normally loved it, but she hated it right now. Hated seeing Read 8:42 P.M. and no sign of Acacia responding.

Cassie [8:44 PM]
Kaysh? I am into Parker's mom

Acacia [8:44 PM]
Yes and?

Cassie [8:44 PM]
No like. I am /into/ her

Acacia [8:45 PM]
What about this is new, Klein?

Cassie was freaking out because Acacia needed to understand.

Cassie [8:45 PM]
I ALMOST TOLD HER I LOVE HER

Read 8:45 P.M. sat there for more than a minute before Acacia started typing back.

Acacia [8:47 PM]
So you figured out you've been dating for the past six months?

Cassie [8:47 PM]
Acacia this is not funny. She is in my apartment ordering dinner and I almost told her I love her???

Acacia [8:48 PM]
1.) It's a little funny 2.) I'm not joking.

Cassie [8:48 PM]
Wtf am I supposed to do

Acacia [8:48 PM]
The same stuff you've been doing bc you've been dating for half a year? Except like, tell Parker

Cassie [8:49 PM]
Jesus Christ I am into PARKER'S MOM

"Hey," Erin said from the doorway, and Cassie almost dropped her phone. Erin grinned. "Didn't mean to scare you."

Erin was in just a T-shirt and underwear, leaning against the doorframe, and Cassie was absolutely, 100 percent into her.

"I'm gonna take a shower while we wait for the food," Erin said. "Wanna join me?"

Cassie swallowed. She wanted to, yes, but she wanted to get her shit together more.

"Nah," she said. Erin's face fell a little, and Cassie rushed to recover. "If I join you we're gonna be a lot longer than it takes the food to get here."

Erin laughed. "Touché. See you in a bit."

She stripped the T-shirt off right there and tossed it at Cassie. Cassie caught it before it hit her in the face. Erin threw a smile over her shoulder when she headed down the hallway.

Cassie [8:51 PM]
Shit Acacia it's /bad/

Cassie [8:51 PM]
Why didn't you tell me it was this bad

Acacia [8:52 PM]
I'VE BEEN TELLING YOU FOR MONTHS

Cassie knew that, of course, but seriously, couldn't Acacia have tried a little harder? She might very well be in love with Parker's mom. She needed like a full sit-down intervention.

Cassie [8:53 PM]
I know, I know. Just like . . . wtf man wtf am I doing

Cassie thought about it. Thought about all the time she'd spent with Erin, all the time she'd spent telling Acacia they weren't dating. She thought about how Erin made her feel—warm, and happy— and knew that was the case long before now. She thought about what she'd heard Erin say to Rachel, and she made a decision.

Cassie [8:55 PM]
It doesn't have to change anything tho

Acacia [8:56 PM]
???

Cassie [8:56 PM]
You've said I was into her all along, right? So just because I know now doesn't mean anything has to change

Acacia [8:57 PM]
This sounds like a bad idea

Cassie [8:57 PM]
Why? We do what we've been doing for the rest of the summer, and when I head to Caltech, I find someone else to fuck and get over it

She felt fake even writing that, but she could do it. She was Cassie Klein; she could do anything.

Acacia [8:58 PM]
Just get over it, that sounds easy

Cassie [8:58 PM]
Well what do you think I should do, Kaysh?

Acacia [8:58 PM]
Talk to her. It's not like this whole thing has been one-sided. She's probably into you, too

Cassie [8:59 PM]
No, she's not.

Acacia [8:59 PM]
Cassie just give it a chance

Cassie [8:59 PM]
I'm telling you she's not. I heard her talking to her friend about it

Acacia [9:00 PM]
What?

Cassie [9:00 PM]
She said we weren't dating just because I was good in bed

Cassie added a smirking emoji, tried her usual bravado. It didn't work. She thought about that day, wondered if the way her stomach dropped was less about Erin's tone and more about Erin's words. Wondered how many things she'd lied to herself about when it came to Erin.

Cassie [9:01 PM]
It doesn't matter. I gotta go. She's in my shower and food's gonna arrive soon. I'll talk to you later

Acacia [9:01 PM]
Cassie. Are you okay at least?

Cassie [9:02 PM]
I'm fine, babe. Just had great sex and about to eat delicious Chinese food

Acacia [9:02 PM]
Remember how you're not supposed to tell me about your sex life?

Cassie [9:02 PM]
You asked

Cassie heard the shower turn off as she got dressed. She was fine, really. Being into Erin was not a big deal. She deleted her recent messages and went to get cash for the delivery guy.

• • • •

Erin woke Cassie up with her mouth.

Cassie came two minutes before she needed to be awake for work.

"Good timing," she said when she realized it.

"I checked when your alarm was," Erin explained. "And acted accordingly."

Okay, who wouldn't be into this woman?

Cassie had convinced herself the whole *I love you* almost-slip was only because of a couple orgasms. She didn't love Erin; she was just into her. Which was still scary as fuck, but she could handle it.

And she was handling it. Dinner last night had been fine. Erin was so easy to be around; even when Cassie was having a minor panic attack about being into her friend's mom, Erin had made her feel comfortable. They shared orange chicken and chow fun and crab Rangoons. Cassie had said *you're perfect* instead of *thank you,* and Erin gave an adorable little smile in response.

Now she'd given Cassie an orgasm without making her even a minute late for work. It was totally reasonable that Cassie was into her, and it wasn't a big deal.

Over breakfast, Cassie asked, "Did you have a patient yesterday or something? Why'd you come down?"

"No patient," Erin said. "You said you were having a long day, and I thought I'd surprise you."

Cassie flushed. She wondered if it was right before her period or something—she swore she wasn't usually this stupid about having feelings for someone.

"And maybe I've been thinking of surprising you ever since you gave us your spare key." Erin shrugged, then lost the battle to a grin.

"You wait two months and then picked this week to surprise me? Did you forget I'm coming up for a long weekend?"

"Speaking of, what if you came up Friday night instead of

Saturday?" Erin asked. "That way you can meet Acacia at the airport, too."

"I would, but Parker's at Adam's isn't she?"

"Why do you think I'm asking you to come up early?" Erin smirked and waggled her eyebrows. "I'll even make you dinner first."

Cassie ignored the way her stomach churned. Erin obviously wasn't using her for sex—she'd come down to the city just because Cassie had had a bad day. Even if she *were* using Cassie for sex, who cared? Getting used for sex by a MILF was basically a porno fantasy. Cassie should be honored, not upset.

Last night was their first night alone since spring break. Sure, Cassie snuck down the hallway most Saturday nights—and one particularly memorable one, Erin had done the sneaking—but Parker was always there. They had to be careful, and quiet, and quick. An entire night just the two of them, no worries about Parker or work in the morning?

"I'll head up after work."

When they said goodbye, Erin kissed her on the street by her bike, dirty and long, tugging a bit at the collar of her riding jacket.

"See you Friday." She made it sound like a promise.

Yeah, there was absolutely no way Cassie was doing anything to fuck this up. Feelings or not, she did not want this to stop.

Midmorning, Acacia texted.

Acacia [9:50 AM]
Did you survive the night?

Cassie updated her on the situation, how being into Erin wasn't a big deal and she was going to keep it up for the rest of the summer.

Acacia [9:53 AM]
Yeah since being in love (maybe?) with someone who doesn't love you the same way is always so nice

Cassie [9:54 AM]
She can't hurt me like Seth did, Kaysh. We've never been any
sort of exclusive—she wouldn't be breaking my heart sleeping
with someone else or anything

Cassie hated the thought, but it wouldn't be a big deal. She de-
flected.

Cassie [9:54 AM]
Just like I wouldn't break her heart if I banged your brother

Acacia [9:54 AM]
Ew

Acacia [9:55 AM]
Also you're not getting out of this conversation by talking about
my brother

Cassie [9:55 AM]
Kaysh, I'm fine, seriously. If you want to bother me about it, do
it in person when you come up THIS WEEK

Acacia [9:56 AM]
All right I'll let you off the hook but only bc OMG I'M SO EX-
CITED TO SEE YOU AHHHH

Twenty-Four

ERIN

Erin hadn't planned to invite Cassie up for Friday. But Monday night with her was so goddamn nice. The sex was some of the best yet—Erin had almost passed out at the sight of Cassie with the strap-on jutting out between her legs. So amid the post-coital hangover of the next morning, Erin had simply asked for what she wanted.

Now that Cassie had agreed to it, Erin didn't know why she hadn't been coming up on Friday nights the whole summer. They needed to take advantage of any time they could.

Erin danced around the kitchen as she gathered the ingredients for dinner. It'd been too hot all week, the kind of weather she tried to remember in the middle of winter but that also meant she wasn't willing to turn on her oven. So she was making cold noodle salad with a spicy peanut sauce. There were butterflies in her stomach at the thought of making Cassie dinner. It was ridiculous—she'd made Cassie dinner more than a dozen times by now. It felt different tonight. She'd never cooked just for Cassie. Like a date.

She allowed herself to think about it. Just this once. Everything she'd said to Rachel still applied, but there was no harm in admitting—if only inwardly—that Rachel had been right, too: Erin and Cassie were basically dating. Before spring break, their relationship probably landed more in the friends with benefits category. The benefits weren't even that frequent—they'd flirted, but never sexted after Valentine's Day. After their night in Boston—which had definitely been a date—they'd started making dinner together over FaceTime. Since summer break started, they'd had plenty of benefits, Cassie coming up before Parker came back from Adam's or sneaking down the hallway after she'd gone to sleep, but they'd had dates, too. The times Erin was in Boston for work and they'd go out to dinner before going back to Cassie's apartment. The times Erin pretended she was in Boston for work then drove down, just to meet Cassie. Once they'd gotten lunch and hadn't even had time for more than a kiss goodbye.

And now Cassie was on her way over for dinner, just the two of them. Tonight, Erin let it feel real.

Cassie arrived while Erin was cutting cucumbers. She didn't wait for her to finish before kissing her.

"How was your ride?"

"Good," Cassie said, running a hand up Erin's arm. "This is better, though."

Goose bumps followed Cassie's touch, but Erin shook her head. "Patience is a virtue."

"I've never been particularly virtuous." Cassie kissed her again. "Can I help with anything?"

"Nah," Erin said. "There's not much to do."

Cassie let out an exaggerated sigh and took one of the stools at the kitchen island. They chatted about their weeks while Erin sliced radishes. Whenever Erin glanced over her shoulder, Cassie's eyes were on her, interested, intent. Erin forced herself to focus. It was that or slice open a finger.

She hadn't realized Cassie had moved closer until she set down the knife and was suddenly pulled back, Cassie's hips pressing flush against Erin's ass.

"Maybe dinner could wait?" Cassie murmured.

Erin fought not to melt in Cassie's grip. "Once the water boils, I'll take a break while the noodles cook."

"I don't want to kiss you while the noodles cook," Cassie said, nuzzling her nose just below Erin's ear. It was embarrassing how little pressure it took on Erin's waist to turn her around. "I want to kiss you now."

She did just that.

Perhaps dinner *could* wait. It'd taste better if the vegetables marinated longer, but it wasn't a deal breaker. And really, who cared how dinner tasted when Cassie tasted this good?

Erin broke their kiss only long enough to push the cutting board and radishes out of the way so she could boost herself up onto the counter. Cassie stepped between her thighs and Erin locked her ankles behind Cassie's back. Before she could get her lips on Cassie's again, Cassie leaned slightly away and grinned up at her.

"I thought patience was a virtue."

"Turns out I'm not particularly virtuous either," Erin said.

She scratched her fingernails against Cassie's scalp and thought about scratching them down her back later. Cassie practically purred.

At some point, there was a noise, Erin's brain wasn't working well enough to identify it, and she pulled away from Cassie to look in the direction it came from and—

"What the fuck is going on here?"

Erin knew this was bad, but if anyone was going to walk in on them, she was glad it was Adam. She didn't give a fuck what he thought of her.

Cassie leapt back, but Erin merely slid off the counter, not bothering to put space between her and Cassie.

"None of your business," she said. "You could've knocked."

"I could have knocked?! You could have not been *making out* with our daughter's friend!" Adam was already shouting. His eyes were narrowed, his face going redder by the second.

Erin's heart was beating triple time in her chest, but she ignored it and raised her eyebrows. "Why are you here, Adam?"

He kept yelling. About how she was disgusting and what was

wrong with her and he couldn't believe she would ever blah, blah, blah. She truly did not care what he thought about her. None of it was anything worse than she'd already told herself.

As he was lecturing her on appropriate behavior, though, Parker appeared behind him.

Erin moved out of Cassie's orbit. Her heart bottomed out. Dropped to the soles of her feet, maybe further, maybe it disappeared altogether. She didn't know. Couldn't think. She could no longer hear Adam. The sound in her ears had gone static. Her vision tunneled to Parker's face, which was blank, blank, blank, her mouth a flat line. Maybe if Erin could think, she would've reacted quickly enough to stop this before it got worse—Parker technically hadn't *seen* anything. Maybe if Erin said something, interrupted, *anything,* Parker wouldn't have found out. Instead, Erin stood frozen while Adam circled back.

"How about this—I'll knock from now on as long as you don't fool around with your child's friend."

Parker's face didn't change, but she did open her mouth. "Dad."

Adam jumped. Apparently he hadn't noticed her come in, while Erin hadn't taken her eyes off Parker since she'd arrived.

"Parker, honey, what are you doing here? I'm so sorry you had to—"

"Dad. Go home," Parker said.

"What?"

"Go home. I'll get the Switch and meet you there."

"Parker, I—"

"Go home." Parker's voice was steel.

Erin closed her eyes and tears leaked out of the corners. Adam's opinion didn't matter. He could hate her all he wanted. But Parker. Erin felt like she was drowning, like she knew there was no hope but she was struggling anyway. It was already over.

She couldn't look at Cassie.

Adam left, but not without one last glare at the two of them, a disgusted shake of his head. The front door closed behind him—Erin heard it this time—and the three women stared at each other.

Erin finally found her voice.

"Parker, let me explain. I—"

"Don't bother," Parker said, and Erin wanted to throw up. Then: "I already know you're dating."

"You know?" Erin said, at the same time Cassie said, "Dating?"

Parker turned to Cassie, her eyes narrowing. "Where the hell is your phone?"

Erin looked at Cassie for the first time since Adam had arrived. Her hair was a disaster, the ponytail half pulled out from Erin's fingers combing through it while they'd kissed. Her eyes were wide, bewildered, blinking at Parker like she had no idea what was happening. Erin was in the same boat.

"I've been texting you for twenty minutes trying to prevent what just happened," Parker said.

"What?"

"Dad said he wanted to get the Switch so he could beat me at Mario Kart, which, like, as if, but then he said he'd just pick it up on his way home from work, and I know you said you weren't coming up until tomorrow, but, I mean, I don't want to think about what y'all would do with a night alone, but I'm not an idiot."

Erin blushed four shades of red, even as her brow felt permanently furrowed. Parker was mad . . . that Cassie hadn't seen her messages? She knew Cassie and Erin were planning to spend the night sleeping together behind her back, but that didn't seem to be an issue?

"When you weren't answering any of my texts, I tried to beat him here but obviously that didn't work. Now that's gonna be a whole fucking mess."

"Language," Erin said automatically.

Parker raised her eyebrows, an amused grin on her face. "Really? I think we have bigger fish to fry than me saying 'fuck.'"

"Sorry, you're right. Habit," Erin said.

She tried a smile, and Parker's smile grew in response. Cassie looked at them like they'd gone off the deep end. Erin felt like maybe she had, but Parker knew she and Cassie were sleeping together, and she wasn't mad. Erin wasn't about to look a gift horse in the mouth, even if she was still thoroughly lost as to how any of this had happened.

"I've known since Valentine's Day," Parker said like it was nothing. Like it didn't matter. Like she didn't care.

Erin was nauseated. Parker knew they'd sexted on Valentine's Day?

"I was on Cassie's computer when you texted her thanks for the flowers," Parker explained, and Erin's stomach settled. "I'm over it. You can thank Acacia for me not killing you."

Cassie blinked at her. "Acacia?"

"It took her a long time to convince me, but she's the reason I realized how happy you make each other."

Cassie let out a shuddering sigh. "I need a minute," she said.

That made sense—Erin needed a minute to come to terms with Parker knowing, too. What didn't make sense was why Cassie headed for the foyer, where her shoes and jacket were. Erin followed her, Parker close behind.

"You're going?"

"I'll be back in a bit," Cassie said.

Erin wanted to give her all the time she needed, but she didn't want her to *leave*. Something must have shown on her face, because Cassie added, "I'll leave my stuff here, okay? I promise I'll be back."

And then she was gone, the saddlebags from her bike still on the foyer table. The garage door opened. Her bike engine revved then faded away as she rode off.

"Aren't you gonna go after her?" Parker asked.

"I want to give her space if she needs it," Erin said, which was true, even if the way Cassie had fled made Erin's heart tighten into a fist. But there was a bigger reason she was staying put. "And I feel like, maybe, we should talk?"

Parker chuckled, and the anxiety in Erin that spiked as Cassie left mellowed some.

"Yeah, that's probably a good idea."

They both just stood there. Erin didn't know how to start. *I'm sorry* or *It wasn't supposed to happen* or *I love you so much*. When she took too long searching for the right words, Parker laughed at her.

"Okay, let's stop being weird and just sit down." She climbed onto a stool at the kitchen island. "I mean, it's gonna be weird, *obviously*, but we don't have to be."

She patted the stool beside her, and Erin came to sit on it.

"I love you," she said. "So much."

She expected Parker to roll her eyes or something similar. Something typical of a teenager. Instead, Parker grabbed her hand and squeezed.

"I know, Mom. I love you."

"I didn't mean for any of this to happen. I—" Tears sprung to her eyes. She wanted to beg for forgiveness, even though Parker was acting like she hadn't done anything wrong. "It didn't—it wouldn't have—if I had known—"

"Mom," Parker said, squeezing her hand again.

Erin was supposed to be the adult here. She was supposed to be mature, wise, a role model. She wasn't supposed to need her daughter to hold her hand.

She took a breath. "You said you've known since Valentine's Day. But it started—it started well before that. Before I even saw you at school."

"Tell me about it."

"Family Weekend." It was surreal to talk about. "You went to dinner with your dad Friday night, and I went to a bar." As long as they were being honest, Erin figured she should go all in. "It's hard, sometimes, being divorced. I mean, being divorced with a kid. It was one thing if your dad was your favorite when we were married, but

I don't know, it can feel like a competition now. I don't want it to, and it's not healthy, I know, but it can. So I went to a bar to distract myself. And I . . . met a woman."

There was honesty, and then there was giving your kid details about your sex life. Erin skipped over that part.

"When you 'introduced' us at breakfast the next morning, I— God, I still don't know. I was terrified."

"I had no idea," Parker whispered. "I mean, Acacia told me y'all had met then when I grilled her about it on Valentine's Day, but at the time—I really had no idea."

"Yeah, that's kind of what we were going for."

"Right."

"I thought it would be okay. You hadn't been at school long. Maybe you'd fall in with a different group. I didn't think you'd invite her to visit over winter break."

Parker was still holding her hand. She didn't look mad, or disgusted, or any number of things Erin thought she would be. She'd thought of this moment a hundred different ways over the last six months, but she'd never imagined it would be this easy.

"I didn't want anything to happen," Erin said. "You and I were doing well, with you at school. It was hard, for a while, with the divorce, and my work, and just everything, right? But you're so important to me. You're the most important thing in my life. The most important person. The best thing I ever did."

"Mom, stop."

"I'm serious. I would do anything for you. All I want is for you to be happy."

They were veering away from the point of the conversation, but this was important.

"My mom taught me to care about what other people thought. She taught me that other people's opinions mattered, that that's what I needed to pay attention to. I don't want you to think that. I want you to do anything you want to. It's *your* choice. Not your father's, not mine, not your professors'. You get to find what's right for you. You get to make mistakes along the way. It's your life." Erin wiped away the tears that escaped her eyes. "Sorry, I know that's not what this conversation is supposed to be about, but . . . it's important."

"It is kind of what the conversation is about, though," Parker said. "You and Cassie. That's you picking what's right for you, yeah?"

Erin half laughed and wiped harder at her tears. "Yeah, I—I think you're right. Cassie's just—she's—"

"She's pretty great, huh?"

"She is."

Erin's chest warmed at the thought. Cassie was so great.

"Look, Mom, it's not like I want y'all to date."

Erin didn't comment on Parker picking up y'all from her time at school.

"I mean—it's not what I would've ever thought I wanted," Parker said. "When I saw your texts on Valentine's Day, I . . . I never wanted to talk to either of you again. I hated you both so much."

Erin nodded. She'd hated herself, too.

"I made Acacia tell me everything she knew. Which—we all owe her a lot, to be honest. I made her be kind of a shitty friend. She *never* would have told me anything about you and Cassie, but I made her. And I'm glad I did, because she helped me see it for what it was. You make each other so happy, Mom."

Erin cried some more.

"I was so mad at both of you, but I could also see how happy you were. You haven't been this happy in a long time." She shrugged. "So I got over it."

"You're allowed to be mad," Erin said. "Even now. Even if you're 'over it.' We shouldn't have lied to you. Or gone behind your back. I am so sorry. I should have been honest with you from the beginning."

"What, like at breakfast?"

"Okay, maybe not the exact beginning."

Parker chuckled. "I guess yeah, maybe I'm still a little mad. But I love you both. And I get it. And I'm happy for you."

"How'd you turn out so good?"

"Maybe you were a good role model after all," Parker said. "So, what are you going to do now? With her going to Caltech and all."

Erin's balloon burst. "I don't know. I . . . I don't even know how she feels, honestly. We haven't talked about it."

"You've been dating for seven months and you haven't talked about it?"

"We didn't—I mean, we haven't exactly called it dating. We haven't called it anything. Talking about it would have made it real, and it couldn't be real."

"Y'all should probably talk about that, huh?"

"Ya think?"

"I gotta go talk Dad down anyway."

Erin cringed. "I'm sorry about that," she said. "I don't care what he thinks of me, but I can't imagine it's going to be a particularly fun conversation for you."

"I'll definitely threaten to come back and spend the night here if he's a dick about it," Parker said. "But I won't, 'cause"—she waved her hands vaguely—"I don't want to mess up your . . . date night or whatever."

As though their night hadn't already been thoroughly messed up. "I'm more than happy to go back to pretending you don't know rather than have you allude to my sex life."

"Yeah, me too." Parker shuddered like she was shaking the contamination off. "Anyway. I'll deal with Dad. Don't worry about it."

Adam wasn't who Erin was worried about dealing with though.

She had no idea what was going through Cassie's head. Hopefully the other woman was simply overwhelmed, which would be understandable.

Erin watched Parker's car pull away and then kept watching, like Cassie was going to immediately show up again. She bounced her leg. The street was empty.

After a minute or two, she convinced herself to finish making dinner instead of staring out the window.

A watched pot never boils.

Twenty-Five

CASSIE

Cassie drove too fast and left her helmet visor open. She couldn't cry with the wind stinging her eyes.

She didn't know where she was going. Took roads she hadn't taken before. She just wanted to get *away*. Riding usually cleared her mind, but her thoughts were too messy.

The whole semester. Parker's distance. Their fight. Acacia, stuck in the middle. None of it was what she'd thought it was.

The way Erin didn't disagree with Parker's claim they were dating.

That one made even less sense than the rest.

Cassie knew it looked like they were dating. Acacia had been telling her that for months, and Cassie could see it. They enjoyed each other's company and liked having sex. It took Cassie until this fucking week to realize it was anything other than that. But Erin didn't want to date her. That was what she'd told Rachel.

Maybe not in those specific words, but that was the gist.

She pulled off the road at a park.

This was so messed up. She needed to talk to her best friend.

Acacia picked up the phone with: "Did Parker get ahold of you?"

Cassie twisted her ponytail around her fist and yanked, the pressure and pain grounding her. "Not until after Adam walked in on me and Erin making out in her kitchen."

"Shit."

"Tell me about it."

"He didn't kill you, at least. Unless this is your ghost calling me."

Cassie laughed quietly at that. Dialing Acacia, she'd been ready to cry, but she couldn't help herself when it came to this idiot.

"Still alive, unfortunately," she said.

"Agree to disagree on the fortunateness of that fact."

"Okay but it'd be easier to be dead than deal with this."

"It'd be easier to be dead than to figure out what to eat for dinner every day, too, doesn't mean it's unfortunate to put a frozen pizza in the oven for the third night in a row."

"Forget Adam," Cassie said instead of admitting Acacia had a point. "How'd you convince *Parker* not to kill me?"

"Yeah, that took some work," Acacia said. "And almost two months."

"So she wasn't just like, really obsessed with Sam after Valentine's Day?"

"No, she definitely was. She just also wanted to murder you."

Cassie huffed out another laugh. "Yeah, that sounds about right."

Acacia made everything easier. Everything was still a mess and Cassie was still going to have to figure her shit out, but talking to Kaysh, it didn't feel as impossible.

"I'm sorry I didn't tell you," Acacia said. "She knew—on Valentine's Day, she figured out that I'd known. I don't know, my face or something when she told me about the texts. But I didn't tell her any specifics, really, just that you were kind of hung up on her mom."

Cassie tugged on her ponytail again. "Understatement of the year, it turns out."

"Yeah," Kaysh agreed. "Honestly, I wasn't surprised Parker came to terms with y'all dating before you did."

Cassie wasn't sure they had yet. Erin didn't want to date her, right?

There was a beat of silence, and then Acacia's voice was quiet as she asked, "You're not mad at me for lying to you?"

"I'd love to be," Cassie said. "But it'd be a little too much pot calling the kettle, so nah."

"That's very mature of you."

"Yeah, I'm trying." Didn't feel like she was mature enough for Erin, though. "Except I did basically run away from Erin and Parker because I got overwhelmed."

"That's okay," Kaysh said without an ounce of judgment.

Things had gotten, if not scary, then at least intense, and Cassie had fled. Then again, when had she done anything else? This spring, she'd let Parker pull away from their friendship with almost no fight. And at the beginning of the school year, when her friend group had chosen Seth, she'd just . . . let them. It was easier to let people go than to admit you wanted them in your life. At least that way you wouldn't have to chance rejection.

The only thing Cassie had ever admitted to wanting was Caltech. But that was . . .

Caltech had always been her dream, but not for the school itself. It was about getting away from home, from anyone who looked at her with pity. It was about a whole new life, sunshine and palm trees and no one who even knew enough about her to pity her. She'd been trying to run away from her life since she literally ran away from her mom's trailer at twelve. She'd slept on the floor of Acacia's closet and they'd told no one where she was. It was three days before her mom had even realized she was gone. The Webbs bought Acacia a trundle bed after that.

Cassie didn't want to escape anymore.

She'd found a life worth staying for.

"You wanna talk about it?" Acacia asked.

She did. She wanted Acacia to tell her what to do. How to handle this. How to fix it. Kaysh would know. She had always been better with people than Cassie.

But Cassie needed to figure it out herself. She'd gotten herself into this mess. Acacia had already done enough work getting her out of it with Parker. If Cassie wanted to stay, she had to prove it.

"I think I gotta do this one on my own, babe." She doubted herself even as she said it.

"It's okay to need other people, you know?"

"Good, 'cause I'd be a fucking disaster without you."

"We're both disasters anyway," Acacia said. "But you got this, okay?"

Cassie tried to believe her. "Okay."

Her phone buzzed in her hand. She switched Kaysh to speaker to check her messages.

Parker [6:34 PM]
You okay?

Cassie stared at the text. She had no idea if she was okay. She answered with what she knew.

Cassie [6:34 PM]
I'm sorry for lying to you

Parker [6:34 PM]
Thank you

"You gonna pick me up at the airport tomorrow with Parker?" Acacia asked.

"She just texted actually," Cassie said. "I'm still pretty fucking lost on how she doesn't hate me, but it seems like she doesn't, so yeah, I'll be there tomorrow."

The last six months of her life had been turned upside down in the past week. All of it—what she'd been doing with Erin, what happened between her and Parker, all the shit she'd put Acacia through. But she was on the other side of it now. And she still had Acacia to give her a pep talk over the phone. She still had Parker texting her to check in.

Parker [6:35 PM]
We'll talk about it tomorrow, yeah? Rn I gotta go calm my dad
down, and you're gonna go back to my mom's, right?

Did Cassie still have Erin? Maybe she could, if she actually talked
to her about it.

"I should probably head back to Erin's," Cassie said, sending a
text to Parker along the same lines.

"You know what you're gonna say?"

Cassie didn't. "Not yet."

"You got this," Acacia said again.

"I'll figure it out, anyway."

"I love you."

"I love you."

"See you tomorrow."

"Fuck yeah."

No matter what happened the rest of the night, tomorrow Cassie
was going to go with one of her best friends to pick up the other for
a long weekend. Things weren't all bad.

After hanging up, Cassie didn't give herself time to second-guess
before getting back on her bike. But she didn't head straight to Erin's. She didn't want to show up empty-handed. Plus, a longer ride
meant more time to figure out what the hell she was going to do.

Because she could do this. She could admit to wanting Erin.
Make herself vulnerable. Ask for something she wanted. Risk having
to see Erin's face when she said no.

Maybe Erin didn't want to be with her. Cassie didn't know—
she'd heard what Erin said to Rachel, but she hadn't heard the entire
conversation. Maybe she'd missed something. She must've, since
Erin hadn't disagreed when Parker had said they were dating.

Cassie tried not to talk herself out of it. Erin liked her. She liked
her enough to look for apartments for her. She liked her enough to
sleep with her, even when that should've fucked up her relationship

with Parker. She liked her enough to drive an hour and a half to surprise her, just because she'd had a long day.

Liking her and wanting to date her were different things, of course, just like Cassie had been telling Acacia. But they were in the same galaxy, following similar orbits. Cassie just had to figure out how to get them to collide.

Okay, the metaphor kind of fell apart there, but the point was: Cassie needed to do something.

It should probably be something mature. That was probably the biggest hang-up here, right? That Cassie was barely old enough to drink while Erin was turning forty in six months? Now that it turned out Parker was okay with it, the age difference had to be the biggest obstacle. But Cassie had no idea how to prove she was old enough, mature enough, to be worthwhile. There was nothing romantic in showing off tax returns, and Erin already knew Cassie had a job that paid her bills. Cassie had been taking care of herself since she'd hit double digits.

And anyway, fuck should.

Besides, her relationship with Erin—now that she could admit this was the right word for it—wasn't about being taken care of. She didn't give a shit that Erin was older than her. She cared that Erin was funny and smart and made her feel safe. It didn't hurt that she was hot as fuck.

Erin made Cassie happy. And Cassie wanted to make her happy. That was what their relationship was about.

Cassie needed to go back with something that said this. Yeah, she could do wine or chocolate or something traditionally romantic and boring. But Erin wasn't boring. She deserved so much more than boring. She deserved her clinic and winter vacations to anywhere near the equator and scuba diving.

Scuba diving.

It would be ridiculous, maybe. It certainly wasn't going to prove Cassie's maturity. But it would say what Cassie wanted to say.

She pulled over to the side of the road, plugged Dick's Sporting Goods into Google Maps, and drove off to buy scuba gear.

A regular sporting goods store, it turned out, did not carry scuba gear. Also, a Google search indicated scuba gear was fucking expensive. Cassie bought swim fins instead, in purple, Erin's favorite color.

It wasn't until Cassie got back to her bike that she remembered she'd left her saddle bags at Erin's. How was she supposed to carry these ridiculous flippers on her bike?

Might as well be even more ridiculous, she thought as she stuffed them up the back of her jacket.

If Erin said no, this was going to break Cassie's dignity in addition to her heart.

She wanted to pretend it wouldn't. Even in her mind, she wanted to deflect with a joke. Instead, she got on her bike one more time.

The ride to Erin's was too short. When she pulled up in front of the house she'd been pulling up in front of almost every weekend that summer, Cassie wasn't ready. She hadn't figured out the perfect thing to say. Erin would understand, right? If Cassie told her she wanted to go scuba diving with her. Scuba diving was scary as fucking shit, but Cassie would go with Erin. That meant something.

If she was going to do this, she had to do it. Adrenaline was already flying through her veins and she wasn't even off her bike.

Erin must have heard her pull up, though—the front door was still open behind her as she marched toward Cassie. Well, at least Cassie no longer had to figure out if she should knock or just walk in. She couldn't read Erin's face, but it didn't matter. Cassie had decided to do this. She needed to.

She leapt off the bike before Erin got there and held up her hands. "Okay, stop, wait, I have to say this."

Erin stopped.

"I'm sorry I left," Cassie said. "I shouldn't have."

She closed her eyes because it was easier to get everything out if she wasn't analyzing Erin's face for any sign of agreement. "I know there're a million reasons not to—I'm young and honestly so dumb when it comes to feelings that I didn't even realize I had them for you until this week and just because it turns out Parker's okay with it doesn't mean other people are going to be and God, so many other reasons. But I should have stayed because I want to stay. I want you to stay. I know you maybe don't want to, but I want to do this, for real."

Erin might have smiled, but Cassie didn't let herself look. She unzipped her jacket instead—the flippers fell out the back and to the ground.

"What in the . . . ," Erin said so quietly Cassie wasn't sure she even meant to give voice to the question.

Cassie picked up the swim fins. This had seemed like a good idea at the time, but she felt ludicrous now, thrusting them out toward Erin.

"I want to go scuba diving with you."

That was supposed to have been enough, but Erin stared at her like she expected some kind of follow up.

"Like, the ocean is huge and terrifying and unknown, but if you want to go scuba diving, I want to," Cassie explained. "I want to make you happy. Or do the things that make you happy with you. And, I don't know, maybe it won't be so scary if I'm with you. 'Cause *life* is kinda huge and terrifying and unknown, right? But I never think about that when I'm with you."

"Cassie," Erin said, a tenderness in her voice that Cassie wanted to wrap her arms around. She hadn't taken the flippers.

"I don't know," Cassie said. Her arm holding the flippers out to Erin dropped to her side and she shrugged. "It made sense when I bought these."

"It makes sense," Erin said, and then she was right in front of Cassie, one hand on her face and the other on top of Cassie's hand clutching the swim fins, Erin's fingers curling around Cassie's. "It's maybe the sweetest thing anyone has ever said to me."

Cassie couldn't breathe. "Really?"

"Really," Erin said.

"Cool."

Erin laughed like she had said something funny, though Cassie wasn't sure what. This didn't necessarily mean—thinking someone was sweet wasn't the same as wanting to date them.

Cassie took a deep breath and tried to be brave. "I know you said you didn't want to date me, but I thought—"

Erin pulled back, her brow furrowed. "When did I say that?"

"Last weekend," Cassie said. "You told Rachel you weren't going to date me just because I was good in bed. And—"

Erin cut in. "That was *not* what I was saying. I was trying to talk myself out of telling you how I felt. If that's all you heard then you missed me—" She cut herself off, and Cassie would really like to know what she'd missed. "You missed a lot, okay? The entire point of that conversation was how much I do want to date you."

Cassie blinked. "Really?"

"*Yes,*" Erin said, pressing their foreheads together before sneaking a quick kiss. One of her hands was still on Cassie's, both of them holding the flippers together. "It feels so good to say it out loud."

"Even though Parker—"

"Is fine with it?"

Cassie supposed that was true. "Well, yeah, but Adam—"

"Can fuck off," Erin growled. "His opinion means absolutely nothing to me."

"Okay, fair. There's still the thing where I'm an idiot and only figured out I have feelings for you like three days ago."

Erin smiled at her, so gently. "I want to be with you even though you refuse to stop coming up with reasons I shouldn't."

Cassie chuckled and shrugged. She couldn't help it. This didn't feel real.

"I want to go scuba diving with you." Erin laughed and waved her hand around. "Or whatever the equivalent is for you. Like, I want to go to Caltech with you. Or at least come visit you every month."

Cassie bit her lip, half smiling. "About that . . ."

Erin tilted her head, like a confused puppy.

"I, uh, might have been considering going to MIT instead."

Erin's face lit up so suddenly it seemed laughable Cassie had ever not been sure she wanted to be with her.

But Erin didn't celebrate right away. "Not just for me, right? I don't want you to change your dream for me."

"Not just for you," Cassie confirmed. "Mostly because I'm too much of a baby to be that far from Acacia, if I'm being honest. I mean, yeah, and you, and Parker. And my job, too. I didn't really notice while it was happening but, uh, I kind of made a life for myself here that I really like."

Erin's smile made Cassie's chest feel light.

"You really only figured out you had feelings for me this week?"

Cassie groaned. "I told myself we were friends with benefits. It was easier, I guess, than risking getting hurt if that's what you thought we were, too. I don't know. It probably wasn't that deep, really—I'm just bad at feelings."

Erin took the flippers from her and tossed them to the ground, which Cassie wasn't exactly thrilled with. She made up for it by cupping Cassie's face in both hands.

"Since you're so bad at feelings, I want to make sure you get this," Erin said. "When I say I want to go scuba diving with you, I mean I love you."

Cassie felt like she was flying.

"That—I'm probably still bad at it, but I know that feeling," she said. "Like, I mean, me too. Like, I love you, too."

What an embarrassing way to say it for the first time. She was *definitely* bad with feelings. But Erin beamed at her anyway, and kissed her, and *loved* her.

It definitely felt fucking surreal.

They were still in the driveway for fuck's sake.

Twenty-Six

CASSIE

Cassie was used to waking up beside Erin. Being woken up by Erin sliding one arm underneath her head and wrapping the other around her, skin pressing against skin, wasn't unusual.

"Morning," Erin murmured into Cassie's ear.

"Morning." Warmth spread throughout Cassie's body.

She still wasn't fully awake yet, but when Erin's hand started wandering, Cassie was *ready*.

It wasn't the first or even the tenth day they'd woken up with morning sex, but it was different. This time, with her fingers inside Cassie and their faces close, close, close, Erin nudged her nose into Cassie's and said, "I love you."

Cassie came.

Acacia's flight was due in a little before noon. Parker picked Cassie up from Erin's on the way to the airport.

Cassie met her in the foyer, trying not to be awkward. It seemed Parker didn't have to try. She threw her arms around Cassie and held on tight.

"You okay?"

"Yeah," Cassie said, still only half believing it. "You?"

"Yeah. My dad managed not to have an aneurysm yesterday, which is probably the best we could hope for. We didn't totally fuck up your night, did we?"

Cassie laughed. How were they even talking about this? "I mean, kinda. But we managed."

"Good," Parker said. "You ready to go or do you need to kiss my mom goodbye first?"

She cackled at whatever Cassie's face did in response. Cassie wasn't even sure what it was—something between a cringe and an attempt at a smile.

"I'm ready."

"Be back in an hour, Mom!" Parker called on their way out the door.

The last time she'd gone to the airport, Cassie had fallen asleep in the front seat, Erin's hand gentle on her thigh. It was supposed to have been the end of whatever was between them. It was the last rule Erin had made and the last they broke. Six months later, Parker asked if Cassie wanted to kiss Erin goodbye before they left. Other than that, though, she acted normal the whole ride: talked about how excited she was to see Acacia, who all was coming over to swim today, where they'd watch the fireworks tomorrow. She cranked the volume on the radio and belted along to Olivia Rodrigo.

Cassie spent the whole time trying to believe Parker was being sincere. She gave no indication she wasn't, but Cassie still had a hard time trusting it. It felt too easy. Then again, everything with Erin had always felt too easy.

Acacia was waiting on the sidewalk outside of arrivals. Her hair was still shaved close on the sides, but the top was a little longer now, styled in 360 waves. Cassie rolled down her window as they approached.

"Best friend!" she shouted, earning a glare from the airport security guard near the door.

"Best friends!" Acacia shouted back.

Cassie was out of the car before Parker had put it in park. She had never needed an Acacia hug so badly. Kaysh held on tight until Parker made it out of the car and demanded a hug of her own.

"Calm down, there's enough of me to go around," Acacia said as she hugged Parker.

Cassie piled into the back seat with Kaysh for the drive back. Just like talking to her on the phone last night, things felt easier with her around.

"I can't believe you've gotten to spend any weekend you want here, while I was stuck in Chicago with Emerson," Acacia said.

"Please," Parker said, glancing at them in the rearview mirror. "Don't pretend like you're not insanely close with your brother. Not as close as Cassie, but still."

Cassie groaned. "It was *one* time."

"That you made out with my brother? Yeah, we remember."

Cassie regretted what she said next before it was even out of her mouth. "And now that everyone in this car knows why I made out with your brother over Family Weekend, maybe we could stop giving me shit for it?"

Acacia's mouth dropped open, but Parker burst out laughing.

"Nah, I'm definitely going to keep doing it," she said.

Cassie buried her head in her hands. Acacia leaned over to pat her thigh. It wasn't even that bad, actually. If being teased about making out with Emerson to avoid thinking about Erin was the worst thing that came out of this, Cassie could handle it.

Cassie had spent most of her free time this summer sharing the same air as Parker and Erin at the same time. But when they got back, after Erin hugged Acacia hello, the four of them just stood there, awkward as hell. Cassie wanted to smile at Erin, she always wanted to smile at Erin, but she was stuck with something more like a wince on her face, watching Parker out of the corner of her eye. She didn't know what was allowed.

"I'm gonna take Acacia's stuff to Cassie's room for now," Parker said. "We can figure out sleeping arrangements later."

Cassie wanted to die. Did Parker know about all the nights Cassie had snuck down the hallway to sleep in Erin's bed?

"I'll come with you," Acacia said. "You can give me the tour."

It was a transparent excuse to let Cassie and Erin have a moment, but Cassie seized it, let Parker and Acacia disappear up the staircase.

"How was it?" Erin asked.

Cassie took a step toward her, would've liked to collapse against her but held back. "Normal? Shit, I don't know. It was normal, which was fucking weird."

Erin closed the space Cassie had left between them and wrapped her arms around her. Cassie wished the feeling of being held didn't make her sag in relief, but it definitely did.

"You okay, babe?"

Cassie shrugged.

"It's a lot to get used to," Erin said.

"Yeah," Cassie said. "But I mean. She might actually be okay with it? It seems like it, anyway? Or she's plotting ways to kill us."

Erin smiled. "There's always that option. But I don't think she'd leave us alone if that were the case."

"Yeah."

"And she's done it a lot this summer," Erin said, rubbing Cassie's back. "All while apparently knowing about us."

It was true. There had been so many times when Parker had left them alone, and always for longer than she'd needed to. Coming back from Adam's late or taking too long at the store or in the shower. And she'd known the whole time.

It was *weird,* but it made Cassie's heart jump.

"So maybe she doesn't want to kill us after all."

Erin chuckled and brushed a kiss against Cassie's cheek.

"Cassie!" Acacia called from upstairs. "Come put your suit on! We're going swimming!"

"Duty calls," Cassie told Erin.

They stepped back from each other, Erin trailing her hand down Cassie's arm to catch her fingers.

"You gonna swim with us?"

Erin shook her head. "You don't think it's weird enough without me around?"

"I do," Cassie said, "but it'd definitely be better if you were."

"I think I can give you three a day without me," Erin said. "I've got some work to do anyway."

Parker and Acacia came barreling down the stairs. Cassie immediately dropped Erin's hand, then felt bad about it, but Erin waved her off.

"C'mon, slowpoke," Acacia said.

"We're not waiting for you," Parker said, and they didn't, heading straight outside and to the pool.

"Go," Erin said. "I'll be here if you need me."

It was a pretty normal Saturday, all things considered. Having Acacia splash in the pool with them was so great, most of the time Cassie forgot things were supposed to be weird. Caleb showed up, said Lila and Madison would be by after they picked up Haylee from the train station.

About a half an hour later, Erin came out to say hi to Caleb. Cassie didn't hear any part of their conversation, because Erin had on white cutoffs, and her legs went on forever. It wasn't fair. Cassie kept staring after her even though she'd disappeared inside.

"Um, Cassie?"

Cassie snapped her head around to look at Caleb. "Yeah?" she said, sounding breathless instead of nonchalant.

Caleb waved a deck of cards at her, then started to shuffle them. "I asked you three times if you wanted to play continental rummy?"

"Cut her some slack," Parker said. "She's easily distracted by her girlfriend."

Cassie didn't mean to squeak, but she definitely did. Caleb

stared at Parker, and then at her, and then toward the house. Back to Parker.

"What?"

"She's dating my mom."

The cards shot out of Caleb's hands. Acacia had been about to get into the pool, but she took a step toward Cassie, like she was going to need to run interference. Cassie backed up.

"Right," she said. "Well. I'm—uh—is anyone else thirsty? I'm going to get a drink. Anyone need anything?"

"'Thirsty' is definitely the word I'd use," Parker said, not looking up from her magazine.

Cassie fled instead of waiting for the others' answers.

She found Erin in the kitchen. Before Erin could say hello, Cassie wrapped her arms around her middle and dropped her forehead onto Erin's shoulder. "Caleb knows we're dating."

Erin sighed. "Of course he does." She held Cassie gently. "Are you okay with that?"

"I mean, yeah," Cassie said, her voice muffled against Erin. "It's obviously part of this whole dating thing. It would've just been nice for Parker not to drop that into conversation without warning me."

Cassie's head moved with Erin's shoulder as she shrugged. "That's Parker, babe," Erin said. "Besides the fact that she tells Caleb everything, she's going to make us suffer a bit for lying to her."

"How do you know she doesn't hate us?"

One of Erin's hands found Cassie's face to tilt her head up, make her look at her.

"If she hated us, she wouldn't be here," Erin said. "Her dad lives ten minutes away. She wouldn't have picked you up this morning if she hated you. She would do a lot worse than make you uncomfortable if she hated you."

Cassie remembered last semester, remembered weeks going by without ever seeing Parker, and knew Erin was right.

"It still sucks."

"It does," Erin agreed. "But . . . I can do this without worrying about who's around."

She kissed Cassie, softly, sweetly, and neither of them looked over their shoulder to see if they'd been caught.

"Okay," Cassie said. "I guess it's worth it."

"You guess?"

Cassie grinned. "Maybe you should do it again to convince me."

Erin was very convincing.

That night, after Erin barred her from helping clean the kitchen anymore and Acacia disappeared to call Donovan, Cassie knocked on Parker's bedroom door.

"Come in."

Cassie opened the door and took a couple steps into the room. Parker was fiddling with things on her dresser, not paying Cassie any attention.

"Parker . . ."

"Mm-hmm?" She was completely nonchalant.

"Can we like—talk?"

"Sure, bud. What's up?" Parker sat cross-legged on her bed and looked at Cassie.

Cassie flapped her hands awkwardly. "I'm serious."

Parker sighed. "I know. So talk."

Parker had been nice to her, really, all day. Parker had been good. But Cassie had been a mess. Any time she'd actually thought about things, she'd been confused and awkward and distant and there was no way she was going to get past that until she did this.

She cracked her knuckles. "I'm sorry for lying to you," she said. "I'm really fucking sorry for lying to you and sorry this whole thing got way bigger than I thought it was and fucked up a lot between us. I can't really—I can't say I wish it didn't happen. Because I'm in a really good place right now. But I wish I hadn't lied to you about it."

Parker stared at her. Cassie would like to be on her bike, hugging curves on the backroads up to Nashua. She'd like to be in the lab, even though she'd spent too many hours there this week. She'd like to be under a car in a hot garage, sweaty and covered in grease. She'd like to be pretty much anywhere that wasn't this bedroom, with her best friend staring at her like she didn't know her.

But then Parker sighed again, and shifted over on the bed, patting the spot next to her.

"So come tell me about it, and be honest."

Cassie approached Parker's bed slowly. "Tell you about me and your mom?"

Parker didn't even flinch. "Yeah. And I'll tell you about how I went from wanting to kill you to realizing you were still my friend. Kiss and make up, you know?"

Cassie sat beside Parker on the bed, her legs hanging over the edge, feet on the floor like she might bolt at any moment.

"What do you want to know?" she asked.

"Start at the beginning," Parker said. "But leave out like, sex stuff, please, God."

Cassie laughed. "I think I can do that."

She breathed. And then she explained. Calmly, for the most part. She picked at Parker's comforter as she talked, eventually swinging her legs up onto the bed and lying down. Staring at the ceiling was easier than looking at Parker's face.

Parker stayed quiet until Cassie said that she had figured out Cassie had feelings for Erin before Cassie herself had. "What do you mean?"

Cassie closed her eyes. Parker had known she'd been lying to her for months. Parker had known but she had no idea what an idiot Cassie had been.

"I mean I figured out I was into your mom on Monday, Parker."

"What?" Parker sounded so fucking confused. "Mom said you hadn't talked about it, but you didn't even know? When you've been—for like months. You sent her Valentine's Day flowers."

"I know," Cassie said. She could feel everything bubbling in the

back of her throat, all of the things she hadn't been able to stop thinking about, all of the ways she'd fucked up. Parker had asked her to be
honest, and she was going to be fucking honest. "Acacia kept trying
to tell me there was something there, and looking back on it, I look
like a complete fucking moron, right? We texted daily, sent each other
pictures every day. We made dinner together while FaceTiming. It's
fucking ridiculous that I didn't figure my shit out." She paused. Took
a breath. "But I couldn't be dating my best friend's mom. I couldn't
want to date her. We were friends with benefits, that's what I kept telling Kaysh. And that's what I thought, honestly. Because the last time I
dated, I got my heart crushed. Because she's your mom. Because we live
hundreds of miles apart. It's so complicated it was easier just to think
we were friends with benefits. No stakes. No one could get hurt."

Cassie swallowed. She refused to blink. She'd been so stupid
about everything. Acacia had warned her it was all going to blow up
in her face and she'd ignored her. Cassie had spent months being so
stupid and hurting her best friend. Both her best friends.

Parker uncrossed her legs and lay down next to Cassie. She
bumped their shoulders together, caught Cassie's hand.

"I hated you," she said, and Cassie laughed, didn't reach to wipe
the tears that fell so Parker might not notice them. "I did. I hated
you for it. Because she's my mom and because you lied and because
it felt like you didn't care about me."

"No, Parker, I—"

"I let you talk," Parker said. "It's my turn."

Cassie nodded.

"Acacia tried to tell me you had feelings for her but so what? You
were a shitty friend and I was so mad. And dating Sam gave me an easy
excuse to not hang out with you. I wanted to make you feel as crappy
as I did, even while Kaysh tried to get me to give you a chance. How
was I supposed to broach that subject? 'Hey, I know you're banging
my mom, but I want to give you a chance to explain yourself'?" Parker
chuckled. "Though I guess that's where we are right now, huh?"

Cassie squeezed Parker's hand. "I wouldn't have done a good job then, anyway. Back when I thought we were friends with benefits."

"You think if I had asked earlier you'd have figured it out earlier?"

"God, I don't know." Probably not, to be honest. Cassie had been committed to her ignorance.

"Well, regardless. I'm glad you did eventually," Parker said. She took a breath. "Back then, I hated you, but I missed you, too. And Acacia wore me down. And so, I came up with a plan to figure out if you actually cared about my mom or if you were just fucking her. To see if you'd fuck someone else who I knew you were into."

Things clicked into place in Cassie's head. "Gwen."

"Gwen," Parker confirmed. "When you turned down Gwen, I figured this thing with my mom was real."

"I know I'm not supposed to be interrupting you, but I have to," Cassie said. She couldn't let this go. "This thing is real, but I wouldn't have slept with Gwen in that situation even if I didn't know Erin. I was serious when I said I didn't want to fuck things up with you."

Parker leaned her shoulder into Cassie's. "I had thought I was okay with it at school. Like, I had accepted it. I could tell from talking to both of you that y'all were making each other happy. So, whatever, it was fine." Parker picked at the comforter. "It was something else to see you together."

Cassie dug her teeth into her bottom lip instead of grimacing.

"But at the same time, it like, wasn't weird at all. It should've creeped me out or something, right? But fuck, the way y'all look at each other. You're so obviously in love."

Cassie choked on her saliva. Obvious to everyone but her, apparently.

"So," Parker said, her I'm-in-charge voice on. "It's still shitty that you lied, but I'm over it. And it's still weird that you're dating my mom, but it's cool. I've known for longer than you have apparently—almost half a year at this point; I've pretty much worked through it. We're good."

"We're good," Cassie said.

Parker squeezed her hand.

"You're my best friend," she said.

Cassie's breath caught in her throat. "You're my best friend."

After a moment, Parker said, "Don't tell Acacia."

"Never," Cassie said with a grin.

Acacia herself joined them a few minutes later, pushing Cassie into the middle of the bed and climbing in.

"How we doing, kids?" she asked.

"We're good," Parker said.

Cassie interlaced their fingers. "We're good."

They just lay there, snuggled together, for a while. Cassie was almost asleep when there was a quiet knock on the doorframe, Erin standing in the hallway.

"Night, girls."

All three said good night back, and Erin clicked the hallway light off as she left.

Parker elbowed Cassie in the ribs. "Don't you have somewhere to be?"

"Tomorrow, maybe," Cassie said. She was sandwiched between Parker and Acacia. "Right now, I'm exactly where I want to be."

The next day Cassie actually started to believe things might be okay. It was the Fourth, and they started their day with homemade blueberry pancakes with strawberries and whipped cream.

"This is the most patriotic breakfast I've ever had," Cassie said.

"This is the most patriotic I've ever been and it's not even 10 A.M.," Acacia said.

They spent the day in true American style: drinking by the pool. Erin made homemade sweet tea, and Cassie drank two glasses before bothering to add alcohol, because it tasted so good. The whole crew from yesterday showed up early. Lila had UV Blue and Cassie only mocked her a little for drinking like a high schooler. Erin joined them in the early afternoon, happily taking the drink offered to her by underage Haylee.

"If any of you get drunk enough to crack your head open, you're cleaning it up," she said, then took the lounger next to Cassie, without being told this time.

Acacia was on the other side of Cassie. She bumped her arm and whispered, "Your girlfriend's kind of awesome." Cassie's whole body flushed.

She and Erin might have said *I love you,* but they hadn't come close to using the word girlfriend yet. Cassie sure as shit liked when other people used it though.

It was no surprise, then, that pretty soon Cassie and Erin ended up tipsy and making out inside.

"*Um,* what are you doing?"

Cassie pulled back from Erin—just a little, Erin kept her hands on Cassie's hips and didn't let her go too far—to see Rachel gesturing wildly at them.

"What are you doing?" Rachel said again. "I could've been Parker!"

Erin burst out laughing. Cassie smirked.

"Erin!" Rachel snapped.

"Parker knows, Rachel. It's all right."

Rachel's mouth hung open. "She knows you two are—"

"Dating," Erin said quickly.

"Dating," Rachel repeated, and Cassie wondered what she would've said had Erin not clarified. Rachel looked at her suddenly. "Cassie, don't you want to go swimming and give me some time to interrogate my best friend?"

Cassie chuckled and looked at Erin, who rolled her eyes but nodded. Cassie kissed her quickly.

"Go easy on her," she told Rachel as she headed outside.

Apparently Caleb had put down some blankets at a park yesterday, so they had a great place to watch the fireworks from that night. The park was nearby, and when dusk settled, they all headed down the road.

Cassie wished she were drunker—no one was much past tipsy

by this point. If she were, she wouldn't be so worried about what was appropriate with Erin. Everyone they were with knew they were together, thanks to gossip and their lack of subtlety when drunk. But they were meeting up with Caleb's dad, and some other people, and Adam. And they were dating, yeah, they'd established that, but this was very public. There were other people walking in the same direction, and when they got to the park, it was already packed.

Cassie wouldn't have admitted to being the hand-holding type, but she wondered if she could get away with a hand on Erin's lower back or something. Erin looked beautiful, and Cassie wanted to touch her.

Their group was big, spread over four blankets. They said a surprisingly cordial hello to Adam and then settled as far away from him as possible, Cassie made sure of it. She was beside Erin, Parker and Acacia in front of them.

The crowd sent up a cheer when the streetlights went out and three fireworks went up. They exploded in red, white, and blue, and Cassie caught Erin's hand in the dark.

She watched Erin's face almost as much as she watched the fireworks. Erin was beautiful, and she *loved* her, and Cassie was so fucking happy.

"Oh for God's sake, if you're going to stare at her like that, you might as well just kiss her," Parker said.

Cassie looked at Parker, stunned. Erin squeezed her hand.

"I'm not kidding," Parker said as purple sparks exploded above them. "I'd rather you kiss her than go ridiculously heart eyed. It's gross."

She turned back to watch the fireworks and Acacia bumped their shoulders together, laughing. Cassie looked at Erin.

"Well, I mean," Cassie said. "If Parker insists."

Erin laughed and kissed her and Cassie felt the fireworks everywhere.

CASSIE

Cassie's head buzzed pleasantly as she matched the final three jewels to beat the level.

Parker was graduating in two days. There'd be plenty of events with way too many people, but for tonight, after a stiffly polite dinner with Parker's parents, she, Acacia, and Cassie were having a best friend night in Acacia's hotel. They'd played like preteens in the pool, soaked in the hot tub, and then gotten drunk in Acacia's room.

Acacia was next to Cassie on the bed, giving a spirited lecture about which exercises were best for your lats, despite neither of her best friends listening. Parker was on the other bed, which she got to herself since she was the graduate.

"Cassie," Parker said, a snap in her voice like this was *important*.

Cassie locked her phone, put it in her pocket, and gave Parker her undivided attention. "What's up?"

"Why aren't you married to my mom?"

Acacia whipped her head toward Parker. Cassie's mouth went dry.

"What?"

"Why aren't you married to my mom?" Parker asked again. "Like, you're not even engaged? It's been like four years."

Cassie swallowed. Her adrenaline was through the fucking roof.

She was either too drunk for this conversation, or decidedly not drunk enough.

"Uh—" *Good start, Klein, good start.* "Because—"

"Do you not want to marry my mom?"

"No, I do," Cassie said immediately. "I mean, like, I want to be with her forever—I don't really care if that means we get married or—"

"You don't care if you get married?"

Cassie felt like she was fucking this up. Acacia was watching like it was a tennis match, back and forth and back again.

"Look, Parker, you know I'm crazy insanely in love with your mom. She's—she's everything, honestly, and if she wanted to marry me and you were cool with that, yeah, fuck, absolutely, I would love to marry Erin."

She'd never said any of that out loud before, had hardly even thought it, to be honest. They'd never talked about it. It wasn't like her genes had a great track record with commitment of any kind, and Erin had a marriage go south already. Marriage had always seemed like a worthless piece of paper, really, but the idea of being married *to Erin*? Cassie couldn't help the way she grinned.

"If I was cool with that?" Parker said.

"Yeah," Cassie said. "Like. I know some people ask the father first or whatever? I'd definitely ask you."

"First of all," Parker started, and Cassie was certain she was about to get a feminist rant, but Acacia cleared her throat and Parker reined it in. "I won't even get started on how fucking ridiculous it is that you would need anyone's permission but my mom's. And second of all, here's my blessing. Marry my mom. I'm cool with it."

Cassie's face split wider with her smile. She fished her phone out of her pocket and was halfway to writing a message when Acacia pulled it from her hands. Cassie looked up at her quizzically.

"Maybe a drunk message is not the best way to propose?" Acacia said gently.

"Holy shit, I have to *propose*," Cassie said. "You guys, oh my God, help me, what should I do? It has to be *perfect*, you guys."

Parker groaned. "She's not gonna shut up the rest of the night. I never should have said anything."

ERIN

Erin knew Cassie would say yes.

After all, she'd been the one to suggest it when they were buying the lake house.

"Would this all be easier if we were married?" Cassie had asked their real estate agent.

"Well," the agent had said, noticing the way Erin's eyes had bugged out, even if Cassie hadn't. "A joint bank account would have simplified the paperwork, but it doesn't make much of a difference, and the contracts have already been prepared."

Cassie shrugged. "Figured I might as well ask. It's not like I'm not gonna be hers forever anyway, you know?"

It was a throwaway line, like it was no big deal. When Erin had kissed her senseless the moment they were alone, Cassie—once she'd gotten her breath back—had gaped at her and said, "What was that for?"

That was when Erin had decided to propose.

She'd already known she'd be Cassie's forever, too, but that made her want to make it official. Standing up in front of their family and friends, announcing it, *This is my person*—she wanted that.

Erin also knew she could've proposed to Cassie at breakfast, or in the car, or the grocery store, or anywhere. Cassie was hardly the type to need a big production. Erin wanted to give her one anyway. Or—she at least wanted to make it special, because it was. She wanted to make it fit her feelings on the whole situation—that even if a marriage license were just a piece of paper, the idea of marrying Cassie meant a lot to her.

It'd be different this time around. With Adam, Erin had had grand dreams about marriage, about what their life would be like together. This time, she and Cassie had already been living together for two years. Erin had bought that house herself, halfway between Boston and Nashua. She was full time at her free clinic then, and Cassie was on her way to running her own lab with UAL. Erin had been ready to move on from the house she'd shared with Adam, regardless of whether Cassie had wanted to live with her or not, but it wasn't exactly a surprise when Cassie had said yes.

It wouldn't be a surprise this time, either, even if it was a bigger question.

In the end, Erin didn't go with a big production so much as a sentimental one.

She'd told Parker, whose eyes had shone in delight, and Rachel, who'd said, "It's about fucking time." She'd had a ring made, with aquamarine, Cassie's birthstone, and pieces of meteorite on either side. It was unique, and beautiful, and a little silly, just like her girlfriend, who still wore that rocket ship necklace from four Christmases ago.

And then she waited.

For the Fourth of July, the entire Turner family joined them at the lake house, plus Acacia and Rachel. It was most of the crew from that first Fourth, the night that had felt something like their first official date. There were no city fireworks at the lake, the way there were in Nashua. Instead, it would be random neighbors at varying times, though they'd all agreed to wait until after sunset.

Erin's stomach churned all day. She cut watermelon and grilled hamburgers and her hands shook. Cassie seemed to notice, though she never asked, just stayed close, almost always within reach, but usually with a hand in the pocket of her Bermuda shorts, casual and present, not making a big deal of how needy Erin was being. Twice, Erin almost dropped to one knee right then and there, just to get it over with.

She managed to wait until sundown, though, when they all headed toward the dock to watch the neighborhood light up. Acacia had brought a hefty load of fireworks herself, but for now, she joined the rest of them on the dock. Must've been waiting until it was darker out to set the fireworks off from shore.

Cassie thrummed beside Erin. She loved fireworks, obviously— things that went fast *and* blew up? Win-win in Cassie's book. Erin could feel the excitement coming off her in waves, or maybe it was just a reflection of Erin's own nervous energy.

"Wait a minute," Erin said, tugging Cassie's arm before she could sit on the edge of the dock. She wanted to do this while Cassie was standing up.

"What's up?" Cassie said. Her hand slid into her pocket.

"There's something I've been wanting to do," Erin said.

She pulled the focus of everyone on the dock: Melissa, Jimmy, and Noah, who were already seated, Mae and Caleb standing beside them, Rachel, who was playing at disinterest, Parker and Acacia, who already had their phones out. *Way to be obvious,* Erin thought, even as she liked the idea of there being a video record of this moment.

Erin dropped to one knee.

"No!"

Cassie shouted the word, and Erin blinked up at her.

"No?"

Cassie tripped over her words. "No. Not no. Just—keep going. I'll explain in a minute."

Your girlfriend yelling no when you knelt in front of her seemed like a bad sign, but the way Cassie was beaming at her made Erin think otherwise. So, she kept going.

She'd spent a long time thinking about what to say. In the end, she'd decided on the simplicity of what Cassie had said to her to make them official.

"I want to go scuba diving with you for the rest of our lives."

She popped open the ring box.

Cassie's hand was still in her pocket. She lifted the other to her mouth, bit down on the knuckle of her pointer finger, somehow still smiling. She hadn't even glanced at the ring. Her eyes stayed on Erin's, tears welling in them as Cassie nodded.

"Yeah?" Erin asked.

"Yes, Erin, Jesus," Cassie said, and yanked her to her feet so she could kiss her.

Cheers went up, first for them, and then again, louder from the rest of the neighborhood, after the first firework exploded above the lake. Erin only saw its reflection in Cassie's eyes.

"You gotta look at the ring," she said. She plucked it from its box as Cassie offered her left hand.

"Aquamarine?"

"And meteorite," Erin confirmed, sliding it on Cassie's finger. "For my astronaut."

Cassie's laugh was watery. "Is it my turn now?"

"What?"

Cassie's hand dipped into her pocket again, removing something this time. Something small and dark and—

Erin gasped as Cassie went down onto one knee.

"You kinda stole my thunder."

There were more fireworks going off now, but Erin barely registered them. She could only see Cassie and the open ring box in her hand.

"True to form, I'm such an idiot with feelings that it took Parker asking me why we weren't married for me to realize I was allowed to do this," Cassie said.

Erin glanced at her daughter, a few steps away, shakily holding her phone. There were tears in her eyes, too.

344 | MERYL WILSNER

"I always thought it was stupid when guys proposed with 'will you make me the happiest man in the world' but fuck, I can't imagine how anyone could be happier right now," Cassie said. "I almost did this so many times today, and so many times before today. As soon as I bought the ring I wanted to give it to you. I wanted to beg you to be my wife."

"You don't have to beg."

"Could you be quiet? I'm trying to propose here." She rubbed at her eyes. "God, you did this so much better than me with that scuba diving line, why didn't I think of that?"

Erin knelt beside Cassie, her hands coming up to hold Cassie's face. "You're doing it perfectly."

"I told you to be quiet," Cassie said. "And what are you doing? You're supposed to be standing."

"Shut up and kiss me."

Rachel let out a whoop and suddenly Erin remembered they had an audience.

"Your proposal's perfect," she said. "And if you've got more to say you can say it in a minute, okay? Just kiss me."

"You heard the woman!" Acacia yelled.

But Cassie didn't do what she was told. She took Erin's hand instead, held the ring at the edge of Erin's finger.

"You gonna be my wife?" she whispered.

"And you're gonna be mine," Erin whispered back.

Cassie grinned, sliding the ring on fully. "I suppose if I'm gonna be this ridiculously heart eyed over you, I might as well kiss you, right?"

And kiss her she did.

ACKNOWLEDGMENTS

Honestly, God bless Patrice Caldwell. She became my agent at a time I desperately needed her enthusiasm, support, and utter competence. I'm not sure I would've found my footing without her. The same goes for Vicki Lame, who helped remind me that writing is something I love to do. She's the type of editor I wish on every author.

Thanks to the whole team at New Leaf, especially Leah Moss, Trinica Sampson, and Joanna Volpe, who answered every one of my way-too-many questions while Patrice was out of office. Thanks also to the team at Griffin, especially Rivka Holler, Brant Janeway, Sarah Haeckel, Kiffin Steurer, Justine Gardner, Hannah Jones, Joy Gannon, Angelica Chong, and Vanessa Aguirre. I'm so grateful to have such a beautiful book, and for that I thank Gabriel Guma, Soleil Paz, Olga Grlic, and Petra Braun.

The first draft of this book came long ago, and I'm lucky enough that it brought some friends along with it. Zabe Doyle, thank you for always being a disaster with me. Jas Hammonds, I can't believe the first thing of mine that you ever read is a real book! Tash McAdam, you yelling at me about this was the first time I ever felt like being an author was something I could really do.

And then there are newer friends I picked up along the way. Rosie & Ruby, aka clit crew, the best romance writer group chat. Jen St. Jude is one of the kindest and most giving people I've ever met. Anita Kelly is an amazing writer and I'm a better writer for knowing them. Courtney Kae is a fountain of joy and light. I'm grateful Mary Randall has let me get to know her, even if she'd rather not be perceived. Emma Patricia is my little crustacean. Thank you for letting me force you to become friends with me through Zoom. And thanks for being on your best behavior the first time we Zoomed with Ashley Herring Blake, so we could trick her into being friends with us, too. Ashley, I almost dedicated this book to you just because of how much you blush when we call you a MILF.

Thank you to Ashley, Anita, Dahlia Adler, Olivia Dade, and Denise Williams for taking the time to read and blurb this book, even though in the early copy they read, there were about four thousand more instances of eye-rolling.

As always, to my number one, Brooke. It's embarrassing, as a writer, but I don't have the words to explain how much you mean to me, how much you make my life better. There's a reason I had to write poetry to woo you—you make me feel in metaphors.

ABOUT THE AUTHOR

MERYL WILSNER writes happily-ever-afters for queer folks who love women. They are the author of *Something to Talk About* and *Mistakes Were Made*. Born in Michigan, Meryl lived in Portland, Oregon, and Jackson, Mississippi, before returning to the Mitten State. Some of Meryl's favorite things include: all four seasons, button-down shirts, the way giraffes run, and their wife.